BRILLIANCE

BRILLIANCE

MARCUS SAKEY

Text copyright © 2013 Marcus Sakey

Published by Thomas & Mercer

PO Box 400818
Las Vegas, NV 89140

ISBN-13: 9781611099690
ISBN-10: 1611099692
Library of Congress Control Number: 2012922334

For the three amazing women in my life:
My mother, Sally
My wife, g.g.
My daughter, Jocelyn
Never was a man so lucky.

Excerpted from the *New York Times*, *Opinion Pages,* December 12, 1986

LATELY MUCH HAS BEEN MADE of Dr. Eugene Bryce and his study of the so-called "brilliants," that percentage of children born since 1980 with exceptional abilities. While the full scope of their gifts is unknown, it's clear that something remarkable has happened: savants are being born not once in a generation, but every hour of every day.

Historically, the term "savant" was generally paired with another word, to form an unkind but not inaccurate phrase: idiot savant. Those rare individuals with superhuman gifts were generally crippled in some way. Broken geniuses, they were able to recreate the London skyline after only a moment's glance, yet unable to order a cup of tea; able to intuit string theory or noncommutative geometry and yet be baffled by their mother's smile. It was as though evolution was maintaining equilibrium, giving here, taking there.

However, this is not the case with the "brilliants." Dr. Bryce estimates that as many as one in a hundred children born since 1980 have these advantages, and that these children are otherwise statistically normal. They are smart, or not. Social, or not. Talented, or not. In other words, apart from their wondrous gifts, they are exactly as children have been since the dawn of man.

Perhaps unsurprisingly, public discussion has focused on cause. Where did these children come from? Why now? Will this continue on forever, or will it end as abruptly as it began?

But there's a more important issue. A question with shattering implications. A question that is on the tip of our collective tongues, and yet that we do not discuss—perhaps because we fear the answer.

What will happen when these children grow up?

PART ONE: HUNTER

CHAPTER 1

The radio host had said there was a war coming, said it like he was looking forward to it, and Cooper, coatless and chilly in the desert evening, was thinking that the radio man was an asshole.

He'd chased Vasquez for nine days now. Someone had warned the programmer just before Cooper got to the Boston walk-up, a brick rectangle where the only light had been a window onto an airshaft and the glowing red eyes of power indicators on computers and routers and surge protectors. The desk chair had been against the far wall as if someone had leaped out of it, and steam still rose from an abandoned bowl of ramen.

Vasquez had run, and Cooper had followed.

He'd gotten a hit on a forged credit card in Cleveland. Two days later a security camera tagged Vasquez renting a car in Knoxville. Nothing for a while, then he'd picked up the trail briefly in Missouri, then nothing again, then a near-miss this morning in a tiny Arkansas town called Hope.

The last twelve hours had been tense, everyone seeing the Mexican border looming large, and beyond it, the wide world into which someone like Vasquez could vanish. But with each move the abnorm made, Cooper got better at predicting the next. Like peeling away layers of tissue paper to reveal the object beneath, a vague form began to resolve into the pattern that defined his target.

Alex Vasquez, twenty-three, five eight, a face you wouldn't notice and a mind that could see the logic of computer programs unfolding in three dimensions, who didn't so much write code as transcribe it. Who had waltzed through MIT's graduate program at age fifteen. Vasquez had a talent of wondrous power, the kind they used to say happened only once a generation.

They didn't say that anymore.

The bar was on the first floor of a small hotel on the outskirts of San Antonio. Cooper made himself a bet as he walked in. *Neon signs for Shiner Bock, smoke-stained drop ceiling, jukebox in the corner, pool table with worn felt, chalkboard with specials. Female bartender, a blonde showing dark roots.*

The specials turned out to be on a dry-erase board, and the bartendress was a redhead. Cooper smiled. About half the tables were occupied, mostly men but a few women too. The tabletops held plastic pitchers and cigarette packs and cell phones. The music was too loud, some country-rock act he didn't know:

Normal was good enough for my grand-daddee,
Normal's all I want to be,
Normal men built the USA,
Normal men taught me how to play.

Cooper pulled out a high-backed stool, sat down, tapped out the beat on the bar with his fingertips. He'd heard once that the essence of country music was three chords and the truth. *Well, the three-chords part still stands.*

"What can I get you, hon?" The roots of her red hair were dark.

"Just coffee." He glanced sideways. "And get her another Bud, would you? She's about done with that one."

The woman on the stool beside him was peeling the label off her longneck. The knuckles of her right hand brightened for a

4

moment, and her T-shirt tightened at the shoulders. "Thanks, but no."

"Don't worry." Cooper flashed a wide smile. "I'm not hitting on you. Just had a good day, thought I'd share the mood."

She hesitated, then nodded, the motion catching light on a slender gold necklace. "Thanks."

"No trouble."

They went back to looking straight ahead. A row of bottles lined the back of the bar, and behind them faded snapshots had been tacked up in a collage. A lot of smiling strangers hanging on each other, holding up beer bottles, all of them seeming to be having a great time. He wondered how old the photos were, how many of the people in them still drank here, how their lives had changed, which had died. Photographs were a funny thing. They were out of date the moment they were taken, and a single photograph rarely revealed much of anything. But put a series together and patterns emerged. Some were obvious: haircuts, weight gained or lost, fashion trends. Others required a particular kind of eyes to see. "You staying here?"

"Sorry?"

"Your accent. You don't sound local."

"Neither do you."

"Nope," Cooper said. "Just passing through. Be gone tonight, everything goes well."

The redhead returned with his coffee, then pulled a beer from a cooler, the bottle dripping ice water. She spun an opener from her back pocket with easy grace. "Four dollars."

Cooper set a ten on the bar, watched the woman make change. She was a pro, returned six singles rather than a five and a one, made it easy for him to tip extra. Someone at the other end of the bar yelled, "Sheila, sweetheart, I'm dying here," and the bartendress headed away with a practiced smile.

Cooper took a sip of coffee. It was burned and watery. "You hear there was another bombing? Philadelphia this time. I was listening to the radio on the way in. Talk radio, some redneck. He said a war was coming. Told us to open our eyes."

"Who's us?" The woman spoke to her hands.

"Around here, I'm pretty sure 'us' means Texans, and 'them' means the other seven billion on the planet."

"Sure. Because there aren't any brilliants in Texas."

Cooper shrugged, took another sip of his coffee. "Fewer than some other places. The same percentage are born here, but they tend to move to more liberal areas with larger population density. Greater tolerance, and more chance to be with their own kind. There are gifted in Texas, but you'll find more per capita in Los Angeles or New York." He paused. "Or Boston."

Alex Vasquez's fingers went white around her bottle of Bud. She'd been slouching before, the lousy posture of a programmer who spent whole days plugged in, but now she straightened. For a long moment she stared straight ahead. "You're not a cop."

"I'm with the DAR. Equitable Services."

"A gas man?" Her pupils dilated, and the fine hairs on the back of her neck stood up.

"We turn out the lights."

"How did you find me?"

"We almost had you in Arkansas this morning. That's ten hours and change from the border, too far to make in daylight. You're smart enough to plan to cross during the day, when it's crowded and the guards are sloppier. And since you're more comfortable in cities, and San Antonio is the last big one before the border..." He shrugged.

"I could have just hidden somewhere, laid low."

"You should have. But I knew you wouldn't." He smiled. "Your patterns give you away. You're running from us, but you're also running toward something."

Vasquez tried to keep a straight face, but the truth was revealed in half a hundred tiny tells that glowed like neon signs to his eyes. *You could give this up and play poker,* Natalie had once told him, *if anyone played poker anymore.* "I thought so. Not working alone, are you?"

Vasquez shook her head, a tight, controlled gesture. "You're awfully pleased with yourself."

Cooper shrugged. "Pleased would have been catching you in Boston. But keeping you from releasing your virus counts as a win. How close were you?"

"A couple of days." She sighed, lifted the beer bottle, and tilted it to her lips. "Maybe a week."

"You know how many innocent people that could have killed?"

"It only targeted guidance systems on *military* aircraft. No civilian casualties. Just soldiers." Vasquez turned to look at him. "There's a war, remember?"

"Not yet there isn't."

"Fuck you." Vasquez spat the words. The bartender, Sheila, glanced over, and so did a couple of people at nearby tables. "Tell that to the people you've murdered."

"I've never murdered anybody," Cooper said. "I've killed them."

"It isn't murder because they were different?"

"It isn't murder because they were terrorists. They hurt innocent people."

"They *were* innocent people. They could just do things you couldn't imagine. I can see code, do you get it? Algorithms that confound straights are just patterns to me. They come in my dreams. I dream the most beautiful programs never written."

"Come in with me. Do your dreaming for us. It's not too late."

She spun on her stool, clutching the beer bottle by its neck. "I bet. Pay my debt to society, right? Stay alive, but as a slave, betraying my own people."

"It's not that simple."

"You don't know what you're talking about."

Cooper smiled. "Are you sure?"

Her eyes sparked and then narrowed. She drew a shallow breath. Her lips moved as if she were whispering, but no words came out. Finally, she said, "You're a gifted?"

"Yes."

"But you—"

"Yes."

"Hey. You all right, ma'am?"

Cooper broke the gaze for the split second he needed to take the man in. Six one, 220, fat over hard muscle that came from working, not the gym. His hands in front of him, half raised, knees slightly bent, balance good. Ready to fight if it came to that, but not anticipating it would. Cowboy boots.

Then he turned back to Alex Vasquez and saw what he had expected when he noticed the way she was holding the beer bottle. She had taken advantage of the distraction to swing at him backhanded. Her elbow was up and she put her back into it, and the bottle was whistling around to shatter on his skull.

But he was no longer there.

All right, then. No way to know for sure how the cowboy would react. Better to be safe. Cooper slipped sideways and snapped a left hook into the cowboy's jaw. The man took it well, rolling with the impact, then lashed out himself. It wasn't a bad punch, probably would have laid a normal man out. But Cooper saw the flicker of motion at the man's eye, the tightening of the deltoid, the twist of the obliques, caught it all in an instant the way a straight might recognize a stop sign, and the meaning was as clear to him. The punch was a jackhammer, but for Cooper, who could see where it would be, avoiding it was the easiest thing in the world. Out of the corner of his eye, he saw Vasquez slide off the stool and sprint for a door on the far wall.

Enough of this. He stepped in close, cocked his elbow, and slammed it into the cowboy's throat. All the fight went out of the man in an instant. Both hands flew to his neck, the fingers clawing at the skin, carving blood trails. His knees wobbled and gave.

Cooper thought about telling the man he'd be all right, that he hadn't crushed the trachea, but Vasquez was already vanishing through the far door. The cowboy would have to figure it out for himself. Cooper pushed past and wove through the crowd, most of them frozen and staring, a few starting to move but too slowly. A stool was toppling as a man leaped off, and he read the pattern of the man's muscles and the arc of the falling stool and split the difference, jumping the metal legs without engaging the guy. The jukebox had switched to Skynyrd, Ronnie Van Zant asking for three steps, mister, gimme three steps toward the door, which would have made him laugh if he could've spared the time.

The door had a sign that read HOTEL GUESTS ONLY. Cooper caught it just before it closed, yanked it all the way open to be sure Vasquez wasn't waiting on the other side—he would have noticed a weapon on her, but she could have stowed it before she came into the bar—and then, seeing it was clear, spun around the frame. The hallway continued forward to another door, probably the lobby. A staircase carpeted in a bland pattern of orange and gray went up. He took the stairs, the music and bar sound fading, leaving the sound of his breathing echoing off the cinder-block walls. Another door led to a hallway, hotel rooms lined up on both sides.

He raised his right foot to take a step down the—

Four possibilities.

One: An unplanned panic sprint. But she's a programmer; programmers deal in logic and anticipated possibility.

Two: She's thinking of taking a hostage. Unlikely; she wouldn't have time to try more than one room, and no guarantee she could handle the occupant.

Three: Going for a hidden weapon. But that doesn't change the equation; if you can see her, she won't be able to hit you.

Four: Escape. Of course, the building was surrounded, but she would have known that. Which means an alternate route.

Got it.

—hall. Eleven doors, ten of them identical except for the room number. The door at the end was plainer and unmarked. Janitor's closet. Cooper ran to it, tried the handle, found it unlocked. The room was a dingy five by five. Inside was a cart of cleaning supplies and mini-toiletries, a vacuum, a steel rack of folded towels, a deep sink, and, bolted to the near wall, an iron ladder to a roof hatch. The hatch was open, and through the square he could see the night sky.

She must have set this up after checking in. The hatch had probably been locked; Vasquez must have cut it or broken it, leaving herself a neat little escape. Clever. The hotel was a squat two-story in a row of similar buildings, and it wouldn't be hard to move from one to the next, then climb down a fire escape and stroll away.

He reached for one of the slender rungs and hauled himself up. Spared a moment to be sure she wasn't waiting at the top to brain him with a rock, then grabbed the lip and crawled onto the roof. Sludgy tar clung to his feet. Even through the wash of city lights, stars spilled across the horizon. He could hear traffic from the street below, and yelling as his team moved into the bar. Staying low, he glanced left and then right, saw a slender figure with her back to him, hands planted on a three-foot abutment that marked the edge of the roof. Vasquez pushed herself up, hooked a knee on the ledge, then rose to stand.

"Alex!" Cooper drew his sidearm as he stood but kept it low. "Stop."

The programmer froze. Cooper took a few careful steps closer as she turned slowly, her posture conveying a mix of frustration and resignation. "Goddamn DAR."

"Get off the ledge, then put your hands behind your head."

Light from the street revealed her face, eyes hard, lips set in a sneer. "So you're gifted, huh?" Another glint of gold from her necklace, a delicately wrought bird. "What is it for you?"

"Pattern recognition, especially body language." He moved up until only half a dozen paces separated them. Kept the Beretta lowered.

"That's how you moved so fast."

"I don't move any faster than you. I just know where you're going to hit."

"Isn't that sweet. And you use that to hunt your own kind. Do you like it?" She put her hands on her hips. "Does it make you feel powerful? I bet it does. Do your masters pat you on the head for every one of us you catch?"

"Get down, Alex."

"Or you'll shoot me?" She glanced across the narrow alley at the building opposite. The leap was far but doable, maybe six feet.

"It doesn't have to go this way. You haven't hurt anyone yet." He read the hesitation in her body, the tremble in her calf and the tension in her shoulders. "Get down and let's talk."

"Talk." She snorted. "I know how you DAR boys talk. What's that term the politicians like? 'Enhanced interrogation.' Very pretty. It sounds so much nicer than torture. Just like 'the Department of Analysis and Response' sounds so much nicer than 'the Bureau of Abnorm Control.'" Her body told him she was making up her mind.

"It doesn't have to go this way," he repeated.

"What's your first name?" Her voice soft.

"Nick."

"The man on the radio was right, Nick. About a war. That's our future." A strange resolve came over her, and she slipped her hands into her pockets. "You can't stop the future. All you can do is pick a side." She turned, glancing back at the alley.

Cooper saw what she intended and started forward, but before he'd taken two steps, Alex Vasquez, hands tucked deep in her pockets, dove off the roof.

Headfirst.

CHAPTER 2

Cooper spent all night and most of the following day cleaning up.

The broken body of Alex Vasquez was the least of it. The medical examiners took care of that, joking about cause of death as they loaded her onto a gurney. He and Quinn had watched, the other agent holding an unlit cigarette, spinning it, sliding it between his lips, tucking it behind his ears. It wasn't that he was trying to quit. He just savored the tension between holding the cigarette and the moment he lit it. Cooper watched facial muscles as Quinn finally took a deep drag and was pretty sure that the smoke itself was a letdown.

"I always wondered if someone would be able to do that." Quinn looked up at the roof of the hotel thirty feet above. "Must be hard to fight the survival reflexes, keep her skull leading the way."

"She put her hands in her pockets before she jumped."

Bobby Quinn whistled. "Shit, Cooper. What did you do to her up there?"

They'd found her missing datapad in her hotel room and a stamp drive in her pocket. He'd given both to Luisa and Valerie, told them to hit the San Antonio field office and check them out.

Vasquez had claimed the virus needed another week of coding. If she was telling the truth, the thing was far too complex for another programmer to easily finish.

I dream the most beautiful programs never written.

About two in the morning he'd put in a call to Drew Peters, director of Equitable Services. Despite the hour, his boss sounded wide awake. "Nick, good. What's the word?"

"Alex Vasquez is dead."

There was a pause. "Was that necessary?"

"She killed herself." Cooper hated talking on the phone. He felt handicapped when he couldn't see the other person, the play of their muscles and the change in their pores and the widening of their pupils. When he couldn't see someone, he had to take their words for what they were instead of reading the meaning beneath them. He'd heard that some readers actually preferred the phone because it stripped away the wild dissonance between what people said and what they were thinking, but for him, that was akin to cutting out his tongue because he didn't like the way something tasted. "I couldn't stop her."

"Too bad. I'd have liked to have talked to her."

"I think that's why she killed herself. We spoke before she jumped, and she mentioned interrogation. It scared her. Not the process, but what she might tell us."

Another long pause. "Hard to see an upside to that."

"Yes, sir."

"All right. Well, still a success, even if not total. Nice work, son. Get everything settled and come home."

After the call, there had been cops to deal with, and jurisdiction issues. The department wielded broad powers no local dared question, but government work always had a CYA factor, and there had been forms to fill out, authorization codes to pass, after-incident reports to write. His team had questioned the other patrons, making sure that Vasquez didn't have a partner among them. He'd arranged to have the body shipped back to DC—thirty years since the first brilliants, and the scalpel crew still liked to take their brains apart—and put in calls for regional law enforcement to deliver the bad news to next of kin. Vasquez had a mother in Boston and a father in Flint, both normals. One brother, Bryan, also normal, a once-promising engineer turned dropout, last seen peddling weed in Berkeley.

The previous days had been a long run, and Cooper felt raw and exhausted with the forms and the procedure, all the trappings of civilized law enforcement. Patience for bureaucracy wasn't his strong suit even when he wasn't worn out. When he finally got on the charter jet back to DC, the reclining seat felt like a featherbed. He glanced at his watch, figured a three-hour flight with an hour time difference, plus a ride from Dulles to Del Ray, call it ten o'clock. Late but not too late. He leaned back in his seat and closed his eyes. Found a vision of Alex Vasquez waiting for him, that quarter turn she made when he had realized her intention, the way she had thrust her hands deep in the pockets of her jeans. The way she had planted herself off her right foot as she bent into her leap.

I dream the most beautiful programs never written.

Cooper was asleep before wheels up. If he dreamed of anything, he didn't remember it.

A hand on his shoulder woke him. He blinked, looked up, saw the flight attendant smiling down at him. "Sorry. We're landing."

"Thanks."

"No problem." The woman held the smile. It was a coquettish look, but he could see that it was practiced. "You need anything?"

"I'm okay." He rubbed the sleep from his eyes and glanced out the window. DC was smeared with rain.

From the seat across the aisle, Quinn said, "I think she's sweet on you."

"That's because she doesn't realize I work for the government." He stretched, the joints in his shoulders and elbows popping. The jet was a commercial charter, nicer than the military gear they often used. He and Quinn were the only passengers. Luisa Abrahams and Valerie West, the other two members of his team, would be catching flights home tomorrow, after they'd finished wrapping up in San Antonio. *Speaking of...*

"Any word on the virus?"

"Good news, bad news. Luisa says the virus is, and I quote, 'one vicious cunt of a piece of code.' Good news is it's not finished, and Valerie doesn't think another programmer would be able to pick up where it leaves off. Says *she* definitely couldn't."

"What's the bad news?"

"Vasquez wouldn't have been able to use it. It would have to get past military security protocols. Those are designed by our best twists."

Cooper shot him a look.

"No offense. Anyway, Luisa said that to work, it would have to be introduced *inside* the firewall."

"So Alex Vasquez had a contact. Someone inside the military."

"It would need to be someone with serious juice. Think that's why she took her final bow? So she wouldn't give up the name?"

"Maybe." The fear of betraying a friend or lover might have given her the strength. Cooper wasn't the suicidal type, but he imagined that if you were going to go by jumping, you'd want somewhere high and certain, a place where the ground was an abstraction. Vasquez would have been able to see every mark on the concrete, every piece of gum trod black, every bit of broken bottle sparkling up. It must have taken tremendous will to tuck her hands in her pockets and hurl her head at the concrete.

The jet touched the runway, bounced once, and then settled in, the roar of air and engine growing as they braked to a taxi.

"Got word from the office, too. Something's brewing."

"What?"

"No specifics yet. Just a lot of chatter at this point. But it's got everybody keyed up."

What a surprise. Everybody's been keyed up since 1986.

That was the year Dr. Eugene Bryce had published a study in the science journal *Nature* formally identifying the brilliants, the oldest of whom were six. At that point, they were a curiosity, a weird phenomenon that people expected would likely be linked to pesticides or vaccinations or the deterioration of the ozone layer. An evolutionary blip.

It had been twenty-seven years since that study, and though thousands more had followed, the world was no closer to understanding the causes.

What was known was that slightly under one percent of children were born brilliant. The vast majority had fourth- and fifth-tier gifts: calendar identification, speed-reading, eidetic memory, high-digit calculation. Incredible abilities, but not problematic ones.

Then there were tier ones like Erik Epstein.

To Epstein, the movements of the stock market were as obvious as code had been to Vasquez. He'd racked up a net worth of $300 billion before the government had shut down the New York Stock Exchange in 2011. Most nations had followed suit. Global markets remained shuttered to this day. Debt holders had gone crazy. Property-rights lawsuits were on the docket in every country. Entrepreneurialism had vanished overnight; small caps had folded; the Third World had gotten even more screwed up than usual.

All because of one man.

Normal humanity could see the writing on the wall. What had once been a curiosity was now a threat. Whatever you called them—brilliants, gifted, abnorms, twists—they changed everything.

Hence the Department of Analysis and Response, an attempt to deal with a radically shifting world. Though only fifteen years old, the DAR already had unspecified funding greater than the NSA. The agency handled testing, monitoring, research; it advised lawmakers and occupied a cabinet post. And every time a gifted engineer jumped technology forward a decade, the DAR got another half a billion. Still, as long as abnorms were productive members of society, good citizens who obeyed the laws, they were afforded the same rights and protections as everyone else.

It was the ones who didn't play nice that Equitable Services was concerned with.

"Anyway, sounds like it's all hands on deck to find the signal in the noise. No rest for the virtuous." Bobby Quinn spoke through a yawn. "You drive here, or should I call for a ride?"

"Call a ride." He pulled his bag down and then dug out his keys.

"Umm, Cooper?"

"Yeah?"

"Aren't those car keys?"

"Looks like."

Quinn rolled his eyes. "Must be nice to be Drew Peters's fair-haired boy."

"Let me know if you find anything." Cooper walked down the aisle, toward the open door. The flight attendant smiled as he passed. He smiled back, then walked down the stairs to the runway.

■

The weather had driven DC indoors, and he made good time. Del Ray was at the north end of Alexandria, a cozy neighborhood of single-family homes nuzzling close against one another. The houses were well maintained and solidly middle class, with a sodden flag dangling from every fourth porch.

Natalie's was a tidy Folk Victorian, two stories, bright blue, and dotted with windows. A picket fence framed a postage-stamp yard, within which a black dirt bike lay on its side under a maple. Cooper pulled into the drive and killed the engine. He slid the

Beretta and holster off his belt and locked both in the case beneath the passenger seat. The downstairs lights were on; he might not be too late after all.

The rain had picked up, and Cooper hurried up the walkway, still wishing for a jacket. As he approached the front door, he heard footsteps behind it. There was the click of a deadbolt, and then the door swung inward. His ex-wife wore striped pajama bottoms and a worn T-shirt with a Greenpeace logo. Natalie's feet were bare, her hair pulled into a ponytail. She smiled at him. "Nick."

"Hey," he said as he stepped inside. He gave her a hug and was briefly enveloped in her familiar smell. "I'm sorry it's late. I wanted to see them."

"They're asleep."

"Can I pop in anyway?"

"Sure," she said. "I just opened some red. Want a glass?"

"Bless you. Yes." He bent over to untie his shoes, left them on the mat next to a jumble of sneakers. "I won't be long."

The hall light was off, but Cooper had climbed these stairs ten thousand times. He padded up, skipping the squeaky step at the top. Gently, he opened the door to their room and stepped in. Pale light filtered in the windows, and he paused to let his eyes adjust.

The room smelled of children, that sunlight smell over socks and sweat. The left side had posters of dinosaurs and nebulae, a big framed image of the earth rising from the moon. There were toys in heaps, robots and knights and cowboys.

His son was curled on his side, hair in disarray, mouth open. A thin trail of spit ran from his lips to the pillow. His comforter was a bundle at his feet. Cooper eased the blanket up to cover Todd's Spider-Man pajamas. The boy stirred, made a soft sound, and then rolled to his other side. Cooper bent over to kiss his forehead. *Nine years old already. Won't be long before he'll stop letting me kiss him.* The thought was a bittersweet spike through his chest.

Kate's side of the room was neater. Even in sleep she looked composed, lying on her back, her features calm. He sat on the edge of her bed and stroked her hair, feeling the warmth of her, the unbelievable softness of her four-year-old forehead. Skin as fresh and new as a May morning. She slept with the zombie depth of a child, and he watched the easy rhythm of her inhales and exhales. Something in him was refreshed at the sight, as if she slept for them both. He lifted Fuzzy Bear from the floor and tucked him against her side.

Walking back downstairs, he heard music playing softly, one of the obscure female folk groups Natalie liked. He followed it to the living room, found her on the couch, feet tucked girlishly beneath her, a magazine on her lap. She looked up as he walked in and gestured to a syrah on the coffee table. "The kids good?"

He nodded, poured, sat down at the other end of the couch. "Sometimes I can't believe we made them."

"Our best work." She held up her glass, and he clinked it. The wine was full and rich. He sighed, rolled his head back, and closed his eyes.

"Long day?"

"I started in San Antonio."

"Someone you were chasing?"

He nodded. "A woman. Programmer."

"Did you have to kill her?" Natalie looked at him steadily. She'd always been blunt, to the point that people sometimes mistook her for cold. In truth, she was one of the warmest people he had ever met. It was just that she had the honesty of someone with nothing to prove. That was part of what had drawn him to her, all those years ago. He rarely met people whose thoughts and words and actions so closely synced.

"She killed herself."

"And you feel bad."

"No," he said. "I feel fine. She was a terrorist. The computer virus she was working on could have killed hundreds—maybe thousands—of people. Crippled the military. Only thing that bugs me is…" He trailed off. "Sorry. Do you really want to know?"

She shrugged, the ripple of her trapezii graceful beneath her thin T-shirt. "I'll listen if you need."

He wanted to tell her, not because he was troubled by Vasquez's death or because he needed Natalie's benediction, but simply because it felt good to talk, to share his days with someone. But it wasn't fair anymore. They'd always love each other, but it had been three years since the divorce. "No, I'm okay." He sipped the wine. "This is good. Thanks."

"You're welcome."

The room was warm and comfortable, scented with cinnamon from a candle on the coffee table. Outside, the rain fell soft and steady. A gust of wind stirred the trees. He wouldn't stay long—they were good about boundaries—but it felt nice to sit in this sanctuary with his children asleep above him.

Until Natalie took a tiny sip of wine and then leaned forward to set the glass on the table, swinging her legs to the floor. She took a breath and folded her hands in her lap.

Ahh, shit. "What is it?"

Nat glanced at him sideways. "You know, that used to drive me crazy. Just because you can tell I've got something on my mind doesn't mean you shouldn't shut up and wait for me to get to it."

"As I recall, there was an upside to me being able to read your body language."

"Yes, Nick. You were very good in bed. Better?"

He smiled. "What's on your mind?"

"It's Kate."

He stiffened, immediate paternal protectiveness leaping, the part that would always fill in the worst possible ending to any statement that began, *It's Kate.* "What is it?"

"She arranged her toys today."

It was such an innocuous statement that he almost laughed, his head full of all the sentences he'd imagined: *It's Kate, she fell down and hit her head. It's Kate, the neighbor has been touching her. It's Kate, she has meningitis.* "So? She likes things neat. Lots of girls do."

"I know."

"*You* like things neat. Look at this place." He gestured to the framed photos, dustless and aligned, to the square edges of the rug and the couch, to the basket on the coffee table that organized remote controls. "She's just trying to be like Mom."

Natalie stared at him for a long moment. "Come with me." She stood and started for the arch into the kitchen.

"Where—"

"Come on."

Reluctantly, Cooper rose, bringing the wineglass. He followed her through the kitchen to the sunroom that doubled as the playroom. Three walls were glass; on the fourth Natalie had painted a mural, a scene from *The Jungle Book*, the big bear Baloo floating on his back in a river, Mowgli lying on his chest. She was a capable artist; she had once filled notebooks with sketches, back when they had been teenagers who thought love was a noun, a thing you could possess. Natalie flipped on the overhead light. Todd's side of the room was chaotic, the lids of toy bins open, a train under attack from a stuffed panda, an unfinished Lego creation that might one day be a castle.

Kate's side was neat as a surgery. Her toy box was closed, and the spines of her picture books looked as if they'd been aligned with a ruler. A low shelf held dolls and stuffed animals—Raggedy Ann, a brontosaurus, a plastic crocodile, a boxy fire truck, a stuffed Goofy missing an eye, a parrot, Tinker Bell, a pudgy unicorn—all in line like a Marine formation.

"I get it," he said. "It's neat."

Natalie made a short, sharp sound. "Sometimes I don't understand you, Cooper."

It was never a good sign when she called him by his last name. "What?"

"You have these amazing abilities. You can look at someone's credit card statements, what books they've read, their family photo album, and from that know where they'll run, what they'll do. You can track terrorists across the whole country. Can you really not see this?"

"It doesn't mean anything."

"Doesn't *mean*—aren't you the one who says that if you want to understand how abnorms think, all you need to know is that the whole world is patterns? That all the rest of it—whether a gift is emotional or spatial or musical or mathematical—is secondary to the fact that brilliants are more tuned in to patterns than everybody else?"

"Let's just give her some time. There's a reason testing isn't mandatory till age eight."

"I don't want to get her tested, Nick. I want to deal with this. I want to figure out what she needs."

"Nat, she's *four*. She's imitating. It doesn't—"

"Look at her stuffed animals." Natalie walked over and pointed, but her eyes stayed on him. "They're not neat. *They're alphabetical.*"

He'd known that, of course, had spotted it the moment the lights flickered on. But his little girl, tested and labeled? There were rumors about the academies, the things that happened there. No way would he let Kate end up in one.

"Look at the spines of her books," Natalie continued, relentless. "They're arranged by color. And in the spectrum, from red to violet."

"I don't—"

"Kate's an abnorm." Her tone was matter-of-fact, a simple statement. "You know that. Probably for longer than I have. And we have to deal with that fact."

"Maybe you're right. Maybe she is a twist—"

"Not funny—"

"But maybe she's just a little girl whose father is one. Maybe it's not you she's imitating. Maybe it's me. Or maybe she does have a gift. What do you want to do? Test her? What if she's tier one?"

"Don't be cruel."

"But what if she is? You know that means an academy."

"Over my dead—"

"So then—"

"I'm saying that we need to deal with this. Figure out what her gift is and help her explore it. She might need help, tutoring. She can learn to control it."

"Or maybe we could leave her alone and just let her be a little girl."

Natalie squared her pelvis and put her hands on her hips. It was a pose he knew, his ex-wife digging in her heels. Before she could speak, his phone rang. Cooper gave her a *what can I do?* shrug and pulled the phone out. The display read QUINN— MOBILE. He hit TALK, said, "Not a good time. Can this—"

"Sorry, no." Bobby Quinn's voice was all business. "Are you alone?"

"No."

"Call when you are." His friend hung up.

Cooper slipped the phone back in his pocket and rubbed at his eyes. "That was work. Something's going on. Can we talk later?"

"Saved by the bell." Natalie's eyes still had fire in them.

"I was always lucky."

"Cooper—"

"I'm not saying we can't talk about it. But I've got to go. And there's no need to decide tonight." He smiled. "The academies don't accept entrants at this hour."

"Don't joke," she said, but she wrinkled her nose, and he knew the topic was safe for the moment.

She walked him to the door, the hardwood floors creaking with each step. The wind gusted outside, the storm picking up.

"I'll tell them you came by," Natalie said.

"Thanks." He took her hands. "And don't worry about Kate. It will be okay."

"It has to be. She's our baby."

In that moment, he remembered Alex Vasquez just before she'd gone off the roof. The way the light had caught her from below, throwing her features into contrast. The determination in her pose. The way her voice had softened as she spoke.

You can't stop the future. All you can do is pick a side.

"What is it?" Natalie asked.

"Nothing. Just the weather." He smiled at her. "Thanks for the drink." He opened the front door. The rain was louder, and the wind cold. He gave his ex-wife a final wave, then jogged down the path. It was one of those soaking storms, and his shirt was plastered to his shoulders by the time he reached his car. Cooper yanked open the door and slid inside, shutting out the storm. *I really need to invest in a jacket.*

His phone was DAR issue, and he activated the scrambler before he dialed, then tucked it between ear and shoulder as he pulled the case from beneath the passenger seat. "Okay." The case was brushed aluminum, locked with a combination. He popped the latches. The Beretta was nestled in the clip-lock holster atop black foam. Funny, all the ways the gifted had jumped the world forward, and firearms technology remained fundamentally the same. But then, it hadn't changed all that much since the Second World War. Guns could be faster, lighter, more accurate, but a bullet was essentially a bullet. "What's going on?"

"Are you secure?"

"Sure."

"Coop—"

"The scrambler's on, and I'm sitting alone in a car in the middle of a hurricane outside my ex-wife's house. What do you want me to say?"

"Yeah, all right. Sorry to interrupt, but get here. Someone you're going to want to talk to."

"Who?"

"Bryan Vasquez."

Alex Vasquez's older brother. The burnout with no last known address. "Stuff him in an interview room for the night. I'll get to him tomorrow."

"No can do. Dickinson is already with him."

"*What?* What is he doing with my target's brother?"

"I don't know. But you know how our records showed that Bryan was a loser? Turns out, not so much. He's actually a big shot at a company called Pole Star. His sister must have hacked their records, and ours. Pole Star is a defense contractor. Know what they specialize in?"

Cooper switched the phone to his other ear. "Guidance systems for military aircraft."

"You've heard of them?" Quinn sounded surprised.

"Nope."

"Then how—"

"Alex needed someone to plant her virus. They were working together?"

"Yeah," Quinn said. "Not only that. He claims they were working with John Smith directly."

"Bullshit." Cooper picked up the Beretta, checked the load, then leaned forward and attached the holster to his belt.

"I don't know. You should see the light in this guy's eyes. And there's more." Quinn took a deep breath, and when he spoke again, his voice sounded muffled, as though he were cupping a hand around the receiver. "Cooper, he says there's going to be an attack. A big one. Something that makes his sister's virus look tame."

The air in the car had grown cold, and Cooper's flesh goosebumped under the wet shirt. "Her virus would have killed hundreds of people."

Bobby Quinn said, "Yeah."

"Some of my best friends are normal. I mean, not that there's anything wrong with that."

—COMEDIAN JIMMY CANNEL

CHAPTER 3

Like most institutions of its kind, the Department of Analysis and Response wasn't much to look at from the street. There was a granite sign fronted by a neatly tended flowerbed, and half a dozen security gatehouses. A dense line of trees screened everything beyond.

The guards who stepped out were trim and serious looking, dressed in tactical blacks, with submachine guns slung on shoulder straps. One of them circled the car, a heavy flashlight in one hand; the other moved to the driver's side window.

"Evening, sir."

"Hey, Matt. I told you, it's Cooper."

The man smiled, looked down at the ID Cooper held, then back up at his face. His partner shone the flashlight into the backseat of the car, the fingers of his right hand resting lightly on the grip of his weapon. "Hell of a night, huh?"

"Yeah."

The flashlight spearing through his rear windows snapped off. The guard glanced over the car roof, then said, "Have a good one, sir."

Cooper nodded, rolled the window up, and pulled through the gate.

To a casual eye, the road might have seemed designed for aesthetic reasons, winding as it did around nothing in particular. But the design concealed the protective measures. The curves limited speed, reducing the chance a car bomb could reach the complex. The manicured grounds assured excellent sight lines for sniper towers not quite hidden by clusters of very precisely pruned trees. Half a dozen times, the steady hum of his tires hiccupped as he rolled over retracted spike strips. From the parking lot, Cooper could just make out the tips of the antiaircraft clusters mounted on the roof of the building.

Hell of a long way from the beginning. Had it really been seven years ago that he'd followed Drew Peters into the old paper plant? Cooper could still taste that faded fart stink, could see the slanting shafts of sunlight through high factory windows. The building had been shuttered for a decade, cheap, clean space hidden back in a Virginia industrial park. The director had led the way, followed by Cooper and eighteen others, all handpicked, all nervous, and all trying not to show it. Twenty highly skilled individuals who comprised the newest division of the DAR, the razor tip of a unique spear. Equitable Services. "The believers," Peters had called them.

And for eighteen months, belief was about all they had. They worked on card tables in that drafty warehouse. Funding was so tight that there were a couple of months when they went without pay. After the first terminations, the justice department launched an investigation to shut them down. Half the believers quit. Drew Peters remained steadfast, but circles began to form beneath his eyes. There were rumors of a pending congressional subcommittee, of a public excoriation. What they were doing was extreme, a privilege never granted to an agency—the right to hunt and execute civilians. Peters had assured them that he had support at the highest levels, that what they did was outside the traditional legal system. But if he was wrong, they'd face jail and possibly the death penalty.

Then an abnorm terrorist named John Smith walked into the Monocle, a Capitol Hill restaurant, and butchered seventy-three people, among them a US senator and six children. Suddenly, Drew Peters's vision didn't seem so extreme. Within a year, the paper plant hummed with activity; within two, Equitable Services had earned a reputation as the most prestigious subgroup of the DAR.

The rain had downshifted to a drizzle as Cooper parked and jogged to the front door. The internal security measures were just as stringent: a two-stage entrance, each requiring an ID scan and a video capture, a metal detector that his ID allowed him to bypass, an explosive-trace detection system that it did not, all overseen by men with body armor and automatic weapons. He went through it on autopilot, mind replaying the conversation with Quinn, running the angles. Wondering if it was possible that Alex and Bryan Vasquez really did work for John Smith. Wondering what it would mean if they did.

The vast portion of the department was given over to the analysis side of the job, which employed thousands of scientists and bureaucrats. They funded research and explored theory and advised politicians. They designed and redesigned and forever refined the Treffert-Down Scale, the test administered to children at age eight. They maintained the files on tier-one and tier-two gifted, tracking and collating every piece of data in the system, from medical records to credit history. They facilitated budgets and logistics and questions of jurisdiction. It was work done in cubicles and conference rooms, over the phone and the net, and the offices looked pretty much like any corporate headquarters.

Equitable Services, not so much.

The command center was dominated by a wall-size tri-d map of the United States. Actions and interventions were highlighted across the country. Analysts constantly fed data into the system, tracking the movements of targets. Cooper paused to scan the board, taking in the shifting colors, green to yellow to orange: the

Unrest Index, a visual representation of the mood of the country that aggregated everything from frequency of graffiti tags to information on tapped phone lines, from protest marches to target terminations, mixed it all up and laid it over the map like weather patterns. A red pinpoint in San Antonio marked yesterday's takedown of Alex Vasquez. Not a terribly public action, but even so, the people in the bar, on the street, they'd been affected. No matter how smoothly you tossed a stone into water, there were always ripples.

Alongside the tri-d, monitors and digital crawls ran news from every major source. There was a low hum of muffled phone conversation; direct lines ran to the Pentagon, the FBI, the NSA, and the White House. The air had a faintly ionized taste, like biting a fork.

The command center was the hub of the wheel, with hallways spoking off. He ran his ID through a reader and yanked open a heavy door. The clerk glanced up from behind a desk, his expression changing from boredom to sycophancy as he recognized Cooper. "Hello, sir. What can I—"

"Dickinson. Which interview room?"

"He's in four, along with his suspect."

"*My* suspect." Cooper unclipped the holster from his belt, dropped it on the man's desk.

"Yes, sir. But…"

"Yes?"

"Well, Agent Dickinson asked not to be disturbed."

"I'll be sure to apologize." Cooper walked down the hall, shoes squeaking on the polished tile floor. He passed wooden doors with—

Dickinson knows Alex Vasquez is my case. He's risking a beat down for meddling above his pay grade. Possible reasons:

One: Bryan Vasquez turned up in a separate investigation. Unlikely.

Two: Dickinson heard about the John Smith connection and is risking pissing me off for a chance to catch the big fish.

Three: Dickinson is trying to find evidence that I mishandled Vasquez.

Four: Both two and three. Asshole.

—reinforced glass windows centered in them. Two of the first three were occupied by nervous men and women sitting at plain tables under bright light. There was a rumor—a joke? Hard to tell at the DAR—that the fluorescent bulbs were the result of a multimillion-dollar program specially engineered to offer the most hopeless light possible. Cooper didn't know about that, but they did make everyone look two weeks dead. Even Roger Dickinson, who had the kind of strong jawed good looks of quarterbacks in football movies.

The heavy door of interview room four muffled the shouting within, rendering the words indistinct. But through the window Cooper could see Dickinson leaning over the table, one hand planted knuckles down, the other up and pointing, inches from the face of a man with the same cheekbones and brow line as Alex Vasquez. Dickinson was stabbing the air with his finger, jamming it back and forth as if he were pushing a button.

Using the shouting as cover, Cooper gently opened the door and slipped inside, catching it with one hand as it closed and easing it shut.

"—had better come clean with me, do you hear? Because this isn't some speeding ticket. It's not an eight ball of blow. You're looking at terrorism charges, my friend. I will vanish you. Just"—Dickinson straightened, held his hands out in front of him, and stared at them in mock bewilderment—"where'd he go? Wasn't there a guy here a minute ago? Some twist lover? Poof, he's gone, no one knows where, never seen again." He leaned forward again. "Do you hear me?"

"I hear you," Cooper said.

The agent whirled, one hand blurring to his empty holster. *Man, he's fast.* When he saw Cooper, he looked briefly sheepish, but that faded quickly, buried by naked dislike. "I'm in the middle of something."

"Yeah? What?" Cooper spared a glance at Bryan Vasquez, saw no sign he'd try something stupid, so turned his attention back to Dickinson. "What exactly are you in the middle of? Which case? Who's the target?"

Dickinson gave a wolfish smile. "Just following a lead. Never know where it's going to go." The other agent squared up to him. "Until I get there."

Cooper flashed to a schoolyard brawl, one of a hundred. Military brats were always the new kids in town, the outsiders. They always had to fight for their place. But being an abnorm in a world that had only just begun to acknowledge the phenomenon took it to a different level. Seemed like every time he landed in a different school some bigger kid wanted to play Pound the Freak.

One time he'd tried to submit, see if that made things easier. His father had just been posted to Fort Irwin, a couple of hours outside Los Angeles. Cooper was twelve at the time, and the bully was fifteen, a big-toothed kid with red hair. Red seemed no more dangerous than any other bully, so Cooper decided to let him get a few hits in. Maybe if the kid got to show off for his posse, exert his male dominance, then he'd move on with no real damage done.

It might have worked if Cooper had been a normal kid, one in a line of victims. But he was different. And difference, as he learned that day, inspired a particular kind of savagery.

His algebra teacher had found him in a bathroom stall, curled at the base of a toilet, the porcelain bowl drenched with his blood. His eyes had been swollen shut, nose broken, testicles bruised, two fingers crushed. The kicks he'd taken on the ground cost him his spleen.

Dad had asked who'd done it, and so had the doctors and the teacher who found him, but Cooper never said a word. He just gritted his teeth and bore up for the three months it took to heal.

Then he went looking for the bully and his posse. And that time, Cooper didn't submit.

"Something on your mind, Roger?" He met the man's posture and gaze. The ritual was stupid and primitive, and he didn't enjoy it, but it was a dance that needed dancing. "Something you want to say?"

"I said it." Dickinson didn't blink or flinch. "Want to let me work?"

He's not a coward. An insubordinate bigot with boundless ambition, but at least not a coward. So what do you say, Coop? How far do you want to take this?

"Gentlemen." The voice behind them was cotton padding over hardened steel. It snapped the schoolyard moment like a twig. Cooper and Dickinson turned as one.

With his conservative suit, rimless glasses, and impeccable shave, Drew Peters looked like a clerk or a pediatrician, not a man who routinely ordered the murder of American citizens. "Join me in the hall."

The moment the heavy wooden door slammed shut, Peters turned. "What was that?" His voice quiet and firm.

Cooper said, "Agent Dickinson and I were just conferring about the best way to handle Bryan Vasquez."

"I see." Peters looked back and forth. "Perhaps that kind of discussion should be had in private?"

"Yes, sir," Dickinson said. Cooper nodded.

"And how is it, Agent Dickinson, that you happen to be interviewing Vasquez at all?"

"My team discovered that the files on Bryan Vasquez had been altered. The current file lists him as a loser with no last known address. But the original file showed he lived and worked in DC."

"Someone hacked our system?" For the first time, Peters sounded genuinely annoyed.

"Yes, sir. Either that, or…" Dickinson shrugged.

"Or?"

"Well, it could have been done by someone inside the agency."

Cooper laughed. "You think I was covering for Bryan Vasquez? All us twists hang out together on Friday nights?"

Dickinson shot him a glare. "I'm just pointing out that it would have been easy to alter the files from inside the department. Under the circumstances, I thought it best to detain Vasquez immediately. Since Agent Cooper wasn't present, I began the interview myself."

"Very proactive," Peters said dryly. He turned to Cooper. "Take over as primary."

Dickinson said, "But, sir—"

"Vasquez is his target, not yours."

"Yes, but—"

The director cocked one eyebrow, and Dickinson swallowed whatever he had been about to say. After a moment, Peters said, "Grab a coffee."

Dickinson hesitated, then said, "Yes, sir," and started away. To Cooper's eyes, the tension and fury radiating from every muscle made the man seem almost wreathed in flame.

Cooper said, "He's a problem."

"I don't think so. He's a good agent, almost as good as you. And he's hungry."

"Hunger I appreciate. It's running a one-man witch hunt that I don't like."

"The man who burns a witch—does he do it because he likes seeing people on fire, or because he believes he's fighting the devil?"

"Does it matter?"

"Enormously. Both men are doing a terrible thing. But the first is entertaining himself, while the second is protecting the world." The director took off his glasses and polished them with a handkerchief. "You and Dickinson are a lot alike. You're both true believers."

"The only thing Dickinson believes is that I'm in his way. You can't honestly think that someone inside the department altered those files."

Peters waved the idea away as he put his glasses back on. "I don't doubt Alex Vasquez had the skill to hack our systems."

"And Dickinson knows that. But he's throwing accusations anyway."

"Of course. And I'm sure he does want your job. More than that, he probably genuinely doubts you. Remember, many people haven't really accepted that abnorms aren't the enemy. Oh, they'll hold forth on it at a cocktail party, how it's not norms versus abnorms, it's civilization versus anarchy. But in their hearts…"

"I'm a big boy, Drew. I don't need Roger Dickinson's love. There are plenty of people here who don't like me. I'm an abnorm hunting abnorms, and that makes people nervous."

"It's not just that. It's also the power you have. Everyone else at Equitable Services operates within much stricter latitudes than you. Know why that is?"

"I've been here since the beginning. And my record is better."

"No, son," the director said gently. "It's because I trust you."

Cooper opened his mouth, closed it. After a moment, he nodded. "Thanks."

"You've earned it. Now. Can you and Dickinson cooperate on the interview?"

"Sure. Of course." He had a flash of Dickinson leaning over the table, red-faced and yelling. "Though I guess I'll be playing good cop."

"In that case," Peters deadpanned, "God help Bryan Vasquez."

CHAPTER 4

"What's the attack?"

"I already told you, I don't know." Vasquez's voice was at once exhausted, frightened, and eager to please. "All I know is that there's going to be one."

"Yeah, so you keep saying." Dickinson tapped his fingers on the metal table. "Thing is, you're not giving me any reason to believe you."

They'd been at it half an hour, and Cooper had spent most of that time letting Dickinson run through the preliminaries. Interrogation was a dance, and while the early steps were important, they weren't delicate, so he'd used the time to size up Bryan Vasquez, to note his tells and ticks, to read the energy coming off him. One of the peculiarities of his gift was that he sometimes saw people almost as colors. Not literally—he didn't have optical manifestations—but connotatively. The combined effect of a hundred subtle muscle movements—the level of dissonance between what someone was sharing versus what they held back—took on shades in his mind the way hot soup tasted red or a forest smelled green. Natalie was the cornflower blue of a clear winter morning, honest and cool. Director Peters was the heather gray of an expensive suit.

In Cooper's mind, Bryan Vasquez was an awkward orange, simmering with tension, angry but unfocused, withholding but not doing it well.

"Haven't you read a history book? This is a revolution. It's set up in discrete cells so that we can't betray one another. I can't tell you what the attack will be because I don't know. He set it up that way on purpose."

"'He' being John Smith," Dickinson said.

"Yeah."

"You spoke to him?"

"Alex did."

Cooper said, "Personally?"

"No." The hesitation was almost imperceptible. "Over the phone."

You lying little shit. Your sister met with John Smith personally. *No wonder she went off the roof.* But what he said was, "How do you know she was telling you the truth?"

"She's my sister."

"Did you help her code the virus?"

Vasquez looked stunned.

"We know about it, Bryan. We know she was working on a virus to incapacitate the guidance of military aircraft." He leaned into the table. "Were you the one who was going to execute it?"

"No." His voice came out weak, and he started again. "No. I helped with the technical specs. Alex knows everything there is to know about computers. But airplanes…" He laughed. "I'm not sure she'd know how to buckle her seat belt. But the virus needed to be released inside military firewalls, at root level. It would take someone with clearance way, *way* higher than mine."

"Who?"

"I don't know." His eyes were steady, his pulse elevated but no higher than it had been. He was telling the truth. Cooper said, "So how would it work?"

"I'm supposed to deliver it to someone the day after tomorrow."

"Who?"

"I don't know. I just show up and he'll approach me."

"How do you know it's a man?"

"That's what Alex said."

"Where? "

Bryan Vasquez crossed his arms. "You think I'm an idiot? I won't tell you for nothing. I don't even know for sure that you have Alex."

Dickinson leaned in, his face hard. "Do you have any idea the world of shit you're in? I wasn't kidding about vanishing you." He turned to Cooper. "Was I?"

"No," Cooper said, watching for the reaction. Saw it, the bob of the Adam's apple, a bead of sweat on the cheekbone. But Bryan held himself together, said, "I'm not the only one in trouble. You are, too."

"How do you figure?" Dickinson with that wolfish grin again, the dangerous one.

"Because whatever the attack is, it's coming soon, and it's big. Big enough that what we were doing was only a corollary to it. Do you understand?" Bryan leaned in. "Alex and I were crippling the ability of the military to respond to the *real* attack. So you tell me, who's in a world of shit?"

Cooper thought back to his conversation on the plane with Bobby Quinn, how Quinn had said there was a lot of chatter, that everyone was keyed up. Equitable Services routinely monitored phone and digital communications on a national basis. If an attack of significant scale was planned, it would be preceded by all kinds of coded communication. Cooper saw Alex Vasquez again, just before she jumped off the building. The turn of her head, the golden glint of her pendant. The way she tucked her hands in her pockets.

"I don't get it," Dickinson said. "You're normal. Why help her?"

Bryan looked as if he'd bitten something foul. "That's like asking why a white man would march with Martin Luther King. I'm helping because it's the right thing to do. Gifteds are people. They're our children, our brothers and sisters, our neighbors. You want to label them and track them and exploit them. And those you can't control, you kill. *That's* why."

Cooper kept his face bland, but his mind was racing. He was getting a read on Vasquez. Helping his sister was only part of the agenda. He also thought he was David, taking on Goliath. The undiscovered hero with the potential for immortality. It was precisely the kind of personality a revolutionary leader would exploit. *Could he really be just one level of contact away from John Smith?*

The idea was staggering.

Seventy-three people dead at the Monocle alone. Hundreds at his orders since then, and God knows how many to come. The most dangerous terrorist in the country, and this man might lead you to him.

Dickinson let the silence linger just long enough for Vasquez's righteousness to cool. "That's nice. It's kind of moving, even." His tone was metered. "Thing is, you aren't marching beside Dr. King, asshole. You're making planes fall out of the sky."

Vasquez looked away. Finally he murmured, "She's my sister."

The fluorescent lights hummed. Cooper weighed a play in his mind, turning it over. Decided to try for it. "Bryan, here's the thing. Thus far, you aren't really guilty of much. But your sister is in serious trouble. She'll go to prison for the rest of her life for that virus. That's if she's lucky."

"What?" Vasquez straightened. "No. She didn't execute it. Legally, you can't charge her just for planning—"

"It's a terrorist attack against the military," Cooper said, "by an abnorm. Trust me when I say that we can, and we will."

Bryan Vasquez opened his mouth, closed it. "What would I have to do?"

"Lead us to the meeting."

"That's all?"

Cooper nodded. "Assuming your contact shows, of course. If he doesn't, or if you warn him, deal's off."

"And in return—"

"I'll personally guarantee that we won't charge your sister."

Dickinson's head jerked sideways to stare at Cooper.

"That's not good enough," Vasquez said. "I want it in writing."

"Fine."

"Cooper, are you—"

"Be quiet, Roger." He locked eyes with the other agent, saw the man wrestling with himself, remembering that Peters had named him primary, weighing that against a deal to free a known terrorist. Saw Dickinson wondering if it was a twist thing, if he was showing sympathy to one of his own kind.

Vasquez looked from one to the other, then said, "And I want to see her."

"No."

"How do I even know that you have her?"

"I'll prove it," Cooper said. "But you're not going to see her until after. And if you mess with me, you'll never see her again."

Orange hate radiated in waves off Bryan Vasquez's face. Cooper could see him trying to decide if he was the kind of man who would jump a table and attack a government agent. See him knowing that he wasn't that man, that he never had been, and that fury didn't change facts. Finally, Vasquez steepled his hands in front of his face and blew a long exhale into his palms. "Okay."

"Good. We'll be back in a minute with your document."

The interview rooms were kept stuffy on purpose—warm, thick air made people sleepy, which led to slips—and the air-conditioning in the hallway felt great. He waited till he heard the door of the interview room click shut before he turned around.

"Are you out of your mind?" Dickinson's eyes were bugged. "Letting a terrorist—"

"Get that document drafted," Cooper said. "Make it simple and clear. If Bryan does what we want, we won't charge his sister, period."

"I don't work for you."

"You do now. You got proactive, remember?" Cooper stretched, popped his neck. Tired. "And when you're done with that, go downstairs and get a necklace from Alex Vasquez's personal effects. It's gold, a songbird. Bring that back up for Bryan, to prove we have his sister."

Dickinson looked confused. "Downstairs?"

"Yeah. In the morgue." He turned and started to walk away, then spun back. "And Roger, make sure there's no blood on it, would you?"

PIERS MORGAN: My guest tonight is David Dobroski, author of *Looking Over Our Shoulders: The Crisis of Normalcy in the Age of Brilliants*. David, thank you for coming.

DAVID DOBROSKI: My pleasure.

PIERS MORGAN: There has been no shortage of books about the gifted and what they mean. But yours frames things differently.

DAVID DOBROSKI: To me, it's a generational issue. A generation is born, it matures, it comes into power, and eventually it passes that power on to the next. That's the order of things. And yet it's been disrupted. People fixate on technological advances, or the New Canaan Holdfast in Wyoming, but what it comes down to is far simpler—the natural order of things has changed. And my generation is the one facing that.

PIERS MORGAN: But doesn't every generation fear the one after it? Doesn't every generation believe the world is, if you'll pardon the expression, going to hell in a handbasket?

DAVID DOBROSKI: Yes, that's perfectly natural.

PIERS MORGAN: So what's the difference?

DAVID DOBROSKI: The difference is, we never had our time. We never got to shine. I'm thirty-three, and I'm already obsolete.

CHAPTER 5

"You let him think his sister is alive?" Bobby Quinn smiled over the lip of his coffee. "You, my friend, are a bad, bad person."

"Whatever. I don't disagree with what he said about abnorm rights, but blowing shit up isn't the way to fix it. He and his sister would have killed hundreds of soldiers, and I'm supposed to be weepy about lying to him?" Cooper shrugged. "Not feeling it."

Last night's rain had given way to one of those pale, chilly DC days. A patchwork of clouds pressed down on the city, shading the daylight a tarnished silver. The wind was cold, but Cooper finally had a coat on. That and the half dozen hours of sleep he'd snatched had done wonders for his mood.

12th and G, Northwest. Bland office buildings loomed on all four corners, the windows reflecting back the cold sky. Between them was a public square of concrete and stone. Escalators ran up from the open mouth of Metro Center Station, vomiting men and women in business attire, all of them checking watches and talking on cell phones. According to Bryan Vasquez, all he was supposed to do was show up and stand on the corner. His mysterious contact would do the rest.

"It's a mess," Quinn said. "High visibility, multiple escape options, way too many civilians."

"And whoever is meeting Vasquez could watch from any one of these buildings." Cooper leaned back, spun in a slow circle. "Perfect position to make sure he's not being followed."

"It could be a team, too. Spotters in the buildings, maybe security on the ground. An extraction crew. Decoys. Plus, we won't know who we're looking for until they make contact. Tactically, they have every advantage."

"Can we do it?"

"Sure." Quinn smiled. "We're gas men."

"Never liked that nickname."

"You know where it's from, right? Victorian era, the streetlights used to have to be extinguished by hand. The people that did it, they called—"

"Yeah, I know, Professor. My point is, doesn't it seem a tad bloodthirsty?"

"Well, we terminate brilliants. We're lifeguards at the gene pool."

"So that's a no."

"That's a no."

"May the lord forgive you your wicked ways." Cooper made the sign of the cross. "All right, you're my planner. How do you want to set it up?"

"Teams there"—his partner gestured with the coffee cup—"and there. Put 'em in a FedEx truck and a phone company van. Plus a couple of agents dressed as civilians on the street. Women, preferably. If the bad guys are amateurs, they'll be less likely to suspect women."

"Are Luisa and Valerie back?"

"This afternoon, commercial flight. Luisa wanted to know, and I quote, 'whose nutsack she needs to gargle' to score a seat on the jet next time."

"Woman has a way with words."

"She's a poet." A bus pulled up to the corner, the brakes loud. Quinn gestured at it. "Check it."

The side of the bus had been tagged with graffiti. Letters six feet high, orange and purple. I AM JOHN SMITH.

"Are you kidding me?" Cooper shook his head.

"Been seeing that all over. Other night I was at a bar, somebody had put that on the wall above the urinal. And somebody else had added, AND I AM PEEING ON MY SHOES."

Cooper laughed. "When do we get the teams in place?"

"We can get the phone company van here today, have the team sleep in it. The FedEx we'll roll up half an hour before the meet. We'll stuff it with packages, get an agent running in and out of the building. We should plant a tracker on Vasquez."

"Two."

"Two?"

"One on him, and one in the drive he's supposed to hand off. Just in case. Also, I want snipers with clean firing lines."

Quinn cocked his head. "I thought you wanted his contact alive."

"I do. But if something goes wrong, I'd rather take him down here than let him get away. And I want an airship above. Infrared, image-recognition package, the whole works."

"Why? Alex was the primary target, and we got her. That virus needs someone with high security clearance to activate it. What are the chances someone like that is going to come himself? It'll be a lackey, someone disposable." Quinn tossed his coffee cup, spread his hands. "I mean, you're the boss. You want me to put this in play, I will. But isn't this an awful lot of effort for one target?"

"It would be, yeah. Except that it's not just a target. It's a target that might lead us to John Smith."

Quinn sucked air through his teeth. "Smith is going to know that we were onto Alex Vasquez. It took, what, nine days to catch her? She'd have gotten word to him."

"Maybe. But she was running for her life. And it's not like he's got a phone number. He's got to stay mobile, every night a differ-ent place. He must suspect the search protocols we've had running

for him since the Monocle. The new version of Echelon was written by academy coders. Tier one, as good with a console as Alex
Vasquez. Anytime John Smith speaks into a phone, anytime he
logs on to a computer, he's playing hide-and-seek with about five
thousand professionals who want him dead. He may have set this
into motion and then stepped back specifically so that Vasquez
couldn't burn him."

His partner looked thoughtful. "I don't know, man."

"I do. Set it up." Cooper checked his watch. Ten a.m. The drive
would take almost three hours. He could requisition a helicopter
but didn't feel like explaining why. Plus, tear-assing through the
mountains of West Virginia sounded like fun. There was a reason
he drove a 470-hp Charger that cost half a year's salary. And it
wasn't like he'd get pulled over for speeding; the transponder in
his car would ID him to police as Equitable Services. "Can you get
a ride back?"

"Sure. I'll be here a while anyway. Where are you going?"

"To watch John Smith grow up."

CHAPTER 6

The boy was about nine, pale and bony, with full lips and a mop of black hair. There was something lush about him despite his scrawny build; it was in the brightness of his mouth, the curls in his hair. He held up his hands like a boxer from a previous century, thin forearms scant protection.

The other's punch was clumsy, more flailed than swung, but hard enough to snap the child's head sideways. Stunned, the boy dropped his guard, and his opponent swung again, this time splitting a lip and bloodying his nose. The boy fell to the ground, struggling to cover his face with one hand, his crotch with the other. His opponent, a blond kid four inches taller than he, dropped on top of him and began throwing wild blows, the belly, the back, the thigh, whatever wasn't defended.

The ring of children surrounding them grew tighter, fists waving. The glass of the office window was double-paned, and Cooper could hear only the barest hint of the ragged yelling below, but it was enough to bring him back to a dozen schoolyards, to a memory of toilet porcelain cool against his battered face. "Why aren't those teachers breaking it up?"

"Our faculty is experienced." Director Charles Norridge steepled his fingers. "They'll step in at precisely the right moment."

Two floors below and forty yards away, in a white beam of West Virginia sun, the blond had moved to straddle the younger boy's chest, knees digging into shoulders. The black-haired boy tried to buck, but his opponent had weight and leverage.

Now comes the humiliation, Cooper thought. *It's never enough to win. Not for a bully. A bully has to dominate.*

A glistening ribbon of spit slid out of the blond kid's mouth. The younger boy tried to turn his head, but the blond grabbed a handful of his hair and banged his head against the ground and then held him still so that when it snapped, the string of spit landed square across his bloody lips.

You little shit.

A whistle blew. A man and a woman hurried across the playground. The children scattered, retaking the monkey bars and resuming games of tag. The blond kid sprang to his feet, stuffed his hands in his pockets, and assumed a sudden interest in the western sky. The younger boy rolled onto his side.

Cooper's knuckles ached from clenching. "I don't understand. Your 'faculty' just watched a ten-year-old beat another child senseless."

"That's a bit of an exaggeration, Agent Cooper. Neither boy will suffer permanent damage," the director of Davis Academy said mildly. "I understand that it's startling to watch, but this kind of incident is central to our work."

Cooper thought of Todd the way he'd seen him last night, asleep in Spider-Man pj's, skin warm and soft and unmarked. His son was nine, about the same age he guessed the black-haired boy to be. He imagined Todd on a playground like this one, pinned under an older kid, his head throbbing, rocks digging into his spine, a circle of faces surrounding him, faces that belonged to children he had been playing with only moments earlier, and who now jeered at every wound and shame done to him. He thought of four-year-old Kate, who alphabetized her toys and organized her picture books according to the color spectrum. Who had a gift that, despite what he'd said to Natalie, showed every early indication of being quite powerful.

Maybe even tier one.

Cooper wondered if he grabbed Norridge by his gray tweed lapels and hurled him into the window the director would break through in a rain of sparkling shards or just bounce off. And if he did bounce, whether a second throw might do the trick.

Easy, Coop. You might never have seen it firsthand, but you knew these places wouldn't be rainbows and unicorns. Maybe there's more here than you understand.

Try not to kill the director until you do.

He forced a neutral tone. "Central to your work? How? Is the older boy a plant?"

"Heavens, no. That would defeat the purpose." The director walked around his desk, pulled out a leather chair, gestured to one on the opposite side. "It's crucial that all of the children here be gifted. Most are tier one, although there are a handful of twos who demonstrated significant aptitude in other areas. Unusually high intelligence, for example."

"So if they're all abnorms and none of them are in on it—"

"How do we incite incidents like this one?" Norridge leaned back in his chair and folded his hands in his lap. "Though these children all possess savant-level abilities, they remain children. They can be manipulated and trained just like any other. Disagreements can be fostered. Betrayals engineered. A confidence whispered to a trusted friend can suddenly be heard on everyone's lips. A favorite toy can vanish only to reappear, broken, in the room of another child. A stolen kiss or the secret arrival of menstruation can become common knowledge. Essentially, we take the negative formative experiences that all children experience and manufacture them according to psychological profiles and at a dramatically higher rate."

Cooper imagined rows of cubicles with men in dark suits and thick glasses listening to late-night confessions, to the frantic sound of masturbation in a toilet stall, or to the sobs of homesickness. Analyzing it. Charting it. Calculating how each private shame could be exploited to maximum effect. "How? How do you know all these things?"

Norridge smiled. "I'll show you." He activated the terminal on his desk and began to type. His fingers, Cooper noticed, were long and graceful. Piano-player fingers. "Here we are."

He pressed a button, and sound came out of the computer's speaker, a woman's voice.

"...there. It's not so bad."

"It hurts." The child stretched the word out into three syllables.

"I told you to be careful with that one. That boy is trouble. You can't trust him."

A moan, and then a quiet sob. "They were all laughing at me. Why were they laughing? I thought they were my friends."

Something cold snaked through Cooper's belly. The woman, he presumed the one he'd seen break up the fight, continued. "I saw them all laughing at you. Laughing and pointing. Is that what friends would do?"

"No." The voice was thin and forlorn.

"No. You can't trust them either. *I'm* your friend." Her voice saccharine. "It's okay, sweetie. I've got you. I won't let anyone get you now."

"My head hurts."

"I know it does, baby. Do you want some medicine?"

"Yes."

"Okay. I can make it all better. Here. Swallow this—"

Norridge tapped a key, and the sound vanished. "Do you see?"

Cooper said, "You have the whole *place* bugged?"

"That was our solution for the first years. However, in a facility of this size, and given the outdoor spaces, the rough play, it's impossible to assure coverage. Now we have a better way." Norridge paused, the ghost of a smile playing on his lips.

Why would that be? What would make the man so pleased with himself?

"It's not the school you wire," Cooper said slowly. "It's the children. Somehow you're bugging the children."

The director beamed. "Very good. When subjects enter an academy, Davis or any other, they are given a thorough physical examination. This includes inoculation against hepatitis, PCV, chicken pox. One of those shots implants a biometric device. It's a dazzling piece of work, not only recording physiological statistics—temperature, white blood cell levels, and so forth—but also relaying an audio broadcast to receivers placed all over the school. It's quite something. Advanced nanotechnology, powered by the child's own biological processes."

Cooper felt dizzy. His job didn't really entail any overlap with the academies, and so while there had always been rumors about them, he hadn't really imagined they might be true. Yeah, every few years some journalist tried to write an exposé on the places, but they were never granted access, so he'd chalked up the more outrageous claims to sensationalism. After all, there were rumors about Equitable Services, too.

His first taste of the reality had come on his way in, when he'd passed a group of protesters on the road. Demonstrations had become a fact of everyday life, part of the background that people didn't really notice anymore. There was always someone protesting something. Who could keep up?

But this group had been different. Maybe it was the size of the police response. Or that cops were arresting people rather than just containing them. Or maybe it was the protesters themselves, sane-looking people in decent clothes rather than shaved-headed radicals. One in particular had caught his eye, a woman with pale, slack hair who looked as if she might once have been lovely but now was shrouded in sadness; sadness draped her shoulders, sadness hugged her chest. She held a placard, two pieces of poster board stapled across a wooden handle. The sign bore a blown-up photo of a grinning child with her cheekbones, and the markered text I MISS MY SON.

As two cops had closed in on her, she'd locked eyes with Cooper through the windshield and made a tiny gesture with the sign, just raised it an inch. Visually underlining it. A plea, not a screech. But with his eyes, he could see the turmoil beneath.

"Who's the boy?"

"I'm sorry?"

"The boy who got beaten. What's his name?"

"I know them mostly by transponder number. His name is…" Norridge clicked at the keyboard. "William Smith."

"Another Smith. John Smith is the reason I'm here."

"There are many John Smiths."

"You know the one I mean."

"Yes. Well. He was before my time." Norridge coughed, looked away, looked back. "We've thought about discontinuing use of the name, but that seemed a victory for terrorism. Anyway, I'm afraid there's no relation between this one and the one you're looking for. We reassign all of the children's names when they arrive. Every boy here is Thomas, John, Robert, Michael, or William. Every girl is Mary, Patricia, Linda, Barbara, or Elizabeth. It's part of their indoctrination. Once a child is admitted to an academy, they remain here until they graduate at eighteen. For our work, we find it's best that they not be distracted by thoughts of the past."

"Their past. You mean their *parents*, right? Their family, their home."

"I understand that this is startling to witness. But everything we do here has a careful logic behind it. By renaming them, we emphasize their essential sameness. It's a way of demonstrating that they have no value until they have finished the academy. At which point they are free to choose their own names, to return to their families if they choose. Though you might be surprised to learn that a large percentage do not."

"Why?"

"Over their time here, they have built a new identity and prefer it."

"No," Cooper said. "Why do this? I thought that the purpose of the academies was to provide specialized training in their gifts. To raise a generation that had mastered its potential."

The director leaned back in his chair, elbows on the armrests, fingertips touching in front of him. Anyone could read the cold defensiveness, the go-for-the-throat approach of the embattled academic. But Cooper saw more to it. Something in the easy way Norridge maintained eye contact, the steadiness of his speech as he said, "I would have thought that an agent of the Department of Analysis and Response wouldn't need to be told."

"This isn't really my area."

"Still, surely you could have gotten these answers without a trip—"

"I like to see for myself."

"Why weren't you academy trained, Agent Cooper?"

The suddenness of the topic change wasn't what surprised Cooper—he'd seen it coming in the fold of the man's lips and the crinkle of his eyes—but the content threw him. *I never told him I was gifted, or that I was tier one. He could tell on his own.* "I was born in 1981."

"You were in the first wave?"

"Technically second."

"So you would have been thirteen the year the first academy opened. Back then we could barely manage fifteen percent of the tier-one population. With the opening of Mumford Academy next year, we expect to be able to train one hundred percent of them. That's not public knowledge, of course, but imagine it. *Every* tier one born in America. A shame you were born so early."

"Not from my perspective." Cooper smiled and imagined breaking the administrator's nose.

"Tell me, how did you grow up?"

"Doctor, I asked a question, and I want an answer."

"I'm giving you one. Indulge me. Please, your childhood."

Cooper sighed. "My dad was army. My mother died when I was young. We moved around."

"Did you know a lot of children like you?"

"Military brats?" The old snide side coming out, the part that didn't handle authority figures well.

But Norridge didn't bite, just mildly said, "Abnorms."

"No."

"Were you close to your father?"

"Yes."

"Was he a good officer?"

"I never said he was an officer."

"But he was."

"Yes. And yes, a good one."

"Patriotic?"

"Of course."

"But not a flag worshipper. He cared about the principles, not the symbol."

"That's what patriotism means. The others are just fetishists."

"Did you have a lot of friends?"

"Enough."

"Did you have a lot of fights?"

"A few. And you've about hit the limit on my patience."

Norridge smiled. "Well, Agent Cooper, you *were* academy trained. Your childhood is essentially what we try to replicate. We turn up the intensity, of course, and we also provide access to programs to develop their gifts, resources your father couldn't have dreamed of. But. You were lonely. Isolated. Often punished for being what you were. You never had the opportunity to learn to trust other abnorms, and because you so often had to defend yourself for being one, you were unlikely to seek them out. You didn't have many friends and lived in a constantly shifting environment, which means you placed special value on the one rock in your world—your father. He was a military man, so concepts like duty and loyalty came easily to you. You grew up learning all the lessons we teach here. You even ended up working for the government, as the majority of our graduates do."

Cooper fought an urge to lean over and bang Director Norridge's face into the desk three or four times. It wasn't the things he was saying about Cooper's life, all of which were true, and none of which had stung him for years. It was the condescension and, worse, the bullying gleefulness of the man. Norridge didn't just want to make his point. Like the blond boy on the playground, he wanted to dominate.

"You still haven't answered my question. Why?"

"Surely you know."

"Indulge me," he said.

Norridge gave a tip of his head to acknowledge the returned volley. "The gifts of the vast majority of abnorms have no significant value. However, a rare handful have abilities that make them equivalent to the greatest geniuses of our history. Individually, that is reason enough to harness their power. However, the real concern is not the individual. It is the group. You, for example. What would happen if I were to attack you?"

Cooper smiled. "I wouldn't recommend it."

"What about someone more skilled? A boxer, or a martial artist?"

"Training can teach you how to defend yourself. But unless you were very, very good, your body would still reveal what you were about to do. That makes it easy for me to avoid."

"I see. And what about, say, three martial artists?"

"They'd win." Cooper shrugged. "Too many attacks to track."

Norridge nodded. Then he said, quietly, "And what about twenty totally average, out-of-shape, slightly overweight adults?"

Cooper narrowed his eyes—

He said "our history" and "their power." He doesn't see abnorms as human.

Despite that, he knows us so well he could identify your gift. That knowledge has been applied to every facet of life here.

He dissected your past and the sensitive spots in it based just on this conversation.

He could have illustrated this current point a hundred different ways. But he chose combat as a metaphor.

—and said, "I'd lose."

"Precisely. And we must always hold that advantage. It's the only way. The gifted cannot be allowed to band together. So from their youth we teach them that they cannot trust one another. That other abnorms are weak, cruel, and small. Their only comfort comes from a single *normal* figure, a mentor like the woman you heard earlier. And they learn core values like obedience and patriotism. In that way, we protect humanity." Norridge paused, then smiled toothily. It was a strange expression, knowing. It looked like given the chance, the man might take a bite out of him. "Does that make sense?"

"Yes," Cooper said. "I understand you now."

Norridge cocked his head. Whether he caught the real meaning or not, he'd at least caught the tone. "Forgive me. Getting me started can be dangerous."

No kidding.

"I should mention the tangible benefits, too. Academy graduates have made enormous breakthroughs in chemistry, mathematics, engineering, medicine—all of it government controlled. That recording device I mentioned? The nanotechnology is the work of a former pupil. All the latest military equipment is designed by abnorms. The computer systems that connect us. Even the new stock market, which is, ironically, immune to abnorm manipulation.

"All these things come from academy graduates. And thanks to our work, all are managed and controlled by the US government. Surely you can agree that as a nation—as a people—we can't afford another Erik Epstein."

Which people, Doc? Cooper could feel a scream boiling inside of him, a rage that he very much wanted to give in to. Everything here was worse than he had imagined.

No. Be honest. You never let yourself imagine it. Not really.

Still, now that he knew, what could he do about it? Kill the director, then the staff? Tear down the walls and blow up the dormitories? Lead the children like Moses out of Egypt?

It was either that or get the hell out of here. He stood.

Norridge looked surprised. "Are you satisfied, then?"

"Not even close." But if he stayed another minute he was going to explode, so he stalked out of the office, down the polished halls, past the narrow windows with their rocky evergreen vistas. Thinking, *This cannot be the way.*

And, *John Smith was raised in an academy. Not this one, but they'll all be the same, and there will be a Norridge heading all of them. An administrator who holds all the power, a skilled manipulator who understands and hates his pupils.*

John Smith was raised in an academy.

John Smith was at war from his earliest days.

CHAPTER 7

"Ground one?"

"We're go."

"Ground two?"

"Go."

"Three?"

"Freezing my tits off, but go." Luisa, bringing her usual flair.

"Crow's nest?"

"Two positions, overlapping sight lines. Go."

"God?"

"The view from on high is divine, my son." Behind the voice came the buzz of rotors. At the elevation the airship was flying, it was nothing but a darker gray spot against a bright gray sky. "God is good."

Cooper smiled and pressed the transmit button. "Peace be with you."

"And also with you. But woe betide the sorry shitbird who tries to run, lest we hurl a thunderbolt."

"Amen." He clicked off and gazed down through the double-thick glass at the meet site.

Today looked pretty much like yesterday, which was one of those things you could say about a lot of DC days between

November and March. The sunlight was weak tea, and gusts of wind tugged at the coats of powerbrokers, the scarves of businesswomen.

Ground two was the FedEx truck. It was parked on G Street, on the northwest corner. The back door was up, and an undercover agent was loading boxes on a dolly, checking each one against a manifest. Behind a makeshift shelf, four more agents were jammed together out of sight. It was a tight, uncomfortable space, but even so, they had it better than ground one; the utility van had been parked on 12th all night.

Cooper had done recon in those things before. They were dark and uncomfortable, boiling in the summer and frigid in the winter. Movement had to be restricted to the absolute minimum, and the air always reeked of urine from the quart jars they used. One time a junior agent had broken a jar, and after six scorching hours, the team had been ready to forget the target and beat the hell out of him.

11:30. The meet was set for noon. Good planning on the bad guys' part: lunchtime, and the corner below would be even busier as all the people in the surrounding buildings scurried from their cubicles.

"Camera feed good?"

"Better than." Bobby Quinn sat at a polished wood table twenty feet long. He'd co-opted the law firm's presentation system for his mobile headquarters, and the air in front of him shimmered with ghost images, video feeds from various angles. "The intersection is wired like a tri-d studio."

"Show me the transmitter."

Quinn gestured, and a map of the city streets glowed. "Green dot is this." Quinn tossed him the stamp drive. It looked perfectly normal, down to the half-rubbed-out logo on the side. Cooper pocketed it. His partner continued. "The red dot is Vasquez, the man himself."

"How'd you wire him?"

"His colon," Quinn deadpanned. Cooper glanced over sharply, but his partner continued. "Shiny newtech, just in from R and D. Some academy bright boy came up with a tracker in a gelcap. Enzyme-bonds to the lining of the large intestine."

"Wow. Is he…is it—"

"No. Bonds dissolve in about a week, and out it goes with the rest of the junk mail."

"Wow," Cooper repeated.

"Gives new meaning to the phrase 'stay on his ass.'"

"Been waiting to use that?"

"Since the moment they handed me the gelcap." Quinn looked up and smiled. "Learn anything useful yesterday?"

"Yeah. I learned Smith has a right to be pissed off."

"Hey, hey, whoa." Quinn dropped his voice. "Dickinson would flip if he heard you say that."

"*Screw* Roger Dickinson."

"Yeah, well, you know he'd be happy to screw you. So be careful." Quinn leaned back. "What's really going on?"

Cooper thought of yesterday afternoon, the relief he'd felt as he hit the road. The Monongahela National Forest blurring around him, huddled trees and ragged mountains, prefab housing dropped at random.

I MISS MY SON, the pale woman's placard had read.

"They aren't schools, Bobby. They're brainwashing centers."

"Come on—"

"I'm not being poetic. That's literally what they are. I mean, I'd heard things, we all have, but I didn't believe it. Who could treat children this way?" Cooper shook his head. "Turns out the answer is, we can."

"We?"

"They're government facilities. DAR facilities."

"But not Equitable Services."

"Close enough."

"It's not 'close enough.'" Quinn's voice sharp. "You are not personally responsible for the actions of an entire agency."

"See, that's where you're wrong. We all—"

"Do you believe that Alex Vasquez was trying to make the world a better place?"

"What?"

"Do you believe that Alex Vasquez—"

"No."

"Do you believe that John Smith is trying to make the world a better place?"

"No."

"Do you believe that he is responsible for killing a whole bunch of people?"

"Yes."

"Innocent people?"

"Yes."

"Children?"

"Yes."

"Then let's go get him. That is what we do. We take down bad people who hurt good people. Preferably *before* they hurt the good people. That's our responsibility. After that," Quinn said, "we go out for beer. Which you buy. That's your responsibility."

Cooper chuckled despite himself. "Yeah, all right, Bobby. I hear you."

"Good."

"That was something." Cooper stood. "Getting all *righteous* on me. Didn't know you had it in you."

"I am multilayered. Like an onion."

"That part I'll buy." Cooper clapped his friend on the shoulder. "I'm going to check on Vasquez."

"Calm him down, will you? He's sweating so bad I'm afraid he might somehow shake that tracker loose after all."

"And thank you for that image."

"Here for you, boss." Quinn yawned and put his feet up on the polished wood table.

Cooper strolled down the hall, passing a gold logo with the names of three white guys followed by 'LLC.' The law office was in a building overlooking the Metro station where the meet was to take place. Quinn had reached out to them yesterday, and the partners had been delighted to help Equitable Services. Cooper had met one of them earlier, a trim guy with a halo of white hair who had wished him good hunting.

Good hunting. Shit.

Two guards stood outside the corner office, their tactical blacks today replaced by bland business suits. The submachine guns were still ready-slung. He nodded at them. One said, "Sir," and opened the office door.

Inside, Bryan Vasquez stood by the window, his hands against the glass. At the sound, he jumped, turning with an expression that was part guilt and part nerves.

Fever Orange, Cooper decided to name the color. He thanked the guard, then stepped inside.

"You startled me," Bryan said. He had one hand pressed against the glass, the other to his chest. Ghostly white dots of condensation marked where the pads of his fingers had rested on the window. There were sweat stains at his armpits, and his chest rose and fell swiftly. He licked his lips as he shifted his weight from right to left.

Cooper slid his hands into his pockets and—

He's dedicated to his sister, but he's also a believer. He's worried about his own safety but would never admit it. He's attracted to the idea of plots and secret worlds, to comrades in arms.

He needs a strong hand, but not so strong he shatters. He needs to be pumped up and sent out to do his piece for a better world.

—stepped into the room. "Sorry about that. I always get jumpy before these things, too." He pulled out the chair, spun it around, then sat with his arms on the back. "This part drives me crazy."

"What part?"

"The waiting. Too much time in your head. Once things start, it gets better. You know what you have to do, and you just do it. It's easier. Don't you think?"

Bryan Vasquez cocked his head and turned to lean against the window with his arms crossed. "I don't know. I've never had to betray something I believe in to save my sister before."

"Fair point." He let the silence hang. Bryan looked like a man who expected to be punched; slowly he realized the blow wasn't in the air. A faint wind howled along the edge of the glass, and somewhere far away, a car horn sounded. Finally, he moved to the desk and slumped awkwardly in the chair on the other side, all angles and elbows.

"I know this is hard," Cooper said. "But you're doing the right thing."

"Sure." The word drifting across the table.

"Can I tell you something?" He waited until the other man looked up. "Everything you said the other day about the way gifted are treated? I agree."

"Right."

"I'm an abnorm."

Bryan's face crinkled in conflicting directions: surprise and disbelief and anger. Finally the guy said, "What is it for you?"

"Pattern recognition, a sort of souped-up intuition. I read intention. That can be really specific, like knowing where someone is going to throw a punch. But personal patterns work, too; I get to know somebody, my gift forms a picture of them, helps me guess what they'll do."

"So if you're gifted, what are you doing—"

"Working for the DAR?" Cooper shrugged. "Actually, pretty much the same reasons you helped your sister."

"Bullshit."

"It's not. I want my children to live in a world where abnorms and straights coexist. The difference is, I don't think you get there by blowing things up. Especially when one group vastly outnumbers the other. See, normal people, like *you*"—he gestured with palms together—"if you decided to, you could wipe out all the people like *me*. Every one of us, or close enough it wouldn't matter. It's a numbers game. You have ninety-nine to every one of us."

"But that's exactly why—" Bryan Vasquez stopped. "I mean."

"I know how you feel about the way Alex is treated. But you're an engineer. Think logically. The relationship between norms and brilliants, it's gunpowder. You really want to strike sparks?"

He pulled the stamp drive from his pocket, set it on the desk, halfway between them. "Don't forget," Cooper said, "you're not doing this for me. You're doing it for Alex."

It was a calculated play, backing up the philosophical get-out-of-jail-free card with a personal imperative. And it was far from the first time he had lied to a suspect.

So why am I feeling guilty about it?

The academy. Seeing that place had stirred up issues he thought he'd made peace with. Cooper pushed away thoughts of the playground, of the woman with the placard, and locked down his expression.

Bryan Vasquez took the stamp drive.

Cooper said, "Let's go."

■

"This is Quarterback. The ball is in play; repeat, Delivery Boy is moving. Headquarters, confirm."

"Confirmed," Bobby Quinn's voice crackled in his ear. "Both signals are strong."

The square across the street looked as planned and uninviting as ever, the black branches of manicured trees tossing in the wind. A couple of hardy souls huddled around the entrance to the nearest building, rocking from foot to foot as they sucked on cigarettes. The entrance to Metro Center Station had a steady stream of traffic. A row of newspaper dispensers, bright red and orange and yellow, ran along a low wall; at the end of it a man in a wheelchair shook a paper cup at passersby.

Cooper kept his stance casual, pitched his voice low. "God, what have you got?"

"Delivery Boy is heading north on 13th."

"Clear view?"

"God sees all, my son."

Everything is in place. You're about to be a step closer to catching the most dangerous man in America.

Across the street, the agent at the FedEx truck finished loading his dolly and started for the near building. In a bench on the square, two women in business casual chatted as they picked at salads. One looked like the assistant principal of a middle school; the other was petite and lithe as a soccer player.

"How you doing, Luisa?"

"Never thought I'd say this," dabbing at her lips with a napkin to cover the motion of her lips, "but I actually wish I was back in that cow-humping Texas backwater we just left."

Luisa Abrahams was barely over five feet, pretty but not beautiful, famous for talking like a trucker, and perhaps the most stubborn person he knew. He'd picked her for his team after a mess of an op where her agent in charge had lost communication with her. The AIC hadn't realized that her cover was blown and she needed support, so Luisa had chased a target two miles on foot, finally run him down, finished the job, and then called the AIC using her target's cell phone. The insults she'd hurled at him had circulated the agency for weeks.

Now she sat on a bench alongside Valerie West, the two of them pretending to be on their lunch. Val was a whiz with data analysis, but nervous in the field. Cooper was watching her shred her napkin, and weighing whether it was worth it to say something, when Luisa touched the other woman's knee, said something off-mic. Valerie nodded, shrugged her shoulders back, and tucked the napkin in her pocket. Good. Normally Cooper would have discouraged a romantic relationship between teammates, but the two often seemed better agents because of it.

Half a block away, Bryan Vasquez appeared in the crowd, walking behind a pair of tourists draped in cameras.

"All eyes," he said. "Delivery Boy is here."

Cooper ran through a mental checklist, making sure that everything was in place. Between the tracker, the cameras, the airship, and the agents, they had the corner locked down tight. Whoever came to meet Bryan Vasquez was going to be sitting in an interview room within an hour, bathing in that hopeless light and wondering just how true the rumors about Equitable Services' "enhanced interrogation" privileges were.

Too bad we can't let them walk and follow them to others. The payoff could be sweet, but the risk was simply too great; with an attack imminent, if their only lead got away, it could cost God knew how many lives.

Through the earpiece Cooper could hear the calls and confirmations of his team tracking Bryan Vasquez. The man was walking on the other side of the street, and Cooper carefully didn't look quite at him. Just loosened his stance and opened up his senses, trying to take in the whole scene, to parse it, filter for the pattern beneath. The faded yellow blur of a taxi. The texture of a tweed coat. The smells of auto exhaust and cooking grease from a fast-food restaurant. The dull platinum glow of the sky and the shadowless noon it created. The determined set of Bryan Vasquez's shoulders as he stepped onto the sidewalk and turned to look around. The clanging of a flagpole halyard driven to dance by the wind. The bright red and yellow newspaper dispensers behind Vasquez. The muted rumble of the Metro and the rot smell of the sewer grate and the squeal of brakes two blocks down and the very, very pretty girl talking on the cell phone.

A man in an oxblood leather jacket crossed the street toward Vasquez. There was purpose in his stride, a vector Cooper could see as if it was drawn with an arrow.

"Possible ID, leather jacket."

In his ear, the team confirmed the sighting. On the bench, Luisa set down her salad and put a hand on her purse.

Vasquez turned to face the guy, his eyes a question.

The man in the leather jacket slipped his hand into his right front pocket.

Vasquez's eyes darted from side to side.

Cooper forced himself to hold. He had to be sure.

The man stepped up to Vasquez...and then past him. He pulled a handful of change from his pocket and began to feed the newspaper dispenser.

Cooper let out his breath. He turned back to Vasquez, wanting to send him strength with a look, to let him know it was all right, it was under control.

Which is what he was doing when Bryan Vasquez exploded.

CHAPTER 8

The flames blew outward like the spray from a sunset ocean, orange and yellow and blue, ripples of fire spilling and sloshing. In slow motion they had an ethereal beauty. The fire roiled and twisted. In front of the blast, dark shapes surfed, indistinct and spinning. It was really quite lovely.

Until the torn metal slivers riding the shockwave struck Bryan Vasquez like a thousand whirling razor blades.

"That's precision work," Quinn said. "See the way the explosion is shaped? Boom, straight out of the newspaper box. Whoever set it up designed their charges with care. All the force was projected forward through packed metal shavings. Result is a cone wide enough to guarantee they got their target, but not much else."

From Cooper's perspective, the thousands of metal shavings had looked like a swarm of locusts tearing Vasquez apart. The explosion had stunned his ears, and even now Quinn's voice seemed to be coming through a thick bath towel. He had a throbbing headache and burns on his hands from the metal trash can that he'd touched dragging a shrieking woman away from the fire.

For a short moment after the bomb went off, the world hovered in surreal balance. Thick smoke billowed from the wreckage.

The limbs of a tree burned with pale orange fire like autumn leaves. Sound was disjointed, disassociated, effect not seeming to follow from cause. A woman wiped at her face, smearing blood and hair that had once been Bryan Vasquez.

It was as if, Cooper thought, the bomb had been inside of Bryan, as if he himself had been an explosive device.

People stared at one another, unsure what to do, what this disturbance to their daily lives meant. But bombings had grown more frequent in the last years, and if one had never happened to them, they had at least seen it on TV and assembled their reaction from that. Some ran away; some ran to help. A few screamed. Sirens began to fill the noon air. Agents poured out of the FedEx truck and the phone company van. Then the real chaos started, cops and firemen and EMS and news crews converging from every direction.

A nightmare. What should have been a quiet little operation was now looping on CNN. Drew Peters had immediately played the national-security card, shutting down any connection to the DAR. There had been a half a dozen bombings this year alone, mostly by abnorm-rights fringe groups, and for now, it was easy enough to pass this off as just another one. But a bomb going off in Washington, DC, half a mile from the White House? That would get more attention. Chances were someone would dig up the DAR's involvement.

That wasn't Cooper's problem. He stayed out of politics. What bothered him was that John Smith had beaten them. He'd taken away the only lead they had on a major attack. "Who triggered it? The guy in the leather jacket?"

Quinn shook his head. They'd finally made it back to DAR headquarters, and he had the explosion footage up on one of the big monitors. He pressed a few keys, and the crimson slag heap sucked inward and upward to become Bryan Vasquez. The flames retreated, waving like banners. The door of the newspaper dispenser shut the explosion behind it. A man in a leather jacket put a copy of the *New York Times* back in the neighboring machine. "See? He's beside the blast. He lost an ear—which doesn't matter, because he damn sure lost the hearing in it—and the docs are working now to see if they can save his left arm."

"Could have been a suicide run," Luisa said, way too loud. She'd been closer to the bomb than any of them.

"Maybe, but why? Besides, if he was doing the martyr dance, why not wire him instead of setting up a fake newspaper machine?"

"Maybe because it was supposed to be a secure area? Maybe because that should have been the only way to get a bomb in at all?" She was small but fearless, and Cooper had seen her leap into fights with men twice her size. "I thought you had the whole scene under control."

"I *did*," Quinn said too fast, his hands up. He looked from Luisa to Valerie, saw no support there either. Neither had been in the path of the shrapnel, but the shockwave had tossed them both like rag dolls, and neither looked inclined to forget it. Quinn turned to him. "Nick, shit, I was there all day yesterday, and the team in the van spent the night. We've got twenty hours of footage from a stack of cameras. Nobody planted the bomb."

Cooper coughed. His partner reddened. "I mean, no one planted it while we were there. They must have put it there in advance."

"And you didn't check." Luisa's voice had a dangerous edge to it. "I got an idea, Bobby. How about next time *I* secure the scene, and *you* sit on the park bench in a skirt?"

"Weezy, I'm sorry, but—"

"Don't you dare, you piece of—"

"Enough," Cooper said. He rubbed at his eyes and listened to the sounds surrounding them, the clacking of keys, the quiet voices of analysts and operators speaking into microphones. Even in the face of this, and of the looming attack, there were still thousands of tier-one abnorms to track, dozens of active targets. "Enough. Two days we lost here. Two days and nothing to show for it." He straightened, looking from one to the other. "You all need to get it through your heads. John Smith is not just a twist with a grudge. He may be a sociopath, but he's a chess master, the strategic equivalent of Einstein. I'll bet he had that bomb in place weeks ago. You hear me? *Weeks ago.* Probably before Alex Vasquez even left Boston."

Luisa and Valerie looked at each other. He could read the fear in Valerie's eyes and the protectiveness that elicited in Luisa's. Quinn opened his mouth as if he was waiting for the words to come on their own. Finally he said, "You're right. I'm sorry. I should have checked everything inside a hundred yards of the meet."

"Yeah, you should have. You screwed up, Bobby."

Quinn lowered his head.

"And I should have told you to check. So we both screwed up." Cooper took a deep breath, blew it out hard. "Okay. Let's start with who triggered the bomb. Val, you're our analysis expert."

"I haven't had time to review—"

"Gimme your gut."

"Well, if it was me, I'd do it remotely. All you need is a detonator and a clear view."

"How would you trigger it?"

"A cell phone, probably," she continued. "Cheap, dependable, won't arouse suspicion if you're caught with it. Just dial the—" She broke off, her eyes going wide. "Bobby, move."

"Huh?"

"*Move.*" She pushed the man out of his chair, then took it herself. Her fingers flew over the keyboard. The big screen flickered, and the frozen video of the explosion vanished, replaced by columns of numbers.

Cooper said, "If you can access the local cell towers and isolate calls made within a few seconds of the explosion—"

"I'm on it, boss."

A voice from behind said, "We need to talk."

Dickinson. Damn, but he walks softly for a big man. Cooper turned, met the agent's eyes. Saw the anger crackling there. Not rage, nothing so out of control. More like anger was the fuel his engine burned.

To his team Cooper said, "Keep on it. This won't take long." He started away, jerking his head for Dickinson to follow without waiting to see if the man would. Alpha-dog posturing, stupid but necessary. He led the way to a dead space beside the stairs, put on a smile because he just couldn't resist, and said, "What's on your mind?"

"What's on my *mind*? How about what's on your collar?" Dickinson gestured. "That wouldn't be a little Bryan Vasquez, would it?"

Cooper glanced down. "No. That blood belonged to a woman I pulled away from the fire."

"Are you actually proud of yourself?"

"That's not the word I'd choose, no. You got a point?"

"I found Bryan Vasquez. I brought him in. We had one lead, *one*, and I brought him in. And you just let him get blown up."

"Yeah, none of us really liked him. We took a vote, decided what the hell—"

"Is this a joke to you?"

"Tell me, Roger. What would you have done differently?"

"I wouldn't have put him on that street corner in the first place."

"Oh yeah? Just lock up his twist-loving ass and throw away the key?"

"No. Handcuff his twist-loving ass to a chair and go to work."

"A little recreational enhanced interrogation?" Cooper snorted, shook his head. "You could waterboard him till he grew gills, and it wouldn't change the fact that he didn't know anything."

"You don't know that. And now we never will."

"We're agents of the United States government, not some Third World dictator's private security force. That is not the way we work. We don't have a torture chamber in the basement."

"Yeah, well." Dickinson stared at him, his gaze level, eyes unblinking. "Maybe we should."

Yikes.

"Roger, I don't know what your problem is. I don't know if it's a personal grudge, or ambition, or if you just need to get laid. But we have a fundamental difference of opinion on what our mission is. Now if you'll excuse me, I'm going to go do my actual, legal job." He started away.

"You want to know what my problem with you is? Seriously, do you want to know?"

"I already do." Cooper turned. "I'm an abnorm."

"No. It's got nothing to do with that. I'm not a bigot. The problem," Dickinson said, stepping forward, "is that you're weak. You're in charge, and you're weak. And Equitable Services needs strong people. Believers." He held the glare for a moment longer, and then he brushed past.

Cooper watched him go. Shook his head. *I'm going to go with needs to get laid.*

"Everything copacetic?" Bobby Quinn asked as he returned to the workstation.

"Sure. What have we got?"

Valerie West said, "The nearest cell tower reports a dozen calls within ten seconds. Eight of them local. When you triangulate the location, only one set of GPS coordinates makes sense: 38.898327 by -77.027775."

"Which is…"

"Right about…" She zoomed in on the map. As she did, Cooper felt that intuitive tingle, like a tickle in his brain, his gift jumping ahead to tell him what he was about to see. "There." The screen showed G Street, half a block east of 12th. The entryway to a bank. He recognized it.

He'd been standing right beside it.

Cooper closed his eyes, thought back. The movement of the moment, so many things he'd been taking in. The faded yellow blur of a taxi. The smell of auto exhaust, cooking grease from a fast-food restaurant. The muted rumble of the Metro and the rot smell of the sewer grate and the squeal of brakes two blocks down and the very, very pretty girl talking on the cell phone.

You gotta be kidding me. He turned to Quinn. "Do we have video of that spot?"

"My cams were all pointing across the street." His partner looked at the screen, pinched his lips, then snapped his fingers. "The bank. It would have security cameras."

"Get in touch. See if you can find a picture of our bomber."

Quinn snatched his suit coat from the back of the chair. "On it."

Cooper turned back to the two women. "We need to get out ahead of this thing. Valerie, we have Alex's and Bryan's cell phones, right?"

She nodded. "SOP would be to dupe his when we arrested him. And analysts are probably already working her phone, pattern building based on the contact info."

"Good. Initiate a search. I want digital taps on every number in their cell phone. To two degrees of separation."

Luisa's mouth fell open. "Je-sus," she whispered.

Valerie was doing that thing with her hands again, only without the napkin to shred this time. "Two degrees?"

"Yeah. I want taps on every contact in both phones. Then, any number that has connected with any of those contacts? I want them tapped, too. Going back...six months."

"Christ on a chorus line." Luisa stared. "That'll be hundreds of people."

"Probably more like fifteen or twenty thousand." Cooper glanced at his watch. "Get the academy coders on board. Pull them off the Echelon II scans we're running for John Smith if you have to. If anyone out there says anything, *anything*, that sounds related to this attack, I want analysts digging in fifteen seconds later. You get me?"

"I get you." Valerie's face showed the early traces of excitement. It was a dream for someone like her. The keys to the kingdom. He had essentially made this the single biggest investigative priority in the country and then put her in charge of it.

"Boss," Luisa said. "I don't mean to second-guess. But twenty thousand NatSec taps, all initiated without a judge? Not to mention pulling the resources, what a monster bitch of a bill this will come with? Are you sure? I mean, you know what they'll do to you if it doesn't work, right?"

"I'll be sent to bed without supper." Cooper shrugged. "Make sure it works out. If it doesn't, we have bigger things to worry about than my career."

CHAPTER 9

The Monocle on Capitol Hill was an institution. Located just a few blocks from the Senate offices, the place had hosted DC's powerbrokers for fifty years. The walls were covered with autographed eight-by-tens of every politician of influence for five decades, every president since Kennedy. It was busy even on a Monday evening.

A Monday evening like the one when John Smith strolled in.

He was broad shouldered but lithe, a quarterback's body wrapped in a decent suit, with a white shirt open-collared beneath. Three men followed him, their movements almost synchronized, as though they had practiced the act of stepping into a restaurant.

Smith ignored them. He paused in the entrance, looking around as if to memorize the scene. When a pretty hostess touched his arm and asked if he was meeting someone, he smiled as he nodded, and she smiled back.

The restaurant was split between bar and dining area. The former was boisterous, a deluge of laughter and conversation. Half a dozen flatscreens ran the Wizards game; three minutes to the end, and they were down ten points. The patrons were mostly men, ties tucked between the third and fourth buttons of their shirts. Smith walked through, past the stools holding lawyers and tourists and clerks and strategists. The three men followed.

The restaurant portion was mood lighting and high-backed booths, patrician, with the feel of a previous era. An appellate judge clinked cocktail glasses with a woman not his daughter. A family from Indiana took in the scene, Mom and Dad chatting around mouthfuls of steak while Junior used the scraps of his hamburger to buttress the walls of Fort French Fry. A corporate headhunter put the recruitment moves on a twentysomething in nerd glasses.

John Smith walked past them all to a booth on the right-hand side. The upholstery was dimpled and worn with use, and the table had the polish of decades. On the wall, Jimmy Carter beamed down, the words "Best crab cakes around!" slanting above his signature.

The man in the booth wore hair gel and pinstripes. His moustache was more salt than pepper, and the nose that had delighted caricaturists was crisscrossed with broken capillaries. But when he turned to look at John Smith, his eyes were bright and alert, and there was in that movement more than an echo of the figure he had cut, the once-feared and still-respected senator from Ohio, onetime chair of Finance, former presidential hopeful with a strong chance until the Panamanian thing.

For a moment the two men looked at one another. Senator Hemner smiled.

John Smith shot him in the face.

The three bodyguards shrugged out of their coats, revealing cross-slung Heckler & Koch tactical submachine guns. Each took the time to extend the retractable metal stock and brace the weapon against his shoulder. The red light of an exit sign fell like blood against their backs. Their shots were precise and clustered. There was no spraying, no wide sweeps. They double-tapped a target and moved to the next. Most of the victims hadn't even risen from their chairs. A few tried to run. A man made it halfway to the entry before his throat exploded. A woman in a dress rose, cocktail glass shattering in her hand as the bullet passed through it to her heart. Screaming and more shots came from the bar, where a second team had entered. A third team had broken through the back door and was shooting immigrants in chef whites. The mother from Indiana slid beneath the table and yanked her son with her, clutching him in her arms.

When the guns were empty, the men reloaded and began firing again.

Cooper touched the screen of his datapad, and the image froze. The security camera had been mounted near the stairs to the conference rooms, and the angle was at once disjointed and horrifying, the violence more real because of the lack of Hollywood techniques. The pause had caught a teardrop of white fire exploding from a submachine gun barrel. Behind the three, John Smith stood with his pistol at his side, his face attentive but not involved, a man watching a play. The body of Senator Max "Hammer" Hemner had fallen back against the booth, a neat hole punched in his forehead.

Cooper sighed, rubbed at his eyes. Almost two in the morning, but though he was tired and sore, sleep hadn't come. After lying in bed for forty-five useless minutes, he'd decided if he was just going to stare at something, better it was the case file than the ceiling.

He put a finger on the touchscreen and moved it slowly. The video scrubbed in response. Forward: a shooter released the magazine on his gun, let it fall to the ground as he slotted a replacement and aimed again. Backward: a shooter pulled the magazine from his gun as another leaped up from the floor and inserted itself into the weapon. The whole thing was Zen, smooth and clean and practiced. Almost the same forward or reverse.

Cooper used two fingers to zoom, then panned until Smith's face filled the screen. His features were balanced and even, strong jaw, good eyelashes. The kind of face a woman might find handsome rather than hot, the kind that belonged to a golf pro or a trial lawyer. There was nothing that hinted at barbarism or rage, no hint of giggling madness. As his soldiers killed everyone in the restaurant—every single man, woman, and child, busboy, tourist, and senator, seventy-three in all, seventy-three KIA and not one wounded—John Smith simply watched. Calm and unaffected. When it was done, he walked out. Strolled, really. Cooper had watched the video hundreds of times in the last four years, had grown inured to the obvious horrors, to the spray of blood and the lethal calm of the soldiers. But one thing chilled him still, a thing perhaps especially frightening to a man with his eyes. It was the total lack of impact the massacre had on the man who started it. His shoulders were down, his neck was relaxed, his steps light, his fingers loose.

John Smith strolled out of the Monocle as if he'd just popped in for a quiet drink.

Cooper dumped out of the video, tossed the datapad on the table, and took a long swallow of water. Vodka sounded better, but it would make tomorrow morning's jog less pleasant. The ice had mostly melted, and the glass was slick with cold sweat. He rocked his neck from side to side, then picked the pad back up and began punching through the rest of the file, not looking for anything in particular. The headlines, ranging from dispassionate (ABNORM ACTIVIST SLAYS 73; SENATOR KILLED IN DC BLOODBATH) to incendiary (A GIFT FOR SAVAGERY; MONSTERS IN OUR MIDST). The stories that accompanied them, and the ones that ran in the weeks to follow. Reports of abnorm children beaten at their schools, a tier two lynched in Alabama. Columnists who appealed for calm and decency, who pointed out that the actions of a single individual should not be held against the group; other pundits who spewed smoke and ash, who whipped the baser demons to howl. The event had dominated headlines. But when John Smith hadn't been caught in months, and then years, the story had faded from the foreground of public consciousness.

There was more. Text and video of speeches Smith had made for abnorm rights before the massacre. He'd been a terrific speaker, actually, at once inspiring and intimate. Detailed logs of the Echelon II protocols running to find him. Incident reports from half a dozen near misses. Biographic details, genetic profile, personal data. Lengthy analyses of his gift, a logistical and strategic sense that had made him a chess grand master at eleven. Transcriptions of every ranked chess match he had played. Terabytes of data, and Cooper had read every word, watched every frame.

And still, today.

A few more stabs at the datapad, and the headlines were replaced by the VCS. Virtual Crime Scenes—there was a piece of newtech he wasn't sure he was glad of. A photorealistic, completely manipulatable model of the inside of the Monocle as John Smith had left it, down to every smear of blood and spatter of brain matter. Cooper could pan and twist and tilt to any angle, could view the mess from the height of the ceiling or the intimacy of inches. It was an incredibly useful forensic tool that had been instrumental in solving many cases, but that didn't make it any easier to take when he scrolled down beneath the table where Juliet Lynch had dragged her son, Kevin. Being able to see the angle of her body, the star-shaped hole in her face, that was forensically handy. But the ability to see her expression, the remnants of the face of a woman who had without warning watched her husband's head explode, who had in an incomprehensible instant gone from the simple happiness of a family vacation to howling chaos and the abyss, that Cooper didn't need or want. It was one thing to understand she had died knowing—not fearing, knowing—her son would die, too; it was another to see the holes in the hand she had stretched out to protect him, as if a mother's palm could stop bullets.

Screw the jog. Cooper pushed himself up from the couch and walked to the kitchen. The fluorescent light seemed surreal at this hour, and the standard-issue black-and-white floor tile was grim.

He dumped the rest of his water in the sink, dropped a couple of ice cubes into the glass, and poured chilled vodka over them.

Back in the living room, he picked up his phone and dialed. Took a sip, savored the icy bite.

"Hey, Cooper," Quinn said, his voice thick with sleep. "You okay?"

"I was just watching the Monocle."

"Again?"

"Yeah. What are we doing, Bobby?"

"Well, we're not sleeping."

"Sorry about that."

"S'okay. Just busting your balls. So. The Monocle."

"The VCS. That woman under the table."

"Juliet Lynch."

"Right. I was looking at that again, and it hit me, that could have been Natalie. And the kid, it could have been Todd."

"Shit. Yeah."

"What are we doing? All of us, I mean. Ever since I visited the academy, I haven't been able to shake it."

"Shake what?"

"The feeling that things are about to get a lot worse. That we're on the brink, and nobody seems to want to step away from it. All these horrors we're creating. The academies, the Monocle, they're the same. Flip sides of the same horror. And meanwhile, I've got two kids."

"And mentally you're putting Kate in an academy and Todd at the Monocle."

"Yeah."

"Don't."

"I know."

"All of this stuff, it's a mess. I know. We all know. Not just DAR. The whole country, the whole world, knows it. We've been on this collision course for thirty years."

"So why aren't we swerving?"

"Got me, boss. That's above my pay grade."

Cooper made a sound that wasn't a laugh. "Yeah."

"You know what I do, these thoughts hit me?"

"What?"

"I pour myself a stiff drink."

"Check."

"Good. Listen, I know you want to take this on. But all we can do is our job, one day at a time. I mean, at least we're in the game. We're *trying*. The rest of the world is just hoping things work out okay."

"He's out there right now. Somewhere. John Smith. He's out there, and he's planning an attack."

"You know what he's not doing?"

"Huh?"

"He's not calling his best friend to agonize over whether the world is going to shit. That's how I know we're the good guys."

"Yeah."

"Get some sleep. For all we know, Smith's attack is coming tomorrow."

"You're right. Thanks. Sorry for the hour."

"No worries. And Coop?"

"Yeah?"

"Finish that drink."

■

He made himself jog the next morning as planned. Cooper did five miles twice a week, hit the gym opposite days, and sometimes enjoyed it, though not today. The weather was nice enough, warmish and bright for a change, and last night's insomnia cocktails didn't affect him as much as he'd feared. But part of the pleasure of exercise was losing himself in the physical, offlining the analytical side of his brain for a while and just concentrating on his breathing and the rhythm of his muscles and the beat through his headphones. This morning, unfortunately, John Smith jogged with him. The length of the run, all Cooper could think about was something he had said yesterday. *He may be a sociopath, but he's also a chess master. The strategic equivalent of Einstein.*

The trick was to figure out how to beat a man like that. Cooper was the top agent at arguably the most powerful organization in the country. He had enormous resources at his disposal; he could access secret data, tap phone lines, command police and federal agencies alike, deploy black-ops teams on American soil. If an abnorm had been designated a target, Cooper could kill without legal consequence—and had, on thirteen occasions. He could, in short, bring incredible force to bear…but only if he knew where to focus it.

His opponent, meanwhile, could attack wherever he wanted, whenever he wanted. Not only that, but even a partial success was a victory for him, where for Cooper, anything less than complete triumph was a failure. Prevent half the casualties of a suicide bomber, and you still had a suicide bomber and a lot of dead bodies.

Brooding on it made a five-mile run seem like ten. And in one of those charming little ironic moments, when he passed the convenience store at the end of his block, he saw that the locked security roll door had been freshly graffitied: I AM JOHN SMITH.

What you are, pal, is an asshole with a can of spray paint. And man, *do I wish I'd rounded the corner as you were finishing up.*

Inside his apartment, he peeled off the sweaty T-shirt, caught a whiff—yow, laundry time—and headed for the shower. When he was done, he flipped on CNN as he toweled his hair.

"…a significant increase in the so-called Unrest Index, to 7.7, the highest level since the measurement's introduction. The jump is largely attributed to yesterday's bombing in Washington, DC, which claimed…"

In the closet he chose a soft gray suit with a pale blue shirt, open collared. He checked the load on the Beretta—it was full, of course, but army habits died hard—and then clipped the holster to his hip.

"...controversial billionaire Erik Epstein, whose New Canaan Holdfast in Wyoming has grown to seventy-five thousand residents, most of them gifted, and their families. The twenty-three-thousand-square-mile area, purchased by Epstein through numerous holding companies, has become a polarizing factor not only in the state, where New Canaan's occupants comprise nearly fifteen percent of Wyoming's total population, but in the country at large with the introduction of House Joint Resolution 93, a measure to allow the region to secede as a sovereign nation..."

Breakfast. Cooper broke three eggs in a bowl, beat them frothy, and dumped them in a nonstick pan. He toasted a couple of slices of sourdough, poured a coffee big enough to dock a yacht, slid the scrambled eggs on the toast, and squirted sriracha on top of that.

"...culminating in an opening ceremony at two o'clock this afternoon. Developed to be impregnable to individuals like Mr. Epstein, the new Leon Walras Exchange will function as an auction house. Instead of the former NYSE's real-time trading of every stock, company shares will be offered in daily auctions with descending bid prices. Final prices will be locked in according to the average at which they are purchased, thus removing the possibility..."

He'd overcooked the eggs a little, but the hot sauce made up for it. Hot sauce made up for most everything. Cooper finished the last bites, licked his fingers, and glanced at the clock. Just after seven in the morning. Even with traffic, he'd be at headquarters early enough to review the highlights of the phone taps before the weekly target status review meeting.

Cooper set his plate in the sink, dusted off his hands, and headed out. He skipped the elevator and took the three flights to the ground. It really was a lovely morning. The air was warm and rich with that ionized smell he usually associated with thunderstorms, but the horizon was clear and bright. As he reached the car, his phone rang. Natalie. Huh. His ex-wife was many things—sincere, clever, a wonderful mother—but "morning person" was not on that list. "Hey, I didn't know you could manage to dial a phone at this hour."

"Nick," she said, and at the sound of her voice and the sob that cut her off, all light vanished from the morning sky.

And that was before he heard what came next.

CHAPTER 10

Cooper's apartment in Georgetown was eight miles from the house he and Natalie had shared in Del Ray. Like most DC drives, it had moments of grandeur set among long stretches of drab ugliness, all divided into agonizingly short blocks with lights at every damn one. Add city traffic, and the eight miles usually took twenty-five minutes, thirty if you skipped 395 and stuck to surface streets.

Cooper made it in twelve.

He opted for the Jefferson Davis, a distinctly unpretty street, but four lanes each direction. The transponder in his Charger broadcast a signal that marked him as a gas man to every cop within a mile, and so he treated speed limits as jokes and red lights as suggestions. When a cascade of brake lights bloomed before him, he downshifted to third and bumped the car up on the median.

He slowed when he pulled down her street—lot of kids on the block—parked, flipped off the car, and climbed out all in one motion.

Natalie was already coming out to meet him. She was dressed for work, in boots, a gray skirt to the knee, and a soft white sweater.

But even though her eyes were dry and her mascara unsmudged, to his eyes she was bawling. He opened his arms and she came into them hard, threw her own around his back and squeezed. There was a humid sense to her, as though tears were coming out her pores. Her breath smelled of coffee.

Cooper held her for a moment, then stepped back and took her hands in his. "Tell me."

"I told you—"

"Tell me again."

"They're going to test her. Kate. They're going to test her. She's only four, and the test isn't mandatory until she's eight—"

"Shhh." He ran his thumbs across her palms, squeezed in the center, an old gesture. "It's okay. Tell me what happened."

Natalie took a deep breath, then exhaled noisily. "They called. This morning."

"Who?"

"The Department of Analysis and Response." She put a hand to the side of her head as though to brush her hair back, although none had fallen. "You."

His belly was cold stone. He opened his mouth but found no words eager to come out.

"I'm sorry," she said, glancing away. "That was shitty."

"It's okay." He huffed a breath of his own. "Tell me—"

"Something happened. At school. There was 'an incident.'" She made the air quotes audible. "A week ago. A teacher witnessed Kate doing something and reported it to the DAR."

Gifts were amorphous in children, often indistinguishable from simply being bright, which is why the test wasn't mandatory until age eight. But people in certain roles—teachers, preachers, full-time nannies—were supposed to report behavior they found particularly compelling evidence of a tier-one gift. One of many things Cooper hated about the way things were going; for his money, the world didn't need more snitches. "What incident? What happened?"

She shrugged. "I don't know. The gutless bureaucrat wouldn't tell me."

"And so—"

"And so he asked whether it would be more convenient to test my daughter next Thursday or Friday. I told him that she was only four, that you worked for the DAR. He just kept saying the same thing. 'I'm sorry, ma'am, but this is policy.' Like he was the phone company and I had a complaint about my fucking bill."

Natalie doesn't swear. The thought drifted pointlessly through his mind. "Have you talked to her about it?"

"No," she said. Then a pause. "I'll—we'll—have to. Nick, she's gifted. We know she's gifted. What if she's tier one?" She turned away, eyes finally wet, the tears he had seen the moment he arrived now there for the world. "They'll take her from us, send her to an academy."

"Stop." Cooper reached out, took her chin in his hand, turned it back to face him. "That's not going to happen."

"But—"

"Listen to me. That is not going to happen. I'm not going to let that happen. Our daughter is not going to an academy." *I MISS MY SON,* her sign had read. "Period. I don't care if she's tier one. I don't care if she's the first tier zero in history and can manipulate space-time while shooting lasers from her belly button. She is *not* going to an academy. And she's not getting tested next week."

"Dad!"

Natalie and he exchanged a look. A look older by far than either of them, a look that had bounced between women and men as long as they'd been mothers and fathers. And then they broke apart to face the children sprinting toward them, Todd in the lead, Kate right behind, letting the screen door bang behind her.

He dropped to a squat and opened his arms. His children flew into them, warm and alive and oblivious. Cooper squeezed them both until they nearly popped and then made sure his face was innocent as he leaned back. "Uh-oh. Uh-oh!"

Kate looked up, concerned; Todd smiled, knowing what was coming.

"Uh-oh, I gotta go! I gotta go, who's coming with me?"

"Me!" Kate, all glee.

"Me too." Todd, caught between childish joy and the first hints of self-consciousness.

"Okay then." He stretched out his arms. "Take your seats. In the event of a sudden loss of cabin pressure, oxygen masks will drop from the ceiling. Please swing from them like monkeys. Ready?"

Kate was on his left arm, body wrapped around it like, well, a monkey. Todd had his right locked, their fingers gripping one another's forearms.

"Okay. Prepare for liftoff. Three." He rocked up, then back down. "Two." Again. "One!" Cooper lunged from a squat, using the force of his legs to send them into a spin and then half hurling, half falling into it. Todd was really getting too heavy, but screw that, he just cranked harder and planted his heels and then they were going. The world was the faces of his children, Katie giggle-screaming and Todd smiling pure and wide, and beyond them a blur of green lawn and brown tree and gray car. He pushed harder, feet moving like a dancer's, arms rising wide, the kids floating now, momentum doing the work for him. "Liftoff!"

Later, he would remember the moment. Would take it out and examine it like the faded photograph of a war veteran, the last relic of a life from which he was adrift. An anchor or a star to navigate by. The faces of his children, smiling, trusting, and the world beyond a whirl of green.

Then Todd said, "I want to fly!"

"Yeah?"

"I waaaannaa flyyyiyiyiyyy!"

"Oh-kay," he said, and gritted his teeth and spun faster, one more revolution, two, and then as he came around on the third he forced his right arm up, and Todd let go of it and he let go of

Todd, and he had a stutter-second view of his son in midflight, arms up and back, hair wild around his face, and then momentum spun him out of sight. Katie clutched his arm as he slowed, one rev, Todd coming to the ground, two, Todd on his back laughing, three, touchdown, Cooper's world a little wobbly as the revolution brought Katie down to bump gently against him. When he stopped he let go of her arm but kept close, waited for her to catch her balance, the endless parental quest to make sure his baby girl didn't fall and crack her skull, didn't run into sharp things, didn't feel the rough edges of the world.

What if she's tier one? They'll take her from us. Send her to an academy...

Cooper shook his head and straightened his smile. He bent down, elbows to knees. His daughter stared at him with solemn eyes. His son lay on his back on the ground. "Toddster? You good?"

His son's arm shot skyward, thumb up. Cooper smiled. He glanced up at Natalie, saw her look, the happiness a veneer on the fear. She caught him, touched her hair again, said, "We were about to eat. Have you?"

"Nope," he lied. "Whatcha say, guys? Breakfast? Some of Mom's famous brontosaurus eggs?"

"Dad." Todd scrambled up and brushed grass off his pant legs. "They're just regular eggs."

Cooper started on the old routine—*You ever seen brontosaurus eggs? No? Then how...*and found he couldn't do it. "You're right, buddy. How about some regular eggs?"

"Okay."

"Okay." He gave Natalie a look no one else would have noticed. "Help your mom get started, would you? I'll be right in."

His ex reached down and took her son's hand. "Come on, flyboy. Let's make breakfast."

Todd looked briefly baffled but followed Natalie as she led him inside. Cooper turned back to Kate, said, "You want to fly again?"

She shook her head.

"Phew. You're getting so big, pretty soon you're going to be doing that to me." His shoelace had come undone, and he knotted it quickly.

Kate said, "Daddy? Why is Mommy scared of me?"

"*What?* What do you mean, honey?"

"She looks at me, and she's scared."

Cooper stared at his daughter. Her brother had been a restless baby, and many, many times Cooper had spent the ghostly hours of night rocking his son, soothing him, talking to him. Often he wouldn't want to move once Todd had finally fallen asleep, certain that any shift, no matter how gentle, might wake his infant boy. And so he had played a game with himself, looking at his son's thick dark hair—now faded to sandy brown—and the broad forehead and lips that looked like they'd been taken directly off Natalie's face, and the ears that belonged to Cooper's grandfather, big outward-facing things, and he had tried to find himself there. Other people said they could see it, but he never really could, at least not until Todd got older, started making expressions identical to his own.

Kate, though. He'd seen himself in his daughter since the day she'd arrived. And not just in her features. It was in the way she held herself, the way she observed things. *It's like the world is a system,* he'd said to Natalie, years ago, *and she's trying to break it but knows she doesn't have all the data yet.* Kate had mostly been calm, but when she wanted something, boob or bed or fresh diaper, she had made it goddamn clear.

"What makes you think she's scared, baby?"

"Her eyes are bigger. And her skin is more white. It looks like she's crying but she's not crying."

Cooper put a hand on—

Dilated pupils.

Blood diverted from the skin to the muscles to facilitate fight-or-flight.

Enhanced tone in the orbicularis oculi.

Physiological responses to fear and worry. The kind of stimuli you can read like a billboard.

—his daughter's shoulder. "First of all, your mom isn't scared of you. Don't you ever believe that. Your mom loves you more than anything. So do I."

"But she was."

"No, sweetheart. She wasn't scared of you. You're right, she was upset. But not because of you or anything you did."

Kate stared at him, the corner of her lip sucked between her teeth. He could see that she was wrestling with the dissonance between what he had said and what she had seen. He understood that. It had been part of his life growing up, too.

Actually, it was still pretty much SOP.

Cooper dropped from his squat to sit cross-legged on the ground, his face a bit below his daughter's. "You're getting to be a big girl, so I'm going to tell you some things, things that you may not understand all the way right now. Okay?" When she nodded solemnly, he said, "You know people are all different, right? Some are tall and some are short and some have blond hair and some like ice cream. And none of that is right or wrong or better or worse. But some people are very good at things that other people aren't. Things like understanding music, or adding really big numbers together, or being able to tell if someone is sad or angry or scared even if they don't say so. Everybody can do that a little, but some people can do it really, really well. Like me. And, I think, like you."

"So it's good?"

"It's not good or bad. It's just part of us."

"And not other people."

"Some of them. Not a lot."

"So am I…" She sucked her lip back in. "Am I a freak?"

"What? No. Where'd you hear that?"

"Billy Parker said that Jeff Stone was a freak and everyone laughed and then no one would play with Jeff."

And thus are human relations boiled down to their essence. "Billy Parker sounds like a bully. And don't use that word—it's mean."

"But I don't want to be weird."

"Sweetheart, you're not weird. You're perfect." He stroked her cheek. "Listen. This is just like having brown hair or being smart. It's just a part of you. It doesn't tell you who you are. You do that. You do it by deciding who you want to be, one choice at a time."

"But why was Mommy scared?"

And you thought you might dodge that one. Sharp girl. What do you say, Coop?

When Natalie had been pregnant, they'd had lots of conversations about the way they would talk to their children. Which truths they would tell, and when. Whether they would say that Santa Claus was a real person or just a game people played, how to answer questions about dead goldfish and God and drug use. They had decided that the thing to do was to be essentially honest, but that there was no need to dwell on things; that obfuscation was preferable to outright lying; and that there was an age when saying, *Well, where do you think babies come from?* was preferable to charts and diagrams.

Funny thing, though, they'd never imagined what it would be like if their child could see right through them. Dozens of studies had shown that a gifted parent wasn't any more likely to have a gifted child, and that if they did, there was little connection between the parent's gift and the child's. In fact, young gifted children rarely exhibited a specific savant profile. At Kate's age, it was usually more an uncanny facility with patterns that could manifest itself mathematically one day and musically the next.

And yet his daughter could read and interpret miniscule movements of interior eye muscles.

She's tier one.

"There are some people," Cooper said, choosing his words carefully and controlling his expression, "who like to know about people like us. People who can do the things you can do, and the things I can do."

"Why?"

"That's complicated, munchkin. What you need to know is that Mommy wasn't scared of you. She was just...surprised. One of those people called her this morning, and it surprised her."

Kate considered that. "Are they bullies?"

He thought of Roger Dickinson. "Some of them are. Some of them are nice."

"Was the one who called Mom a bully?"

He nodded.

"Are you going to beat him up?"

Cooper laughed. "Only if I have to." He stood, then reached down to hoist her to his hip. She was getting too old for it, but right then he didn't care, and she didn't seem to either. "Don't worry about anything, okay? Your mom and I will take care of everything. No one is going to—"

If the test says she's tier one, they'll send her to an academy.

She will be given a new name.

Implanted with a microphone.

Raised to mistrust and fear.

And you will never see her again.

"—hurt you. Everything is going to be fine. I promise." He stared into her eyes. "You believe me?"

Kate nodded, chewing her lip again.

"Okay. Now let's go have some eggs." He started for the door.

"Daddy?"

"Yes?"

"Are you scared?"

"Do I look scared?" He smiled at her.

Kate shook her head no, then stopped, nodded yes. Her lips pinched. Finally, she said, "I can't tell."

"No, baby. I'm not scared. I promise."

It's not fear I'm feeling.

No, not fear.

Rage.

MAX VIVID IS TRYING TO OFFEND YOU
***Entertainment Weekly*, March 12, 2013**

Los Angeles: You can call him an ingenious ring-master with his finger on the pulse, or the most offensive, degrading television host since Chuck Barris. What you can't call Max Vivid is polite.

"Social conscience is boring, darling," Vivid says, downing a triple espresso at Urth Caffé. "F-k political correctness. I'm here to entertain."

If ratings are any proof, his latest show, *(Ab)Normal,* is precisely the entertainment America is looking for. The reality show, which pits gifted individuals against teams of normals in competitions that include mock assassinations, daring robberies, and even hand-to-hand combat, regularly draws 45 million viewers a week.

It also garners criticism for at best exacerbating social tensions—and at worst, being explicitly racist.

"In Rome they watched slaves fight lions. Entertainment's a blood sport, baby," Vivid responds. "Besides, how can it be racist? We're all the same race, f-ktard."

It's a typical comment from the inflammatory host, who revels in insulting detractors and fans alike. Nor does he stray from controversy. In this season's most infamous *(Ab)Normal* episode, three gifted contestants were tasked with infiltrating the Library of Congress and planting explosives. While the bombs were fake, the security was genuine—and failed to protect the library from the television terrorists.

It was a shocking display in an age when domestic terrorism is a very real threat, and neither the FCC nor the FBI was amused. The former has levied extensive fines against the network, while the latter has opened an active investigation to determine whether criminal charges should apply.

"I think of it as a public service," says Vivid. "I'm pointing out the weaknesses in the system. But bring 'em on. I've got a 42 share. I can afford all the lawyers in the world."

CHAPTER 11

Cooper used the drive to work to run scenarios. He got no small amount of grim pleasure from the one in which he tracked down the gutless bureaucrat who had called Natalie this morning and beat him bloody with the handset of his desk phone. Unbelievable. What kind of a job was that? Sitting in a cubicle, cold-calling families to tell them that something had happened, you couldn't say what, but their son or daughter needed to take the Treffert-Down Scale Assessment the following day. Hiding behind a call sheet and a flowchart of responses. Sorry, sir, sorry, ma'am, it's just policy.

Drew Peters will be able to help. There had to be some advantage to being the best that the best of the DAR had to offer. Seven years of dedication, of brutal hours and relentless travel and blood on his hands. It had to count for something.

He remembered a conversation he'd had with Natalie back when Peters first recruited him. He'd already been with the department, first as a military liaison, then, when his term with the army was up, full-time. But Equitable Services was a whole new world. Instead of just tracking and analyzing brilliants, he would be actively pursuing some of them.

"Our task," said the neat, calm man with steel in his eyes, "will be to preserve balance. To ensure that those who would upset the order of things are held in check. In certain cases, preemptively."

"Preemptively? You mean—"

"I mean that when the evidence is clear and the danger is real, we will act before they do. I mean that instead of waiting for terrorists to attack our way of life, instead of allowing them to push this country toward a war against its own children, we will act to prevent one."

To the average person, it might have been a stunning statement. But Cooper was a soldier, and to a soldier it was simple logic. Turning the other cheek was a lovely sentiment, but in the real world, it mostly resulted in matching bruises. Better still, why wait until after you're hit to hit back? Neutralize the threat before it hurt you. "Will we have authorization to do that? Terminate citizens?"

"We have support at the highest levels. Our team will be protected. But what we will do will require the sharpest mind, the clearest moral sense. I need men and women who understand that. Who have the strength and intelligence and conviction to do difficult things in service of their country. I need," Director Drew Peters had said, "believers."

"He needs," Natalie had said, when he recounted the conversation later, "killers."

"Sometimes," Cooper had said. "Yes. But it's more than that. This isn't some evil CIA spinoff group whacking political rivals. We'll be protecting people."

"By killing gifteds."

"By hunting terrorists and murderers. Some—okay, most—of which will be brilliants, yes. But that's not the point."

"What is?"

He'd paused a long moment. A beam of dusty sun tracked across the scuffed hardwood of their apartment. "You know that moment in a movie when the good guys stand together? Against incredible odds, and for something important, and with total faith that their brothers will stand with them?"

"You mean like at the end of a rom-com, when the best friend rushes the guy to the airport to catch the girl?"

He'd mock-pushed her, and she'd laughed. "Yeah, I know the scenes. You get all teary. You play it off, but I can always tell. It's cute."

"I get teary because I *believe* in it. In heroism and duty, in sacrifice for justice and equality. All that good stuff. That's why I became a soldier in the first place."

"But now you'll be fighting against other gifteds. People like you."

"I realize it's weird." He'd taken her hands. "Twists—"

"Would you stop it with that word?"

"Okay, *abnorms*, they'll think I'm a traitor, and some of my new straight colleagues won't trust me. I get it."

"So why—"

"Because we have a son."

Natalie had been about to respond, but his answer threw her. She looked down at her hands in his. "I just—I don't want you to end up hating yourself."

"I won't. I'll be fighting for a world where it doesn't matter if my son is gifted or not. That's a cause I can kill for." As if on cue, Todd had stirred in his crib. They had both held their breath. When he settled, Cooper continued. "Besides, I want to be able to protect you both if things do get worse. There's no better place to be able to do that."

Time to test that theory.

The Equitable Services command center was as busy as ever. Shifts ran twenty-four hours, and day or night analysts keyed in their data, argued over meaning and relevance, and updated the video wall that showed every action in the country. There were more oranges and reds overlaid today than yesterday, measurements of the nation's growing tension. The bank of monitors played cable news, two channels dedicated to that evening's reopening of the stock market, a third showed a conservative pundit drawing on a chalkboard, the fourth running an earlier press conference in which a reporter buttonholed President Walker about the New Canaan Holdfast in Wyoming. The president looked tired but handled himself well, reminding the world that the gifted were also American citizens, and that the NCH was legally purchased corporate land.

Cooper headed for the stairs. Behind him, a woman called his name. He ignored her and started up the stairs. Valerie West hurried after him. "Cooper!"

He turned his head but didn't stop. "I'm busy."

"No, listen, one of the taps turned something up. You've got to hear—"

"Later."

"But—"

He whirled. "I said *later*, okay? I don't know how much simpler I can make it."

Valerie reacted as if slapped. "Yes, sir."

Cooper hurried up the stairs, one hand trailing the railing. A balcony ringed the command center, executive offices, and conference rooms. Director Drew Peters's office was mostly glass, allowing him to keep an eye on the video wall and the activity below. Now, however, the blinds were closed. His assistant, Maggie, a stylish woman in her early fifties with a pleasant smile and ice water in her veins, looked up as Cooper approached. She'd been with Peters for two decades, and her experience and security clearance made her more executive officer than secretary.

"I need to see him."

"He's on a call. Have a seat."

"Now, Maggie. Please." He let some of the turmoil show on his face.

She examined him calmly, then turned to her keyboard, typed something. A moment later there was a ding of the returned instant message. "Go ahead, Agent Cooper."

The office was tidy and tastefully lit, small for a man of Peters's standing. There was a couch in one corner under the de rigueur framed portrait of President Henry Walker. But it was the other photographs that always caught Cooper. Instead of the predictable dick-measuring images of Peters with world leaders, the walls were decorated with shots of active targets. Pride of place was given to a black-and-white photo of John Smith holding a microphone and addressing a crowd on the Mall, leaning into the microphone like an evangelist.

From behind the desk, Peters gestured at a chair and continued speaking into the phone. "I understand that, Senator." A pause. "It means just that. I understand you." Peters rolled his eyes. "Well, perhaps you shouldn't have sold him half the state, should you?" Another pause. "Yes, well, you're certainly welcome to do that. Now if you'll excuse me, I have an appointment." He hung up, pulled off the slender earpiece, and dropped it on his desk. "Our distinguished senator from Wyoming. Erik Epstein bought twenty-three thousand *miles* of his state, an area the size of West Virginia, and the good senator didn't trouble himself to wonder why." The director shook his head. "The world would be a better place if people stopped voting for folksy candidates they could have a beer with and started voting for people smarter than they are." Peters leaned back in his chair and looked at Cooper quizzically. "What's on your mind?"

"I need help, Drew." In public it was always *Director* or *sir*, but the intensity of their job had taken things beyond the merely professional. Peters was a cool one, maintained decorum, but it wasn't every agent he referred to as *son*.

"What's going on?"

"It's personal."

"All right."

"You've met my children."

"Of course. Todd must be…eight now?"

"Nine. But it's Kate that I need to talk to you about. Her mother got a call this morning from someone in Analysis. Apparently there was some sort of incident at school. They want to schedule a TDSA."

Peters winced. "Ah, Nick. I'm sorry. I'm sure it's nothing, just a precaution."

"That's the problem." Cooper took a deep breath, blew it out. "It's not nothing."

"She's gifted?"

"Yes."

"You're certain?"

"Yes."

The director sighed. He took off his rimless glasses, pinched at his nose. "That's hard."

"I'm asking you for a favor."

Peters replaced his glasses. Looked sideways, at the photos, the Wall of Shame, where John Smith leaned into a microphone. "It's strange, isn't it? There was a time, not so long ago, when every parent hoped their child would be born gifted. And now…"

"Sir, I know what I'm asking, and I'm sorry to do it. But she's only four years old."

"Nick." A hint of reproach in the tone.

Cooper met his gaze, didn't waver. "I need this, sir."

"You *know* I can't."

"*You* know how much I do here. How many times I've killed for you."

The director's eyes hardened. "For me?"

"For Equitable Services. For," he said, spreading his hands, "God and country. And in all that time, I've never asked for a thing, not one personal favor."

"I know that. You believe in what we do here. That's what makes you so good at your job."

"My children are what make me good at my job," Cooper said. "Everything I've ever done here, it's to make the world better for them. Because I believe that what this agency does is the only way to get there. And now that agency wants to take my daughter."

"First," Peters said, "that's an overstatement. Don't lose your head. This test is given to every child in America—"

"At age eight. She's four."

"—and 98.91% of the time, it comes up negative."

"I'm telling you, she's gifted."

"And only 4.91% are ranked as tier one." Peters took a deep breath, then leaned into the desk. Sympathy radiated from every muscle in his body. "There are times I hate this job, you know. You're not the first agent to have a child be scheduled for an early TDSA. I have to do this about once a year. But you've heard of Caesar's wife? Well, we're Caesar's palace guard. Being beyond reproach isn't just a noble idea. It's mandatory. We cannot put ourselves above the law. If we do, we become the Gestapo."

Cooper understood the principle, understood the need for it. Yesterday, if he'd been in the director's shoes and Quinn had come to him for the same favor, he would have made the same argument. *But this time it's* my *child.* "But—"

"I'm sorry, Nick. I truly am. I wish there was something I could do. It's not that I don't want to help you. It's that I can't. I literally can't."

Cooper said, "Were your children tested?"

Peters's eyes narrowed. For a moment, raw emotion slipped past the cool gray wall of the man, and Cooper was surprised by the intensity of it, the anger. Then the director said, "You know I lost my wife."

Cooper had never met Elizabeth; she'd died the year before Peters recruited him. In the photos he'd seen, she had that inner glow that made her seem much prettier than she objectively was. One shot in particular had caught him, Elizabeth in the midst of a laugh, her head thrown back, eyes shut, given over entirely to the moment.

"Forty-one years old, and one Wednesday morning she found a lump. Eighteen months later, she was gone, and I was raising three daughters. She's buried in her family mausoleum in Oak

Hill. They're wealthy from way back; her however-many-times-great-grandfather was in Abe Lincoln's cabinet. Her father, Teddy Eaton, handled the private fortunes of half of Capitol Hill. God, he was a bastard." Peters's usually quiet voice hit the word with inflection. "As his daughter was dying, the old man begged her to let him bury her with them. 'You're an Eaton, not a Peters. You should be with us.'" Peters stared out at the middle distance.

"I'm sorry, Drew."

"The day we buried her in Oak Hill, I thought that was the worst day of my life." Peters's eyes focused. He locked them on Cooper's with an almost audible click. "Were my children tested? Of *course*. And I was wrong. The day I buried the woman I loved in a place where I won't get to lie next to her, that wasn't as bad as it gets. When my daughters got tested, that was the worst day of my life. Both times. And when Charlotte turns eight this spring, *that* will be the worst day of my life."

A numb feeling crept up Cooper's body. He had a flash of a sleepless night years ago, when Kate was a newborn, seven pounds of tiny helplessness, crying by Christmas lights as he tried to soothe her. All that time. All those hours. All the pain and pleasure of fatherhood.

There has to be a way.

"I know this is difficult, Nick. But you're Equitable Services. Focus on that."

"You think I don't—"

"I think," Peters said, "that when family comes up against duty, it's hard to choose. But never forget that there are people who believe a war is coming. Some of them want it to. And we're all that's standing against that."

Cooper drew a deep breath. "I know."

"There's one thing you can do to help Kate." The director's eyes were pale blue and sharp edged. "Your job. Do your job, son."

CHAPTER 12

Lacking any better ideas, Cooper did just that. There was still an attack imminent, still lives on the line.

Besides. You have a chance to catch John Smith. You want leeway? Catch the most dangerous man in America. Then see if the answer is the same.

He went looking for Valerie West—there'd been no need to snap at her that way, especially when it sounded like she had something—and found his whole team together and frenetic. The monitor in front of Valerie had a live satellite image, a rectangle maybe half a mile by a mile of tightly packed houses and narrow streets. Luisa Abrahams leaned over her shoulder, talking fast into the phone. Bobby Quinn, bulky with a vest, was checking the load on his weapon. As Cooper approached, all three turned to look at him. Then all three started talking at the same time.

Twenty minutes later he was in the back of a helicopter, the rotors thumping as the pilot flew over fields and forest, suburbs and golf courses. To the east the Chesapeake was a thin blue ribbon nicked by diamond sparkles of sunlight.

"It's thin," Cooper shouted over the noise. He'd unfolded his datapad from his pocket and snapped the display fabric taut. On the screen was a transcript of a conversation recorded three hours earlier between a man named Dusty Evans and an unknown caller.

DE:	*"Hello?"*
UNK:	*"Good morning. How are you?"*
DE:	*"Great. Looking forward to the fishing trip."*
UNK:	*"Everything ready?"*
DE:	*"Got all our gear packed. Everything you asked for."*
UNK:	*"How's the water?"*
DE:	*"Clear as glass."*
UNK:	*"Glad to hear it. We're going after the big one today."*
DE:	*"Yes, sir. It's going to be a thing of beauty."*
UNK:	*"Yes. Yes, it will. Good work."*
DE:	*"Thank you. It's an honor."*
UNK:	*"The honor's mine. We'll talk again later."*

"You said you wanted anything off the taps," Quinn yelled back. "We got two dozen hits; this is the only one the analysts cleared."

"It's obviously coded, but what else? Who's Dusty Evans?"

"Electrician, unmarried, twenty-four. Tested tier four in '92—mathematical—joined the army in 2004, washed out of basic. Punched his sergeant, apparently. A couple of speeding tickets, an assault charge for a bar fight."

"He was in one of the Vasquezes' cell phones?"

"No. About three months ago he called a woman named Mona Appismo, who was in Alex's cell phone."

"That's it?" Cooper felt a sinking inside him. For a moment he'd thought he had conjured a miracle by sheer force of will. But now he felt himself drifting back to questions for which he had no answers. "This is a waste of time. He's probably a nobody talking to his pot dealer."

"Only if he's got a thing for ditch weed." Quinn grinned. "Unknown number turned out to be a cell phone in Wyoming. It's from inside New Canaan. Belongs to a guy named Joseph Stiglitz."

"And you're thinking Joseph Stiglitz, JS, John Smith?"

"I'm not thinking it, boss. The analysts are."

"The voice doesn't match, does it?" For the last five years, they'd been running the most sophisticated computer search algorithms ever devised to find John Smith. Either the man had never once picked up the phone, or, more likely, he was disguising his voice. Easy enough to do on digital lines.

"No," Quinn said, "but the phone was bought last month and never used. So who buys a phone but doesn't even turn it on for a month?"

"Someone who plans ahead. Good thinking. Local cops on alert?"

"Yeah. They know to stay back, too. Luisa is coordinating, and I think they're afraid of her."

"Good." Cooper slid his fingers across the face of the datapad, scanning the hurriedly assembled file on Dusty Evans. An arrest record from the assault charge listed him as six two and 230, hair black, eyes brown, no scars, a skull-and-snake tattoo on his right bicep. In the mug shot Evans looked like a pissed-off young man, his glare at the camera pure contempt.

There was an address in Elizabeth, New Jersey, a working-class burg forty-five minutes west of Manhattan. Vehicle registration for an older Ford pickup. His brief military service record: a fine shot, good fitness, but discipline problems.

The helicopter banked, shifting Cooper against the frame. On the horizon he could see a low industrial city, Philadelphia, he thought. City of Brotherly Love. He remembered talking to Alex Vasquez by bar light, the sour taste of the coffee as he told her that there had been a bombing in Philadelphia that day. It had been a post office, after hours. A silly, pointless target.

Two thoughts rang in his head. First, if Joseph Stiglitz really was John Smith, then Cooper was closer than anyone had ever been to catching the man. And second, there was going to be a major terrorist attack on America today. Or at least starting today; it could be a multiphase strike. For all they knew, Smith could be about to march on the White House. Cooper didn't have the information to say.

Trying to analyze a situation without enough data was like looking at a photograph of a ball in flight and trying to gauge its direction. Is it going up, down, sideways? Is it about to collide with a baseball bat? Is it moving at all, or is something on the blind side holding it in place? A single frame didn't mean a thing. Patterns were based on data. With enough datapoints, you could predict just about anything.

It was no different with Cooper's gift. It often felt like intuition: he could go through a subject's apartment, look at their photographs, the way they organized their closet, whether there were dishes in the sink, and from that he could make a leap, oftentimes a leap that banks of computers and teams of researchers could not. But it wasn't a matter of visions from the Almighty, and it couldn't be forced. Without data, he was just as clueless as anybody else looking at the photograph of the ball.

All he had right now was one Dusty Evans, a man he'd never even heard of yesterday. A loser with no prospects, no special skills, no connections that made him valuable. He seemed an unlikely conspirator for someone like John Smith. On the other hand, he was a pissed-off young man—young *abnorm* man—which was a demographic Smith fared well with.

Philadelphia had grown large out the window. Cooper checked his watch; about half an hour till they landed. They'd know soon enough if Evans had anything to offer them. He turned, saw his partner looking at him. "What?"

"There's something else." Quinn scratched at a temple. Uncomfortable, Cooper could see, and stalling.

"Am I supposed to guess?"

"Right. Let me send it to you." Quinn tapped at his own data-pad, and then a notification box appeared on Cooper's, asking if he would accept a file. He clicked yes, and a photograph filled the screen.

It didn't capture the fluidity with which she moved, the graceful transfer of weight in each step, the elegance of her posture. But the girl talking on the cell phone was still very, very pretty. Probably about twenty-seven, full lips, brown hair in a chic cut that highlighted a dancer's shoulders. Skin color said Mediterranean, or Jewish, maybe. Her mascara was thick, but as she wore no other makeup it seemed exotic rather than cheap. She was slender enough that he could mark her clavicles beneath her fitted T-shirt.

Very, very pretty indeed.

"That's our bomber," Quinn said. "The photo is from an ATM security camera. Thankfully, all the major banks use newtech lenses these days to discourage fraud, so the quality is good. Five years ago she would have been a black-and-white blur. Anyway, Val checked the time stamp against the cell tower logs and the GPS coordinates. It's her."

Cooper said nothing, just looked at the woman. She had the hint of a smile on her lips, like she knew a secret.

"Thing is…" Quinn hesitated.

"I was right beside her."

"Yeah."

Cooper laughed through his nose, then took a deep breath. "I was afraid of that." He caught Quinn's look and said, "Yesterday, when we found out where the call came from, I was thinking back, and I thought I might have been."

"Did you notice her at the time?"

"Look at her."

"But you didn't…"

Cooper shook his head. "Not a clue." He laughed again and saved the photo to his desktop. "We got anything on her?"

"Nothing."

"What about the phone she used?"

"It belonged to a woman, dental hygienist, named Leslie"—Quinn checked—"Anders. We talked to her; she noticed her phone was missing last night, thought she'd left it somewhere. We're confirming, but I think she's clean. My guess is Foxy Brown there lifted it from her purse."

"We recover it?"

"Nah. Probably in the sewers." Quinn shook his head. "She whupped us good, boss. Twenty agents, an airship, cameras all over the place, snipers, and she strolled right in and blew up our witness." His partner didn't explicitly mention that the girl had stood beside Cooper while she triggered the bomb, but that was only because the words were in parentheses.

Cooper sighed. Crushed his d-pad into a square and jammed it in his pocket. "Well, one thing's for sure."

"What's that?"

"Roger Dickinson is having a better day than I am."

■

By one o'clock they were rolling through Elizabeth in a black Escalade commandeered from a DAR tactical response team. Bobby Quinn was expanding on one of his theories, and Cooper was driving and trying not to listen. The truck had been rebored and given twin turbochargers, and the result was a roar of muscle Cooper was digging on.

"So I finally figured out those anti-Wyoming people," Quinn said. "I used to think, you know, why not? I mean, who needs Wyoming? You ever been there? Of course not. No one has. And maybe it would take some of the pressure off things if abnorms had a place they knew was safe. No big surprise Erik Epstein named the place New Canaan, right? Tap into the Jewish sympathy, parallel the situations."

"Mmm," Cooper said. He glanced at the map on the Escalade's GPS. Outside the window Elizabeth looked exactly the way he had imagined. The houses were mostly two stories, small but tidy, nestled close. Older domestic cars were parked in squat driveways beneath crisscrossing power lines. The kind of neighborhood where a nurse and a plumber could own a home, raise a family.

"But then I figured it out. It's like Risk."

"Like risk?" Cooper asked, drawn in despite himself. "Who likes risk?"

"No, *Risk*. You know, Risk, that board game, the one with all the little plastic pieces and the map of the world? Risk."

"Oh. Okay." Cooper paused. "Yeah, still not getting it, Bobby. What's like Risk?"

"You ever play it?"

"I don't know. A long time ago."

"My nephews were in town, we'd done the zoo already, the Mall, and I was going crazy for something to entertain them. See, the goal of the game is to take over the world—"

"That's your revelatory realpolitik understanding of New Canaan and norm-abnorm relations? 'The goal is to take over the world'?"

"Just listen. You start with a certain number of pieces in different countries, and you attack the countries next to them. You get more armies every turn depending on what countries you hold. Well, continents, really, you get armies for continents, but anyway, the point is, you get different amounts for different continents."

"Okay." Cooper turned onto Elm Street. Evans was at 104 Elm. He checked his mirror; no sign of police cars, nothing to startle the man. The sky was white.

"So say you own Australia. And you feel pretty good about yourself, right? You took it over a bit at a time, and the rewards are coming in now, a few armies every turn. And you've got all that water between you and the rest of the world. You're rolling."

"Right."

"Wrong. Because someone out there has Asia. And they get like three times the armies you do. Every single turn, bam, you get two armies, they get six or seven. Over one turn, it's not a big deal, right? You started out equal, so the few extra armies make a difference, but not a crucial one. Australia is still in the game. But after a few turns, things get dicier. Asia has a lot more power already. And Australia can see that it's going to get worse. Given ten or twenty turns? Forget it. There's no comparison between the two. They may have started at the same place, but now one is totally at the other's mercy."

98, 100, 102, 104. A single-story house of no discernible architectural style, painted the color of old cream cheese. A Ford pickup was parked in the driveway. The license plate matched. Cooper drove past, then pulled the Escalade to the curb half a block down and killed the engine. "So brilliants are Asia in this. We do all the growing and advancing."

"Yeah. Thirty years ago, humans were all basically the same. I mean, sure, try telling that to a kid in Liberia, but you take my point. Then for whatever reason, vaccinations or livestock hormones or the ozone layer, you guys come along. And wham. I mean, it's not an *opinion* that you're better than us. You empirically are." Quinn shrugged. "Better at everything. All the technology, the software, engineering, medicine, business. Hell, music. Sports. No straight can compete. The absolute best normal computer programmer in the world, could he match Alex Vasquez?"

Cooper shook his head as he checked his Beretta. Habit; the load hadn't changed since this morning.

"And it's only going to get worse. Right now we're only a few turns into the game. But in another decade? Two?" Quinn shrugged. "And the problem is, it's hard for Australia not to do the math. Not to see that if things go on, they will become totally irrelevant. We, normal humans, will become totally irrelevant."

"Ready to go?"

"Yeah."

They opened the doors and climbed out. Cooper took the lead, giving the streets a quick glance as they walked east. Bobby unbuttoned his suit jacket, took out a cigarette, spun it between his fingers. The air was cool but pleasant, more fall than winter. Not far away, someone was playing basketball.

"Here's the problem with your theory," Cooper said.

"Hit me."

"You said Australia and Asia, right? But there are only, what, forty thousand gifted born every year in the US. So across the last thirty years we're looking at 1.2 million, give or take. Two-thirds of those are under twenty. Call it four hundred thousand adult abnorms."

"Right."

"Meanwhile, there are three hundred *million* straights." They came to Evans's house and started up the walk. Cooper kept his stride calm and his eyes on the windows. "We're not Asia, my friend. We're not even Australia. We're a tiny minority surrounded by a very freaked-out majority. A majority that's desperate to own a newtech TV so they can watch Barry Adams stroll through a defensive line in tri-d, but wouldn't want their daughter to marry him."

"You kidding? Adams's contract with the Bears is a hundred sixty-three million dollars. When my ex and I have the Talk with my daughter, it's going to be, 'Sex is only for when two people are really in love, or when one of those two people is Barry Adams, in which case remember what we said about always giving your very best effort.' Hell, I *pray* my little girl will marry him." Quinn spread his arms like a television preacher. "Lord, please, I say puh-*lease*, bestow upon your faithful servant a rich twist son-in-law."

Cooper turned, laughing, and that was when a hole blew through the front door in a hail of splinters and a boom that muffled the world, and Quinn staggered back, the front of his suit shredded and a look of childish confusion on his face. Another hole punched beside the first and somewhere behind them glass shattered, and then Cooper clotheslined his partner across the sternum while kicking out the back of his knee, Bobby not falling so much as dropping and Cooper still spinning, his right hand pulling the Beretta and leveling it at the door and taking three shots and then two more, best-guess suppressive fire. The first crack was the loudest, the others seemed farther away. He didn't give the man on the inside a chance to collect himself, just took two quick steps, yanked open the door, and spun in, adrenaline driving him forward. His nerves screamed at the move, but fight was better than flight, and he needed to *see* the shooter; he couldn't read him if he couldn't see him.

A living room, sparsely decorated, couch and coffee table. A man was standing next to an arch that looked like it might lead to a dining room. About six foot, long hair, and a black T-shirt, a shotgun in his hand, the barrel swinging and—

Shotguns are bad news; the wide spread of buckshot cuts down your edge.

But the holes in the door were small, fist-size.

He's firing double- or even triple-ought shells. Call it six nine-millimeter pellets in each. Incredibly lethal, but intended for tactical operations, which means a full choke in the barrel for precision. The lead will only spread about eighteen inches over fifty yards.

And he's not even ten feet away.

—his finger tightening on the trigger, and Cooper stepped sideways ten inches as a blast of fire bloomed from the barrel of the shotgun and metal shards hurtled through the space he had been standing in. He raised the Beretta and sighted down it. The man in the T-shirt leaped back into the dining room, taking cover around the corner. Cooper tracked the motion, lowered his aim about two inches, and fired. The bullet tore through drywall like Kleenex. The man screamed and collapsed. The shotgun clattered on the hardwood floor.

Cooper moved fast, came around the corner with his weapon up. The man was on the ground, weeping and moaning and squeezing his thigh. Thick streams of blood pulsed between his fingers. The room had a card table and two chairs; there was another archway through which he could see the kitchen. No other targets. He picked up the shotgun, locked the safety, tossed it back toward the front door. "Where's Dusty Evans?"

"My goddamn leg!" His face was pale and sweaty as he rocked back and forth. "Jesus, oh Jesus Christ, it *hurts*."

"*Evans*. Where is—"

A sound from the other room, a squeak and then a bang. Cooper jumped over the man's extended legs and the growing pool of blood and sprinted into the kitchen. A wooden door stood open; the sound had been the storm door slamming. He shouldered his way through into a small backyard. A tangle of rosebushes, all thorns and no flowers; a small toolshed; a grill beside a picnic table. The whole thing was framed by wooden privacy fencing eight feet high, which Dusty Evans was in the middle of hauling himself over. Cooper grabbed his leg and yanked.

The man landed on his feet, came up ready to fight, six foot two inches of pissed-off bar brawler. Cooper still had the gun in his hand, but the thing with guns, they had unpredictable consequences. Bullets didn't necessarily stop in flesh, and in this neighborhood, that flesh could belong to a kid. He waited until Evans made his move, a feinted cross that concealed a jab, then stepped where the punch wasn't and brought his gun hand into the side of the man's neck in a brutal chop. Evans collapsed like his bones had vanished. By the time he could move again, Cooper had patted him down and cuffed his hands behind his back.

"Hi," Cooper said, then jerked the man to his feet by his bound wrists.

"Ow, *shit*."

"Yes." He pushed the man forward. "Walk."

The inside of the kitchen had the burned smell of gunfire. Cooper pushed Evans ahead of him. "Bobby?"

"Yeah." The reply sounded heavy, forced. "Here."

He marched his prisoner into the dining room. The wounded shooter flopped on the floor, pushing down against his thigh with cuffed hands. "Jesus Christ, oh Christ."

Cooper ignored him, looked at his partner, who leaned against a wall, one hand holding his sidearm, the other hugging his chest. "The vest catch everything?"

"Yeah." Quinn forced the word through clenched teeth. "Broke at least one rib, though."

"Messed up your suit, too."

His partner barked a laugh and then winced in pain. "Shit, Coop, don't."

The adrenaline was beginning to fade, leaving Cooper with that rubbery-limbed feeling. He holstered the Beretta, then flexed his fingers, took a deep breath. "You check the house?"

Quinn nodded. "Clear."

Cooper took another deep breath and a look around. The place had a dorm-room feel, everything cheap and secondhand. The couch was Salvation Army. There were no pictures on the wall. Shelves of cinder blocks and boards were packed with books, mostly politics, some memoirs, a row of electronics manuals. The tri-d was the only expensive thing in the place; it was a recent model, its hologram field sharp and unwavering, the colors vivid. It was tuned to CNN, tickers and ribbons hanging in midair, the head and shoulders of an anchor ghostly as she talked about the grand opening of the new stock exchange. An open bag of Doritos sat on the coffee table, along with half a dozen beer bottles.

Cooper turned to his prisoners. "You guys having a party?"

"You have a warrant?" Evans glared. "Some ID?"

"We're not cops, Dusty. We're gas men. We don't need warrants. We don't need a judge or jury, either."

Evans tried to lock down his expression, but fear flashed across it like a spotlight.

Quinn said, "Still think this lead is thin, boss?"

Cooper laughed and pulled out his phone. They'd need to let the cops know what the gunfire was about before some local got twitchy and rolled in. And Director Peters would want to know that they had their targets. Not only that, but the first credible recording of John Smith's voice in three years.

Of course, the bad news was that meant an attack was likely to happen today—

Wait a second.

The beer. The Doritos. The tri-d tuned to CNN.

Oh *shit*.

■

A horn blared. Cooper yanked the Escalade hard right, the tires popping up the curb shoulder, gravel spitting behind them, clearing the pole of a streetlight by inches. The man in the passenger seat screamed. They'd tied a kitchen towel around his thigh, but the blue-checked terrycloth was crimson now. He was trying to keep pressure on it, his hands still bound, fingers and handcuffs covered in gore. In the backseat, Quinn grunted, but said nothing. Beside him, Dusty Evans had recovered his screw-you face.

Cooper jammed down on the gas, cleared the van in front of them, and then bounced back into his lane. He had both the siren and the flashers going, but he also had the accelerator nearly to the floor, and it seemed like they were outrunning the sound.

The clock on the dashboard read 1:32. He glanced at the GPS. A thirty-minute drive, and they didn't have thirty minutes. He pushed the accelerator a little farther down, the speedometer breaking 100 now, Highway 1 a blur of concrete barriers and low warehouses. Airplanes bound for Newark International cut crosses from gray skies.

"Hey," Cooper said. "What's your name?"

"I need a doctor, man, I need a doctor bad."

"We'll get you a doctor soon. I promise. What's your name?"

"Gary Nie—"

"Don't tell them *nothing*," Dusty Evans said from the backseat. "This is Gestapo bullshit. This is what we're fighting against."

"Listen, Gary," Cooper said, ignoring the outburst, "we don't have a lot of time." The back of a semi loomed, brake lights flaring as the trucker tried to pull over, but Cooper was going too fast, had to skim between the lanes, the left mirror inches from the concrete barrier, the right almost touching the truck panels. He was good at driving fast, enjoyed the dance of hurtling steel, but the circumstances were making it tricky, the chaos of sirens and lights and horns and screams and blood, not to mention the stakes, a vision of what he feared was about to happen. "I need you to answer some questions. First, where exactly is the bomb?"

"How do you know about the—"

"Don't say anything, you hear?" Evans again. "You hear me?"

There was the snick of metal against leather. Cooper spared a quarter second to glance in the rearview. Evans had turned into a statue, his eyes rolling but muscles locked. Bobby Quinn didn't look away from the pistol he held to the man's temple. "Go ahead, Coop. I think the backseat is out of opinions."

"Thank you." Cooper put on his best mild grin. "Now. We know you planted the bomb." They hadn't, of course, until Gary confirmed it a moment ago, but there was no point saying that. He pulled past a sedan, saw a patch of blessedly empty straightaway, and floored it. "These are the things I need to know. Where *exactly* is it? What kind of bomb? How powerful? How is it detonated? When?"

Gary moaned and rocked forward, his hands clenched over his left thigh. The backs of his hands were caked in dried blood. His features were pale. "Jesusgod this hurts. I need a doctor."

"Elevate it."

The man looked at him, and Cooper nodded. "Go ahead."

Gary fumbled to undo his seat belt, then spun so that he was leaning against the side door. He raised the leg awkwardly, bracing a boot against the console and moaning as he did.

"Better? Good. Now listen. Where exactly is the bomb? What kind is it? How powerful? How is it detonated? When?"

"I don't." He gasped as the Escalade hit a pothole at 112 miles an hour, bouncing on the heavy shocks as they blew past a tour bus. "Goddamn it! Take me to a hospital."

Cooper glanced over. Gary Nie-whatever's long hair was scraggly and matted with sweat. His body was broadcasting agony, all of his muscles tensed, and trying to read the subtleties beneath that was dicey at best. One thing was for sure, though: the man looked smaller when he wasn't holding a shotgun.

Slowly and carefully, he asked again. "Where is the bomb? What kind is it? How powerful? How is it detonated? When?"

Gary looked over, his eyes glossy with tears. His lips quivered, and then he whispered something.

"What?"

"I said." The man fought a breath in. "Screw you, Gas Man. I am John Smith."

The road was two lanes of blacktop in each direction under steel-gray skies. Half a mile ahead, a bridge stretched across the listless brown of the Passaic River. Cooper checked the side mirror. Clear.

He leaned across Gary Nie-whatever's chest and yanked the door handle at the same time as he jerked the steering wheel left. Centripetal force and the weight of the man's body threw the door open.

For a fraction of a second, Gary hung weightless as a balloon, his mouth open, arms in front of him, the chain of the handcuffs still swinging between them as a roar of wind filled the world.

Then Cooper jerked the wheel to the right, narrowly dodging the lane divider. The door slammed shut. In the rearview mirror Gary's body hit the pavement at a hundred miles an hour, smearing and bouncing. There was a squeal of air brakes as the tour bus behind them fought to stop, and then his body vanished beneath its wheels.

Quinn said, "Jesus *Christ*! Cooper—"

"Shut up." Cooper looked in the rearview. Dusty Evans had both hands to his mouth, the muscles of his throat twitching. His eyes stared, unbelieving. Cooper waited until he turned back to the front, locked gazes. "Now. Where *exactly* is the bomb? What kind is it? How powerful? How is it detonated? When?"

CHAPTER 13

In a very real sense, the south end of Manhattan is the center of the universe. The concrete canyons of Broad and Wall, of Nassau and Exchange and Maiden, have for a century served as the financial epicenter of the world. The largest of the Federal Reserve Banks is located there. AIG, Morgan Stanley, Deloitte, Merrill Lynch. And until abnorms like Erik Epstein forced the government to shut it down, $153 billion flowed through the New York Stock Exchange every single day.

It is a landscape of marble and glass, of cobblestone streets thronged with tourists and traders, of the rumble of delivery trucks on Broadway and blasts of warm air from the subway, of enormous American flags and somber statues. During the workday the population swells 600 percent. Under the very best of circumstances, it is not easy to navigate quickly.

Cooper was not finding today to be the best of circumstances.

The new Leon Walras Exchange was located in the grand old building that used to house the NYSE. Though popular opinion focused on Erik Epstein, the twenty-four-year-old billionaire had in truth been only the most successful of a number of abnorms whose gifts broke the global financial system. For two hundred years, the market had existed on the myth that all people were equal. It was a nonsensical statement, but an easy one for most people to swallow when the prospect of financial gain was involved.

It was a myth that couldn't survive the gifted. Epstein and others like him had pillaged the market as easily as Cooper could have dodged a slap.

Two years ago, the United States had bowed to the inevitable and dissolved the stock market. It was a nuclear option, and while it had worked, the side effects were disastrous. Without the free market to support it, American industry had to pay for itself—and found it often couldn't. Small-cap companies became endangered species. Entrepreneurship plummeted. Protests on Wall Street raged to this day. Meanwhile, fortunes were wiped away, and the grandmother who stored cash in her mattress suddenly had the right savings plan.

If it was to survive, America had to develop a new system of exchange, one that would be impervious to the gamesmanship of gifted individuals. By functioning as an auction house and averaging the bids to arrive at a final price, the Leon Walras Exchange had in one stroke stripped out the volatility, excitement, and emotion of investing, while still offering the potential for businesses to raise capital. It was a step backward to a more archaic age that had taken two painful years to move through the political process.

And today, March 12, 2013, at 2:00 p.m., General Electric would become the first public offering of the new financial reality. At 2:00 p.m., history would be made.

Which meant that now, at 1:51 p.m., lower Manhattan was a nightmare. Wall Street had been cordoned off for blocks in each direction. Foot police redirected traffic on Broadway, blowing whistles and gesturing impatiently. Half a dozen school buses had been parked along Liberty, and harried teachers fought to corral children hyped up on the excitement of an afternoon out of class. A line of protesters shoved against a police barricade, raising placards and shouting slogans. A marching band played in

Trinity Churchyard, the brass mostly lost in the noise but the bass thumping uneasily through every stomach. Media helicopters circled above. Bobby Quinn's datapad showed a live feed of a podium on the steps where the former CEO of the NYSE chatted with the new CEO of the LWE and the first deputy mayor of New York, the three of them surrounded by men in dark suits and sunglasses.

If there was a worse place for a bomb to go off, Cooper couldn't think where it would be.

"*I don't know nothing about how to make bombs, man. I'm an electrician.*" All the hard-guy attitude had vanished from Dusty Evans in the instant his friend skidded across the concrete. "*I just did what I was told. The company I work for did some of the wiring on the new Exchange. Mr. Smith had me steal a key and then use it to plant the bombs.*"

"*Bombs? More than one?*"

"*Five of them.*"

Ahead of them two cops were walking a police barrier into place. Cooper burped the siren, pointed at his chest, then at the street beyond. The nearer cop nodded and rotated the barrier out of their way. Cooper tossed them a salute as he steered the Escalade through the gap. Every nerve in his body was screaming for speed, but in the crowd of tourists and sightseers they had to creep forward at five miles an hour. Someone banged on the back window of the truck. A blonde stopped right in front of him to pose for her pimply-faced boyfriend. Cooper laid on the horn.

1:53.

"*What did they look like?*"

"*Like in the movies. Blocks of gray putty. They weighed about fifteen pounds.*"

"*Total?*"

"*Each.*"

It had gone on like that the whole ride in, every question leading to an unhappy answer. Eventually Evans had started repeating himself. When it was obvious they'd gotten out of him all they were going to, Quinn had used a second pair of cuffs to secure his hands to his opposite ankles. It was an awkward, uncomfortable position, and the big man was bent nearly in half, weeping softly.

"Shut it," Quinn said. He'd climbed up to the passenger seat, and when he saw Cooper looking at him, he cocked his head and took a breath, his nostrils flaring. It was a look that read, *Well, we're in it now.* "We could evacuate."

"The politicians, maybe." Cooper rode up on the curb to pass a cop on a horse. "Not all these people."

"Some of them. Use the cops, SWAT—"

"It'd be panic, people trampling each other. Besides, we don't know it's on a timer. If Smith sees everyone running, he'll blow it early." Ahead, a row of fast-food vendors had parked right in the middle of Broadway. He grimaced, thought about plowing through the falafel truck, threw the truck into park instead. 1:56. "I'm going to have to try to stop this myself."

"Yourself? Bullshit. I'm coming—"

"You have at least one cracked rib."

"I can take the pain."

"I know you can. But you'll slow me down. Besides, all I know about disarming bombs comes from old cop shows. Unless I just pull the red wire, I'm going to need help." He popped the magazine on the Beretta. Eight rounds left. "I need you to get me a bomb squad."

"They'll never make it. Not in this crowd."

"Then get them ready to talk me through it. I'll be on the earpiece. And call Peters, let him know what's going on." He took a deep breath, then opened the car door. The crowd noise enveloped him. "And, Bobby, just in case—"

"Arrange ambulances and emergency services, I know. But make sure it doesn't come to that, okay?" The fear in his partner's eyes wasn't for his own safety or for Cooper's. It ran deeper than that, and broader. Cooper recognized it because the same thoughts had been running through his head. It was a fear of what would be unleashed if he failed. A fear of the cracking of the world.

Cooper slammed the door and began to push through the crowd. 1:57.

The ceremony won't start on time. These things never do. And John Smith likes theater. He'll wait until every camera is watching.

But then he will *blow it. Unless you stop him.*

He ran, trying to move between the bodies that mobbed the street. Cooper hated crowds, felt assaulted by them. All those intentions crossing and crisscrossing, it was like trying to listen to a thousand conversations at once. But where his mind would turn the noise of a thousand conversations into gray noise he could ignore, he couldn't tune out body language and physical cues. They came at him all at once and from every direction. All he could do was try to focus, to put his attention on the woman right in front of him and the angle of her shoulder that meant she was about to shift her bag. To the man about to speak to his friend. To the little girl who looked a lot like Kate—*no, push that away, no time now to think about Kate*—reaching up for her mother's hand.

When he couldn't find a hole, he made one, barreling through with one elbow up like the prow of a ship. Yells rose behind him, and curses. Someone shoved at his shoulder.

"Cooper." Quinn's voice in his ear. "Peters is trying to reach the officer in charge on the scene, but it's madness right now."

"No kidding." He surged past a cluster of schoolgirls. "What about my bomb squad?"

"Scrambling now. ETA fifteen minutes."

Fifteen minutes. Damn, damn, damn. There was a bank on the corner, and he raced through the revolving door. The lobby was sweet relief. Velvet ropes, bland colors, stale air, a manageable number of people. He sprinted across. A manager rose from his desk. The security guard yelled something. Cooper ignored it all, focused on making it to the opposite door.

And then he was on the corner of Wall and Broad, where history was about to be made, and the whole world was noise and howling chaos.

People were packed shoulder to shoulder. He winced at the tangled skein of vectors in front of him, at the collective motion of the crowd, the herd, something he could never read or understand, his talents all aimed at the individual, the person, the pattern.

Focus. There's no time.

To the south was the magnificent façade that had once belonged to the NYSE, with its six massive columns supporting an intricate sculpture above. Beneath was a stage and podium, dignitaries milling nearby, security orbiting them like planets around a star.

He started pushing south, gently where he could, roughly where he couldn't. Somehow he had to get to the Broad Street entrance. In a door off the lobby he would find a janitor's hallway and a freight elevator that would take him to the basement, where he could access the wiring tunnels where Dusty Evans had placed his bombs.

Sure, Coop. Just get through the crowd, past the security, through the lobby, down to the basement, into the tunnels, and then all you have to do is figure out how to disarm five separate bombs placed at strategic structural locations.

1:59.

Body odor and thrown elbows, hairspray and curses. He pushed forward one agonizing step at a time. Everyone seemed to be yelling, even when their mouths were closed. A wave of frustration washed over him, and he fought the urge to pull his gun, fire into the air. This was pointless. It would take too long to get to the front, and even if he made it, security would be too tight. He needed a better plan. Cooper pushed over to a newspaper dispenser—quick flash of Bryan Vasquez disintegrating—and climbed up on top of it.

The Broad Street entrance was too tight. But maybe back on Wall Street? There must be side entrances. They'd be guarded too, but security would be lighter, and if his rank didn't get him in fast enough, then he'd find another way. He scanned the crowd, planning his move, eyes falling across businesspeople in business suits, parents with cameras and weary expressions, locals here for the free theater, a homeless man shaking a Dunkin' Donuts cup, a group of protesters holding signs, a very, very pretty girl heading west—

Holy shit.

He leaped off the dispenser, tumbling into a burly dude holding a giant soda. Man and drink flew in opposite directions. Cooper kept the inertia going, went through the hole the falling man had made, heading away from the ceremony. "Bobby, I've got our bomber in sight, the woman in the photograph. She's on Wall Street heading west."

"Roger. I'll alert the police—"

"Negative. Say again, negative. If she spots someone coming after her, she'll blow the bombs."

"Cooper—"

"*Negative.*" He pushed forward, forcing himself not to sprint. It was just like John Smith to have her on scene, gauging the exact moment to trigger the bomb. Timing it for maximum damage.

But that planning was going to work against Smith this time. Bombs Cooper knew nothing about, but a bomb*er* he could handle.

He shoved through the crowd, throwing elbows and stomping on feet. He found her, lost her, found her again. The farther he went from the podium, the more things opened up, until he was able to read individual body language again. He went as fast as he dared, and yet though she was walking at a calm pace, she seemed to be getting farther ahead of him with every step. Somehow people seemed to be always moving out of her way. Two singing drunks in soccer jerseys swayed into a crowd of people, clearing a hole just in front of her. A father hoisted his son onto his shoulders, and she slid behind them. Two cops pushed through the crowd, opening a lane she followed for half the length of a building. It was like watching Barry Adams strut across a football field untouched by an entire defensive line. As if she was looking at things not as they were, but as they would be when she reached them.

She's an abnorm.

No surprise, really; most of Smith's top operatives would be. But it explained how she'd beaten them so handily in DC. If she had a gift for patterning anything like Barry Adams's, then the whole world would be moving vectors to her. Walking through the security perimeter would be simple. She'd probably even pegged Cooper as the leader. Blowing the bomb while standing ten feet from him was her way of giving the bird.

That made his belly burn, and he quickened his pace. He was twenty yards behind her and moving fast. She hadn't looked back, not once. Concentrating on the terrain in front of her. Which suggested that she was near her goal. He looked ahead and saw it. A side entrance to the Exchange.

Two cops stood nearby, their postures relaxed. She walked past them, overshot the entrance by a few steps, and then paused to look at her watch. One of the cops hitched up his belt and said something that made the other laugh, and she pivoted lightly and slid around behind them. Cooper couldn't believe it. If she'd raised one slender arm she could have tapped the cops on the shoulder, and yet they were completely unaware of her. It was the strangest thing, a virtuoso display of ability that practically rendered her invisible, and it would have been gorgeous to watch—except that she pushed open the door of the Exchange and slipped inside.

"Shit. She made it into the building. I'm going after her."

"Do you want—"

"Hold on." Cooper walked toward the police. The girl had somehow been able to slip right through their blind spot, but he didn't know how to do that. *Sorry, fellas.* "Excuse me, Officer, do you know where the stage is?"

"Round the corner, buddy." The cop pointed. "Follow the—"

Cooper bobbed down and hammered a left hook into the man's exposed kidney, placing it in the fabric portion of the bulletproof vest. The cop gasped and staggered. As he did, Cooper grabbed the front of his shirt and shoved him at his partner as hard as he could. The two collided and went down in a tangle. Cooper followed them, driving his knee into the solar plexus of the second cop, then scrambled to his feet and through the door.

A marble entrance, broad and bright. Sunlight poured in the windows. People milled about, holding champagne glasses and chatting. A string quartet played in the corner, the notes bouncing off marble and glass. Stepping out of the crowd was like surfacing for air. He glanced around, saw the woman vanish around a corner to the right, and hurried after her. Figure thirty seconds, tops, before the cops had caught their breath, radioed in, and come after him.

Ten steps took him to the corner. He rounded it, blood singing in his veins. The woman stood halfway down the corridor, in front of a painted metal door. In one hand, she held a ring of keys. In the other, a cell phone.

No.

Cooper abandoned all attempts at subtlety for a headlong sprint. Time drew out like a blade. His eyes caught details: the smell of fresh paint, the buzz of the lights. At the sound of his footfalls, the woman looked up. Her eyes, already huge with mascara, widened further. She dropped the keys but raised the phone. Cooper pushed as hard as he could. Everything came down to his hurtling progress, that against-the-wall feeling that he simply could not go any faster, his mind replaying yesterday and the explosion in DC, the slow-motion spill of fire, the way Bryan Vasquez had melted into a red mist; she was doing it again, only this time it wasn't one man she was executing, it was hundreds of people on national television, and the phone had reached her face and her eyes locked on him and her lips parted to speak just as Cooper's arm lashed out in a forehand slap that knocked the cell phone from her fingers. The device hit the floor and broke on the bounce, plastic pieces skittering across the marble.

She said, "Wait, you don't—" and then his fist slammed into her belly and doubled her over. He didn't like punching women, but damned if he was going to take a chance with this one.

"I got her," he said. "Target in custody." Bobby Quinn hooted in the earpiece.

A wave of relief washed over Cooper. Jesus, but that had been close. He spun the woman around, pulled one arm behind her back, and dug for his cuffs with the other.

"Listen," she said, gasping between the words. "You have…to let…me go."

He ignored her, snapped the cuff on one wrist, reached for the other. Spoke for his partner's benefit. "Bobby, I had to take out a couple of cops on the way in. Can you reach out to NYPD and calm them down real fast? I don't want to—"

But before he could finish the sentence there was a crack of planets colliding, and the ground vanished beneath him, he was flying, his arms out and twisting, and everything—

CHAPTER 14

The noise came first. An overlapping mishmash of sound. Cries of pain. Urgent, indecipherable yells. Rasping, scraping. Solemn voices counting. Sirens farthercloserfarther.

He wasn't aware of it, really. It was the water he floated through.

Then, slowly, the formless syllables began to shape themselves into words. The words had taste and heft. Hemorrhaging. Amputate. Crushed. Concussed.

The scraping became the wooden legs of a chair or table dragged across concrete.

The men counting backward punctuated the arrival of zero with an exhalation of effort, as though they were heaving something.

The sirens stayed the same. He just came to realize how many he was hearing, some moving, some still, some nearby, some a good distance away.

Cooper opened his eyes.

Canvas stretched above him. The pattern was indistinct, and the colors moved and swirled. For a moment he faulted his vision, then realized it was active camo, smart fabric that chameleoned to match the environment. Military issue. He blinked eyes dry and swollen. The noises around him took no notice, just kept insistently on, each cutting across the other.

"…need more O over here…"

"…breathe, just breathe…"

"…my husband, where is…"

"…it hurts, God, it *hurts*…"

Cooper took a deep inhale, felt tings and stabs of pain as his chest swelled. Nothing too bad. He raised his right hand and gingerly patted the back of his head. The flesh was hot and swollen and sore, the hair sticky. He must have hit it. How?

Slowly, he rolled onto one side, then swung his legs off the edge of the cot. Also military, he noticed. This was an army triage tent. For a moment the world swam. He clamped down on the edge of the cot with both hands. The pain came now, a whirling thumping, dull and looming.

"Go slow."

Cooper raised his head and opened his eyes. A trim man in scrubs spattered with blood stood beside him. Where had he come from?

"How did I get here?"

"Someone must have brought you. What hurts?"

"My—" He coughed. His throat was full of dust. "My head."

"Look at this?" The doctor had a penlight out. Cooper obediently stared into it, followed as the man moved it back and forth. A triage center, he was in a triage center of some sort. But how? He remembered fighting through the crowd, the surging, roiling chaos of all those people. Stalked by two o'clock when…the bombs. He had been trying to stop bombs from going off. He had seen—

"*Where is she?*" Cooper whipped his head around, felt the pain as a promissory note, ignored it for now. He was in a large field tent packed with rows of cots, the beds nearly touching. Men and women in scrubs pushed across the rows, speaking insistently to one another as they tended the wounded. Maybe twenty racks in here, he couldn't see all of them, she could be in one.

"Hey." The doctor's voice was firm. "Look at me."

The pain paid what it owed, a crushing feeling like there was a vise in the middle of his skull. Cooper groaned, looked back at the doctor. "Where is she?"

"I don't know who you're talking about," the man said, fitting a stethoscope to his ears, "but I'm sure she's fine. Right now I need you to relax so I can see how badly hurt you are."

It all clicked together, finally, the scattered pieces coalescing into a whole. He had been chasing John Smith's agent, the woman who could walk through walls, the cell phone bomber with the big eyes. He had caught up with her inside the Exchange. But not in time.

"How bad is it?" Cooper felt like something was falling through his chest.

"That's what I'm checking. Deep breath."

Cooper did as he was told, the air rattling in his lungs. "Not me. I mean, how *bad* is it?"

"Oh. Deep breath." The doctor stared into the distance as he listened to Cooper's chest. Whatever he heard seemed to satisfy him. "I don't know how to answer that."

"How many people…"

"I'm focused on the ones in front of me." The doctor looped the scope around his neck and glanced at his watch. "You have a mild concussion. There was a lot of smoke and dust inhalation, but nothing I'm worried about long-term. You're very lucky. You should avoid sleep for a while, eight, ten hours maybe. If you start to feel dizzy or nauseous, go to the hospital immediately." He started away.

"Wait. That's it?"

"You can stay if you feel weak, but if you think you can walk, we could really use the space."

"I can walk." Cooper took a deep breath and a look around. "Can I help you?"

"Do you have medical training?"

"Basic first aid."

The doctor shook his head. "Too many people trying to help already. Best thing you can do right now is get out of the way." And then he was gone, on to the next cot.

Cooper sat on the edge of the rack for a moment, letting his whirling thoughts slowly die down. Collecting himself, rebuilding the memories. He'd had her, hadn't he? Slapped her cell phone away, had cuffs in hand. He'd won. He'd caught the bad guy. Girl.

And yet, this.

He took a long breath that made him cough until he tasted dust on the back of his tongue. Then he stood up. If the bombs had gone off, there would be victims far worse off than he seemed to be. Best to clear the cot.

He looked in the other beds before he left, but she wasn't there.

Moving slowly to keep the pain from splashing around his skull, Cooper walked to the exit, pushed the canvas door flap aside, and stepped outside.

Into a graveyard.

For a moment he thought he was hallucinating.

The sky had been replaced by a thick gray scrim of whirling dust. The air tasted charred. In the dim light, trees were skeleton-limbed silhouettes, pointing like Charon across the river to the underworld. And all around him were tombstones. Marble tombstones inscribed with names and dates.

Cooper reached out to touch the tent, pinching the material between fingers scraped and sore. It was covered in a thin layer of dust, but had the tight, satisfying feel of canvas. This was real. It was happening. So, then, the graves...

Trinity Church. This is the churchyard. Alexander Hamilton is buried here somewhere.

It made sense. In crowded Manhattan, space for triage tents would be in short supply. Still. There was an ugly symbolism. He had fallen asleep in one world and awakened in another. The first had been sunlight and fanfare; this one was dust and ash.

There were people all around. Some of them seemed to be part of the organized rescue effort. They carried stretchers and shuttled medical supplies and directed ambulances in a busy dance. But many others seemed dazed. They stood and stared, looked up at the towering spire of the church, or back toward Wall Street, where the smoke thickened.

Wall Street. The Exchange. Maybe she was still there.

Cooper started through the cemetery. His head hurt and his body was sore, but more than anything he just felt thick, altered. Like a guy driving home, singing along with the radio right up until the semi T-boned him and sent the car end over horrifying end, the world spinning, flashes of colors, sky, ground, sky, ground, and then the impact, the sickening crunch, and in that instant, when the world had shifted completely, when everything that had mattered a moment before no longer even rated, the radio would still be playing the same song.

He felt like the song.

Slowly, he picked his way through the churchyard. He climbed the low fence to Broadway, crossed the street where food trucks had blocked his path. Someone bumped him, their shoulder hitting hard, and the novelty of that struck him. He hadn't been bumped like that in a long time. The world was water; nothing was permanent, all was shift and change. A cop started to wave him back, but Cooper felt through his pockets, found his badge. The man let him pass. The smoke was thicker, and he couldn't see more than ten, fifteen feet. Beyond that the best he could do was make out flashing colors, police lights. He moved toward them. People staggered the other way, their faces dirty, clothes torn, expressions shocked. They leaned on one another. Soldiers carried stretchers.

Cooper walked, slow and steady, four-four time in a world gone off measure.

Every step stranger. The bones of buildings had torn through their stone skin and lay exposed. Collapsed walls buried the cobblestones. Shattered glass dusted the scene with razor-edged glitter. The dust clouds were lit brighter by a dozen fires burning out of sight. He reached the corner where he had spotted the woman who could walk through walls. Firemen dug through the rubble, masks on their faces and reflective stripes on their uniforms.

To the south, he could see the New York Stock Exchange, a building that had stood for a hundred years, weathered depressions and wars and unimaginable social change, been a symbol for the unstoppable power of capitalism until that power was, indeed, stopped by the arrival of his kind; a building that had, ever so briefly, represented the hopes of a world struggling for a new balance when every conviction had been upended, every fact proved unstable, every belief turned fragile; a building of stone and steel that by its simple presence declared that the engines that powered the world were running fine. It was in ruins.

Of the six massive columns that fronted the building, only one was still in place. The others had cracked and sheared; one of them had fallen outright, the huge stone smashing into the street. The glass wall behind must have blown out as well, four stories of lethal shards surfing the roar of air and fire. Through the open space that had been a wall, he could see the building, naked and raw. Offices exposed, bathrooms torn open, a stairwell lost and sad.

And everywhere, the dead. Bodies.

Bodies in the street, bodies in the building. Bodies beneath fallen columns, bodies dangling in a spiderweb of cabling.

Torn and broken, the colors of their clothes a mockery in this bleak new world.

Hundreds of them. Thousands.

This wasn't supposed to happen.

You were supposed to stop it.

It was a nonsense thought. He couldn't hold himself responsible for everything that went wrong in the world. But he'd been so close. It had been he who ran down Alex Vasquez, who used her brother as bait, who implemented the phone taps that led them to Dusty Evans. It had been he playing against John Smith, again, and he'd lost, again, and all of these people had died.

Cooper spun on his heel and walked away. He walked without direction or purpose, without thought or plan. His companions were Frustration and Rage, and together the three of them stalked Manhattan.

■

A pair of strappy heels on a pair of shapely legs flung akimbo inside a stylish black pencil skirt that ended, along with the body, at the waist.

■

A sidewalk peddler of cheap purses and flimsy umbrellas shoving all of his wares off the folding table that comprised his livelihood to make a cot for a screaming man carried between two firefighters.

■

Gray air moving like fabric, like lint, over swirling gray ash. Gray-faced people in gray-smudged clothes. The world gone monochrome.

And then the pink shock of a child's stuffed animal in the middle of Broadway.

■

A bank of payphones surrounded by a mob of people waiting in line. A true New York mix, a skinhead next to a broker, two men in blue jumpsuits, a fashion model, a hot-dog vendor, a boy and girl holding hands. Everyone patient. No one pushing.

◼

A woman in a business suit walking down the middle of the sidewalk. An expensive leather briefcase slung over one shoulder. Blood trickling down the side of her face. Her arms cradling a potted plant three feet tall.

◼

At the corner of two minor streets, a taxi with open doors, the radio playing at maximum volume. New Yorkers standing near, listening to a stammering news reporter.

"…again, an explosion at the Leon Walras Stock Exchange. I…I've never seen anything like it. The entire east side of the building has been destroyed. There are bodies everywhere. The death toll will be in the hundreds, maybe thousands. No one is saying what caused this, but it had to be a bomb, or bombs. I can't…it's something I never thought I would see…"

◼

On the bright expanse of Columbus Park, a mile from the explosion, three large buses parked on the green of the soccer field. Red Cross mobile donation units. A mob of volunteers, hundreds of people rolling up their sleeves.

∎

Just north of Houston, the building was exploding again.

The tri-d billboard was mounted on the second story of an office tower. Instead of the usual advertisements and spinning corporate logos, an image of the Exchange hovered in the air, the Exchange as it had been hours before, a massive American flag dangling above the stage. The image shuddering and bouncing, the camera swerving vertiginously, and not just the camera, the building, suddenly consumed in thick smoke. There were blurry objects flying through the air, growing chunky and pixelated as they reached the edge of the projection field.

"My God," whispered the woman standing beside Cooper.

The image changed, the smoke suddenly lessening, the angle different. The building was shown ripped open. Firemen sprayed water. Paper and insulation drifted on the eddies. Police guarded the scene as emergency workers looked for survivors. A ribbon at the bottom of the screen declared, LIVE FROM STOCK EXCHANGE EXPLOSION.

"Hadda be the twists," said a rough voice behind him. Cooper fought the urge to deck the bigot. After all, he was right.

"Maybe," said another voice.

"Who else would it be?"

"Who knows? All I'm saying, I don't think they'll know for a while."

"Why not?"

"Look at it, man. Mess like that, how you gonna tell the good guys from the bad guys?"

The video had flashed back to the explosion. They'd probably run that loop for three straight months. But as the eyes of everyone in the crowd watched the building blow up, again, Cooper turned and stared at the men behind him. They looked like guys who bet on sports. As he stared at them, first one and then the other turned his attention to look at Cooper. "What?" The bigger one. "Help you with something, buddy?"

How you gonna tell the good guys from the bad guys?

"Thank you."

"Huh?"

But by then Cooper was already gone, sprinting at full speed.

"It's easy. Everybody else on the field, they look where the opposing line is. I look where they're going to be. Then I just head somewhere else."

——BARRY ADAMS, RUNNING BACK FOR THE CHICAGO BEARS, ON HOW HE WAS ABLE TO RUSH 2,437 YARDS IN A SINGLE SEASON, SHATTERING THE PREVIOUS RECORD (2,105, BY ERIC DICKERSON IN 1984)

CHAPTER 15

Located west of DC's Naval Observatory, Massachusetts Avenue Heights was a charming neighborhood of redbrick row houses whose proximity and small yards belied the affluence within. While not quite equaling the mansions and political swing of Sheridan-Kalorama, it was a wealthy neighborhood, the kind of place people said was great to raise kids, and home to numerous politicians, doctors, and lawyers.

The house on 39th Street NW was quaint and carefully maintained, with a pretty porch, manicured hedges, and an American flag. What wasn't quite as evident were the security cameras mounted not only on the house but along the walkway and in the tree, the steel-reinforced doorframe, and the discreet gray sedan that passed the house at random intervals twice an hour.

Cooper had been here many times. He'd sat on the picture-perfect back patio and sipped beer while the kids played. He'd helped design the security and, for several months, even served as a driver. During a mousetrap operation in which they'd leaked supposed weaknesses to terrorist elements, he'd run a team out of the place, sleeping in the spare room and hoping that John Smith might take the bait. He wasn't a stranger to the house on 39th Street.

Still, showing up unannounced after dark, wearing torn clothes and smelling of sweat and diesel, well, it wasn't something he'd normally do.

He rang the doorbell. Opened and closed his hands as he waited for what seemed a long time, conscious of the security measures trained on him.

When he opened the door, Drew Peters looked at Cooper for a long moment. His accountant's eyes took in every detail and gave nothing back. Cooper didn't say anything, just let his very presence speak for him.

Finally the director of Equitable Services glanced at his watch. "You'd better come in."

■

Cooper had interrupted dinner, so Peters brought him through the kitchen to say hello. The space was bright and homey, with hardwood countertops and glass-fronted cabinets. It had always struck Cooper as out of character with the cool gray he associated with Director Peters.

Of course, at home, he wasn't the director; he was Dad, and Cooper was sometimes Uncle Nick. The girls usually squealed when he came in. Maggie harbored a tweenage crush, while Charlotte often begged helicopter rides.

Tonight, though, Charlotte pushed broccoli listlessly around her plate, and Maggie stared at her hands. Finally, Alana, the eldest, rose. "Hi, Cooper. Are you okay?" She'd been eleven when her mother died, and since then she'd become the de facto lady of the house, watching over the others and taking care of meals. Cooper had often felt sorry for Alana—nineteen years old and forced to act forty. He wondered who she would have turned out to be if Elizabeth had lived. Imagined she wondered that, too.

"Sure," he said. "I'm as okay as everybody else."

"It's awful," she said, and immediately looked as if she wanted to amend that, find a stronger term, a word that could encompass the bodies and the smoke and the pink shock of a child's stuffed animal in the middle of Broadway.

"Yes." If there was such a word, Cooper didn't know it. "I'm sorry to interrupt dinner."

"It's okay. Want something?"

"No, thanks." With that, the small talk sputtered and died.

Peters said, "Let's talk in the study" and then led Cooper through the house, past school photographs and framed macaroni art.

The "study" was a windowless room off the back of the house, with a desk and a couch, a sidebar, two muted tri-ds running the news. There was a silver-framed photograph of Elizabeth, the director's wife, gone eight years now and buried in Oak Hill Cemetery. Was it only this morning Drew had told him that story?

The room sported a few less-traditional features as well: inch-thick plating beneath the drywall, hydraulic steel door, buried hard-lines running to the DAR and the White House, a panic button that would seal the place like a vault and summon an assault team. The director poured two scotches, sat down, and looked at Cooper expectantly.

So Cooper took a breath and a sip of scotch and told him everything that had happened that day, every moment of the pursuit, how close he'd been to the bomber, how he had almost stopped things. And then he shared the idea that had struck him on a NoHo street—*How you gonna tell the good guys from the bad guys?*—the proposal that had driven him back here despite the distance and the impropriety and especially the magnitude of sacrifice it would involve.

Drew Peters said, "That's a preposterous notion. Absolutely not."

"It's not preposterous. It's perfectly feasible."

"I can think of a dozen ways it could fail."

"I can think of a hundred. But it gives us a chance, a real honest-to-Christ chance, to get close to him."

"He'd see through it. See you coming."

"Not if we went all the way with it."

"All the way."

"Yes. That's the only way to get him," Cooper said. "We've been doing this wrong for years."

Peters picked up his silver pen, spun it between long fingers. If he was offended, it didn't show in his offhand "Oh?"

"The way we're working now, we have to bat a thousand just to tie. Say I'd been able to get to the bombs today. If I disarmed four of them and the fifth went off, it's a win for Smith. If I disarmed them all but the press found out they'd been planted, it's *still* a win. He can hit us anywhere, anytime, and any hit is a victory. We have to protect everywhere, all the time, and the best we can do is tie. A perfect defense alone never wins.

"If we want to end this, if we want to keep things from escalating, if we want to *win*, we have to neutralize John Smith. And this is a way to do it."

"Not a way," Peters said. "A chance."

"That's better than no chance." Cooper took a swallow of scotch. He was exhausted, and the drink smoothed some of the rough edges. Cooper waited. The director gave nothing away, but the tiny muscles of his nose, his ears, the miniscule tensing of his shoulders, all said he was considering it.

"You understand what would be entailed? Just naming you rogue wouldn't be enough," Peters said. "I'd have to designate you a target."

"Yes."

"I won't be able to hold back. The preliminary reports I've seen put the dead at more than a thousand. And this attack was in the heart of Manhattan. There will be no half measures. I'd have to cast you down like Lucifer. I can keep you off the news—probably—but within the agency, there'd be nothing I could do for you."

"I know."

"You'll be more hated than John Smith ever was. Because you were one of us, and you betrayed us. Every resource in the department's power will be aimed at you. There will be thousands of people hunting you. Literally thousands. If you're captured, I can reveal the truth. But—"

"But no one is going to try to capture me. If they have a shot, they'll take it."

"That's right. And meanwhile, you're going to be on your own. No resources. No requisitioned helicopters, no phone taps, no surveillance teams. No backup. Nothing."

Cooper just sipped his scotch. Nothing Peters was saying was a surprise to him. He'd had time to think it out on the flight down.

All commercial flights had been grounded, so he'd badged his way onto a Marine Corps C-130 and ridden in with a squad of jarheads. The boys were extra gung ho under the circumstances, but he could see the hurt under the oo-rah. America wasn't used to being hit this way, to an attack in the heart of its strength.

The response would be devastating. There would need to be a blood payment. The country would demand it.

It wouldn't be long before it got out that the bombing was John Smith's work. And in America's overwrought state, most people wouldn't make the distinction between abnorms and abnorm terrorists.

After all, it was abnorms who had forced the stock market to close in the first place. Abnorms who were taking the lead in every field. Abnorms who were making the rest of humanity feel small and secondary.

You can't stop the future. All you can do is pick a side. Alex Vasquez's voice in his head.

Not an easy choice. And more complicated than she would have admitted. Was he a government agent hunting terrorists, or a father whose daughter was in danger? Was he a soldier or a civilian? If he believed in America, did that mean he had to accept the academies?

All right, Alex. I've made my choice. But right now, this hour in the sky, this hour is for me. He'd leaned against the metal skin of the airplane, felt the thrum of the turboprops, the cold of the air rushing past, and he let himself think of what he was about to risk. All that he might lose. The staggering costs of the plan he was proposing.

And when he landed, he'd pushed that kind of thinking aside and begun to act. Now he stared across the table at the director, at the man's pale, calm eyes, and he said, "I can do this."

"There will be no going back. None. You succeed or you die."

"I know."

"Even a *chance* to get rid of John Smith is worth a gamble. If we don't, he may well tip this country into outright civil war." Peters looked away and tapped his fingers lightly on his desk. The news channels were playing footage of the explosion, and reflected in his rimless glasses, the Exchange fell again and again.

Finally, he said, "Last chance, son. Are you sure you want to do this?"

"Yes. I'll kill John Smith for you." Cooper set his glass on the desk and leaned forward. "But there's one condition."

■

Natalie's house.

A tantalizing hint of silhouette flickered across one of the curtains. The lights were on, and the windows glowed buttery warm. Del Ray was too much part of the city for the sky to be truly black, but the queasy purple of light pollution was lonelier than night. It made those windows, and the life within them, all the more attractive.

Cooper stared out of the windshield. Took a deep breath, blew it out. There was an emptiness in his stomach, a hollowness he hadn't felt in years. A childish sort of yearning pain, the way he'd felt when he was twelve and all the rewards he'd ascribed to adulthood—love, freedom, certainty—seemed a million years away. The emptiness of the morning bed after a glittering dream of girls and adventure.

Now that things were in motion, he wanted more than anything to stop it all. To beg the director to call it off. It was too much. The costs were too high.

But then he remembered what this was really about, and he put childish fantasy away.

He climbed out of the Charger—something else he'd have to abandon soon, his beloved car and its even more beloved license-to-speed transponder—and crossed the street. The night air nipped but didn't bite. Everything smelled clean. He was sore and tired, but he tried to record every detail, to move with heightened awareness. It would be a long time before he could walk this path again.

At the front window, he paused just out of the spill of light. The curtains were parted a couple of inches, and through them he could see his children. Todd was staging an elaborate action-figure battle, the pantheons all mixed up, armored knights fighting alongside World War II soldiers and space monsters. The tip of his tongue protruded from the corner of his mouth as he mounted a robot on a horse. Kate sat on the sofa with a picture book in her lap, turning the pages backward and talking softly to herself. Through the open archway he could see Natalie in the kitchen, washing dishes. Her hair was pulled back in a ponytail, and her hips swayed as she scrubbed, semidancing to music he couldn't hear. The quiet peace of the scene, the warmth and safety and domesticity, was a jagged knife through his belly. Cooper closed his eyes. *You've already chosen sides.*

He took out his phone and dialed. Through the window he saw his ex-wife dry her hands on a towel and pull her phone from her pocket. "Nick. Are you okay? I called you a bunch of times and left messages—"

"I know. I'm okay. But I need to talk to you."

Even at this distance, he could see her stiffen. "Is it about Kate?"

"No. Yes. Sort of. Listen, I'm outside. Can you come out?"

"You're outside? Why didn't you knock?"

"We need to talk first. Before the kids know I'm here."

"Okay. Give me a minute."

Cooper pocketed his phone. Took one last look through the window, felt his stomach slip and his heart squeeze, and then stepped away. He moved over to the lone tree, a maple down to a last handful of leaves. Quick flash of memory, the tree as it had been when he and Natalie had bought the house, a runty little thing held in place by wires.

Natalie came out a few minutes later. She paused on the step, screening her eyes from the porch light, then spotted him leaning. The subtle shifts of expression on her face might have barely registered with a stranger, but each emotion was as distinct to him as if the words had been projected on her forehead. Happiness that he was alive. Guarded concern about the way he'd asked to meet her. Fear of what he had to say about Kate. A quickly overcome desire to run back inside and slam the door. "Hey," she said.

"Hey."

She tucked her hands in her pockets and looked him in the face. Knowing him well enough to recognize that he had something to say, and waiting for him to start. That cool, levelheaded forthrightness that he had always loved. A siren sounded nearby, and it quickened his heart. He glanced at his watch. Tick-tock.

"Am I keeping you?"

"No, I…" He took a breath. "I have to tell you something." He glanced at her, at the yard, at the window. Had that been motion in the curtain?

"For Christ's sake, spit it out."

"I'm going to be going away for a while."

"'A while'? What does that mean?"

"I'm not sure. Maybe a long time."

"Something for your job."

"Yes."

"Something to do with today."

"Yes. I was there. Manhattan."

"My God, are you—"

"I'm fine," he said, then shook his head. "No, that's not true. I'm pissed and I'm frustrated and I'm hurting. I was trying to stop it, Nat. I almost did stop it. But I didn't, not quite, and all those people…"

"Did you try as hard as you could?"

"Yeah. I think so. Yeah."

"Then it's not your fault. Nick, what is this? What's going on?" A miniscule widening of her eyes flashed her fear up at him.

"The explosion today. It was John Smith."

"You can't know that yet. Maybe it was—"

"It was John Smith. The worst terrorist attack on America in history, and it was an abnorm who did it."

"But…that's going to…things are going to…my God, it's going to get worse. They're going to come after abnorms. Really come after you."

"Yes." He stepped forward and took her hands in his. "So I'm going after him. John Smith. Not the same as before. Something different."

"What?"

"The only way to get close is if he thinks I'm on his side. So I'm going to be. I'm going to leave the agency and go on the run."

"I don't understand."

"The bombing. They're going to blame it on me."

She stared at him. He could practically hear her mind working. "Wait, no, it doesn't make sense. He'll know. John Smith, he'll know you weren't in on it."

"Right. But he'll also know that all of the DAR thinks I was. That I'm on the run, and that I'm being chased. That the agency I've served for years, the one I've killed for, has betrayed me. That's enough to make someone start thinking differently. And what a coup for him if I came over to his side! Think how much I could help him. Not only what I can do, but what I know."

"But for that to work—"

"Yeah. They're going to have to chase me. Really, truly chase me. I'll be designated a target. No one but Drew Peters will know the truth. Everyone will think I really went over."

"No!" Natalie yanked her hands from his. "No, are you crazy? They'll kill you."

"Only if they catch me." He tried a grin, aborted it quickly. "It's dangerous, I know, but I can do it. And it gives us a chance to get—"

"No. Take it back. Go to the director right now and tell him you've changed your mind."

"I can't do that, Nat."

"Why not? Don't you understand? You have *children*. I hate John Smith as much as you do, but if I had the choice between him being dead or Kate and Todd having a father, I wouldn't hesitate."

"It's not that simple," Cooper said, and held her gaze. It took only a handful of seconds. He watched the revelation hit. Her mouth fell open and her eyes widened.

"Kate."

"Yes," he said. "Kate. If I do this, she won't be tested. *Ever.* That was my price. She gets to grow up and live a normal life. She won't be taken from us. She'll never see the inside of an academy."

Natalie steepled her hands over her nose and mouth. Her fingers were shaking. She stared at his chest. Cooper knew enough to wait her out.

"She's tier one, isn't she?"

"Yes."

She rolled her shoulders and straightened her back. "There's no choice?"

Cooper shook his head.

"The things we do for our children." Natalie managed a thin, tight smile. "When do you have to go?"

"Soon. I want to see the kids first."

"Do you want to...you could stay. The night."

A warm feeling bloomed in his chest. When they'd split up, they'd both agreed that sleeping together was a bad idea, that it would confuse the kids and maybe risk complicating the friendly relationship they had. It had been a mutual decision and a good one; much as they loved each other, neither wanted to be involved romantically, and so it had been years since they'd shared a bed. For her to offer that now, tonight, it touched him. "That's a tempting offer. I really wish I could. But they're going to be looking for me."

"Already?"

"Soon."

"All right. You'd better come in, then. What are you going to tell them?"

"Nothing. Just that I love them."

She blew another breath, wiped at her eyes, then started across the yard. Her shoulders slumped, and the muscles of her neck were coiled cables. Cooper caught up with her, took her hand, and spun her around.

"Listen," he said, then realized he had no idea what to say next. Tell her that there was nothing to be scared of? There was. Even as they stood here, Director Peters was designating him a target. The most powerful agency in the country would be hunting him, thousands of people with billions of dollars. And even if he could manage to escape them, he was walking into the monster's den and begging for an audience.

"I'll be okay," he said.

And for just a second, a tiny moment, he could see that she believed him.

It was enough.

PART TWO: HUNTED

My fellow Americans.

Today our nation, our very way of life, suffered an attack of the most grievous nature. The victims were men and women of all kinds, all walks of life. Social workers and attorneys, bankers and artists. Mothers and fathers and brothers and sisters. Hundreds, perhaps thousands, of lives were snatched away in the most cowardly fashion imaginable—by terrorists who planted bombs in the heart of our great nation.

The individuals responsible want to disrupt our way of life. By killing innocent people, they want to cow us, like children afraid of monsters shivering beneath their blankets.

But this is not a society of children. We do not hide from monsters. We find them, and we defeat them.

Our intelligence community is united in the belief that this attack was perpetrated by gifted terrorists. Our military and security forces are the strongest in history. They are already at work to track down the people responsible. Make no mistake: we will find them, and they will be brought to justice. Anyone who aids them, anyone who hides them, anyone who supports them in any way will face our wrath.

Since the emergence of the gifted thirty-three years ago, our world has faced a challenge never seen in all of history. A small minority of human beings now possesses a massive advantage. How can men and women on both sides of this divide live together, work together, form a single, more perfect union?

The answers will not be simple ones. The road will be difficult. But there are answers. Answers that do not include bombs and bloodshed.

And so tonight, as our nation mourns its dead, I ask you all for tolerance and patience and great humanity. The gifted as a whole cannot be held responsible for the actions of a violent fringe. Just as those who hold hatred in their heart cannot define the rest of us.

It's said that the strongest partnerships are formed in adversity. Let us face this adversity not as a divided nation, not as norm and abnorm, but as Americans.

Let us work together to build a better future for our children.

And let us never forget the pain of this day. Let us never yield to those who believe political power flows from the barrel of a gun, to the cowards who murder children to achieve their aims.

For them, there can be—will be—no mercy.

Good night, and God bless America.

—President Henry Walker, from the Oval Office, on the evening of March 12

March 13, 2013
Op-Ed: AMERICA DIVIDED, AMERICA EXPOSED

Since the end of the Cold War, America has been the world's only superpower. And yet yesterday we learned that we are vulnerable. That no amount of power can protect from a truly ruthless enemy, one willing to abandon the rules of warfare and attack the innocent.

In the days and weeks to come, there will be endless discussion of responsibility. As you read this, our intelligence communities are drawing up a list of likely suspects. One name is certain to top it: John Smith, the activist-turned-terrorist who has long embraced violence as a means to achieve his ends.

But if yesterday's attack showed us anything, it was that the problem is bigger and more dangerous than we imagine. The problem lies in the fact that we are two nations.

The gifted and the rest of us. And a house divided cannot stand.

The gifted are human beings—our children and friends. And most are as horrified, as hurt, by this shameful attack as the rest of us. But the fact remains that their existence is a threat to peace, to sovereignty, to our very lives...

■

March 15, 2013
WALKER CALLS FOR INVESTIGATIVE COMMISSION

WASHINGTON, DC – Speaking before Congress today, President Walker called for the formation of a bipartisan commission to investigate the March 12 explosion at the Leon Walras Exchange.

"The American people have the right to a full and complete account of the events of that day," said Walker. "How did this tragedy occur? Did our security agencies fail? Have they been compromised?"

The proposed commission would have a broad mandate, investigating not only the cause of the explosion, but also the actions of the intelligence community leading up to the attack, as well as police and federal response afterward.

The March 12 explosion, which left more than a thousand dead, is widely believed to have been the result of a terrorist bombing. To date, no group has claimed credit for the attack...

■

March 22, 2013
FOR MANY, MOURNING TURNS TO ANGER

DALLAS, TX – Ten days after the bombing of the Leon Walras Exchange, the shock many Americans felt is becoming rage and a desire for vengeance.

"We all know who did this," said Daryl Jenkins, 63, a truck driver and former Navy chief petty officer. "We've been nothing but generous to them, and the abnorms have repaid that with blood. I say it's time we showed them what it means to bleed."

Mr. Jenkins is not alone in his feelings. In this time of national anguish, many Americans are eager to act. From donating blood to joining the army, the attack has roused the country to action in a way not seen since Pearl Harbor...

■

April 22, 2013
BILL TO MICROCHIP ABNORMS INTRODUCED

WASHINGTON, DC – Senator Richard Lathrup (R-Ark.) today formally introduced a bill (S.2038) to implant a microchip tracking device in every gifted American citizen.

"The Monitoring Oversight Initiative is a simple, commonsense solution to a complex problem," Lathrup said. "With one stroke, we can dramatically reduce the risk of another March 12th."

The proposed tracking devices would be implanted in the neck, against the carotid artery. Powered bioelectrically, they would allow government agencies to track the exact location of implanted individuals.

The bill has numerous opponents, among them Senator Blake Crouch (D-Colo.), who last year became the first gifted member of the US Senate. "I mourn the tragedy of March 12th as much as the rest of America. But we cannot allow ourselves to follow this path. How different are microchips today from the gold stars Jews were forced to wear before the Holocaust?"

The allegation is one dismissed by supporters of the bill. "Yes, this sounds dramatic," Lathrup said, "but all we want is information to protect ourselves. These devices pose no threat to the gifted. Can they say the same to us?"

■

July 5, 2013

DEMONSTRATIONS TURN VIOLENT; 1 DEAD, 14 INJURED

ANN ARBOR, MI – It was supposed to be a peaceful protest. A march by politically conscious college kids on the Fourth of July.

It turned into a bloodbath.

Organized by All Together Now, a University of Michigan student group supporting equal rights for abnorms, the afternoon march drew several hundred students to protest the Monitoring Oversight Initiative. Most wore gold stars, a reference to the designation Jews were forced to wear in Nazi Germany.

"Everything started fine," said Jenny Weaver, one of the march organizers. "Then we turned down Main, and they came out of nowhere."

According to witnesses, several dozen people wearing ski masks and wielding baseball bats attacked the protesters and proceeded to beat them brutally.

Weaver claims she and her co-organizer, Ronald Moore, were specific targets. She says that even after she dropped to the ground, they continued hitting her.

"One of them said, 'My brother was in New York.' Then his boot came down. That's the last thing I remember."

Ronald Moore died of his injuries before an ambulance could arrive. Weaver was rushed to the hospital, where she underwent eleven hours of emergency surgery. She is expected to survive, although her injuries are...

■

August 8, 2013
MICROCHIP BILL PASSES

WASHINGTON, DC – The Senate today passed the Monitoring Oversight Initiative 73-27. The bill will proceed to the House of Representatives, where a vote is expected to take place within a month.

"Today is a great day for freedom," said Senator Richard Lathrup (R-Ark.). "We have taken the first step toward protecting our way of life."

The controversial bill makes it mandatory for all gifted individuals to be implanted with a microscopic computer chip that acts as a tracking device, allowing governmental agencies to monitor their whereabouts.

While the legality of the measure is still hotly debated, the bill has found significant support that crosses party lines...

■

August 13, 2013
CNN.com
TERROR GROUP HACKS SITES, WARNS OF ATTACKS

NEW YORK, NY – This morning, more than a dozen major online destinations were hacked, including social networks, online encyclopedias, major retailers, and this news agency.

Hackers replaced existing code with what appears to be a message from abnorm terrorist groups:

> "All we want is equality. We want peace.
> But we will not sit idle as you build concentration camps.
> Call this a warning.
> Heed it."

Asked to comment on the possible source, a spokesman for the Department of Analysis and Response said...

CHAPTER 16

In early September, six months after the explosion at the Leon Walras Exchange that claimed 1,143 lives, a Jaguar XKR maneuvered through the abandoned streets of Chicago's warehouse district.

The pavement was cracked by the weight of eighteen-wheelers and the relentless cycle of Chicago winters. The sports car had a racing frame with tight suspension for maximum road-feel, and every chunk of broken asphalt vibrated through the driver's teeth. He rode slowly, steering around the worst of the potholes. Unconvincing rain dribbled on the windshield, too much to leave the wipers off but not enough to keep them from catching with a squeak on every backswing.

He passed a series of bland brick buildings screened behind rusting fences. A few blocks north the warehouses had been converted into massive party palaces, the douchey kind of clubs favored by the douchey kind of clubbers. Here, though, the buildings mostly retained their original function. Mostly.

He rolled over a set of long-abandoned railroad tracks, *ku-chunk ku-chunk*, past a graffitied Dumpster, to a two-story building of faded orange brick with a water tower on top. The fence was topped with razor wire, and a security camera stared down. After a moment, the gate slid open. He pulled through and parked next to a polished Town Car with tinted windows.

The gravel crunched under his shoes, and he could smell rain and garbage, and under it, faint, a hint of the river. He took a plain black briefcase from the trunk and left his pistol in its place.

A tortured squeak of metal came from behind, a door opening. A guy in a track suit watched him without expression.

Inside, the warehouse was a wide-open space, cold and unfinished. The light that seeped from the high windows only made the shadows darker. Stacks of unmarked crates took up about half the floor space. A cherry-red Corvette was parked near the roll doors. Someone's legs stuck out from beneath it, one foot tapping to the beat of a radio playing classic rock.

Track Suit said, "I need to check you."

"No," he smiled, "you don't."

Track Suit was one of Zane's muscle guys, not important, but not used to being contradicted. "I know you're the boss's new pet, but—"

"Listen carefully." Still smiling. "You try to pat me down, I'm going to break your arm."

The man's eyes narrowed. "You serious with that?"

"Yep."

Track Suit took a step forward, favoring his left leg.

"Joey." The mechanic was out from under the car. A smudge of grease stained one cheek. "He's okay. Besides, he's not kidding about your arm."

"But—"

"Take him to Zane."

Joey hesitated for a moment, then turned and said, "This way."

"This way" turned out to be to the back of the warehouse, where a metal staircase ran to a loft. Joey moved heavily, grunting as though each step was a task to cross off. A short hallway ran to a door, and Joey knocked. "Mr. Zane? He's here."

It had once been a foreman's office, with windows that looked not out at the world but in and down to the warehouse floor. Since then it had been cleaned up and decorated. Twin sofas sat atop a lush Oriental rug. The lighting was tasteful and low. A tri-d ran CNN, the volume muted.

Robert Zane had come from the street, and neither the Lucy Veronica cashmere sweater nor the $200 haircut could change that. He radiated an ineffable sense of dangerous slickness, and around his eyes and in his posture there always lingered a hint of the days when he'd been bad old Bobby Z. "Mr. Eliot."

"Mr. Zane."

"Drink?"

"Sure."

Joey closed the door behind them as Zane walked to a sidebar. "Scotch okay?"

"Fine." The rug was thick beneath his shoes. He set the briefcase flat on the table, then sat down. The couch was too soft. He leaned back with his hands in his lap.

"You know, I wasn't sure you were serious. What you were offering? Nobody can get hold of that kind of newtech." Zane took ice cubes from a mini-fridge and dropped them into the glasses, then poured two inches into each. His movements as he walked back were light and balanced, a fighter's posture. He passed a glass and then sat on the couch opposite, legs crossed and arms outstretched, every bit the man of leisure. "But here you are. I guess I shouldn't have doubted, huh?"

"Doubt's good. Makes you careful."

"Amen to that." Zane lifted the glass in a toast. On the tri-d, a reporter stood in front of the White House. The ribbon at the bottom read, BILL TO MICROCHIP GIFTED PASSES HOUSE 301–135; PRESIDENT WALKER EXPECTED TO SIGN. The reporter's breath steamed in the cold air, rippling toward them, artifacting a little where it reached the limits of the projection field. "So."

"So."

Zane nudged the briefcase with his toe. "You mind?"

"It's your case."

The other man smiled, leaned forward, and thumbed the locks. They gave satisfying pops as they opened. Zane lifted the lid. For a moment he just stared. Then he blew a breath and shook his head. "Goddamn. Ripping off a DAR lab. You don't mind my saying, you are one crazy son of a bitch."

"Thanks."

"How did you pull it off?"

Eliot shrugged.

"Okay, sure, professional secret. Let me rephrase that. Any trouble?"

—a finger of flame shattering the glass, shards raining sparkling down, the squealing of the alarms lost behind the roar of another explosion, the truck's gas tank going—

"Nothing that will come back on you."

"Goddamn," Zane repeated. "I don't know where you came from, but I'm sure glad you're here. People can say what they like about your kind—you get the job done." He closed the case slowly, almost gingerly. "I'll have the money transferred, same as before. That okay?"

"How'd you like to keep it?"

Zane had been about to sip his scotch, but the words caught him off guard. He froze, the muscles in his shoulders going tense. Dealings in the criminal world were a dance as regimented as a waltz. Everybody knew the steps, and any improvisation was cause for alarm. Slowly, Zane lowered his glass and set it on the table with a faint click. "What does that mean?"

"It means I'll give you those," gesturing at the case, "and you keep your money."

"And you get?"

"A favor." Tom Eliot leaned forward with his elbows on his knees, a confessional pose, man-to-man. "My name isn't Tom Eliot. It's Nick Cooper."

"Okay."

"What I'm about to tell you…" He paused, held it, sighed. "Trust isn't a big part of our business, but I think I can trust you, and I need your help. You know I'm an abnorm."

"Of course."

"What you didn't know is that I used to work for the DAR."

"So that's how you were able to rob their lab."

"No, actually. I'd never been to one before. The labs are on the analysis side. I was response. Equitable Services."

Zane almost controlled his reaction.

"Yeah. We don't exist. Except, of course, we do. Or they do. I left under…well, being gifted at an agency that hunted my kind caused some friction. The specifics don't matter. What does matter is that once I left, I became a bad guy in their eyes."

"I know something about being a bad guy." Zane smiled.

"That's why I think I can trust you. See, they've named me a target. They're trying to kill me. And sooner or later, they'll succeed."

"And you want me to…what? Take on the DAR?"

"Of course not. I want you to help me become someone else."

Zane picked up his drink. Sipped at it. "Why not go to Wyoming?"

"And live with the rest of the animals in the zoo?" He shook his head. "No thanks. I don't like cages. And nobody is going to put a tracking device in my throat. Not ever. So I need a new name, a new face, and the documents to go with it."

"You're asking a lot."

"Those semiconductors?" He gestured to the case. "That's virgin newtech. No one, *no one*, outside of the DAR has seen that architecture. You play your cards right on those, you can make a fortune. And they won't cost you a dime. You're one of the biggest smugglers in the Midwest. You really going to tell me you don't have a hacker and a surgeon in the family?"

The tri-d switched to footage of the Exchange explosion, the same loop of footage he'd seen on the tri-d billboard back in

March. They had played it endlessly for the first months, followed by clips from President Walker's speech, especially "For them, there can be—will be—no mercy." Then, as it had become clear that John Smith wasn't going to be caught quickly, it had slipped out of rotation. But it still ran every time anyone wanted to say anything negative about abnorms. Which was pretty much once an hour.

"Sure, I have the resources. But if I do this for you, then what?"

"I told you. You get those for free."

"I could just kill you."

"You sure?" He smiled.

Zane laughed. "You got balls, man. I like that."

"We have a deal?"

"Let me think about it."

"You know how to reach me. Meanwhile, hold on to the money and the semiconductors. Call it a good-faith gesture." Cooper brushed off his pant legs, then stood up. "Thanks for the drink."

CHAPTER 17

The rain had let up, and by the patch of slightly brighter gray in the western sky, it looked as if the sun might even be trying to shine. Cooper retrieved his weapon from the trunk, then steered the Jaguar off the crumbling streets of the warehouse district and into traffic. The car was a beauty, though he missed the raw, muscular rumble of the Charger.

It had been a risky play with Zane. Hopefully the man was the dirtbag Cooper believed.

He swung south, downtown. The skyline was half lost in clouds. He passed a row of shops, a car dealership. The El banged by overhead, sparks showering down where it banked.

Streeterville was a high-rent district, the kind of place that before he'd never have thought to stay. It was all boutiques and hair salons, shrill dogs and expensive women. He pulled down Delaware and stopped in front of the gleaming opulence of the Continental Hotel. A tall, pale guy in a dark jacket opened his door. "Welcome back, Mr. Eliot."

"Thanks, Mitch." He left the car and strode into the hotel.

The lobby was the definition of modern elegance, all clean lines and lush furniture. A huge paper chandelier glowed above.

Cooper strolled to the elevator and swiped his keycard. It slid into motion without his touching a button. His ears popped as they rose.

"Forty-sixth floor. Executive suites," the recorded voice purred. He pictured her tall, with sleek blond hair and a skirt that showed a little thigh and a lot of shadow.

Cooper keyed into his suite and slid out of his suit jacket. It was gray and Italian and cost more than his entire previous wardrobe. The staff had cleaned the room and drawn the curtains. Outside and far below, Lake Michigan churned silently against the shore. The sky was slowly turning to amber. He called down for smoked salmon and a bottle of gin.

In the bathroom he splashed cold water on his face, then dried himself on a thick towel. Looked in the mirror. The same face looked back, as it always did; only the setting changed. He remembered the first apartment he and Natalie had shared, a dim, narrow space above a Chinese restaurant. That had been back in their early days, before time and his gift went to work on them. Todd had been conceived in that apartment, on a couch that smelled like egg rolls. They'd had their first Christmas together there, and Cooper could still remember Todd sitting wobbly amidst a pile of wrapping paper, a bow stuck to his head. Could remember—

Don't. Just don't.

Back in the bedroom, he dropped his d-pad on the desk, his gun in the drawer. The armchair was where he'd left it, pulled out of place and turned to face the floor-to-ceiling windows, a stunning panorama of lake and skyline. He sat down and sighed.

"Home sweet home," he said.

Six months ago, when he'd shown up at Drew Peters's door with a plan and a stomach full of reckless energy, his main concern had been convincing his boss. He'd known there would be costs, and he'd accepted them. Only after everything had been in motion had he first gotten that pit-of-the-stomach *what now?* feeling.

It wasn't as though he could just e-mail John Smith and say he wanted to change sides. Any attempt to reach out directly would be seen for the trap it was. And so instead, Cooper had to ask himself what he would do if he couldn't do what he'd always done. If he wasn't the good guy who believed that the system, for all its flaws, was the only way to survive; that it was the route to a better tomorrow. If he really had been cast out by the department, if they had pinned the explosion on him, had betrayed and hunted him, what would he do?

And thus began a startlingly lucrative life as a criminal.

There was a knock at the door. He let the waiter in, asked him to put the tray on the desk by the window, signed the check and a tip without processing the numbers. The salmon was perfect, the smoky sweetness offset by the sharp salt of the capers and the brightness of fresh lemon. He washed it down with icy gin, watching the sky slowly change colors.

He'd been careful. He'd planned his moves with a rigorous devotion. After all, he had nothing else to do. No family he could share his life with. No boss to complicate his work. No friends who needed him. For a little while he tried sleeping with a woman he'd met in the hotel lounge. A magazine editor, smart and chic and very sexy, but neither of their hearts was in it, and the thing petered out on its own.

It had been a surprise—and yeah, okay, a pleasure—to realize how very good he was at being bad. The same skills that made him the best agent in Equitable Services made him an exceptional thief and powerbroker. In the last six months he'd hurtled through the underworld.

There had been some thrills on the criminal end, but far more dangerous than his new friends was his old agency. As they'd planned, Drew Peters had laid the explosion at Cooper's feet. He was now one of the top targets of Equitable Services. Three times they'd tracked him down—in Dallas, Los Angeles, and Detroit.

Detroit had been bad. He'd nearly had to kill an agent.

Staying in cities was dangerous, but he had to be on the radar. Vanishing entirely might save him from the DAR, but it wouldn't bring him any closer to Smith.

Six months of hide-and-seek, building his reputation and his wealth. Six months of relentless caution and patience. Six months while his children grew up without him, while Natalie dealt with God knew what, while his former colleagues hunted him. Six months of never making the first step in John Smith's direction.

Until today. He could only hope that the table he'd set for Zane was tempting enough.

He finished the salmon and licked his fingers. The clouds had broken, and the world outside glowed shadowless Easter colors. Magic hour. The double panes of glass canceled sound, turning the world into a mime show, a bright and dazzling spectacle for his eyes alone. That was the lure of wealth, he'd discovered: a throaty whisper in your ear that you were special, that it was all—this wine, this woman, this world—for you. That it in some way existed only so that you might partake of it. He liked it, a lot. Liked being part of the aristocracy, the one percent who had enough money to do whatever they chose.

He'd trade it in a second to be back in the front yard, spinning his children in a whirling arc of joy.

The phone rang. He rocked the chair back on two legs and stretched for it. Let it ring while he checked the display.

Zane.

Cooper smiled.

CHAPTER 18

Funny thing about Chicago's business district—it had a faucet.

Most of the day was a steady trickle, tourists, shoppers, and the like. At night, the faucet was cranked down to a bare drip. But there were certain moments when the thing was opened full stream, and the streets and sidewalks transformed to wild rapids of humanity. The first was the morning commute. The third was the evening rush back to the trains.

Cooper sat in the window of a falafel joint, waiting for the second. Outside the smudged windows, cars weaved slowly south. The concrete-chasm effect was even more claustrophobic here on Wells, where the tracks for the El cut the sky into thin slivers. He checked his watch. Almost...

Lunchtime.

The sidewalks were suddenly thronged, people hurrying and jostling in braided vectors. Cooper picked up his plastic shopping bag and joined them. As always, the crowd made him uncomfortable. Too much stimulus, too many intentions.

The day was clear and cold. He craned his neck upward, saw nothing but the towers of industry rising to a pale blue sky. Half a block north he climbed the stairs up to the El, careful to move within a crowd, a cluster of twentysomething businessmen laughing and talking. His right shoe was tight and awkward, but his body felt loose and strong, tingling with anticipated adrenaline. Cooper swiped his card and walked through the turnstile. A portico shaded the platform. Holographic ads for beauty products and movies danced along the railing overlooking the street. The buildings pressed close; ten feet off the edge, people in office buildings did…well, whatever people in office buildings did. He'd never been sure.

Cooper walked halfway down the platform. He tossed the plastic shopping bag at the trash and missed, the bag landing at the base of the metal can. He left it there and took a seat on the third bench. The portico hid the sky.

In five minutes Zane's hacker would be here, or not. He was betting on not.

A train rounded the curve, ungodly noisy. There had been talk for years of retrofitting the tracks to allow a maglev train, faster and quieter, but the money had never been in the city's budget. Cooper was glad of it; he liked the El the way it was. Old-world thinking, sure, but the rattle and clank made him happy. He rested his arms on the back of the bench, crossed his legs.

As the Brown Line pulled in, the platform erupted into a mass of motion. People jostled to get off as others fought to get on. Conversations, phone calls, music. Excuse-mes and curses. A man rapped to himself as he walked, completely unself-conscious. The wave of humanity crested with a recorded tone and the announcement that doors were closing. The tide pulled away with the train, leaving the platform suddenly empty.

Except for a very, very pretty girl who had not been there a moment ago.

Cooper blinked, startled. His palms went sweaty and the back of his neck tingled.

The Girl Who Walks Through Walls wore boots to the knee, soft tights to the hem of her skirt, a fitted shirt, and a loose jacket that had plenty of space in the cuff to conceal the snub-nosed pistol she was pointing at his chest.

She said, "Get up."

Cooper stared—

She is not part of the plan. She's a surprise on a day with no margin for error. In about sixty seconds, everything is going to explode.

Why is she here? Why now? She can't be working with Zane.

There must be sources within the department. John Smith has informers.

And how the hell does she do that, anyway?

—at her, conscious, suddenly, that his mouth was open. He closed it. Was this how other people felt about what he could do? Her ability to move unseen was uncanny. He could have sworn he'd been looking right at that spot. "You made it out of the Exchange, I guess."

"Stand up. I won't say it again."

He read her intent in the lines of her shoulder, the set of her mouth, the fury in her eyes, and he stood up. Slowly. "I don't work for the DAR anymore," he said. "Shooting me won't help your boss."

"I'm not here for that. I'm here for Brandon Vargas."

His bafflement must have shown on his face. Her lips tightened. "Of course. You don't remember. He was just another number to you. Walk." She gestured with her head, not the gun. A pro.

Cooper glanced in the direction she indicated. The nearer exit. She meant to take him off the platform before shooting him. Normally he'd have welcomed that, knowing that every second he was alive he'd have a chance to turn this around. But not today.

Today stepping out from under the roof was a death sentence.

"Listen to me," he said. "There's something you need to know."

"Start moving or I'll shoot you right here."

"I don't think so. You're not actually invisible. You may know how to be where people aren't looking, but I'm betting once they're staring, you're just as screwed as anyone else who fires a gun on an El platform."

"Maybe I'll risk it."

"For Brandon Vargas?"

"Don't you say his name. His life was shit because of men like you. Men like you put him in an academy. Men like you made him a slave. And when he refused to join the government after he graduated, *you* killed him. You're the boot of the system, Cooper. It's your job to step on human beings. And you don't even remember them."

"I shot Brandon Vargas thirteen months ago," he said quietly, "behind a biker bar in Reno. We talked first. He smoked a cigarette, a Dunhill Red. Then he made a run for it, a reckless one. Tell you the truth, I don't think he was trying to escape. I think he wanted me to end things. Wanted me to stop him."

A spectrum of emotions rolled across her face. The detail about the cigarette had been the clincher. Had Brandon been friend, family, or lover? If it was the first, he might be able to talk her down. If it was one of the latter two…

"I remember everyone I've killed," Cooper said. "I didn't go after Brandon because he wouldn't join the DAR. I went after him because he started robbing banks and shooting people. In the last one it was a woman and her two-year-old daughter. The girl was in a stroller. It was an accident, but she's still dead." There was motion in his peripheral vision. People coming onto the platform. He desperately wanted to turn and look, but didn't dare. "Yes, his childhood sucked. But I don't think that buys him a license to shoot two-year-olds. Do you?"

Her eyes were large to begin with, and the mascara made them huge. He stared at them, trying to read her thoughts, and more than that, her next move, whether she was going to pull the trigger just because that was the plan. He could feel the seconds ticking away, and the motion in his periphery drawing closer, and then he could no longer take it, and he turned and looked at the steps.

Just as he had expected. *Zane, thank you for being the traitorous, opportunistic piece of weasel shit I thought you were.*

He turned back to the Girl Who Walks Through Walls. She was on the train side of the platform. The roof would cover her from one direction, but not both. "Listen to me," he said. "Take exactly two steps forward and face east. Do it now, or they'll kill you."

"Who?"

"*Do it now.*" She would listen or she wouldn't. Either way, he had to focus. He turned.

Pouring out of both entrances to the east were men and women with neat hair and good shoes and the chest bulk of people wearing body armor. They carried shotguns and SMGs and pistols, carried them properly, aimed down and left, safeties off but fingers outside trigger guards. Three at the far stair and five at the near. Agents from Equitable Services. His former colleagues. There would be dozens more nearby, scores, covering every block. And for a little salt in the wound, both Roger Dickinson and Bobby Quinn were among them.

Ah, well.

They were yelling, telling him not to move, standard law enforcement technique, disorient and overwhelm. Their guns coming up. The handful of civilians on the platform had turned to stone. Slowly, palms out to show he meant no threat, he raised his hands. Showed that he was complying. They fanned out in a precise tactical arc, giving every agent a clean shot. The barrels of eight guns were locked on his chest. No one pointing at his head, no hotshots. If he so much as twitched his finger, they would blow his chest across the platform. He could see it in the white tension of a forefinger curled on a trigger; in the unblinking fish stare framed by submachine gun sights; in the locked shoulder muscles and flared nostrils. Roger Dickinson's lips were twisted into a snarl that looked almost like a smile. They wanted to shoot. They hated him, and they feared him.

All but Quinn. Quinn wasn't sure. Cooper locked eyes with his friend and partner. Let the sounds wash over him, their yells and howls and the rumble of an incoming train, all of it static, like the burbling of a river, out of sync with the motion of their lips.

And then he used his toe to trigger the remote he'd jammed into the front of his shoe, and the flashbangs in the plastic shopping bag turned the world into a blazing roar.

Even facing east, with his back to them, the glare left spots in his eyes, and now static really was all he could hear. All of the agents in their textbook-perfect arc had been staring directly into eight million candelas' worth of white-hot flare. They reeled back, hands going to eyes, weapons flailing.

Ten seconds.

Cooper turned, saw the girl standing beside him, facing east. She started forward, but he lashed out, caught her wrist. "No!" He was shouting but could barely hear his own voice. "Snipers!" He let go of her, turned to the west, and began to run.

Eight seconds.

The platform ran another thirty yards. Benches and trash cans were strung along the length. He leaned into the run, hoping she could keep up. The beginnings of a potential next step were assembling in his head, and she was at the heart of it. No time. He reached the end of the portion with a roof.

Here went nothing.

Five seconds.

Something angry and hot burned past his arm, and sparks popped off a trash can ahead. He did a quick zag to the left. A patch of concrete burst. He faked right and then went left again. The hipster he passed collapsed, hands clutching at his leg, which seemed to have exploded from the inside. Cooper never heard the shots, hadn't expected to. The flashbang was part of it, but also the snipers—there would be at least three—would be on upper floors hundreds of yards away.

Two seconds.

He hit the end of the platform at a dead run, planted his right foot without slowing, leaped upward, got his left foot onto the railing, and flung himself into space, arms whirling, wind on his face, heart in his mouth.

Below him, the street. Unforgiving concrete and the buzz of cars. Empty air. He just had time to wonder if he would make it, and then he hit the fire escape of the building opposite. It wasn't a graceful landing; he pretty much collided with the railing, ribs banging into it. He gasped, then hauled himself up and over. Turned to see if—

—she landed like a cat, flexing her knees down to a squat crouch, her hands catching and pushing her up.

Goddamn.

Cooper pushed aside his appreciation. They were out of time. A flashbang worked by throwing enough photons that it activated all light-sensitive cells in the eye, temporarily blinding anybody nearby and facing it. But ten seconds was as much as he could hope for before the team would be able to see enough to start moving. Maybe even to risk a shot. He lunged for the corner railing, ripped off the strip of duct tape, and yanked the crowbar free, then whirled and smashed the window with one blow. Hauled it back across the bottom to clear the worst of the shards.

He turned to gesture to the girl, and found her no longer there. Right. He leaped through the window as gunfire cracked behind. He hit something, her, and the two of them tangled and fell. He landed on top of her, not a suave action-hero move but a clumsy, wind-losing collapse. He caught a whiff of female sweat and some spicy sort of perfume, and then they were both squirming to their feet.

A thin man with thinner hair sat on the opposite side of the desk. His mouth was wide open. He stared at them like, well, like they had just exploded through his window. Cooper snorted a laugh—something about a fight, he always found synchronicities and amusements when he couldn't afford them—and went for the office door. She followed. An office like any other, cubicles and filing cabinets and fluorescent lights. He walked steadily, nodding at people he passed, just another office drone. The stairwell was by the elevator. He hurried in and up. His ears rang and his ribs hurt. He went up one flight and then paused on the landing and checked the time.

"Why are you stopping?"

"Waiting for them to get here. All of the units in the area will be rerouted to this building."

"*What?* This is a trap?"

"No. They'll surround it, secure the exits. Then tactical response teams will move in. That's when we move out."

"Screw you. I'm not waiting."

He shrugged. "Okay."

Her eyes narrowed. "You've had this all planned."

"I figured Zane would sell me out."

"Then why show up?"

"Because there was a chance that he wouldn't. Besides, I've run a million of these. I know the playbook."

"Right," she said, her voice cold. "You've run a million of these on other gifted."

"Yes. And right now there are about a hundred agents converging on this building. You think you can slip past them all, be my guest. Otherwise, do what I say, and we get out of here."

"Why would you help me?"

He paused, mind racing. He'd figured Zane would betray him; had been depending on it, in fact. The DAR was no doubt paying a hefty bounty. Not only that, but while the agency didn't care about common criminals, it had pull with agencies that did. Selling Cooper out might buy Zane insurance later. It was simple math to assume he would call the DAR, and that the department would come in full force. Come loudly and publicly. Which had been the purpose of the whole exercise. It was a test balloon. A message. It would show John Smith that Nick Cooper was, beyond a doubt, no longer on the DAR's payroll. And just maybe it would be the first step toward the terrorist.

What he hadn't imagined was that the Girl Who Walks Through Walls would come to avenge a man he'd killed thirteen months ago. It presented him with one hell of an opportunity. He wanted to reach Smith? Here was one of the terrorist's most trusted soldiers. The woman who had pulled the trigger on March 12 and blown up the Exchange, killing 1,143 people. He fought the urge to knock her unconscious and leave her for his old team.

But she was just a piece. He wanted the player.

"I don't know," he said. "For Brandon Vargas, I guess." He gave that half a second to sink in, then said, "Let's go."

The door bore a sign that read No Entry: Exit on Ground Floor. He put a palm against it and pushed. It swung open. On the way through he pulled off the duct tape he'd applied last night to keep the latch from catching. Wonderful stuff, duct tape.

"Now what?"

He ignored her and strode down the hall. A woman smiled as he passed. A cubicle jock did cubicle jock things. The break room was just a wider space in the hall, a fridge buzzing away, packets of coffee creamer and plastic silverware. The window had been painted a dozen times, thick layers that locked it shut. He slid one end of the crowbar under the sash and jerked downward. The paint cracked, and something squealed. Another jerk, and the thing popped open half an inch. He forced it the rest of the way, then climbed out onto another fire escape, half a block away and two stories up from the one they'd arrived at. A train was pulling into the El station. Perfect.

"You're kidding." She leaned over the railing.

"Nope." He climbed up, balanced for a moment, then leaned forward. Felt gravity begin to take him. At the last second he flexed his legs and leaped off. Below streaked the same unforgiving concrete, the same buzzing cars, the same empty air. Then he hit the roof of the El platform, bending his knees and falling into a roll. The metal bonged and rang at the impact, but the arriving train masked the noise. Behind him he heard the same metallic clatter, softer than his, and then they crouched side by side atop the roof as the silver train drew to a stop. He waited until the flow of riders on and off the train had ebbed, and then, with an easy step, he moved onto the roof of the second car. Lowered himself down and army-crawled to the front, got a good grip on the lip, and braced his feet. The metal was cold and dirty. A moment later, the girl joined him. She looked sideways, shook her head. "Asshole."

He grinned. "Doors are closing. Please hold on."

There was a lurch like an elevator starting, and then the train began to move.

Most of the plan he'd been reasonably sure of. His old agency hadn't yet taken into account the fact that he knew their techniques. They were using the same playbook. So it had been easy to create a situation where the flashbangs would buy him time, where he could use standard protocol to his advantage, where he could lure every available agent to one spot and then double back from it. But he'd never ridden atop a moving train before.

After everything else he'd done in the last few minutes, it turned out to be almost easy. According to his d-pad, on a long straightaway the trains could hit fifty-five miles an hour. He didn't know if they'd be able to hold on under those circumstances, clinging to the slick metal by lousy handholds. Fortunately, they were in the Loop, where trains made a circle before running back the way they'd come. The greatest risk came as they rounded a corner and the train rocked sideways, but he'd anticipated it and braced for the motion. The wind was exhilarating, and the expressions he saw on the faces of people in the buildings made getting shot at worthwhile. They rode through two stops, and he was almost sad when the third came up.

Goddamn, but I'm good. He stood, started for the edge of the train. The doors had opened, and riders were pouring in and out. He'd wait till they were mostly gone and then jump off just before—

She came from behind, her knee knocking out his as her hands took his shoulders. He was going down, no arguing with physics, but why had he turned his back on her in the first place? They hit the roof of the train, bounced. He slipped her hold, twisted, raised one arm to strike.

The Girl Who Walks Through Walls pointed, alarm in her eyes. Cooper narrowed his, risked a quick glance over his shoulder. Passengers leaving the train, men and women, tourists and businesspeople, a flight attendant, a couple of students…and two men in suits.

Roger Dickinson said, "Damn it. I was sure he'd double back."

"You want to check the train again, sir?" Bobby Quinn had a dryly insubordinate tone, but it was the "sir" that caught Cooper's attention. Peters must have promoted the man, probably given him Cooper's old position. That was bad news. Whatever else he might be, Roger Dickinson was very good at his job.

"No, I don't want to check the train again, Bobby. You know what I want? To know you're on the right side."

"I told you, I don't believe Coop's a terrorist."

"Yeah? Even though he blew up the Exchange?"

"He didn't blow up—"

"Right. He just went there seconds before it blew up, then vanished and started robbing DAR labs. And that woman he was holding hands with, she's the one who killed Bryan Vasquez. So tell me again. How is Cooper one of the good guys here?"

"I don't know." Quinn's voice was dogged. "But I still don't believe he's with Smith."

"Get it through your head, Bobby. Your girlfriend, he's a—"

"Doors are closing. Please hold on." There was a loud *bing-bong*, and then the train started moving. Cooper barely had time to grab the lip of the car. A strange and awful heaviness tightened his stomach. He'd been cocky there, had almost stepped right in front of his old colleagues. He'd seen how fast Dickinson was. And Cooper was unarmed. *If I'd jumped down, he'd have killed me.*

When he turned to look at her, The Girl Who Walks Through Walls met his gaze briefly. Then she looked away.

You say you are the master race,
I say you are our disgrace,
You say it's not your fault,
I say destroy all trace.

Put out the lights,
Put out the lights,
Wash the streets with blood,
And put out the lights.

You say you are the future,
I say I wouldn't be so sure,
You say live and let live,
I say scrub our world pure.

Put out the lights,
Put out the lights,
Set the streets on fire,
And put out the lights.

For all the times you kicked us,
And all the times you smiled,
For all the times you tricked us,
And all the times you lied,

Put out the lights,
Put out the lights,
Let the bodies fall,
And put out the lights.

—Severed Bloodlines, "Put Out the Lights"
Resistance Records, 2007

CHAPTER 19

It was a far cry from an executive suite at the Continental.

Bland and generic and mildly soul-killing, the Howard Johnson was on the unfashionable end of State Street. The afternoon light through the curtains was funereal. Behind him, the Girl Who Walks Through Walls said, "Now what?"

"We wait." He moved to the edge of the bed, sat down.

She stepped in as though uncertain whether to stay. Ran a finger along the desk. "Nice digs."

"Yeah, well, I wasn't expecting company." Cooper began to unlace his shoes. "This is just a place to ride out the storm. Once they realize we slipped past them, they'll make a last-ditch effort to catch us while we're close. They'll fan out across the Loop. They'll co-opt the CPD video camera system. They'll get cops to do door-to-doors, popping into every bar and restaurant, looking in the restrooms. They'll check hotels for new arrivals."

"Last I looked, this was a hotel."

"I booked it a week ago. Under the name Al Ginsberg."

She said, "'I saw the best minds of my generation destroyed by madness, starving hysterical naked...'" She parted the curtains, looked out at the brick wall opposite and the street below. "Never really understood the poem, but I like the way the words taste."

"Yeah." Cooper pulled the shoe off, shook it until the flashbang remote fell out into his hand. "Me too. Why'd you do it?"

"Huh?" She turned.

"The Exchange. Why blow it up? You killed eleven *hundred* people."

"No," she said. "I tried to tell you then. I was there to stop it."

"Bullshit."

"It was supposed to be empty. We'd called earlier that day, announced we had bombs in the building, that we would trigger them if they started searching. I was there to make sure it *didn't* blow, not with all those people there."

"Bang-up job. I noticed on the news how it didn't explode."

She crossed her arms in front of her chest. "Destroying it was supposed to be a symbol. The Exchange was built to counter us, to exclude us. We wanted to show that they can't build a future that doesn't include us. How would killing people have made that point?"

Cooper looked up at her. The width of her pupils, the calm in her fingers, the steady pulse at her neck, none of it suggested she was lying. *But this woman could find a way to hide in an airplane bathroom. Controlling her body is part of that.*

"Anyway, who are you to talk? You're the killer. Not me."

"Yeah? What about Bryan Vasquez?"

Her lips drew into a tight line. "He betrayed the cause."

"The defense of every terrorist masquerading as a freedom fighter."

"Said the storm trooper who protects the state by murdering its citizens."

He started to reply, caught himself. *You've got three hours to convince her that she should help you. If she vanishes, you lose.* He tied his shoe. His fingers were clumsy with post-adrenaline shakes, and his ribs hurt from where he'd hit the balcony. Cooper stood, went to the minibar fridge beneath the television. It opened with a squeal. He pulled out two miniature bottles of Jack Daniel's for himself. "You want a drink?" He rifled through. "They've got red wine, cheap champagne—"

"Vodka."

"There's orange juice, I could make a screwdriver."

"Just vodka and ice."

"You want to watch me pour it? Murdering storm trooper and all?"

She stared at him for a long moment, and then one corner of her lips quirked up into a smile. "Gimme the drink already."

The world's tiniest ice tray was in the freezer. He cracked it, shook the cubes into a plastic cup, splashed Smirnoff over them. He passed it to her, then poured his bourbon. The soothing warmth went right to work on his aches and shakes.

"So how long do we need to hang out here?"

"A couple of days."

"A couple of *days*?"

"I've got some canned soup in the closet; we'll eat it cold. But I was only planning for one, so we'll have to ration our provisions."

Her eyes went so wide they seemed to bulge. He cracked, smiled, said, "I'm kidding. Just till the evening rush, so we can get lost in the crowd."

The Girl Who Walks Through Walls laughed. It wasn't a throaty or sultry thing, a laugh as a pose; it was an honest sound of amusement. Cooper said, "That's better."

"Than what?"

"Than calling each other names. Which reminds me—"

"My name is Shannon."

"Nick Cooper."

"I've heard," she said dryly. "So what, we just walk out of here and that's that?"

"Were you thinking we'd pick flower arrangements, send out invitations?"

"Thing is, Nick—"

"Cooper."

"You've put me in a bit of a bind."

"How's that?"

"You're not dead."

"Pardon?"

"I came to kill you. But you're not dead. And to anyone watching, it wouldn't have looked like I was trying to kill you. It would have looked like we were working together."

"So?"

"So the DAR already has me marked as a target for the Exchange. Now that they've seen us together, I'm probably higher priority than you. And now they know I'm here. Not only that, but until I can get to my people, they'll assume I've switched over."

"Why? Didn't they know you were coming for me?"

She shook her head. "This was personal. I didn't tell anyone. And now it'll look like just as the bad guys were descending, I hooked up with Equitable Services' top gun and we made a daring escape. What am I going to do, say, don't worry, all Cooper and I did was talk poetry and revolutionary politics?"

"How would they even know you were there?"

"We have people in the DAR."

"Really." He sipped his drink. He'd known that, worked it out by her appearance on the platform, but there was no reason to let her know that. "And your moles will report that you joined up with me."

"That's right. This burns me. In both directions. *You* burned me."

Cooper shrugged. "Sorry?"

"Listen, you smug—"

"Lady, I didn't burn you. *You came to kill me.* Not my fault you picked the wrong time. Besides, I could have left you. If it weren't for me, you'd be shivering in a white, well-lit room right now."

"And if it weren't for me, you'd be bleeding out on the platform at LaSalle and Van Buren."

They stood on opposite sides of the bed, both tense and braced, bickering like an old married couple, and there was something so backward about it all, about this woman—this terrorist—having saved his life from his former colleagues, about *her* referring to *them* as the bad guys, and about the fact that in terms of his continued survival she had a point, and it was all so absurd that he found himself chuckling.

"What?"

"Long day." He took another sip of whiskey and then crossed to the television—it was an old flatscreen, not a tri-d—and turned it to CNN. There was no way to know if this would make the news, and even if it did, it probably wouldn't be for hours yet.

"...the site of yet another in a string of terrorist attacks in recent weeks." The woman standing on the El platform was plastic-pretty and overeager, a local reporter getting her big break. "Earlier today, an unidentified man planted a bomb during Chicago's lunch rush."

The image cut to her holding a microphone to a man Cooper vaguely remembered from a seminar in DC two years before. The words TERRY STILES, CHICAGO BUREAU CAPTAIN, DEPARTMENT OF ANALYSIS AND RESPONSE were printed over the lower third. Stiles said, "We've been tracking this individual for several weeks and were able to apprehend him before he could detonate a bomb on the El. However, we were unable to prevent him from firing on the crowd. Several civilians were wounded, as well as two agents."

"Who is he?"

"I can't comment on that at the moment," Stiles said, "other than to say that we suspect he was working with abnorm terrorist groups operating out of Wyoming."

"Does he have anything to do with John Smith and the March 12th explosion?"

"I can't comment on that."

The video cut to footage of an emergency crew wheeling out a gurney. The man on it was the hipster caught in the sniper crossfire.

Over the footage, the reporter continued. "Wounded civilians are being rushed to local hospitals and are expected to survive."

Another cut, and the reporter's overly concerned expression again filled the screen. "This sort of scene has become familiar in recent months, and abnorm splinter groups warn that the violence will escalate if the government proceeds with the Monitoring Oversight Initiative. The controversial bill, which yesterday passed the House, makes it mandatory for all gifted individuals to be implanted with a—"

Suddenly the television blinked off. Cooper turned as Shannon tossed the remote onto the desk with a clatter. "I was watching that," he said mildly.

"I can't stand those lies. They make my skin crawl."

"You know the game. Stories like that keep people calm. There was a bad guy, and we stopped him. It's clean and simple. It's better than the alternative, the mass panic and mob violence that would result if—"

"If what? If you told the truth?" Shannon fixed him with a hard stare. "That news report just talked about an abnorm attack, which there wasn't. It said the terrorist—that's you, by the way—shot agents and civilians, when actually the *agents* shot the civilians. And it said that Big Brother had things under control, when in fact we walked free. The only part of it that was true, literally the only part, was that there was a brilliant on the El platform today. Two, in fact."

"What's your point?"

"What's my *point*?"

"Yeah. Apart from the idea that the truth shall set you free, and other lines no one believes. People don't want the truth, not really. They want safe lives and nice electronics and full fridges." He just couldn't seem to avoid sparring with this woman. "You think I *want* abnorms microchipped? You think I *like* the academies? I hate it, all of it. But we are vastly outnumbered. Normal people are frightened, and frightened people are dangerous. The fact is, we, abnorms, brilliants, twists, we cannot survive a war. We will lose."

"Maybe," she said. "But maybe there wouldn't *be* a war if you people didn't keep going on television and saying there was one."

He opened his mouth. Closed it. Finally he said, "Maybe you've got a point. But watch the 'you people' stuff. The department burned me. They needed a scapegoat for March 12th, and so they hung the explosion on me. My old friends are trying to kill me. But let's not forget. It was your boss's handiwork they blamed me for."

"I told you—"

"Yeah, I know. The building was supposed to be empty. But did John Smith plan the attack? Did he arrange the explosives? Did he have them planted?"

She was silent.

"There's nobody here who's clean," he said. The angle was coming to him, the right way to play her. "Not you, and not the DAR. And I'm tired of it. All I want is out of the game."

He dropped to the bed, lay back with his hands crossed behind his head. The ceiling was stucco, and the low light of afternoon turned every bump into a sundial. *Not another word. It's a lousy salesman who talks too much.*

Shannon put her feet up on the bed, legs crossed at the ankle. Leaned back in the chair to pull one drape aside. Her face glowed sunset colors. Still staring out the window, she asked, "What was Zane supposed to do for you, anyway?"

"Get me a new identity."

"What, fake papers?"

He snorted. "I've got a dozen driver's licenses. To Zane I was T. S. Eliot, and to the front desk here I was Allen Ginsberg, and I could walk out of here Chuck Bukowski. But this is the DAR we're talking about. If I want a new life, it'll have to be as a new person. New papers, but also a new history hacked into a hundred places, a new face, the whole thing."

"Why not just go to Wyoming?"

"Right."

"I mean it," she said. "It may not be sovereign yet, but the DAR doesn't plan raids in New Canaan."

"It would be a death sentence. If Zane had come through, maybe, but he didn't." *Let her sell you. Let her think it's her idea.*

"New Canaan is different than the normals' world. Everyone comes there with a past. Everyone has baggage. You can get a fresh start."

"Yeah. Until the brother of someone I killed sets my house on fire. No, if I have to spend my whole life watching my back, I'll do it somewhere prettier than Wyoming." He glanced at the clock, then closed his eyes. "I'm gonna crash for a few."

A long minute passed, and then another, as he stared at the back of his eyelids. *Come on. Come on.*

"There might be a way," she said.

Gotcha. He opened his eyes. "Yeah? What, take a jackknife to my nose, call it plastic surgery?"

"Hear me out. You could be safe in New Canaan, even as yourself." She raised her hands to forestall his objections. "Not as you are now. But if the right person vouched for you, that could change everything."

"I am not a terrorist." He said the words flat and hard. It couldn't look like he was eager. Even the tiniest hint of his true intent and this would all crumble. "I will not work for John Smith."

"I wasn't thinking of him."

"Who were you—"

"Erik Epstein."

Cooper stiffened. "The billionaire? The King of New Canaan?"

"Only straights call him that."

"Why would he speak for me?"

"I don't know. You'd have to convince him. But he's a better chance than a scumbag like Bobby Z. And if you really want a fresh start, well." She shrugged. "He might understand that."

"I just knock on his door?"

"No. You'd need help."

He sat up, spun his legs to the floor. The radiator kicked on, clicking and banging.

"What would you get out of it?"

"Until I square things with my people, which I need to do face-to-face, I can't use any of my old resources. Not my credit, my IDs, my contacts. And meanwhile, your old friends are going to be chasing me as hard as they're chasing you."

Cooper pretended to think it over. "So I get you into Wyoming, and you get me to Erik Epstein."

"Yeah."

"And how do I know you won't bail the moment we're in New Canaan?"

She shrugged. "How do I know you won't sell me out to the DAR to get them off your back?"

"You're saying we trust each other."

"God, no," she deadpanned. "I'm saying we make it worth each other's while."

Cooper chuckled. "All right. Deal." He held out his hand, and after a flicker of hesitation, she shook it.

"Deal," Shannon said. "So. First thing."

"What's that?"

"We need to get some drugs."

CHAPTER 20

"Neurodicin," he'd said, when she explained what she was looking for. "It's a semisynthetic opiate derivative."

"I've never heard of it."

"On the street they call it Shadow or Nada. It's academy-developed newtech, supposed to replace fentanyl. Instead of numbing you, it messes with your memory, so that you forget the pain as it's happening."

"How's it do that?"

"How should I know? Ask the twist who designed it. Anyway, if you want something special for the discerning junkie, Shadow's the trick."

"Where do we get it?"

Which was how they'd found themselves walking north when five o'clock hit and the streets filled with commuters. Before leaving the hotel he'd changed his shirt, and at a tourist shop he bought a Cubs hat and a pair of oversize movie-star sunglasses for her. As disguises went, they were pretty rudimentary, but their real camouflage was the crowd. They stuck to Michigan Avenue: lanes of cabs and buses on one side, towering skyscrapers on the other, and between, a rush of people.

"This woman, she's a friend of yours?"

Shannon nodded. "And she and John have been friends a long time. Since they were in the academy."

So strange to hear him referred to that way. Not John Smith, the terrorist leader; John, the friend from a long time ago. "If she's a friend, why do you need this stuff?"

"You don't show up at somebody's house without a bottle of wine. It's not polite."

"This is some wine."

"Well, it's some favor I'm asking. It's not like I can phone John."

"How does that work?"

She glanced over sharply. "You digging for operational details, Agent Cooper?"

"No, I just..." He shrugged. "I don't understand how he leads people if they can't find him."

"This isn't like the army. There's no chain of command, no rear echelon. No orders."

"What, he just asks nicely?"

"Yes. He's a very nice guy. Anyway, Samantha won't know where he is, but she'll be able to get word to him."

"I hope you're right. This is a big risk," Cooper said. Thinking, *Lady, I will help you steal all the drugs you like if it gets me closer to your boss.*

If anything, the crowd grew denser as they started down the Magnificent Mile. Tourists joined the mix, and shoppers loaded with packages. Crowds were always frustrating to Cooper, but it was worse with Shannon. The concept of a straight line was utterly foreign to her. She slipped and slid and quicksilvered along, finding holes where there weren't any, sometimes stopping dead for no reason he could see. It was unmistakably graceful—Shannon moved the way water flowed—but not easy to walk beside.

He was glad when they reached the gray-and-glass bulk of Northwestern Memorial Hospital. The front entrance was about as inviting as a hospital could be, which was to say not very. The cafeteria was on the second floor. It had fake plants and fake-wood trim and smelled like soup and disinfectant. Cooper bought himself coffee, and they took a table in a corner near the door.

"Did you see the cameras on the way in?" she asked.

"Yeah."

"Cameras are a problem. I can't shift if I can't see the people looking for me."

"You can't what?"

"Shift." For a moment she looked girlishly self-conscious. "It's what I call it. What I do."

"Shift. I like that." The coffee was better than he expected, dark and strong. "The cameras shouldn't be a problem. They'll record us, but I doubt anyone is monitoring the live feed. This isn't a black-ops facility; mostly the security is to foil junkies and keep hospital staff out of the candy jar."

Shannon leaned back, began to run her hands through her hair, letting it fan out between her fingers. "There are two doctors at the corner table."

He glanced at their reflection in a framed poster. "No."

"Why not?"

"White coats and expensive pens. They're administrators. Maybe they have the access to open the dispensary, maybe not."

Cooper took in the room. About fifty people, with more coming in. There were a few scattered patients. A handful of nurses laughed at one table, but they presented the same problem as the administrators. And residents were out.

"There," he said.

Still toying with her hair, she followed his gaze to a middle-aged man in pale-blue scrubs crumpling his napkin and tossing it atop the remnants of a cheeseburger. "How do you know?"

"The hair on his arms thins out at the forearms, and the skin is pinker. That means he washes his hands all the time, washes them hard. Plus, his nails are cut to nothing. Taken together, that tells me he's in surgery a lot. A surgeon will have the access we need.

And look at the circles under his eyes. Exhaustion. Probably working a twenty-four-hour shift. Makes him an easier target."

"You got all that from a quick glance across the room?"

"Yeah, I know, weird way to look at the world."

"No," she said. "No, it was hot."

"Right." He felt oddly self-conscious and gave an aborted laugh.

Shannon leaned back, her expression quizzical. "You need to spend more time with your own kind, Cooper. The straights have you thinking twisted." Before he could reply, she rose and started walking in one smooth motion. It wasn't that she was fast so much as that she was calculated, as if for every motion she applied the exact force needed. It was like watching a cat jump to a table, instinctively determining the precise force and angle needed to land without an inch or calorie wasted.

The surgeon had risen and was walking his tray over to a garbage bin. Shannon circled the table of nurses, slipped between two sad-faced women, cut back across the floor, and then stepped out of nowhere and into the man's path. They collided. He almost lost the tray, the plate and cup slipping to the edge, then managed to get it under control as he apologized, stepping back and blushing. Shannon shook her head, assured him it was her fault, laughed, patted him on the bicep, and came back carrying the man's ID badge.

Cooper smiled into his coffee cup.

They finalized their plan in the elevator. As he understood hospitals, small stores of the most commonly needed medications were kept on every floor. But Shadow wasn't standard stuff. It would be kept in a single location, well secured and carefully monitored.

After they split up, Cooper paused at the corner and counted ten Mississippis. Then he put on a confused expression and started forward.

The dispensary was part storeroom, part pharmacy. A counter opened to a window behind which a man and a woman counted pills. Cooper went to the counter. "Excuse me, can you guys help?" Saying *you guys* to be sure he had the attention of both of them, and leaning on the counter, drawing their eyes away from the back. "I am so freaking lost. This place is huge! It's like a maze. I don't know how you find anything here."

"What are you looking for?"

"I mean, my God. I'm trying to visit my niece. I started out just the way they said. Turned right, went straight, turned left. I found the elevators okay, but that was the last time I knew where I was. I feel like I've been wandering for weeks. Pretty soon I'm going to have to eat my shoe for provisions."

"Well, tell me where you're trying to go and I'll help you."

Over the pharmacist's shoulder, Cooper saw Shannon cross between a row of shelves. She winked at him. He smiled before he could catch himself, then went with it, said, "Sure, sure. That's just what the last guy said. I think he must have had a bet with someone. See how long he could keep a guy wandering. You're probably in on it."

The tolerant expression was starting to slip. "Sir, I can't help you if you won't tell me where—"

"I told you, I'm trying to visit my niece."

"Yes, but where is she?"

Cooper did a double take. "If I knew that, I wouldn't have to ask, would I? You don't listen too good."

"No, what *department*? ICU, pediatrics…"

"Right." He slapped his forehead. "Sorry, sometimes I get to talking, and goddamn if by the time I reach the end of a sentence I haven't forgotten the beginning. It's like the trail of tears. Only, you know, without the dead Indians."

The pharmacist stared at him. It wouldn't have taken Cooper's gift to read his thoughts: *This guy is a moron.*

Not far behind it, though, was *Maybe I should call security.* It was a hospital, after all. There were legitimately crazy people here.

"She had her tonsils out."

"Okay. Recovery." The man gave him directions, speaking slowly and carefully. Cooper nodded, thanked him, and then went back the way he'd come. He barely kept himself from laughing but let the smile spread.

Until he turned the corner and saw a security guard hurrying toward him, along with the surgeon from the cafeteria. Shit. They'd hoped the doctor might not need his badge so quickly, and that even if he did, he'd waste time retracing his steps. Instead, it appeared he had gone straight to security—

The fact that they're here means they checked the computer system. They know his badge was just used to access the dispensary.

They won't waste time talking to the pharmacist. They'll go for the door.

Which is the only exit. She'll be trapped.

—which left Cooper with no choice. He'd do the security guard first, a quick combination, solar plexus–kidney-kidney, then the doctor. Sprint back to the dispensary, hop the counter, take out the pharmacists if they got in the way. Get the Neurodicin, get Shannon, get out.

Someone tapped his shoulder, and he whirled.

The Girl Who Walks Through Walls stood behind him. "Hi."

"You. But." He turned, saw the guard and doctor hurrying past. Neither glanced at them, focused on their goal. "Oh. Huh."

"What?"

"It's just, I thought you were still in there. I was going to…I was about to—"

"Rescue me?"

"Uhh…"

"I'm not a cat up a tree. I can handle myself." Shannon held up an orange plastic bottle, shook it so the pills rattled. "Let's go."

LIFE ISN'T FAIR
MAKE SURE IT'S *YOUR*
CHILD WITH THE HEAD
START

We all want the best for our family. But even the most dedicated and supportive parenting is only as successful as genetics allow.

That's why at Bright Lights Fertility, we only accept donors who:

- Are IQ tested at a minimum of 120
- Have no genetic predispositions to disease
- Are ranked tier three or above on the Treffert-Down Scale

BUT WE'RE FERTILE.
WHY CONSIDER INSEMINATION?

In a word? Your child.

Yes, historically, artificial insemination has been focused mostly on those who have no other means of getting pregnant. But that's changing. And why wouldn't it? After all, what's more important—that your child have the best possible genetic makeup, or that he or she be related to you?

Our donors represent the best humanity has to offer. And while it's not certain why some children are born gifted, common sense says the odds increase if one of the parents is.* If you want to maximize the head start for *your* little gift, the solution is clear.

Anything else is just selfish.

CHAPTER 21

She wasn't what he expected.

Shannon had said that her friend Samantha went way back with John Smith. Cooper had imagined another woman like her, strong, ideologically dedicated, and very dangerous. A soldier.

What he hadn't expected was this tiny, delicate thing with pale-blond hair. She had a woman's face and curves, but couldn't have been more than four foot ten, maybe ninety pounds. It had a strangely erotic effect; she was so small, you couldn't help but imagine what she looked like naked.

"Hey, Sam." Shannon stepped forward, leaning down to hug the woman. "This is Cooper."

"Hi," he said, holding out a hand. As she shook it, he got a whiff of perfume, sweet but clean. Maybe it was that, or the softness of her hand, but he felt himself getting turned on.

"Come in." She stepped aside.

The room looked like a catalog from an upscale furniture store. Twin white sofas sat atop a thick shag rug. A coffee table holding coffee-table books. The only hint of personality was a bookcase packed to bursting. Beyond the floor-to-ceiling windows, only night and the looming, invisible bulk of Lake Michigan.

Shannon said, "Brought you a present." She held out the pill bottle.

"Wow. How did you get your hands on Nada?" Samantha pronounced it like a lover's name. "That's so sweet of you."

Given the upscale apartment and Samantha's style and carriage, Cooper had almost forgotten that she was an addict. But watching her as she held the pill bottle, he could see the raw, curling need inside her, the hunger. She started to open the bottle, stopped herself, tapped the label. "Sweet of you both."

"You're welcome," he said, for want of something to say.

Samantha's eyes were soft brown flecked with gold, and as she looked at him, the addiction was pushed down, replaced by something he couldn't quite identify. She shifted her pose, one foot slightly forward, her hips cocked and back straight. The move was subtle, but it made her look stronger, gave her a ferocity. "I'm surprised a cop would be okay with this."

"I'm not a cop."

"Not anymore, maybe. But you were. Right?" She smiled. "I can always tell. It's the confidence, the way you hold yourself. Like you could handcuff me if you wanted to." There was a small gap between her front teeth, and Cooper remembered reading somewhere that was linked to highly sexual tendencies, and that thought led to a visual of what she would look like riding him, how huge his hands would be on her hips, the way her back might arch so that hair would swing down behind to brush his thighs…

Jesus, man. Lock it down.

"You okay, Cooper?" Shannon wore an amused smile. "You look a little nervous."

He read Shannon's mocking tone, paired it with the movements Samantha had made, the way she had presented herself to him. She was beautiful, no question, but he'd met a lot of beautiful women in his life. There was something more, something in the way she held herself, the frank flirtation—*you could handcuff me if you wanted*—coupled with a bit of distance.

Huh.

"That's a powerful gift you have," he said.

"What's that?"

"Making men sweaty."

It threw her, and in that instant he saw through the pose to the calculations. It was like flipping on the lights in a strip club, the illusion of sensuality revealed as misdirection and razzle-dazzle. He watched as she cycled half a dozen responses, each barely signaled, hinted at rather than adopted. Widening eyes to test a vulnerability angle. Stiffened back and shoulders to go the other way, be fierce and angry. The tiniest hint of a slouch to throw out sassy, feisty, ready to play. Each subtle as a poker tell. It was like she was trying a ring of keys, looking for the one that would unlock the secret of who he wanted her to be.

Through it, Cooper kept himself still, gave nothing away. "You're a reader, aren't you? Only instead of understanding what people are thinking, you see what they want. And then you become it." *My God. What a talent for a spy. She's all things to all people.*

"So show me." Samantha took a step forward. "Stop hiding."

"Why?"

"So I know who to be."

"Just be yourself."

"That's what you want, then? A 'real woman.' I can play that." She laughed and turned to Shannon. "Who is he?"

"DAR. Was, anyway." Shannon dropped to the couch, spread lean arms on the back of the cushions. "Says he's done with it."

"What did he do for them?" The two of them talking like he wasn't there.

"He killed people."

"Who did he kill?"

"That's a good question." Shannon cocked her head. "Who did you kill, Cooper?"

"Children, mostly," he said. "I like a baby for breakfast, start the day right. The portions are small, but you can use the bones for soup."

"He's funny," Samantha said, not laughing.

"Isn't he? A hit man with a sense of humor."

"I heard a hilarious story," Cooper said, "about a building that blew up. Killed a thousand people. Regular civilians just going about their day."

Something tightened in Shannon, her body clenching like a fist. The reaction fast and deep and uncalculated. "I told you," she said. "I. Did not. Do that."

Either she was one of the all-time-great liars, or she really hadn't blown up the Exchange.

Cooper thought back to that day six months ago. Her single-minded focus as she went into the building—into it, not out of it—and her surprise at seeing him, the way she had proclaimed her innocence. What had she said? Something like, "Wait, you don't—" and then he'd hit her, not liking it but not daring to take the risk.

Was it possible she really had been there to stop it?

No. Get your head straight. Just because she's telling the truth as she believes it doesn't mean that she knows what really happened. Smith is a chess master. She's a piece.

"All right," Cooper said. "But I'm not a hit man. So how about a truce?"

She opened her mouth, closed it. Nodded slightly.

Samantha looked back and forth between them. "What are you caught up in, Shannon?"

"I don't know yet."

"Why are you with a former DAR agent?"

"That's complicated."

"Do you trust him?"

"No," she said. "But he could have left me to be arrested, and he didn't."

"Ladies?" Cooper smiled blandly. "I'm standing right here."

"I need your help, Sam." Shannon leaned forward, her elbows on her knees. "I'm in trouble."

The smaller woman looked back and forth between them. Her fingers were tight on the medicine bottle. Finally, she set it down on the counter and moved to the opposite couch. "Tell me."

Shannon did. Cooper sat beside her, listening but also taking in the details of Samantha's room. The novels were all paperbacks, a double-stacked riot of cracked spines and worn pages. Science fiction, fantasy, thrillers. There were no personal photos, and the knickknacks looked like they'd been bought at the same time as the furniture rather than collected across a lifetime. A perfect cover apartment, the kind of place you could walk away from. The kind a spy would favor.

Or an assassin.

The leap was intuitive, but he knew it was correct. She was an assassin.

My God, how good she must be. A woman who could sense whatever a guy wanted, any guy? There was no one she couldn't get close to. No one she couldn't get alone and vulnerable. *How many men has this sweet little thing seduced and murdered?*

Shannon finally reached their shaky bargain: Cooper would see her safely to Wyoming, and in trade she would get him a chance to speak to Erik Epstein.

"That's dangerous," Samantha said. "Both sides are going to be after you."

"Cooper knows DAR protocol. And he's got as much reason to avoid them as I do."

"Are you sure?"

"Still sitting right here," Cooper said.

"This afternoon was no act," Shannon said. "Those agents were trying to kill him."

The other woman nodded. "And you want me to convince our side of it."

"Just tell them," Shannon said, "that I came to you, and what I said. That I'm coming in. Tell *him*."

Samantha's reaction to that last was subtle but sure. A tiny lean. A relaxing of the muscles in her crossed thighs. A stall in her exhale.

She cares about John Smith. Loves him, maybe.

And she knows how to reach him.

It took all his will and all his skill to keep that recognition from his face.

"You don't have to believe me," Shannon said. "Just tell him. Will you do that?"

"For you?" Samantha smiled. "Of course."

"Thank you. I owe you."

"It's nothing."

"Well, then can I ask another favor?" Shannon's lips quirked up in what he was starting to recognize as a trademark expression. "Can I use your bathroom?" She jerked a thumb at him. "You should see the one in his hotel room."

■

Cooper leaned back. Put his hands at his sides. It felt weird. How did he normally hold his hands?

From the other couch, Samantha watched him, something feline in her pose, a languorous, predatory note. Her legs were crossed at the knee, and she was kicking one idly, muscles rippling beneath the smooth skin of her calf. She was barefoot, her toes painted that clear color. Nude, he thought it was called.

"Do I make you nervous?"

"No," he said. "I just don't like being read." He folded his hands. That felt weird, too. Was this how other people felt around him? How Natalie had felt every day of their relationship?

"Have you ever been with a reader, Nick?"

"Cooper," he said. "I've known lots of readers." He stood and walked to the window. Her apartment was on the thirty-second floor, and the view was a partner to the one he'd had at the Continental Hotel, only hers faced east. He could just make out the tracings of waves on the lake, gray on midnight blue. Layered atop it, the ghostly reflection of the room.

"I didn't say *known*." In the glass, she rose, smoothing her skirt as she walked over. "I said *been with*."

Cooper didn't respond. She moved in behind him, small enough that his bulk blocked her reflection. But he could smell her and sense her. "Listen." He turned. "I appreciate what you're doing for us. But drop the sex-goddess act."

"It's not an act. You want the real me?" She traced the outline of her body with her hands, not quite touching. "This is it. I'm the fantasy. What do you want, Cooper? Whatever it is, I'll be it. Hard or soft, helpless or jaded, ashamed or wanton or anything in between. I can be the pliable young innocent or the Amazon only you can conquer." She stepped closer. "You don't even have to tell me, to ruin the fantasy by saying it out loud. Just let me see you."

"You're serious. You want to go off to the bedroom right now?"

"Shannon won't mind. She and I have fooled around before."

That image was almost enough to make his control slip. He took a deep breath, pushed aside the hastily assembled fantasy. "See, I think this is just a game to you. You want to win."

"No games. I want to know you." She put a hand against his chest. "You turn me on. It's your strength. You're so contained. Show me who you are. No one needs to know. I can be your second-grade teacher, or your daughter's girlfriend, the one you won't even admit to yourself that you want."

"My daughter," Cooper said, "is four."

"Just open up to me. I'll sense what your body needs. I know it before you do. I know it even when you don't. What's reality compared to that?"

He looked down at her, at her deep brown eyes and soft skin, at the swell of her breasts and the way the skirt caught at the line of her thigh, at her tumble of golden hair and her pedicured feet. She was stunning, the distilled image of desire, Aphrodite writ in miniature with the corner of her lip caught between bright teeth.

But beneath it all, he could see the need curling inside her, slippery and fanged as an eel.

"Thanks," he said, "but I'll pass."

She had been stretching up, offering pouting lips, and for a moment didn't process his words. When they hit it was like an electric current, her face clenching and eyes sparking. "What?" When he didn't respond, she said it again, angrier this time. "*What?*"

He saw it coming, but he let her have the slap, her hand whistling through the air to smack his cheek.

"No one says *no*. Who do you think you are? Do you know how many men would kill for the chance to be with me?" She planted hands against his chest and shoved ineffectually. "You don't say no. Not to me."

She wound up again, and this time he caught it. In the process, he noticed Shannon, somehow standing in the center of the room he'd been sure was empty.

He dropped Samantha's arm. "I'm sorry," Cooper said. "I didn't mean to insult you."

Her beautiful face had turned red with fury. "Get out. Both of you."

They did. As the door closed, he took a last glance over his shoulder. Samantha had the pill bottle open and was shaking tablets into one perfect palm.

■

Halfway down the extravagantly decorated hallway, Shannon said, "Thanks, Cooper, way to help out."

There didn't seem to be any response to that, or at least none that wouldn't lead to a fight, and he didn't want to fight. So they walked side by side, the sound of their footfalls muffled by the carpet. She thumbed the button for the elevator while he thought back over what he'd seen. He was missing something. It was like a sore in his mouth that he couldn't leave alone.

Her gift had made it impossible to pattern her. The constant chameleon shifting was clearly something she'd done all her life, and half an hour wasn't enough time to break through it. But maybe it was a clue in itself; here was a woman who drew her identity from the wants of others, so much so that she had thrown herself at him just to confirm her own irresistibility. A woman delighted to receive the Shadow, a drug designed to scramble memories of pain.

It didn't make sense. What kind of assassin would a junkie with ego issues make? The pieces didn't add up to the sum.

That usually means that you've got the wrong sum.

The elevator arrived, and they climbed aboard. By the time it drew to a stop in the subterranean parking garage, he had the answer.

A junkie with ego issues that compelled her to fulfill anyone's fantasy would make a lousy assassin.

But a very successful prostitute.

Cooper rubbed at his eyebrow. "I'm sorry," he said. The way Shannon looked over at him, it felt as if she understood that he meant it on more than one level. She started to say something, changed her mind.

After the raid on the hospital they'd picked up his car, and now he beeped the locks and climbed into the driver's seat. Two concrete revolutions saw them to the surface. A heavy gate pulled aside, and then they were merging with Lake Shore Drive, Samantha's expensive high-rise in the rearview.

"It's not her fault," Shannon said, her eyes locked on the road ahead. "She didn't used to be like this. It's getting to her."

"She's a call girl, isn't she?"

"Yeah." The word exhaled slow. City lights danced on her features.

"I thought she was…well, an assassin."

"Samantha?" Shannon asked, startled. "No. I mean, she's got a lot of powerful clients, and I'm sure if John asked her, she'd do it. She'd do anything for him. But he'd never ask."

"Why does she do it?" He checked his mirror and changed lanes. "She's obviously tier one. A reader like that, she could…"

"What? Work for the DAR?"

He looked over, but she kept her eyes ahead. Cooper turned back to the road. An image of Samantha kept appearing to him, that first moment she'd started on him, her tiny step forward and change of posture. There had been such strength in it. But of course, that was all part of the act. He wondered if between her need and her addiction, there was anything left of the real woman.

"Sorry," Shannon said. Her hands were in her lap now, rubbing against one another. "It just gets to me, you know? Seeing her like that. You're right, she's tier one. And she's sensitive, emotionally sensitive. Always was. So that gift for reading others, it translated to empathy. True empathy, trying to imagine what the world was like for others. She wanted to be an artist, or an actress. And even though she was at an academy, she wasn't targeted the way some of them are, the way John was. She might have made it through okay. But then she turned thirteen."

Cooper's fingers tightened on the steering wheel. "Who was he?"

"Her mentor," Shannon said. "You know how academies work? Every kid has a mentor, always a normal, who is their, well, everything. The academies are all about setting us at each other's throats. The mentor is the one person you're supposed to be able to trust. Of course, they're the real monsters, but you don't understand that as a kid. They're just adults who are nice to you. And since you don't have a mom or a dad or brothers or sisters or even a *name* anymore…" She shrugged. "All children need to love a grown-up. Normal or twist, it's in the DNA."

Cooper had that helpless anger again, the feeling he'd experienced when he'd visited the academy, when he'd imagined throwing the director through the goddamn window. He was starting to wish he had.

"Anyway, around the time she turned thirteen, she started looking like she does now. And she had that gift, right? She knew what people wanted. What men wanted." She took a deep breath, then exhaled. "He convinced her it was love. Even promised to sneak her out of the academy as soon as he could arrange it. And until then, he gave her things to make it easier to bear. Vicodin at first, but he moved her up the ladder fast. By the time he did take her out, she was snorting heroin.

"He set her up in an apartment, but he didn't pretend to be in love anymore. Just let her get a taste of withdrawal. Then he introduced her to a 'friend' of his, and told her what she needed to do for her next hit. She's been doing it ever since."

"Jesus," Cooper said. When he'd looked at her before, he'd seen raw need in the shape of a woman. Now he saw a teenage girl, strung out and sold by her father and lover. "Is she…the mentor, is he—"

"No. After John graduated the academy, he went looking for her." Shannon turned to him for the first time since they'd gotten in the car, and he saw that signature smile, lit brake-light red. "Funny thing, her mentor vanished. Never seen again."

Good for you, John. You may be a terrorist with hands bloody to the elbow. But you did that right, at least.

"She's independent now, no pimp or anything. But she never really left her mentor behind. She could have been an amazing artist, or a counselor, a healer, but that's not what the normal world wanted from her. It's not what the normal world had trained her to do.

"What the normal world wanted was blow jobs on demand from an abnorm whore willing to be their daughter. They don't even have to feel bad about it. After all, they never *said* they wanted to screw their daughter; she sensed it. And as for the women, well," Shannon shrugged, "she's just a twist."

She went silent then, the story hanging between them like cigarette smoke as he navigated the darkened city streets. He wanted to argue with her, to tell her that the world didn't have to be that way, that not all normals fit the picture she was painting.

But then, enough did to keep Samantha in an expensive, well-decorated prison as long as she lived. Or until her beauty began to fade.

It was the world. The only one they had. No one said it was perfect.

"Anyway," Shannon said. "Even with that bit at the end, she'll do what she promised. We should be safe from my side, at least until we get to New Canaan. Speaking of which, that's going to take shiny new identities."

"Yeah," he said. "I'm on it. There's just one thing we have to get first."

CHAPTER 22

"I have to admit, I figured you were talking about, you know, assault rifles, or some secret newtech spy toy."

"Disappointed?"

"No," she said, reaching for another slice of pizza, "I was starving."

It was more bar than restaurant, a subterranean joint with brick walls and neon signs. Proper thin-crust pizza, not that thick crap only the tourists ate, with pepperoni and hot peppers. The crowd was casual, baseball caps and jeans, and the tri-d was tuned to the Bears game, good old Barry Adams up there making everyone else look silly.

Cooper spun the lid off the shaker of red pepper flakes and dumped a handful in his hand, then coated his slice with them. Greasy, cheesy, spicy goodness, washed down by a long swallow of a hoppy IPA microbrew.

The crowd all erupted in yells at once; the Bears had scored. Chicago did love its home teams. The replay showed Adams stepping through defensive linemen as if he had a hall pass from the Almighty. Shannon gave a little whoop.

"Football fan?"

"No. A Barry Adams fan."

"I wondered," Cooper said. "The first time I saw you. Well, the second time, really. The first time I just noticed a pretty girl. It wasn't until we triangulated the cell signal that I realized you'd waltzed past my perimeter."

She dabbed at a bit of sauce on her lips. "I wasn't sure if I'd be able to pull it off, if you guys had a file on me."

"No. Nothing."

"I bet they do now."

He laughed. "Yeah, I'd say so. I think the target order probably goes John Smith, then me, then you." It was a strange thing to say, and stranger because it was true. Cover didn't get much deeper than this. He was an enemy of the state. In the last six months he'd raided, robbed, and survived three—no, four, after today—run-ins with agents coming for his life. Earlier tonight he'd stolen experimental narcotics and delivered them to an abnorm prostitute who was a friend and possible lover of the most wanted terrorist in America, and now he was having dinner with one of that terrorist's best operatives, a shadow woman who had probably killed as many times as he had.

He heard Roger Dickinson's voice in his head. *Tell me again. How is Cooper one of the good guys?*

It was an unsettling thought, and he pushed it away. "So what's it like for people like you and Adams? How does it work?"

"My gift, you mean?"

"Yeah."

She picked up her pizza—he dug that she wasn't a knife-and-fork woman—and chewed while staring thoughtfully into some middle distance. "Imagine you're on one side of a freeway and you want to run to the other side. Cars are blurring by, and big trucks that would totally squash you, and motorcycles weaving in between. So what you do is you look in the direction they're coming from, right? You see the relative speeds and distance, and you decide when to run and when to stop based on that."

"Or you use an overpass."

"Or that. But imagine instead you pointed a camera at it and you recorded the next fifteen or twenty seconds. You saw where everything went. How one car switching lanes forced the truck to slow down, which backed up the lane, which made the biker step on the gas."

"You mean twist the throttle. Motorcycles don't have a gas pedal."

"Whatever. The point is, you record all of that. Then imagine you could go back in time to the moment when you started recording, only now you know what's going to happen. You know that the girl on her cell phone is going to change lanes without signaling, and the truck is going to slam on his brakes, and the motorcycle is going around. So avoiding them is easy."

"You mean you see vectors?"

"Sort of. The cars, they're just a metaphor. I can't really do it with them; I can only shift around people. I need the cues from them. I don't really know how I do it, I just—I look at a room, or a street, and I can see where each person is moving and looking."

"Can you tell me what's going to happen in the next fifteen seconds?"

"I don't know what people are going to say, or if someone's going to spill their drink. You don't plan to spill your drink, so I can't anticipate it. But I can see that the guy coming out of the bathroom is going to make it halfway down one row, then he and the waitress will be in each other's way, and he'll back around, only the guy sitting down right there is about to get up, so there will be a logjam. The waitress will stand still, because she's going to the table beyond them, and the others will move out of her way."

Cooper turned to watch. It played out exactly as she'd said. "That sounds exhausting."

She cocked her head. "Most people launch straight into how cool it is, how they wish they could do it."

"Well, it is, and I do. But you must get tired of all of it, all of the time."

"Yours is on all the time."

"Yeah, and I get tired of it," he said. "It's the dissonance. Between what they say and what they mean. Thank God I'm less of a reader and more about pattern recognition and gauging intent. I mean, I can tell when people are blatantly lying to me, when they're bothered, that sort of thing, but I've met some readers who can tell you your deepest secrets after a two-minute conversation about the weather."

"I have, too. Most of them are shut-ins."

"Wouldn't you be? If I were surrounded by the secrets and lies of every person I saw, I'd stay away from people, too."

"So, your patterns. You can tell what people are about to do? Physically?"

"Yes," he said. "And please don't test it by tossing that fork at me."

"Sorry." She smiled and lifted her hand off the silverware. "No wonder John told us not to engage you."

The offhand comment hit like a slap. "John—Smith? He knows who I am? By name?"

"Of course." She was amused. "You thought it only worked one way? He knows all about you. I think he kind of respects you. He vetoed a hit plan on you last year, not too long before the thing at the Exchange. One of our guys wanted to plant a bomb in your car—what was it, a Charger?—to prove that even the DAR's best wasn't safe."

"So what—I don't understand. Why didn't he?"

"John said no."

"I mean, why didn't John? Kill me?"

"Oh. He said that it would only piss the DAR off. That the cost was greater than the benefit."

"He was right."

"He also said that they couldn't be sure your kids wouldn't be in the car."

Cooper opened his mouth. Closed it. Thought about how many times he'd climbed in the Charger, and how he had never once checked for explosives. How many times Kate and Todd had ridden with him. Thought about the car in pieces, flames licking through the windows, and two tiny burned shapes in the back.

Shannon said, "So you must be quite a dancer."

"What? No. No rhythm. I'd be a hell of a partner if someone led, I guess."

"I'll bear that in mind," she said, "case we ever end up on the floor." She folded her napkin atop her half-finished slice of pizza. "So what's next?"

"We need papers that will get us into New Canaan. Driver's licenses, passports, credit cards. I know a guy on the West Side, does great work."

She gazed at him appraisingly. "Why didn't you go to him instead of Zane?"

Damn it. Careful, man. "There's a difference between papers that can get me in the gate, and the power to erase my past, let me start again."

"This guy a friend of yours?"

"No."

Some of the neighborhoods and suburbs west of downtown Chicago were lovely, thriving places, tree-shaded and filled with families.

This wasn't one of those parts.

Cooper, a military brat before he became military himself, had never really put down roots—at least not geographical ones—and so looked at every place fifteen degrees askew as a perpetual outsider. He had a theory going about cities, that the dominant industry of the town filtered into every level of the place, from the architecture to the discourse. Thus in LA, a city built on entertainment and fantasy, there were houses in the clouds and dinner conversation about cosmetic labioplasty. In Manhattan, the business of finance reduced everything, at some level, to money; the skyline was a stock chart and the streets pulsed with currency.

Chicago had been born as a working town, a meatpacking town, and no matter how many chic restaurants opened, no matter the lakefront harbors and the green spaces, its most honest parts would always be covered in rust. They would crowd the banks of the sludge-brown river and huddle in the windowless warehouses of industrial districts.

The building he was looking for was three stories of grim cinderblock. A loading dock ran the length of the face; above it, someone had painted the words VALENTINO AND SONS, LAUNDRY AND DRY CLEANING in five-foot letters. Years of Chicago winters had faded and peeled the paint. Cooper parked the car under a streetlight, though there wasn't much point—no one lived nearby. He popped the trunk and pulled out the duffel bag.

"Dirty laundry?" Shannon asked.

"About six months' worth."

The machinery was audible as they approached the loading dock. A faint sweet humidity radiated from the place. Inside, the room was huge and hot and noisy. Beneath humming fluorescent lights, massive washing machines spun and clanked, men and women moving between them to load the drums or collect clean clothes. The air was soupy and chemical. Although the perchlorethylene used in dry cleaning was supposed to be locked in a contained system, the machines here were old, the fittings bad, and traces of the toxic cleanser were venting into the air. All of the workers had a smallness to them, the mark of people who had spent decades maneuvering through narrow aisles and bending beneath heavy loads. Cooper started down the row, pausing to make room for a withered woman pushing a basket piled with suits. It had been chilly outside, but now he could feel sweat gathering in his armpits and the small of his back.

No one paid any attention as he led Shannon to a narrow staircase at the back. The second floor was hotter than the first, and noisier; here were the massive washing machines and enormous presses used for laundry on an industrial scale, napkins and sheets and towels from a hundred hotels and restaurants. There was a brief snatched glimpse of heavy machinery moving with insectile precision, a trace of music, something Mexican and discordantly upbeat, and then they were heading upward.

Steamiest of all, the top floor was a harshly bright hive of narrow desks jammed together. Scores of people were packed in around them, each squinting into a sewing machine or cutting lengths from fabric bolts. The sound was a hundred woodpeckers at once. Most of the men had stripped off their shirts and worked bare-chested or in wifebeaters, their skin glistening. A fan the size of an airplane turbine spun sluggishly, stirring air that reeked of chemicals and cigarettes and body odor.

Cooper started down the aisle, heading for the office in the back. Shannon followed. "Weird," she said.

"It's a sweatshop."

"I know. It's just, it's like the United Nations. I've seen sweatshops full of West Africans, Guatemalans, Koreans, but I've never seen them all in the same place."

"Yeah," Cooper said. "Schneider's an innovator."

"An equal-opportunity oppressor?"

"Not really. It's still pretty much one subculture being exploited."

"What do you mean?"

"They're all abnorms. All of them."

"But…" Shannon stopped. "How? Why?"

"Schneider makes terrific IDs," Cooper said, shifting the heavy duffel bag from one shoulder to the other. "He specializes in abnorms who want to live as normals. High risk, but big money. Those who can't pay work it off."

"Making cheap clothes."

"Making cheap copies of expensive clothes." Cooper nodded to a woman three desks down. Hair the color of cigarette smoke was pinned in a rough knot at the back of her head. She wore odd glasses, like two jeweler's loupes mounted in granny frames. As they watched, she slid a shirt from a basket on her left side, laid it across her table, kept one hand moving to dip into a cardboard box for an embroidered logo half an inch across, which she placed precisely and then affixed with swift, measured stitches before sliding the shirt into a basket on her right side and reaching back to take another from the basket on her left. The whole process took maybe twenty seconds.

"Is that the Lucy Veronica logo?"

"Beats me." He started moving again, and she followed.

"So how long does it take to pay for a new identity?"

"A couple of years. They need regular jobs to make a living. They're nurses and plumbers and chefs." He paused at the end of a row, looked both ways, moved on. "It's only after they finish that they come here, work six or eight hours off their debt."

"You're saying they're slaves."

"More like indentured servants, but you've got the idea." He glanced down the aisle and saw Schneider talking to a dark-skinned guy twice his weight. "This way." No one paid them any attention. Part of the ethos of the place: no one here wanted to be acknowledged. *After all, that's what they're working toward. Brilliants going blind over menial labor, stitching knockoff clothing so they can earn the right to masquerade as normal.*

Max Schneider was a scarecrow, six and a half feet tall and cadaverously thin. His watch was expensive, but his teeth were a wreck. Cooper figured that for a choice, believed the forger found an advantage in the discomfort it caused other people. Or maybe he just didn't give a damn.

The worker he was talking to was big, fat layered over muscles. His skin was Caribbean black, but Cooper read the tension in him as crackling waves of sickly yellow. "But it's not my fault."

"You introduced the guy," Schneider said. "He was your friend."

"No, I told you, just a guy I met. I told you that when I brought him here. I said I didn't know him, you asked if I was vouching for him, I said no."

Schneider waved his hand in front of his nose like he was clearing away a smell. "And now he gets in a bar fight, gets arrested? What if he talks about me?"

"I didn't vouch for him."

"I should just cut you loose. End our arrangement."

"But I've only got three weeks left."

"No," the forger said. "You've got six months left."

It took a moment to hit, then the man's eyes widened, his nostrils flared, his pulse jumped quicker in his carotid. "We had a deal."

Schneider shrugged. If he was cowed by the size or fury of his employee, he didn't show it. To Cooper, he looked like a man completely in charge, a man who could take or leave the world. "Six months." He turned and started away.

"I didn't vouch for him," the man repeated.

The forger spun back. "Say that again."

"What?"

"Say that again. Say it." Schneider smiled with stained teeth.

For a moment Cooper could see the guy was thinking about it, that he was thinking about saying it and then grabbing Schneider by the neck and squeezing, crushing his strong fingers together. He saw the weight of a thousand injustices bearing down on the abnorm, and the urge to throw them all off at once, to surrender to the momentary pleasure of pretending there was no future.

And Cooper had to admit he kind of wanted the man to do it. For his kind and his dignity.

But the moment passed. The big man opened his mouth, closed it. Then, slowly, he dragged the chair out from his workstation and settled heavily in it. His shoulders slumped. Scarred hands reached for a pair of shears and a bolt of denim, and with a practiced cut, he gave away half a year of his life.

"You," Schneider said, as if he had only now noticed Cooper. "The poet."

"Yeah." He didn't extend a hand.

"You need something?" The forger looked Shannon up and down dispassionately.

"New identities," Cooper said.

"Already? I made you ten last time. You burn them all?" Schneider's brow wrinkled. "That's reckless. I don't work with reckless people."

"It's not that. I need something better."

Schneider snorted, then started walking, gesturing for them to follow. "My work is flawless. The seal, the microchip, the ink. You can look at the edge under a microscope and swear a brand-new card is ten years old. My code rats match my work to the government d-bases. There is no better."

"But this time I'm crossing the border."

"Doesn't matter. They'll work. Mexico, France, the Ukraine, wherever."

"I'm not going to any of those places."

Schneider stopped. Squinted. He leaned over the shoulder of an Asian girl, maybe twenty-two, watched her fingers spin beads onto delicate filigree. Schneider shook his head, sucked air through his teeth. "Too big," he said. "Your spacing is too big. Do it right or you're useless to me."

The girl kept her eyes down, just nodded, began to unstring what she had done.

Schneider said, "You're going to Wyoming."

"Yes."

"You're a twist. You don't need an ID. You can walk right in."

"I don't want to be myself."

"Which self?" Schneider smiled his hideous smile. "Thomas Eliot? Allen Ginsberg? Walter Whitman? Who are you, Poet?"

Cooper met his eyes, returned the smile.

"New Canaan Holdfast is not like other places," Schneider said. "The security there is very strong."

"Very strong" was an understatement of epic proportions, Cooper knew. While the NCH had an open-door policy to immigrating gifted, Erik Epstein and the rest of the Holdfast government had a justified paranoia about being infiltrated. And with the planet's largest concentration of gifted in a single location, they had quite literally the best people in the world securing their borders. DAR agents were allowed in New Canaan—it was still American soil, after all—but only if they identified themselves openly. A few had pretended to go native after badging in; all had been apprehended and politely escorted out by men with prominently displayed sidearms.

"Can you do it?"

"You'll need complete identities. Supporting information in every major database. Recursive consumer profile generation."

"Can you do it?"

"They will catch you eventually. The protocols will change or the search functionality will improve or you'll screw up. And you don't look right. Too much water fat."

"Can you do it?"

"Of course."

"How much?"

The forger sucked his teeth again. "Two hundred."

"Two *hundred*?" It was an outrageous price, several times what he had paid before. Paying for these would wipe out most of the cash he'd accumulated over the last six months of being a bad guy. "You're kidding."

"No."

"How about one hundred?"

"The price is the price is the price."

"Come on. You're screwing me here."

Schneider shrugged. It was the same movement he had given earlier, when he had added six months to an indentured servant's term. A move that said take it or leave it, it didn't matter to him.

Cooper dropped the duffel on an empty work bench, yanked the zipper, and began to count out bundles. Criminal etiquette would have been to do it in private, but he didn't care. Let one of these people jack the forger. Not his problem.

"Here. These are bundles of ten thousand." He pushed the stack of twenty across the bench. Then he reached into the bag, pulled out two more bundles, and dropped them beside the others. "And that's for the other guy. The one you cheated out of six months."

Schneider looked amused. "A noble gesture."

"He gets his ID tomorrow. Same as us." Cooper laid a hand lightly on the stack of money, tapped his fingers. "Yes?"

The man shrugged.

"I want to hear you say it."

"Yes," Schneider said. "Tomorrow morning. Now"—waved a smell away again—"there is work."

Cooper spun on his heel and walked out, Shannon slipping like his shadow. He pushed through the aisle, down the steps, out the door. The night was cool, and he sucked the air deep, stalked to the car. Shannon let almost a mile of pavement slide beneath their wheels before she asked the question he'd seen her wanting to. "Why did you—"

"Because I don't like the way he doesn't even hide the way he sees us. As livestock, or slaves."

"A lot of people do."

"Yeah. But with Schneider, it's truly impersonal. He could watch you burn to death and not make a move to pour water. It's not hate, it's…" He couldn't think of the word, couldn't put his finger on what exactly it was that so pushed his buttons. "I don't know."

"So paying for the guy was to show that you were Schneider's equal?"

"Something like that. Just to make him notice, I guess. Shake him."

"But it didn't. You were still livestock. Like a cow learning to dance: it's amusing, but it's still a cow."

He didn't have anything to say to that, just drove in silence for a moment.

"It's kind of ironic, actually," she said. "Those clothes were knockoffs of Lucy Veronica's new line. You know her stuff?"

"I know her name. She's gifted, right?"

"Jesus, Cooper, pick up a magazine. Her styles have reinvented the fashion industry. The way she sees things—she's spatial—changed everything. Her clothes are fetishized by socialite women. And those rich women are fetishized by middle-class suburban chicks, who want to be like the socialites but can't afford original Lucy Veronica. So what do they do to get the next-best thing to couture designed by a brilliant? They buy a knockoff sewn by a brilliant. In a sweatshop."

"Yeah, well, Sammy Davis Junior got to be in the Rat Pack, but that didn't mean we had racial equality."

Shannon half nodded, a noncommittal sort of gesture. He read her desire to launch into rhetoric, but instead she leaned back, slipped out of her shoes, and put her bare feet up on the glove box. "Anyway. It was nice of you. Paying for him, I mean. A nice thing to do."

"Well, what the hell, right? Got to help each other out." Realizing as he said it that he meant it, that it wasn't just a line to play her. He was finding things murkier out here than he had expected; the relative clarity of his position at the DAR didn't seem to translate. *But you're still with the department. Don't forget that.* "Anyway, it wasn't really my money." He looked over at her, putting on a smile. "Turns out, I'm a pretty good thief."

That got a laugh—he really liked her laugh, full-spirited and adult—which morphed into a yawn.

"Tired?"

"Dodging sniper fire, riding on top of a train, touring a sweat-shop—it'll wear a girl out."

"Wuss."

"I rode. On top of. A train."

It was his turn to laugh. "All right. We'll find a couple of beds."

"I know a place we can go. Some friends of mine. We'd be safe."

"How do you know?"

"Because they're my friends." She looked at him quizzically, the exterior lights glowing off her eyes. "Not everyone's friends shoot at them."

"Yeah, well, how do I know your friends won't want to shoot at *me*?"

She shook her head. "They're not part of the movement. Just friends."

He eased the car left and got on the Eisenhower heading east. A low bank of clouds cut the skyline in half, the lights on the tallest buildings bright as a fairy tale against indigo skies. The Jaguar's tires hummed on the pavement. There were moments driving when he felt a perfect calm, as though he were the car, skimming above the road, power and control and distance. But tonight it felt off. The distance part, maybe. The last six months seemed like they had been all about distance: from his children, from Natalie, from the world he had so carefully built and the sensible position he occupied in it. Though he was a man who enjoyed his own company, talking to Shannon, having a partner, it made him realize he'd been lonely, too. It sounded nice to be around people.

Besides. Getting closer to her is getting closer to John Smith.

"Okay. Where to?"

CHAPTER 23

Chinatown had given the DAR headaches since the beginning.

Not just in Chicago, and frankly, not just the DAR. Whatever the city, law enforcement always had trouble with Chinatown. The places were closed systems, insular worlds that existed within cities, traded with them, drew tourists from them, but nonetheless were never really *of* them. Police working Chinatown carried a bubble around, a small radius of American rule that extended only as far as they could see, that moved with them and left the place unchanged in their wake.

Which made law enforcement difficult. There weren't very many Chinese cops, and the other races stood out like they were backlit. It wasn't just a matter of not speaking the language; they didn't even know how to ask the questions, which questions to ask. And in a world that existed within itself, a tight-knit community with its own leaders and factions, its own sense of and system for justice, what good could an outsider cop do? And all of that was before the gifted came along and complicated the picture.

Shortly after midnight, and the river was a ribbon of black. Light industry and warehouses gave way to dense clusters of brick buildings decorated with green awnings and pagodas, up-down shops with a riot of colorful signs, the characters meaningless as a paint squiggle to him. A handful had English subtitles with awkward phrasing: EAT OR TAKE WITH, THE ALL-BEST CAMERAS, NOODLE FRESH SHOP. Overlapping neon lit the night with science-fiction colors.

"Where's your friend's place?"

"An alley off Wentworth. Park wherever you can, we'll walk."

He found a pay lot on Archer. He was about to get out of the Jag when she said, "Leave the gun."

"Huh?"

"These are my friends. I'm not bringing a gun into their house."

Cooper looked at her for a moment, wishing he had the call girl Samantha's gift, that he could read Shannon, see the real her, understand her intentions. Was this some sort of a trick? Get him unarmed and outnumbered? She stared back. Cooper shrugged, unclipped the holster from his belt, slipped the rig under the front seat.

"Thank you."

Shannon walked half a step in front of him. The windows of shops held a riotous array of crap—waving cats and colorful fans and plastic ninja swords. Tourist junk, but the tourists had gone for the night. Everyone on the sidewalk was a local, and many seemed to know each other. They passed the window of a butcher where the plucked carcasses of birds dangled by their feet. "So how do you know these people?"

"Lee Chen and I have been friends for a long time. He runs a business here."

"Yeah, but how? How did you meet?"

"Oh, you know, in our mutual abnorm hatred of the world we recognized each other as kindred souls in a long battle."

"Right."

She grinned. "We went to high school."

His gift followed the chain back—*school together, but her friend is established here, odds are she grew up in Chicago,* a good starting point if he ever needed to track her down. "Funny to think of you in high school."

"Why?"

"The whole mysterious thing you have going."

"Mysterious thing?"

"Yeah. You keep appearing out of nowhere, then disappearing. Before I knew your name, I called you the Girl Who Walks Through Walls."

She laughed. "Better than what they called me in high school."

"What was that?"

"Freak, mostly. At least until I got breasts." They passed a restaurant called Tasty Place, another called Seven Treasures, and turned down an alley. The glow of the street faded. Dumpsters overflowed, the smell of rotting trash sweet. At the back of an unmarked brick building she stepped into an alcove, knocked on a heavy door painted green.

There was the sound of a heavy lock, and the green door opened. Within was a small antechamber with a metal folding chair, a paperback book split facedown on it. The guard nodded at Shannon, gestured to a door at the opposite wall, and then leaned on a button. Cooper heard an electronic buzz of a lock.

"What is this place?"

"This is Lee's. Social club." She opened the opposite door.

The room beyond was bright with bad lighting, overhead fluorescents battling thick clouds of cigarette smoke. There were eight or nine tables, half of them occupied. No one looked up. The men around the tables—it was all men, mostly older—stared forward, lost in a game played with dominos. Loose stacks of bills were scattered between ashtrays and bottles of beer.

"You mean casino."

"I mean a social club. They socialize over Pai Gow. It's part of the culture. Chance and fate and numbers are more important here." She started around the edge of the room. Sugary pop music played in the background. Reaching a table of seven men, she stopped and stood quietly. The men ignored them, all eyes on the dealer, a younger guy, prematurely balding, who slid stacks of tiles to each of them. The tiles clicked softly as the players arrayed them in sets of two. When the last tiles had been placed, all the players turned them over, revealing patterns of dots, and at once the table exploded in a burst of Chinese. Money moved back and forth.

Shannon touched the dealer's shoulder. He looked up at her. "Azzi." His face broadened into a smile that vanished when he saw Cooper.

"Lee Chen," she said and squeezed his shoulder. "This is Nick Cooper."

The dealer stood up. The man to his left collected the tiles and began to mix them as the remaining players placed bets.

"Hi," Cooper said. He held out a hand. "Nice place."

"Sank you," Lee said. "You po-rice?"

"No. I used to be."

"Not po-rice. Now you are fliend to Shannon."

"Umm. Yeah. Yes, I am her friend." The man's pidgin threw him, one of the classic problems of operating in Chinatown. So much nuance could be lost when only the broad strokes of a question were understood. He'd have to keep his answers simple, be sure not to offend—

Shannon was barely holding back laughter.

Cooper looked at her, then at Lee Chen. "You're busting my balls."

"Yeah, a little bit. Sorry." Lee smiled and turned back to Shannon. "Have you eaten?"

"A while ago. Why, is Lisa cooking?"

"Lisa is always cooking." He gestured at a young man lounging by the bar and barked a short command. The man straightened, hurried over, and took the dealer's place at the table. The play shifted again, an easy rhythm of long practice. Lee put his arm over Shannon's shoulder, and the two started away. "Alice will be happy to see you."

"She's still awake?"

"Her mother made an exception." Lee released Shannon, opened a door marked with characters that even in another language clearly read Do Not Enter, and started up a set of stairs.

"Who's Alice?" Cooper asked.

"My goddaughter." She smiled over her shoulder as they climbed. "She's eight and a beautiful genius."

"And why did he call you Azzi?"

"My last name. My dad's Lebanese."

Shannon Azzi. From Chicago. It sounded so much less dramatic than the Girl Who Walks Through Walls. One was a terrorist operative, a lethal agent of the most dangerous man in America. The other was, well, a woman. Smart, funny, and gifted in both senses of the word. *And damned attractive. You may as well admit that, Agent Cooper.* "Funny to think of you having a dad," he said.

"Enough with that."

Cooper smiled.

The sounds changed as they reached the top, and the smells. Sharp spices, garlic, and fish sauce. A burst of laughter came from down the hall, and a child's happy shriek.

"You having a party?"

"A play date," Lee said. "Friends with kids."

Like most parties, everyone had clustered in the kitchen. A dozen or so men and women, all Chinese, were jammed together around a counter packed with bowls of food. A pot simmered on the stove, a sweet, sour smell rising on wisps of steam. Everyone glanced over as they entered, their smiles slipping only slightly when they saw Cooper, no hostility in it, just surprise.

"You all know Shannon," Lee said. "This is her friend Nick Cooper."

"Hello all." He looked around the room, spotted a slender woman perched on a stool, stylishly dressed, delicately chic in that distinctly Asian-girl way. He read the comfort in her body, said, "You must be Lisa."

She slid off the stool, held out her hand. "Welcome."

"Thank you."

"Are you hungry?"

He wasn't but said, "Starving."

"Good. We have way too much food."

"I wonder how that happened," Lee said dryly, plucking beer bottles from the fridge. He twisted the caps off, passed them to Shannon and Cooper, and kept one for himself.

Lisa ignored her husband, slid her arm into Cooper's. "Let me introduce you."

"Aunt Shannon!" A blur of dark hair and pale skin streaked past him, collided with Shannon, who laughed and wrapped her arms around the girl. The two began firing questions at one another, neither waiting for the answers.

Lisa piled rice on a plate and handed it to him, then began to point out the dishes, saying their names, explaining each as if he'd never eaten in a restaurant. Cooper said how good everything looked and scooped some of every dish, balancing his beer against the plate. Shannon brought the girl over, said, "Alice, this is my friend Nick."

"Hi."

"Hi. Can you do me a favor, Alice? Can you call me Cooper?"

"Okay." The girl took Shannon's hand and dragged her away. "Come on, come play with us."

Cooper ate and drank and moved around the room. Most everyone spoke in Chinese until he joined, then shifted seamlessly to English. He spent half an hour making bland party conversation. Everyone was very nice, but he felt the same discomfort he always had at parties. Small talk wasn't his thing, and he didn't have the knack for storytelling. There was a skill to organizing your life into neatly bundled anecdotes, and he lacked it.

Besides, what are you going to say? "So this one time, I was tracking an abnorm who had played a loophole in Bank of America credit cards and racked up half a million in microtransactions before killing the bureaucrat who came to his door and fleeing into the backwoods of Montana on a snowmobile"?

A cluster of shrieks echoed down the hall where Alice had led Shannon. Cooper helped himself to a fresh beer and followed the noise. He found Shannon in the family room, standing on top of a sectional sofa, counting down with her eyes closed. "Three, two... one...go!"

Seven children, Alice among them, all shifted from foot to foot, ready to dart. Shannon opened her eyes, glanced around the room, then made a languorous fake to the left before leaping off the couch to the right. The boy she lunged at tried to dodge, but she tapped him with one hand, spun, saw two children running toward each other, held half a beat, then tagged them both as they collided. The touched kids stood still as statues, while the remaining four dodged around the edges of the room, using the furniture and their frozen friends as cover. Shannon said, "I'm gonna get you," then turned and tapped a boy who had been sneaking behind her. He giggled and froze.

Cooper watched the game with a broad smile. Shannon stalked the final three children, easing left and right, corralling them. The woman was the indisputable master of freeze tag.

"You have kids?"

"Huh?" He turned, saw Lee had come in behind him. "Two. A boy and a girl, nine and four." He thought but did not say their names. Took a long swallow of beer.

"Greatest things in the world, aren't they?"

"Yes. Yes they are."

"Even when you want to kill them."

"Even then."

Shannon tagged out the final three in rapid succession, getting Alice last, then wrapping her in one arm and tickling her with the other. When Shannon finally let the girl breathe again, Alice said, "Me next!" She moved to the center of the room. But instead of beginning a new round of tag, she said, "Chicago places."

"Navy Pier," said a pigtailed girl.

"600 East Grand Avenue."

"The Zoo!"

"2200 North Cannon Drive."

The other children began to yell out. "Tasty City!"

"My mom's house!"

"The airport!"

"2022 South Archer Avenue, 337 West 24th Place, O'Hare Airport is 10000 West O'Hare, and Midway Airport is 5700 South Cicero."

Cooper's belly tightened as he realized what was happening. As the children kept shouting places, he turned to Lee. "Your daughter is gifted?"

The man nodded. "We started on *Goodnight Moon*, but she prefers the phone book. She'll get on my d-pad and read listings for hours. Not just Chicago, either. She knows New York, Miami, Detroit, Los Angeles. Anytime we go on a trip she reads the phone book first."

Lee's pride radiated in every word and every muscle of his face. Smitten with his daughter, and delighted at her abilities. It stood in such sharp contrast to the typical parental reaction, to Cooper's own reaction. This wasn't a man worried about what the world would think, afraid that she might end up tested or labeled or living in an academy. This was pure joy in the wonder that was his daughter.

"Now you, Zhi." Shannon pointed to the boy who had tried to sneak up on her.

"Okay." He stood ready, a pupil confident before a teacher.

"Use the addresses. Add them."

"34,967."

"Multiply them."

"1.209 times 10 to the 36th."

"Add them with north and west positive and east and south negative."

"Minus 243."

Alice joined in. "The Zoo times Tasty City minus Andrea's house."

"4,448,063."

"Navy Pier divided by the school."

"2.42914979757085…"

The kids were having a ball, and Zhi stood in the center of it, giving every answer without hesitation. Cooper stared, realization dawning. "They're *all* brilliants?"

"Yes," Lee said. "As I said, this is a play date."

"But…" He looked at the children, at Shannon, back at Lee. "Aren't you…I mean…"

"Worried about hiding the fact that they're gifted?" Lee smiled. "No. Chinese culture sees things differently. These children are special. They bring honor and success to a family. Why wouldn't we love that?"

Because someone who works for my old agency could call you at any moment. "The rest of the world doesn't see it that way."

"The world is changing," Lee said softly. "It has to."

"What about the academies?"

The man's face darkened. "Someday, when this is all over, people are going to look back at those in shame. It will be like the internment camps in the Second World War."

"I agree," Cooper said. "Don't get me wrong. I'm an abnorm, too."

"I assumed. Most of Shannon's friends are."

"And my daughter…" He hesitated. Didn't want to say it even now, even here. *Why? Are you ashamed of Kate?*

That wasn't it. It couldn't be. It was fear, that was all. Fear of what would happen to her.

Right. But all that negative emotion, all that desire to have her hide her ability, isn't there some part of you that wishes she were normal? If only so she wouldn't face this risk?

It was an ugly thought. Cooper tilted his beer up again and found it empty. "Aren't you afraid that someone will make them take the test?"

"That's where being Chinatown Chinese has advantages. The government doesn't know about these children."

"How?"

"Some of us went abroad to have our babies. Others use local midwives who don't record the births. It's a risk, because they don't have the resources of a hospital if things go wrong. A stupid, terrible way to do things. But right now it's worth it."

The DAR had long suspected that there was a significant population of unreported abnorms in immigrant communities. It was a loophole the agency meant to close, but like a squeaky staircase in a house on fire, other issues took precedence. These communities rarely made trouble and so had been left alone. But watching the children play—they'd moved to a new game, where a little girl spun once, then closed her eyes and answered detailed questions about everything in the room, down to the number of buttons on Alice's dress—Cooper saw a whole generation of abnorms growing up right under the noses of the DAR, unreported, untested, untracked. The implications were enormous.

Want to call Director Peters, let him know?

"A lot to take in, huh?" Lee smiled. "I'm so used to it that I forget the rest of the world isn't. Don't you love watching them play together? Children who aren't taught, from the earliest age, that they're monsters. That they're *abnormal*. It's beautiful, isn't it?"

"Yes," Cooper said. "Yes it is."

Later, after the party had ended, after parents had collected their children and said their good-byes and left with Tupperware containers of leftovers, Lisa led him and Shannon to a small room off the hallway decorated in pastel shades and posters of Disney princesses. A lamp shaped like an elephant glowed on a night table beside a single bed.

"Alice's," Lisa said apologetically. "She can sleep with us tonight. I'm sorry there's not separate rooms."

Cooper looked over at Shannon, but whatever she might have felt about the arrangement, she didn't telegraph beyond brushing a loose lock of hair behind her ear. "No problem," he said.

"I'll get some blankets."

She returned with a sleeping bag, set it on the bed with a spare pillow, then said, "I hope you'll be comfortable."

"We'll be fine. Thank you." Cooper paused, said, "It means a lot to me that you let us into your home."

"A friend of Shannon's is a friend of ours. Come anytime." Lisa looked around the room, hugged Shannon good night, and came to Cooper. He waited for her to calculate whether he was a hug or a handshake, but she didn't hesitate, just gave him a quick hug. Then she stepped out of the room and closed the door.

Shannon tucked her hands in her pockets. The movement tightened the shirt across clavicles delicate as bird wings. "So."

"I'll take the floor."

"Thanks."

He made a point of facing the other direction as he kicked off his shoes and socks, unbuttoned his shirt. Decided to keep his pants and undershirt on. Behind him he heard the faint rustle of fabric, and his mind flashed an image of her pulling her shirt over her head, imagined a delicate cream bra over caramel skin.

Whoa there, Agent Cooper. Where did that *come from?*

He chalked it up to a long day of shared adrenaline, underscored by male chemistry, and left it at that. He slid into the sleeping bag, rubbed his eyes. A moment later, he heard the click of her turning off the elephant, and the room went dark. Pale green stars glowed on the walls and ceiling, swirling constellations of an idealized night sky, one where the stars had neat points and sharp edges and were only barely out of reach.

"G'night, Cooper."

"Night." He folded his hands behind his head. He was too old to be sleeping on the floor, but too tired to care. As he lay there, staring at the stars of that better sky, he found himself thinking back to the game, the looks on the faces of those kids as they played with toys barely imaginable to most of the world.

It had been six months since last he'd seen his children. Six months of pretending to be someone else, of burying the life he loved in order to fight for it.

When it came down to it, everything he had done was for his children. Even the things he had done before they were born, before he'd even met Natalie. It was a truth he never could have understood until he'd become a parent, and one he would never be able to forget.

The world is changing, Lee had said. *It has to.*

Cooper hoped he was right.

CHAPTER 24

The man was waiting for them.

He was as big as Cooper remembered, broad-shouldered and muscular beneath pudge; a man who didn't lift weights because he lifted heavy things for a living. He looked right at home in the loading dock.

"What the hell?" He spat the words as Cooper and Shannon climbed the steps.

"Excuse me?"

"Paying for my ID. You trying to be the big man? You think you know me?" The abnorm shook his head. "You don't know me."

"Whatever." Cooper started past, but the big man grabbed his arm. The grip was stone.

"I asked you a question. What do you want?"

Cooper glanced down at the man's hand, thinking, *Twist sideways, right elbow to the solar plexus, stomp the arch of the foot, spin back with a left uppercut.* Thinking, *So much for good deeds.* "I want you to get out of my way."

Something in his tone made the man hesitate, and the grip loosened. Cooper brushed his sleeve, walked past.

"I didn't ask for this. I don't owe you nothing."

He stiffened, the irritation growing. Turned. "You do, asshole. You owe me six months of your life. The phrase you're looking for is 'thank you.'"

The man crossed his arms. Held the stare. "I'm not anybody's slave. Not Schneider's, and not yours."

"Bravo," Cooper said. "Congratulations. You're an island, alone unto yourself."

"Huh?"

"I'm so tired of people like you. Of *twists* like you. Schneider claimed six months of your life on nonsense, and you just lay down and took it. Okay, fine, your choice. But then an angel bought you that time back. And what's your first thought? He must want something. He can't just be trying to bear his neighbor's burden. He can't just be an abnorm who doesn't like seeing another one treated that way."

The man's eyes narrowed. "Nobody does nothing for free. Abnorm or not."

"Yeah, well, no wonder we're losing." Cooper turned away and walked for the door. Over his shoulder, he said, "I don't want you to be my slave. I want you to not be one at all."

Then he yanked open the door and stepped inside. Behind him, Shannon chuckled. "You're a piece of work, Cooper."

"Let's go find Schneider."

The forger saw them coming, gestured for them to follow without waiting to see if they would. Cooper felt his irritation growing. *Just get what you came for and get out.* Time to head for Wyoming, find John Smith, and finish this. Maybe it wouldn't solve all the problems in the world. But it would solve one of them. And it might buy a little time for the world to grow the hell up.

For a man of his means, Schneider certainly hadn't spent much on his office. Cinder-block walls painted white, a chipboard desk with a lamp and a phone. The only expensive item was a custom-looking newtech datapad, sleek and machined. The forger sat down, opened a drawer, and took out an envelope. "Passports, driver's licenses, credit cards." He tossed the packet on the desk.

Cooper opened it, pulled out a passport, and saw his picture above the name Tom Cappello. He flipped the pages, saw that he had traveled extensively, mostly in Europe. The document was faded and worn soft. "The microchip matches?"

"What do you think I am?"

"I'm getting tired of that question. The microchip matches?"

"Of course." Schneider leaned back, crossed his ankle over a bony knee. "More important, your information has been hacked into all of the relevant databases. A complete profile—spending habits, mortgages, voting record, speeding tickets, all of it."

Cooper opened the other passport, saw Shannon's picture. It must have been from a security camera somewhere in the building, but the shot was clean, the background suitably bland. Then he saw the name. "Are you kidding me?"

"What?" Shannon moved beside him, took the document. "Allison Cappello. So what?"

"He made us married."

Schneider smiled his dental horror show. "That a problem?"

"I didn't ask for it."

"The profiles support each other. Minimizes the risk of the data insertion."

"Yeah, for you. For us, it means we have to be able to play a married couple."

Schneider shrugged. "Not my problem. Now listen. You both exist, but only at a superficial level. Your new identities have been implanted into the baseline systems. But it will take time for it to propagate. That's the only way to do it. No way to modify every computer that would have a record. Instead, I plant your identities like a seed, and they grow."

"How long?"

"You could probably clear a basic New Canaan security check now. But in a few days you'll have recursive backup, with your identities spread throughout the whole system. Wait till then if you can."

Cooper didn't answer. He put the passport back in the envelope and turned to go.

"And, Poet?"

"Yeah?"

"Come back anytime. I can always use your money." The forger laughed.

When they walked back through the loading dock, the big man was gone. Just as well. In his current mood, Cooper might have used him as a practice dummy.

"We could probably stay with Lee and Lisa for a few days."

Cooper unlocked the car, shook his head. "Let's get on the road."

"You want to drive to Wyoming?"

"Might as well. We need the time, and it's safer than an airport."

"All right." Shannon thumbed through her passport. "Tom and Allison Cappello." She laughed. "If that's your way of trying to get me into bed, you get points for originality."

"Cute." He started the car and pointed it east. "So how did we meet?"

"Hmm?"

"We're married. If we get questioned, we need to be able to look married."

"Right. Well, at work, I suppose. It's true, after all."

The layers of irony in that made him smile. "Maybe a different job, though. Something boring, so no one asks follow-up questions about it."

"Accounting?"

"Anybody asks me about their tax return, we're done. How about…logistics? For a shipping company. No one wants to know how things get from place to place."

"Okay. I worked there first. We met when you were transferred to Chicago. No, Gary, Indiana. No one wants to know about Gary, Indiana, either," she said. "You were smitten with me, of course."

"Actually, I think you chased me. I played it cool."

"It was totally obvious. You kept pulling puppy-dog faces. And making excuses to come by my desk."

"You ever actually have a desk?"

"Sure, in my apartment. It does a great job of holding up my fake plant." She leaned back and tucked a lock of hair behind her ear. "We went to the movies for our first date. You were a gentleman, didn't try anything."

"But you were hot to go. You kept touching my arm and tossing your hair. Fiddling with your bra strap."

"You wish."

"And panting. I remember a lot of panting."

"Shut up."

Cooper smiled and merged onto the highway. Their rhythm was easy, natural. He wasn't flirting, exactly, but the banter was fun. They kept it up, kept it light, as he drove back to Chinatown. Lisa had made them promise to have lunch before they left, and it seemed as though they had the time to spare now. He pulled up a mental map of Wyoming. The Holdfast spanned a good chunk of the middle of the state, an ugly sprawl of desert and badlands cobbled together in a thousand real estate transactions, with a border like a gerrymandered congressional district. He figured it was about a twenty-five-hour drive. They could take it slow, get some rest along the way. Stop somewhere and buy a couple of wedding rings. And he could use the time to make a plan. Getting to Erik Epstein wouldn't be easy, and that was only a stepping-stone on the way to John Smith.

"The Amalfi Coast of Italy," she said. "That's where we honeymooned. We rented a room on the side of a cliff, with a balcony where we drank wine. Every day we swam in the ocean."

"I remember. You looked dynamite in that suit."

"The red one?" She looked at him through dark lashes. "You always liked me in red."

"It's good with your body," he said, the words spilling out before he could stop them. The memory of last night flashed back, the soft whisper of her shirt sliding off, and the image he'd invented. He felt a little heat in his forehead, glanced over at her.

She wore a half smile. "My body, huh?"

"Your skin, I mean. You said your dad is Lebanese—what's your mom?"

"French. All burgundy lips and flowing hair. They were quite the couple. He was a businessman, a very sharp dresser with a pencil moustache. The two of them were like something out of an RKO flick."

"Were?"

"Yes," she said simply.

"I'm sorry."

"Thank you." She set her shoulders, and he read the active change in topic there, marked it to the pattern that she was becoming in his mind.

He was just about to ask where they lived when he saw the Escalade. Traffic had been getting steadily worse as they'd drawn closer to Chinatown, which he'd chalked up to tourists and the lunch crowd. But the truck—

Late-model Escalade, black, tinted windows.

Parked half in, half out of the street. Like it stopped suddenly. Right at the intersection of Cermak and Archer, two of the arteries of Chinatown.

Engine running.

Government plates.

Shit.

—sent a warning tingle down his spine. Cooper sat bolt upright, fingers tightening on the wheel. Shannon picked up the move, followed his eyes, said, "No."

He glanced in the rearview, half expecting to see black SUVs bearing down on them, but there was nothing but a long line of cars. If it was a trap, the other side hadn't swung shut yet. A U-turn? Conspicuous, a last resort. It could just be a coincidence, a DAR crash vehicle down here for something else, with a different target.

"Lee and Lisa," Shannon said, and jerked as if she'd been electrocuted. "No, no, no."

"We don't know—"

"The traffic," she said. "Damn, I should have seen it. Stop the car."

"Wait, Shannon, we can't—"

"Stop the car!"

He saw it then—the traffic hadn't just been slowing. It had been creeping to a stop. This wasn't a matter of a crowded street or a backed-up stoplight. Something was blocking the flow of cars. It could be an accident. A collision, with police on the scene.

Yeah. And I suppose the DAR is here to write tickets.

Cooper bumped the car up over a curb into a small strip mall. Shannon was out the door before the wheels had finished rolling. He shut off the ignition and followed her, the two of them sprinting through the parking lot.

In the distance, a sound, loud and mixed. Not one source, but hundreds overlapping. His first thought was that it was a parade, some sort of festival, but he knew that was wishful thinking. He'd seen SUVs just like that a thousand times, had called them in a hundred times.

The DAR's private paramilitary police force, a blend of riot cop and SWAT team. They wore black body armor and helmets with visors that completely hid their features. The visors functioned as a heads-up display, enhancing targeting, displaying map coordinates, and allowing night vision. The department called the units tactical response teams.

The public called them the faceless.

Ahead of him, Shannon dodged past the end of the strip mall, leaped a short fence, and sprinted for Archer. Cooper poured it on, hit the fence without breaking stride, and pushed himself over it. She was halfway across the street, dodging through the snarled traffic. A small green space surrounded an apartment building, and she blitzed through the middle of it. He lost sight of her as she rounded the building, leaning into the run, his breath coming fast with the sudden transition to motion.

Half a block to the north, another black Escalade was parked at the entrance to a bank. The doors were open, and he spotted three faceless in defensive positions. Bulky with armor and with blank glass for a head, they resembled predatory insects. Each man held a submachine gun with a folding stock. Shannon was racing south now, right down the middle of the street. Car horns added their screams to the roar of the crowd, closer with every step. Cooper caught up to her just as she made an abrupt turn. He followed.

And saw what was making the noise. The sidewalk and alley were jammed with people, most Chinese, all facing the other direction. They yelled and shook their fists. The group was densely packed and pushing forward without making any progress. Over their heads, Cooper saw a dozen faceless with riot shields cordoning off an alley.

The alley where Lee's social club was located.

No.

Shannon had hit the crowd already, slipped into it like an arrow into the ocean, her gift showing holes and vectors. Cooper followed as best he could, shoving his way through. The noise was unbelievable, a fury of anger and fear in a foreign language. As he watched, a man at the front scooped up a stone and hurled it. The rock bounced harmlessly off a shield. The commando stepped forward and snapped the shield into the guy hard enough that Cooper could almost hear the crunch of the man's nose shattering. He dropped, blood pouring, and the crowd roared louder. Cooper looked around frantically, taking in the low buildings, the fire escapes, the alley farther south, trying to find an opening he knew they couldn't risk.

DAR Tactical Response Team Protocol 43: In the event of an extraction from a dense and hostile environment, first establish a perimeter operating zone. Limit force application unless targets possess a significant strategic advantage and a demonstrated intent to employ that advantage.

Translation: unarmed people on the ground just get hit, but if anybody climbs on a building, shoot them.

Shannon had made it halfway through the crowd before stalling out. Even her gift couldn't find a way through the mob. The faceless held the mouth of the alley shoulder to shoulder, with Chinatown's furious residents layered twenty deep against them. Cooper grabbed a man in front of him and yanked, tangling the guy's foot as he went. The man staggered back into the crowd, and Cooper slid in behind Shannon.

"We need to go," he shouted over the roar of the crowd. Right now the primary team would be searching Lee's gambling den and the apartment above. They'd have thermal scans and dogs, and it wouldn't take them long to realize that he and Shannon weren't there. "They'll search the crowd for us."

"They're not here for us," Shannon said. Her cheeks had paled.

"What are you…" He followed her eyes to a prisoner transport van the size of a delivery truck parked halfway down, the back doors winged open. Riot-geared troopers guarded the rear of the truck, weapons at the ready. Another group was shoving two shackled figures down the alley, a balding man and a woman with chic hair, both of them yelling and fighting.

Lee and Lisa.

Cooper's stomach seized. As he watched, a commando buried the butt of his gun in Lee's belly. Lisa screamed, tried to get to her husband. Another grabbed her from behind, stuffed a black hood over her head, and pushed her into the waiting wagon. Seconds later Lee was forced in beside her. Something in Cooper's chest raged and shrieked, railed against the cage of his ribs. He pushed forward, surging against the crowd, feeling more than hearing his yells. He gained six inches, lost them. It was like being caught in a thundering wave; he was rolled and tossed but made little progress. Shannon made even less, her gift useless here. Overhead there was the rotor of a chopper, and sirens from somewhere far away. Glass shattered, a window or a bottle. That triggered a reaction; the faceless locked shields and braced themselves. From behind them, tossed over their head in a lazy arc, came a smoking canister. The tear gas hit someone in the crowd, bounced downward; billows of white streamed up. A second and third canister followed. People began to gag and retch, the motion of the crowd reversing, sweeping Cooper and Shannon along with it.

The last he saw of the alley, before the gas and the panic consumed everything, was a soldier pulling a black hood over the head of eight-year-old Alice Chen.

■

Silence. It had been an hour, and the silence was still loud, and in it he could hear the echoes of the mob.

He'd gotten a pretty good huff of gas as the crowd split and surged. The frantic coughing had left his throat raw, and his eyes still stung and watered. He kept having to fight the speed of the Jaguar, his foot wanting to go heavy on the accelerator. Instead, he moved with the steady flow of traffic and saw the scene again and again. He'd been too far to make out details, but his imagination was happy to supply them: the wide-eyed trembling of the little girl, the pure panic she would have felt as men in black pulled her parents away from her. Her mother's scream as her father was beaten. The stranger's smooth insect mask reflecting her face as he bent over her.

And then the darkness, close and heavy, as the hood slid over her head.

He had seen it, had heard the crowd and felt the gas, and yet he still barely believed it. How could that mission have been authorized? Why take Lee and Lisa and Alice? Why take them that way?

"It had to be us." His voice thin and hollow against the weight of an hour's accumulated silence. "They were there for us."

Shannon didn't respond. She sat at the edge of the passenger seat, shoulders turned away, as if trying to get as far from him as possible.

"I can't believe it," he said.

"Why not?" She spoke to the side window. "This is what it looks like."

"Not normally. Somehow they knew we'd been there. They wouldn't come in like that otherwise."

She turned to look at him then, pure scorn on her face. "Are you serious?"

He searched for a response, but none of the words that came to mind was right. Everything he believed made a lie by the image of a hood going down over a child's face.

"This is how it works, Cooper. Don't you know that? Of course you do. You've ordered that before."

"No. Never."

"You've never sent faceless out? Top DAR agent, and you never ordered a mission?"

"Not like that."

"Like what, then? Did your team bring flowers and cake?"

"My teams were called in on criminals. Terrorists. Abnorms who had hurt someone, or were about to hurt someone."

"I'm sure that's what those men were told, too. That Lee and his family were terrorists. Same way the Gestapo believed the people they rounded up were plotting against the state."

"Come on. You can win any argument with the Gestapo or the Nazis. The DAR is not the same."

"It look like it's heading in the right direction to you?"

"Okay, first, I'm not with the department anymore, remember? Second, maybe this wouldn't have happened if *you* guys would stop blowing up buildings and assassinating people. I hate what I just saw. It makes me physically sick. But you can't throw a bomb and then get upset if people don't like you very much. Those men thought they were going to catch the people responsible for an explosion that killed more than a thousand people."

"Whatever," she said, and turned away again.

A thought struck him. "Wait a second. I didn't know Lee and Lisa. But you did."

"So?"

"So how would the DAR know unless they were tipped off?"

"By who?"

"How about Samantha? Or…" He paused, let her work it out.

"You're suggesting *John* called the DAR and told them where to find us?"

"Did he know about Lee and Lisa?"

"It doesn't matter. He would never have done that."

"Maybe Samantha hasn't gotten the message to him yet. Maybe it was his attempt to take you out."

"Not a chance."

"Shannon—"

"I mean it, Cooper. Drop it."

He opened his mouth, wanting to fight. Wanting to burn out the anger inside of him in a battle, the two of them going for blood. He wanted to tell her about a pink stuffed animal he'd seen amidst the rubble in New York. But then he imagined the scene in Lee's apartment, the door blowing open without warning, the faceless streaming in, his former colleagues shouting, throwing the family down, shackling them on their kitchen floor, the same kitchen he'd stood in last night and chatted with friendly strangers.

It's on John Smith. If there wasn't terrorism, there wouldn't be tactical response teams. Smith's hands were stained with the blood of thousands. Lee and Lisa and Alice were just the latest.

He found himself remembering the evening of March 12, President Walker's speech to the nation. Cooper had caught it the next day, in a hotel outside Norfolk, already on the run. He'd watched it with an edgy stomach, afraid of what he might hear, that the president would be preaching fire and brimstone against abnorms. Instead, the man had urged tolerance. What were the words?

"It's said that the strongest partnerships are formed in adversity. Let us face this adversity not as a divided nation, not as norm and abnorm, but as Americans.

Let us work together to build a better future for our children.

And let us never forget the pain of this day. Let us never yield to those who believe political power flows from the barrel of a gun, to the cowards who murder children to achieve their aims.

For them, there can be—will be—no mercy."

He'd listened to that with a swell of pride, the patriotic equivalent of a hard-on. And the words still moved him. They represented the reason he was undercover now, the reason he hadn't seen his children in six months.

He had to find John Smith. *And for him, no mercy.*

The words were old, a mantra he'd repeated every night. What surprised him was the small voice that followed it. The one that said, *And then what? Back to the DAR? Call in more tactical response teams? Can you really return to that?*

Shannon said, "What will happen to them?"

"They'll be taken to the local field office. Questioned."

"Questioned."

"Yes," he said. "Hopefully, they'll tell the agents about us right away. That will make things go easier. They might get off with a warning."

"Don't lie to me, Cooper."

He glanced at her, saw the intensity in her eyes. Turned back to the road. "They'll be charged. The bar and apartment will be seized. One or both of them will go to prison for harboring fugitives."

"And Alice?"

Cooper gritted his teeth.

"Oh Jesus." Shannon buried her face in her hands. "An academy?"

"It's…it's possible. It depends if she tests as tier one."

"And even if she doesn't, she'll be marked. They'll track her. Now that the microchip bill passed, they'll put a tag in her throat. Embedded up against the carotid, so even microsurgery can't remove it. She'll never be safe again."

He wanted to say something comforting, something to make it better, but he couldn't think what that would be.

"My God. This is my fault. I should never have brought you there."

"There's nothing we can do for them now. We just have to get to Wyoming and get this settled. Get ourselves clear. Then maybe."

"Right." Her laugh had no humor in it. "Goddamn it." She stared out the window, but he doubted she saw anything. "I sure hope you're worth it."

"What?"

The hesitation was tiny, a clenching in her trapezii, a flutter of the fingers. Tiny, but there. "I said I hope it's worth it. Getting to Wyoming."

Cooper held his own reaction back, tapping the steering wheel. Had she just misspoken? Possible. But that hesitation…she was holding something back. Hiding something.

Yeah, well, she's on the other side, remember?

He thought about calling her on it, decided against it. The events of the last twenty-four hours—*my God, is that all it's been?*—had generated a camaraderie between them. And yeah, she was attractive, in every sense of the word. But their friendship, or whatever it was, wouldn't survive this mission. It wasn't as if he could betray her, kill John Smith, and then see if she wanted to grab a cup of coffee sometime.

She was the enemy. Better not to forget that. Play his part, play it to the hilt, and keep an eye on her throughout.

Just get to Wyoming, get to John Smith, and end this.

For all *the children.*

CHAPTER 25

Three days of green and brown and the road humming beneath their tires, of billboards against endless sky, of seemingly identical gas stations and fading radio stations. I-90 west, a long gray ribbon unfurling through the rolling hills of Wisconsin, the flatlands of Minnesota, the sun-bleached scrub of South Dakota. The cities decreased in size as they rode, from the Milwaukee skyline dotted with church towers and brewery signs to the barely there hint of Sioux Falls and the low-slung strip malls of Rapid City.

They could have made the whole thing in a mad run but needed to kill time anyway and so drove eight-hour days and had dinner at chain restaurants. The silence hadn't lasted. By the first evening, they were back to their calculatedly casual routine. They avoided politics, kept things light. Told stories of growing up, of friends and drunken misadventures and favorite books, tales neither intimate nor distant.

Last night they'd stopped at a roadside motel in the Black Hills. Ate delivery pizza and flipped channels on the tri-d, skipping the news networks without acknowledging it. Outside the world was black, just gone, and the sky awash with stars. He'd fallen asleep to the sound of her breathing in the other bed.

This morning they'd risen early and crossed into Wyoming. He'd visited the state only once, a camping trip with Natalie in the Grand Tetons a dozen years before. It had been late summer then, the mountains carpeted in green. He remembered making love in the morning while coffee boiled on the campfire and birds sang in the trees.

Here, though, on the eastern edge of the state, the landscape was low and blasted, thorny underbrush and dry rock. It didn't look like a place where people could live. The towns were tiny things clutching the highway.

Until they came to Gillette. It had once been a quiet place, twenty thousand people, mostly working in the energy industry. Then Erik Epstein had revealed that the massive portion of the state he'd quietly been buying would be combined into one vast new "commune," a place he'd named New Canaan Holdfast, a home for people like him. Twist Territory, people had called it, and laughed at the idea of anyone trying to live there. Laughed, that was, until the full weight of his $300 billion came into play, and in a matter of months the world changed completely.

Gillette was the end point of a road into New Canaan. Along with two even smaller towns—Shoshoni to the west and Rawlins off I-80 to the south—it was one of the only ways to enter the Holdfast. Epstein had constructed broad highways, four lanes in each direction, that ran into the center of a wasteland, a rough-edged slash through some of the least desirable land of the United States. He'd bought the land for dollars an acre, bought it through holding companies and at auction, bought it around existing villages of twenty people, bought sprawling cattle ranches and mineral rights for ranges of oil and natural gas that lay too deep or were too sparse to have been tapped. The result was a patchwork of stony desert, largely contiguous land that had been barely touched in all of human history.

And with that move, the previously inconsequential towns of Gillette, Shoshoni, and Rawlins became nationally recognized as the gateways into New Canaan. Massive truck stops had sprung up, and housing for the thousands of construction workers who built the initial stages of the Holdfast. Restaurants and movie theaters and shopping malls swiftly followed. Finally came tourist hotels and trinket shops and storefront museums and all the rest.

As a kid, Cooper had loved science-fiction movies, especially the ones from the seventies, all gaudy colors and neon and people in jumpsuits. There was something so kitschily appealing about them, the world transformed into a metropolis two hundred stories high. But now, as they waited in a sea of trucks twenty minutes past Gillette, it occurred to him that the future hadn't turned out like that at all. The barren landscape and blinding sun looked more like the past. A cowboy western.

"How long does it take to clear the checkpoint?"

"From here?" Shannon was at the wheel; she craned her neck sideways to see around the eighteen-wheeler in front of them. "Probably fifteen minutes."

"Efficient."

"Has to be. The entrance is basically a massive delivery depot."

"Yeah, I know." Like any DAR agent, he'd had numerous briefings on the Holdfast. While culturally it resembled Israel shortly after the Second World War, NCH faced a unique set of circumstances. Because it was American soil, it had to abide by US law. But $300 billion made for all manner of exceptions. Epstein's lawyers and lobbyists had cobbled together a hundred loopholes, resulting in the Holdfast's being declared a separate county, with its own municipal code. And because the entire NCH was privately held corporate land, access could be controlled. "All the inbound trucks drop off their loads here, and then they're distributed via an internal shipping network. Makes for a lot of jobs."

"Jobs the Holdfast has plenty of. Unemployment is zero. And not only research—trucking, construction, mining, infrastructure, the works."

"Sure. Got to have something for the normals to do."

She laughed. "Not just normals. Plenty of gifted move here to be part of something, but a tier-five calculator or a tier-three musician isn't exactly leading the charge in biomedical research."

"How long have you lived here?"

"I've had my apartment for three years. I don't know that I'd say I live here."

"I know how that is."

Ten minutes later he got his first look at the border. The four lanes of the highway doubled, then doubled again, and then again. The semis edged to the right, filling the bulk of the lanes, with passenger vehicles heading left. Each lane ran to a checkpoint not unlike a tollbooth. Guards in dun uniforms bearing the blue rising-star emblem of the Holdfast moved like ants, hundreds of them, talking to drivers, running mirrors under cars, walking German shepherds. The canopy over each checkpoint looked simple enough, but Cooper knew that it was packed with the most advanced newtech scanning devices in existence. The joke was that to see next year's DAR gear, you just went to Wyoming and walked into a bar. That was the true protection of the Holdfast, the trump card more important than the desolate landscape or Epstein's billions. The best minds in their fields, gifteds who individually jumped technology forward decades, here worked together, and the results flowed outward to the country as a whole.

You don't need an army to conquer America, Cooper thought. *You just need to produce entertainment centers people can't live without.*

Shannon pulled up beneath the canopy, the sudden shadow falling cool into the car. She rolled down the window, and a young guy with a neat moustache said, "Welcome to New Canaan Holdfast may I see your documentation please," without pausing to breathe. They each dug for their passport—they'd discussed it on the way, the importance of not seeming too ready, too eager— and passed them over. The guard nodded and handed them to a woman behind him, who ran each against a scanner. Cooper knew it would be checking not only the validity of the passport, but also recent credit history, driving and criminal records, God knew what else.

Time to see if Schneider screwed us. The IDs and credit cards had worked fine on the way out, but that meant nothing at all. This was the first real test. Cooper forced nonchalant interest, looking around like a tourist.

"Mr. and Mrs....Cappello," the guard said. "What's your business in New Canaan?"

"We just wanted to see it," she said brightly. "We're road-tripping to Portland and thought it would be fun to stop off."

"Any narcotics or firearms?"

"Nope." Cooper had left his gun in pieces in a Dumpster in Minnesota, knowing they'd ask. It didn't matter. He didn't really like guns all that much, and besides, one sidearm wouldn't make any difference.

"Where are you staying while you're here?"

"Thought we'd get a hotel in Newton." The first town in the Holdfast was one of the largest and largely open to tourists. Deeper in, there would be additional security screenings, and proof of business needed. DAR briefings had compared the Holdfast with layers of sieves; each layer screened out more, using additional legal loopholes, ranging from gated residential communities to high-security mining areas to government-affiliated research facilities. As Cooper watched, another guard held up a device he'd never seen, an unmarked rectangle on a pistol grip, and panned it slowly along the car. Checking for explosives? Taking pictures of them? Reading their auras?

The female guard handed their passports back to the one with the moustache, who passed them to Shannon. "Thank you for your cooperation. Please be advised that the New Canaan Holdfast is privately held corporate land, and that by entering you are agreeing to abide by the bylaws of Epstein Industries, to remain within designated spaces identified in green, and to obey all requests of security personnel."

"Gotcha," Shannon said, then rolled up the window and put the car in drive.

And just like that, they were in.

■

It was different than he'd imagined.

Cooper had reviewed hundreds of photos and simulations. From above he'd seen the massive warehouse districts clustered at each entrance, row upon row of hangars that served as way stations for everything from lumber to ethylene dichloride to whiskey, all the products the Holdfast imported. He'd studied the layout of the region, the network of roads that connected the towns and outposts that had grown overnight. He'd read the specs of the solar fields, where miles of black photoelectric panels glittered like the carapaces of insects, all moving in perfect timing as they tracked the sun across the daytime sky and the moon across the night. He knew the populations of Newton, Da Vinci, Leibniz, Tesla, and Archimedes, knew what the specialized role of each town was. He'd sat in lectures about the unique nature of a preplanned society built with near-limitless funding.

What he hadn't done was ride the streets of Newton with the windows down, smelling dust and the ionized discharge from the moisture condensers. He'd never watched a woman park her electric car at a charging station outside a bar and heard the hum of the generators engaging. And despite having read the figures a thousand times, he'd never realized how *young* the place was. It was one thing to know that the oldest recognized gifteds were thirty-three, and another to see a world of teenagers hurrying busily about, kids in construction helmets and driving trucks, children building a new world to a ten-year blueprint. There were older people, too, of course; plenty of families with gifted children had moved here, but they looked oddly out of place, outnumbered like faculty on a college campus.

Shannon's apartment turned out to be on a second floor above a bar. One room with a Murphy bed tucked neatly in, a kitchen that showed no sign of ever having been cooked in, a desk with a plastic plant bathing in sunlight. It reminded him very much of his own abandoned apartment in DC.

She'd ushered him in, then stood looking around for a moment as if trying to recognize the place, as if someone had been there in her absence and moved things around by inches. After a moment she announced she wanted to clean up. Through the wall he could hear the sound of the shower turning on and off in quick cycles—navy showers only, water too precious here to waste. Cooper opened the fridge, saw nothing but condiments and beer, helped himself to one. He paced the room, then stepped out onto the small balcony.

The Holdfast embodied the latest urban-design theory, with wide bike lanes and public squares like Italian piazzas. He winced against the sun and slugged his beer and watched a cluster of twenty-year-olds break into a flirty game of tag, boys chasing laughing girls around, all of them lean and leathery and sunburned, flush with health. He wondered which could dance among the genome, or recall every detail of a face glanced at a dozen years ago. He wondered which of them worked for John Smith, which of them were terrorists, which of them might have once been targets for him to pattern and track and maybe murder.

Murder?

He took another sip of beer, leaning on the railing. A moment later she joined him, wearing a sundress now, a cotton strappy thing that bared her shoulders. Her hair was still damp, and she brushed it with steady strokes. She looked good, smelled of some tropical shampoo, coconuts maybe.

"So we made it."

"We made it."

He turned and leaned against the railing, the metal hot through his T-shirt. He watched her brush her hair and then watched her watch him. "What?" she asked.

"I was just thinking. You're safe now."

"And you're not. It's uncomfortable, right? Someone in a uniform doesn't like the way you look, and next thing you know, you end up in a brightly lit room." She cocked her head. "I know that feeling."

He didn't respond, just held a level gaze.

She sighed. "Cooper, we had a deal. That means something to me. You got us here, I'll get us in to see Epstein."

"Okay," he said. "What do we do? Drop by his office and ask for an audience with the King of New Canaan?"

"I told you, only straights call him that."

"We're standing in his kingdom right now." He nodded to a pair of uniforms down in the square. "Those are corporate security guards, and he pays them."

"That's right, he does. But there are no sweatshops in the Holdfast."

Why are you needling her? She was right: he did feel uncomfortable. For years he'd moved through the world with the certainty of power. Here, he was at best a tourist with a fake passport. And at worst, well, he had no illusions about his safety.

That wasn't what bothered him. He'd expected to feel like a soldier behind enemy lines. Only now that he was here, enemy territory turned out to be a cross between a kibbutz and a campus. It threw him, the feeling that this wasn't the beating heart of the evil empire.

Far from. What you've seen, you like. There was something inspiring about the place, the energy of it, the rational planning and joyful creation. It felt like a place that was building something. Aiming to the future. The rest of the country seemed mired in the past, always longing for a simpler time, even if that simpler time had never existed.

"What's our next move?"

"Step two is tomorrow. We go to Epstein, as I promised. Step three, we go our separate ways, I find my people and explain the situation."

"And step one?"

"Step one is you change your clothes and we go drinking. I'm home, and I want to celebrate."

■

They started in the bar below her apartment. From the outside it looked like any other, and he played his usual game with himself: country rock on the stereo, neon beer signs behind the bar, scarred wooden tables, the sweaty feel of too-bright sunlight pouring through the front windows, a jaded day-shift bartender with tattoos.

For the first time in a decade, he'd gone one for five.

The place was air-conditioned to just above freezing, and the windows had some kind of polarizing effect that stripped the fury from the sunlight without dimming the outside world. The décor was all smooth lines, the lighting indirect and sourceless, as though the air itself glowed. The music was a sexy, vaguely electronic beat. The bartender was a girl about sixteen years old working on a d-pad, her skin leathery but otherwise unmarked.

At least the tables were wooden and scarred. They looked older than the bartender and probably were. Bought wholesale somewhere, shipped in here.

"Two ciders and two vodkas," Shannon had said, then turned to him, flashed one of her quirky smiles, and said, "And the same for him."

At first he'd sipped his drinks, feeling on edge. The second of the icy vodkas had taken care of that, and the cider—distilled here, Shannon told him, apples and pears being two of the handful of things that grew well in Wyoming—was cut with a pleasant bitterness.

"Vitamins," Shannon said. "Most Bs. We eat a lot of meat here, but vegetables are expensive." She took one shot right after the other, chased that with one of the ciders. There was a lightness to her that he hadn't seen before, like she was uncoiling. The security of friendly ground. She laughed and joked and ordered more drinks, and somewhere along the line he decided, why not.

"So," she said. "First impressions."

"I thought you were very pretty, but a bit explosive."

"Cute."

"Thank you." He took a long pull of the cider. "Honestly? Not what I expected."

"How's it different?"

He looked around the bar, at the dozen or so other patrons. Young, all of them, and loud. The tables covered with empty glasses. Laughter that broke like a bomb, a whole table falling apart at a joke, following it with a toast. When was the last time he'd sat in a group like that, been lost in a conversation, lived only for a drink?

The selfish focus, the certainty that this moment was all there was, it was familiar. When he'd been eighteen and a soldier, drinking with his buddies had been pursued with the same relentless energy, the same showy self-determination. But there were differences. Everyone was thinner, with the tight-fleshed look of people who didn't drink enough water, spent a lot of time in the sun. The clothes were light and similar, very functional. Earlier, at the border, he'd thought that the place looked more like the past than the future, and he'd half expected to see big hats and cowboy boots, a generation playing at an older role. He'd been half right; there were a lot of hats, but the boots were all function and bore the marks of hard wear. None of it seemed to follow a fashion, or at least not one he recognized.

"No beer signs," he said.

She cocked her head.

"A bar like this anywhere else, there would be beer signs. You know, the old-school logos, the Clydesdales. And even the new beers, they make signs that consciously reflect the ones that came before. Because that's the way it's done. You brew a beer, you make a sign for it. It's like a pool table in a bar, even though no one really knows how to play pool anymore. Our grandparents shot pool; we get drunk and whack at the balls with warped sticks. No one thinks about it, but it's nostalgia. It's a sense of the past, of the way things are done."

"Like classic rock," she said. "I could go the rest of my life without hearing 'Sweet Home Alabama' again."

"There you go. I mean, the Rolling Stones are great. But Credence Clearwater, or the Allman Brothers for the ten thousandth time? Is anybody moved by their music? Does anybody even *hear* it? It's nostalgia."

"Cars," Shannon said. "Most people live in cities, don't drive more than a few miles through traffic. So why do car companies keep making big cars that go fast and use a ton of gasoline? What they should be is light and electric and easy to park."

"I don't know about that," Cooper said. "I like big cars that go fast."

"Old-world thinking," she said, smiling. "Another round?"

Outside the windows the world turned gold and orange and finally violet.

When they left he was feeling good, not wasted but certainly on the way, the world slippy around the edges. She hailed them an electric cab and gave the driver instructions. Their knees touched in the backseat of the tiny car. Martinis before dinner, and then steaks, an inch-thick rib eye crusted in rock salt and black pepper and grilled a perfect medium-rare. Every bite made him want to melt onto the plate.

He noticed that people around the restaurant noticed them, marked them as tourists, but there didn't seem to be any threat in it. Newton got its fair share of tourists, and probably thought of it as exporting goodwill.

She ordered a bottle of wine with dinner and matched him glass for glass. Things got hazier, the world shrinking. He knew he was drunk, didn't care.

Sometime later they were in a basement club. Sleek plastic furniture and low tables, a smoky haze sweet with marijuana. On a small stage a three-piece band—bongo, violin, guitar—played a strange, highly rhythmic melody somewhere between reggae and jazz, the musicians all heading off on complex tangents like mathematical equations, the sounds nearly, but not quite, discordant. Brilliants, he was sure, musicians who could play anything they'd ever heard once and yet never wanted to play the same thing twice, bored with a pattern explored. Shannon was in the bathroom, and he leaned back, listening to the music. The smarter plan for the night would have been to stay in her apartment, study maps and read Epstein's biography, but he couldn't make himself care.

She came back swaying, partly to shift through the crowd, partly a hip swing that fit the beat from the band, her legs strong and toned and two more drinks in her hand. "Here you are, Mr. Cappello. Tom."

He laughed, said, "Thank you, Allison."

They were on a couch nestled in a corner, and she dropped beside him. She smelled very good. From behind her ear she pulled a neatly rolled joint, then leaned forward and lit it off the candle on the table. "Ahh. Wyoming Sunset."

"The bar doesn't care?"

"The county can't make it legal, so there's a twenty-dollar fine. Which you pay up front when you buy one at the bar." She took another drag, leaned back into the seat. "You were married, right?"

"Yes." He had a flash of Natalie that last night he'd seen her, standing under the tree at the house where they'd once lived together. "Seven years, divorced for four."

"You got married young, then."

"We were twenty."

"Gifted?"

"No."

"Was that the problem?" She offered him the joint.

He started to pass, then figured what the hell. Took a gentle puff, then a deeper one. Felt an immediate rush, a tingle in his toes and fingers that flowed inward. "I haven't been stoned since I was seventeen."

"Go easy, then. We grow it strong out here."

He took another hit, passed it back. For a moment they just sat together, shoulders almost touching. He could feel the warmth of her, and a glow through his whole body.

"Yes," he said. "That was the problem."

"Was she jealous?"

"No, nothing like that. Part of the reason we got married was that I was gifted. Her parents didn't like us dating, and she hated that in them. Used to joke that we were an interracial couple. Then she got pregnant, and that pretty much settled things."

"Were you happy?"

"Very, for a while. Then less."

"What happened?"

"Oh, just—life." He held one hand up, stared at it, taking in the texture of his skin, the flex of the muscles as he wiggled his fingers. "You can't turn it off, you know? What we do. It wore her down. My fault, a lot of it. I was impatient, always finishing her sentences. The thousand weird ways our differences played out, like the fact that she loved surprises but could never plan one for me. I had her patterned too thoroughly. And when things got tense, I'd respond to her anger before she said a word, and that would piss her off more. The end...it came slowly, then all at once."

"That's Hemingway," she said.

He turned to look at her, the wide dark eyes and heavy lashes. Her face swimming a little in his inebriation. "Yeah."

On the stage, the violinist went into a ragged solo, the notes jarring and alien, and yet not quite wrong, and more vivid with the impact of the drug. It sounded like an insomniac Saturday night spent staring out the window and not seeing.

"I was engaged once," she said.

"Really?"

"Christ, Cooper, you don't have to sound so surprised."

He laughed. "Tell me about him."

"Her."

"Really?" He straightened. "But you're not gay."

"How would you know?"

"Pattern recognition, remember? I've got spectacular gaydar."

It was her turn to laugh. "I'm not, really. These days, with everything going on, it just doesn't seem to make as much difference. I mean, maybe if the gifted hadn't happened it would be a whole issue, maybe people would care about sexual orientation, but we've got much bigger reasons to hate each other."

"So what happened?"

She shrugged. "Like you said. I'm not gay."

"You loved her, though."

"Yeah." She paused, took another puff of the joint. "I don't know. It was a lot of things. My gift was part of it, too. It's hard. Loving someone, but not being able to share the way you see the world. Like trying to explain color to someone who's blind. They'll never really get it."

Part of him wanted to argue with her, but it was more from habit than anything else. An attitude he'd had as an abnorm in a normal world. A twist who hunted other twists.

"It was nice, though," she said. "Being loved."

He nodded. They fell silent, leaned back and watched the band. His body felt elastic, pliable and smooth and melting into the cushions. He caught fragments of a dozen conversations, felt a woman's laugh thrill down his spine. Tomorrow felt far off, and with it all the things he would have to do, the battle he would resume. But for now, right this second, it felt good just to sit here and float in a warm haze. To sit next to a beautiful woman in the midst of a strange new world and revel in being alive.

"This is nice, too," he said. "Taking a little break. From everything."

"Yeah," Shannon said. "It is."

"Thank you."

"You're welcome."

The band started a new song.

"Haunting and hypnotic."
—*New York Times*

"Impeccably researched and utterly believable."
—*Washington Post*

"One hell of a read."
—*Chicago Tribune*

Everyone knows the world changed forever with the arrival of the gifted. Now acclaimed social scientist Dr. Donald Masse details what might have been: war with the Middle East, the rise of violent religious fundamentalism, and a planet on the verge of irreversible ecological damage.

- Michael Dukakis would have lost to George H. W. Bush
- The European Union would be facing bankruptcy
- NASA would have abandoned manned space exploration
- American education would have degenerated to standardized testing
- Elephants, whales, and polar bears would be in danger of extinction
- Central America would be embroiled in a brutal drug war
- Heart disease, Alzheimer's, and diabetes would be leading causes of death

Think you know your own world? Think again.
Discover what would have happened…if the gifted had never happened.

CHAPTER 26

Cooper woke with a gasp, a sudden snapping of unconsciousness. Sweaty and tangled and head pounding. Struggled against his bonds, realized it was his clothes, soaked and tight, and a sheet half on him. He blinked, rubbed at his eyes, tried to put things back together.

There was a soft sigh beside him, and he looked over, saw Shannon curled around a pillow, her hair spilling across her bare neck. The bed. They were in bed back at her apartment. Had they…

No, still dressed, both of them. He had a vague memory of more drinks, and finishing the joint. A flash of dancing, the last thing he could remember. She had been a very good dancer, and beside her he'd felt big and clumsy and happy. Then nothing.

Cooper groaned, swung his legs off the bed. He'd managed to kick his shoes off, at least. He rose, head pounding, and wobbled into the bathroom. Peed for about half an hour, then stripped off his clothes and got in the shower. The controls were odd, a temperature gauge and a button. He set it all the way to hot, then pressed the button. A light trickle of water flowed from the showerhead, then shut off ten seconds later.

Right. The evaporators outside of town stripped what water they could from the air, and every building had a catch basin for rain, but water was eternally short here. That was one of the weaknesses of the Holdfast, a tactical advantage he'd seen plans for exploiting: destroy incoming pipes and hit the evaporators with surgical strikes. Estimated population decrease of 17 percent in two weeks, 42 percent by the end of a month, industrial and technical operational ability lowered by 31 percent. He hit the button again, soaked his hair, helped himself to her shampoo when the water cut off. A hit to wash it clear, a hit to soap up, a hit to wash it off. All in all, one of the least satisfying showers he'd ever taken, and no help at all for a hangover.

He toweled dry and put on his clothes. Looked in the mirror. *Game on.*

Shannon was making coffee when he came out. Her hair was limp, and one side of her face creased with pillow marks. "Morning," she said, her back to him. "How you feeling?"

"Dead and buried. You?"

"Yeah." She filled the pot with water, poured it into the machine, her back to him. He watched her hands, the way they fidgeted at nothing. She opened the fridge, stared at the empty shelves. "Breakfast options are limited."

"Coffee's fine." Awkwardness in the air like last night's smoke. "Thanks."

Shannon closed the door, turned to face him. "Listen. About last night."

"Nothing to say."

"I just, I don't want you to…It was a good time, and I needed it, but I'm not…It doesn't change anything."

"Hey, you got me into bed." He smiled, let her know he was kidding. "It was good. Things have been tense. It was nice to just, you know, be normal for a night."

She nodded. Picked up the discarded beer bottles from yesterday, dropped them in the recycling. Opened a drawer, then closed it.

Cooper said, "Why are you second-guessing me?"

Shannon looked up at him. "That the kind of thing that used to bug your wife? Telling her what was on her mind?"

"Sorry."

"It's okay." She took a deep breath, let it out. "You're right. I am."

"Because we got drunk?"

"Yes. Maybe. You're different than I expected. And I'm just wondering if any of it is real." Her gaze was unwavering and unapologetic.

Cooper turned and went to the Murphy bed. Grabbed the edge of the wrinkled sheets, shook them out and laid them smooth. Whacked the pillows, then tucked them in place. He wondered what Natalie would think of Shannon, whether they would like each other, decided that they probably would. "I grew up an army brat. Joined when I was seventeen. Then the agency. All that time, I was trying to fight for something. Trying to protect…everything, I guess. I was one of the good guys. And then when they pinned the bombing on me, I was alone. In a lot of ways I'd been alone my whole life, but this was different."

He moved to the edge of the bed and folded it into the wall on smooth hinges. Turned to her, not sure where he was going even as he went. "The last months, I've been doing things I used to fight against. I've been one of the bad guys, and I've been good at it. So does that mean I was wrong before?" He shrugged. "I don't think so. I liked protecting things. I miss it."

"There are other ways," she said. "Believe it or not, I feel like one of the good guys, too. I *am* one of them."

"Everybody is," Cooper said. "That's what makes life complicated." He knew her well enough to pattern her. She was holding something back, lying to him at least by omission. What, though? Hard to say. And besides, he couldn't blame her. He was lying to her, too.

Ain't we a pair.

"Look," he said. "Everybody's got layers. Nothing's simple. You thought I would be a humorless government operative without conscience or questions. And I thought you would be a two-dimensional fanatic who didn't care about hurting people. Now you know that I have an ex-wife, that I love hot sauce, that I dance badly, that I've read Hemingway and even remembered some of it. And I know a few things about you, too. But there are things neither of us knows. Things we're holding back." He said it lightly. "And that's okay, too. Doesn't make anything less real. Especially," he said, and rubbed at his temple, "my hangover. So how about we let things lie for now?"

For a moment she just looked at him. Then she opened a cabinet, took out two coffee mugs, filled them both. She handed one to him, and when their fingers brushed in the exchange, she didn't jump. "I'm going to go clean up."

"Okay." He sipped the coffee, watched her walk to the bathroom.

She stopped at the door. "Cooper?"

"Yeah?"

"Pills in the drawer by the sink. For your head."

He smiled at her. "Thanks."

■

Two hours later they were three thousand feet up.

An updraft hit, and they bounced a dozen vertical feet. His stomach rolled. "You sure you know how to fly this thing?"

She smiled from the pilot's seat in front of him. "I saw it on tri-d once. How hard can it be?"

The airfield was on the outskirts of Newton, four smooth runways crisscrossing like a pound sign. They'd left his car parked in a gravel lot, checked in at ground control, and gone to the assigned hangar. The glider was futuristic looking, with broad wings and a streamlined body. Made of carbon fiber, it weighed so little that they pushed it by hand onto the runway, where Shannon hitched it to a thick, twisted cable. Inside she put on a headset, spoke in a soft, fast voice to the tower, and a moment later the cable snapped taut and yanked them almost a mile in thirty seconds, the massive winches hauling with force sufficient to hurl them into the air. Cooper didn't mind heights, had ridden in helicopters and jets and military aircraft, and had even jumped out of a few of them, but the glider he wasn't loving.

"How long can this thing stay up?"

"You a nervous flier?"

"No. I just like doing it in a machine with, you know, an engine."

She laughed. "Old-world thinking, Cooper. Gliders have no emissions, the winches are solar-powered, and out here, if you ride the updrafts, you can stay aloft for hours. Easiest way to get from town to town in the NCH."

"Uh-huh." He looked out the window at the patchwork ground far below. The only sound was the wind rushing beneath the broad wings, whistling over the teardrop body. The hull of the thing was about the thickness of a napkin.

"Look," she said. "No hands." She released the stick and held them up above her head.

"Jesus, would you quit? I'm hungover here."

She laughed again and banked in a slow angle that gave him a better view than he really wanted.

Tesla was in the heart of the state, and tacking from updraft to updraft, they made the trip in about two hours. Seeing it from the air was oddly familiar, similar to the satellite images he'd reviewed. Midsize by Holdfast standards, it was home to ten thousand people. The town was a grid revolving around a complex of mirrored rectangles, energy-efficient buildings that rose four stories higher than anything else.

In one of them sat the richest man in the world.

■

The landing turned out to be gentle enough, not much different from coming down in any other small plane. Shannon had touched, bounced once, then smoothed the glider into a long, slow run. Good flying.

There was another security check at the hangar, this one more intense. The man behind the bulletproof Plexi was affable enough, but he ran their passports with care and spent longer than Cooper liked clicking on his datapad. Tesla was well outside of the tourist sections and protected by several more layers of sieves. The whole town was private corporate land, inside a gated community, inside a high-security municipality, a series of legal classifications that basically amounted to "keep the hell out." Cooper smiled blandly at the guard.

Half an hour later, they were pulling into Epstein Enterprises, the mirrored buildings, all sun and sky, too bright to look at. There was another security post, but Shannon had made a call this morning, and their fake names were on a list. They got in with little more than a passport check and a scan of the vehicle.

While Epstein's official headquarters were in Manhattan, this was the true nerve center. From here, the abnorm ran his massive financial empire, not only the development of New Canaan, but the management of thousands of patents, investments, and research projects, the total net worth of which was impossible to calculate. Money at that level was not something that could be counted; it was dynamic, a living thing that swelled and shrank and consumed the money of others, companies buying companies buying companies for fifty iterations.

The top of every building bristled with satellite dishes and security systems, among them batteries of surface-to-air missiles. Defensive, supposedly, and squeaked through on a congressional exemption that must have cost billions. Cooper remembered a plan he'd seen for a coordinated missile launch targeting the compound: expected physical efficacy of 27 percent in an initial barrage, but casualties projected at only 16 percent, less than 5 percent upper managerial.

There were no doubt plans for a nuclear option as well. One thing the DAR had was plans.

"You okay?" Shannon maneuvered the electric car they'd rented into a parking spot in a row of identical vehicles. "You've been quiet."

"The glider," he lied. "Still getting my ground legs back."

She turned off the engine. "There's something you should know. I got us in by dropping John's name."

"John?" he said. "Oh. John Smith. Hmm. Will that make him friendly?" Epstein openly and frequently disassociated himself from the terrorist movements, all of them. He had to; any link to someone like John Smith and the loopholes that kept the Holdfast safe would close swiftly and tightly. The DAR assumed that there must be some back-channel connection, but they'd never been able to find evidence of one.

"I don't know. Publically, Epstein is a pretty vocal critic. But John has a lot of friends here. Using his name was the only way I knew to get a meeting."

"So what's their relationship?"

"I don't really know. John respects Epstein, but I think he feels they're playing different roles. Some people compare them to Martin Luther King and Malcolm X."

"Lousy parallel. Dr. King fought for equality and integration, not building a separate empire, and Malcolm X may have advocated black rights by any means necessary, but he didn't run a terror network that blew up buildings."

"I don't want to argue about it."

"Fair enough," he said. "But I'm not going to pretend to be with Smith."

"You shouldn't. I wouldn't lie to him at all, if I were you."

"Not much point," he said. "I can't ask him for help if I don't tell him why I need it." *Tough tightrope to walk. You have to convince a man who has everything to lose by admitting a connection to John Smith to do just that. All without telling him too much.* He forced a cocksure grin. "Thanks for this. For keeping your end."

"Yeah. Well, we had a deal." She opened the car door. "Come on. Let's go meet a billionaire."

The grounds were deserted, and given the sun blasting down from the big blue sky, he wasn't surprised. The complex had more than twenty buildings—twenty-two, if he remembered correctly—but the one they entered was at the center. It didn't look like much, none of the grand corporate styling he would have expected in Chicago or DC. Though taller than the rest, it was the same featureless solar glass. *Of course. Solar glass bounces the sun's heat, transforms it to energy. Marble is heavy and needs to be shipped in. And ornate carvings are nostalgia.*

Old-world thinking.

■

The lawyer was one of the older people Cooper had seen in the last days. Early fifties, with close-cropped silver hair and hand-tailored suit, he radiated a two-grand-an-hour vibe. "Mr. and Mrs. Cappello. I'm Robert Kobb. If you'll come with me?" He spun without waiting for an answer.

The lobby was a bright atrium with one wall dedicated to a thirty-foot tri-d screen running CNN in stunningly crisp resolution—Epstein held a 30 percent stake in Time Warner—and they'd barely set foot in it when the man met them. Cooper had expected to be kept waiting for hours if they got in at all. Apparently John Smith's name carried a lot of weight here. Was the billionaire in league with the terrorist? If so, the situation was worse than anyone had dared believe.

"How was your trip in?"

"Bumpy," Cooper said.

The lawyer smiled. "Gliders take some getting used to. This is your first visit to New Canaan Holdfast, correct?"

His smile is bullshit. He knows who we are, but he's keeping to the cover story. A knowledge hoarder. "Yes."

"What do you think?"

"Very impressive."

Kobb nodded, led them past a row of elevators to the last in line, and touched his palm to a featureless plate. The doors slid silently open. "It's growing fast. You should have seen Tesla five years ago. Just dirt and sky."

The elevator moved so smoothly that Cooper couldn't say for sure if they were going up or down. He put his hands in his pockets, rocked on his heels. A moment later the doors parted, and Kobb led them out.

One side of the hall was glass floor to ceiling, the sun dialed down from blast furnace to a warm glow. The other side was an ornate garden built into a tiered wall, greenery spilling over the edges of sleek inset planters. The air felt flush with oxygen. "Nice."

"We use what we have here. And we have plenty of sun."

"Isn't it some sort of sin to waste water here?"

"They're gene-modified, spliced with some form of cactus. The water needs are miniscule. I don't really understand it," Kobb said in a way that suggested he understood perfectly well, but suspected you might not. The lawyer led them past several conference rooms, then touched another featureless spot on the wall to unlock a door at the end. "Mr. Epstein's office."

Considering the wealth in play, the room was understated. Seamless glass on two sides that gave way to a tumbling view of the city and the desert beyond, a smooth wooden desk, a conference area with comfortable seating. A pale young girl, Cooper guessed she was ten or so, sat on the couch, playing a game on a d-pad. Her hair was dyed a sickly Kool-Aid green. A niece? Epstein didn't have any children.

The lawyer ignored her completely. "Please, have a seat. Erik will join us in a moment. Can I get you anything? Coffee?"

"I'm fine, thanks. Allison?"

Shannon shook her head. Instead of sitting, she glided to one of the windows, stared out at the view.

"Hi," Cooper said to the little girl. "My name's Tom."

She looked up from the datapad. Her eyes were a green almost as startling as her hair, and far too old for her body. "No it isn't," she said, then went back to her game.

He felt a snap of embarrassment laced with anger, swallowed it. The girl was obviously a reader; even beyond her casual callout on his lie, she had all the signs: antisocial tendencies, a hunger for nonhuman stimulus, the need to physically express her difference. And it wasn't really a surprise to think that Epstein would use the abilities of the gifted around him. He just hadn't expected a child.

She must be exceptionally powerful. The thought came with a wave of discomfort. To a tier-one reader, the whole world was naked emperors. Her knowledge would go beyond knowing that he was lying about his identity; within a few minutes of listening to him, watching him, she would know things that his ex-wife didn't.

It was one of the few gifts that he really considered curses. Every moment, every human interaction, readers swam in the river of lies that made up everyday life. Worse, they picked up on the darker elements of personalities, the universal Jungian shadow of the human mind, the part that relished torture and pain and humiliation. Everyone had that shadow. For most people, it was controlled, expressed in subverted ways: pornography, aggressive sports, violent daydreams. It was part of the human animal, and most of the time, a harmless part. Thoughts were only thoughts, after all, and these were held close.

But readers saw them all around, in every person. Every kindness was underscored by it. Daddy might protect you, but a tiny part of him wanted to hold the babysitter down and do things to her. Mommy might wipe your tears, but something in her wanted to claw your arms and shriek in your face to shut the hell up. Unsurprisingly, readers ran to madness. The healthiest usually ended up shut-ins, locked in a tiny controlled world where they could count on the things around them.

Most committed suicide.

Robert Kobb coughed into a closed fist and said, "You'll have to forgive Millicent. She says what's on her mind."

"Nothing to forgive," Cooper said. "She's right."

"Yes, I know." Robert Kobb gave a bland smile and settled himself on the couch beside Millicent. She shied away from him without glancing from her game. Kobb said, "You're actually Nick Cooper."

"Yeah."

"Erik asked me to clear the time as soon as he heard from you this morning. He didn't tell me what this was in reference to."

Cooper flopped in one of the chairs, measured the lawyer. Something about the man bugged him. The pose of authority, calling his boss by his first name. That and his veneer of aw-shucks normalcy. "He didn't know. Ask you a question?"

"Certainly."

"What's it like helping to build New Canaan when you're not gifted?"

By the window, Shannon swallowed a laugh. The lawyer's smile curdled slightly. "A privilege. Why?"

"Call me curious."

Kobb nodded, made an unconvincing it's-nothing gesture. "What we're doing here matters. It's an incredible opportunity. Never in history has there been an initiative like this. A chance to build a new world."

"Especially with someone else's money. Sounds like a no-lose."

Millicent smiled into her game.

"Hmm." The phone at the lawyer's belt vibrated, and he unclipped it, read the message. "Ah. Erik is about to arrive. He's in Manhattan."

"He flew in for this?"

"No," Kobb said, the smugness back. "He's in Manhattan now."

"Then—"

Before he could finish the question, Erik Epstein appeared behind the desk.

Cooper was halfway out of his chair without realizing he'd moved, his body on full combat alert. His mind spinning, analyzing the situation—

A gift like Shannon's? Has he been here all the time, somehow?

No, Epstein's gift is for data.

Some unheard-of piece of newtech? Cloaking? Teleportation? Ridiculous.

But there he is. Live and in the flesh...

Got it.

—and realizing what he was looking at. "Wow. That is something."

Erik Epstein smiled. "Sorry to startle you."

Now that he'd had a moment, Cooper could see the faint gauziness at the man's edges, as if he'd been smeared. The shadows were off, too; wherever Epstein was, the lighting was different from here. He looked like a special effect from a movie in the eighties, completely convincing until you really looked.

"One of our newest developments," Kobb said. "Fundamentally similar to the technology in a tri-d set, only significantly amplified."

"A hologram."

"Yes," Epstein said. He grinned. "Not bad, huh?"

"Not bad at all." *That's a decade past the best the DAR has ever managed. Even with the academy graduates.*

In person—well, sort of—Erik Epstein looked a little less polished than he did in broadcasts. He still had the boyish good looks, the raffish hair, but he seemed less stiff. Dressed in a summer-weight suit with no tie, he'd have been at home in an expensive country club. "I'd shake your hand, but"—he lifted one arm, flexing the fingers—"One of the limitations. Still, it beats a speakerphone."

"Thank you for meeting us on short notice," Shannon said. She was somehow beside him, settling into a chair.

"Your message made sure of that, Ms. Azzi. I don't like being connected to John Smith that way."

"I understand," she said. "Forgive me for imposing. It was the only way I knew to get your attention."

"You have it," Epstein said. He laid his hands on the desk. The fingertips penetrated the surface, ruining the illusion a bit. "You must be Cooper."

"Agent Nicholas Cooper," Kobb said. "Born March 1981, second year of the gifted. Joined the army at seventeen with father's consent. Detailed as a military liaison to what would become the Department of Analysis and Response, 2000. Joined full-time in 2002. Entered Equitable Services with its foundation in 2004. Made full agent in 2005, senior agent in 2008. Generally considered the best of the so-called 'gas men,' sporting an unmatched clearance rate, including thirteen terminations."

"Thir-*teen*?" Shannon raised an eyebrow.

"Yes," Cooper said, "that's me. On paper."

"Went rogue following the March 12th attack on the Leon Walras Exchange." Kobb looked up from his datapad. "Now the lead suspect in that bombing."

He shouldn't have been surprised. Though part of the agreement with Director Peters was that they wouldn't publicly reveal his identity—a fanatic might have gone after Natalie and the children—most of the DAR would know he'd been designated a target. And the world's richest man would have access to pretty much any information he wanted. Still. It jarred him. He glared at the lawyer, but spoke to Epstein. "I had nothing to do with that."

"Did you, Ms. Azzi?" Kobb asked.

"No," she said. "Not the way it happened."

"But it was John Smith's organization that planted the bombs."

"Yes. But we didn't trigger them."

"How do we know that?"

"Enough, Bob." Epstein spoke with easy command. "They're telling the truth."

"But, sir, we don't—"

"Yes, we do. Millie?"

The girl looked up. "They're both lying. They're lying to each other, too. But they're telling the truth about that."

"Thank you, sweetheart."

The lawyer opened his mouth, shut it. Cooper could see the man simmering, his frustration. A leader in his field, no doubt a powerful political player, overruled by a child.

Kobb's not the only one. Cooper felt like a tennis ball hammered back and forth across a net. Lying to each other? What did that mean? If nothing else, the girl had clearly made him for what he was, and the nakedness came with fear. She couldn't read his mind, wouldn't know about his mission, but picking up on the subcutaneous cues of his loyalty response to the agency, that would be simple for her. No telling how much deeper that could go.

To make it this far and be at the mercy of a ten-year-old girl...

Lock it down.

"So." Erik Epstein smiled, holding out his hands. "With that out of the way. What are you doing here?"

"Shannon and I had a deal. There was an incident in Chicago, a few days ago, and she needed help. I got her home, and she got me a chance to meet you."

"I see. Why?"

"As you know, my former agency is hunting me." *Stick to the facts as much as possible.* "I'm not safe anywhere."

"Mr. Epstein," Kobb said, "you should know that we're on tenuous legal ground. Now that Mr. Cooper's identity is out in the open, we can't claim plausible deniability. This is verging dangerously close to harboring a fugitive."

"Thank you, Bob," the billionaire said dryly. "We can take the risk for a few more moments. I don't think Agent Cooper is here to entrap us."

"No, sir. In fact, I need your help. I'd like to start over here. In New Canaan." He forced himself not to look at the girl. She would know he was lying, or at least not telling the whole truth. The best he could hope was that she wouldn't interject, that she offered an opinion only when asked.

Epstein steepled his fingers. "I see. And for that you need my help."

"Yes."

"Because you have a lot of enemies."

"Yes. But I could be a good friend to you."

Kobb said, "Mr. Epstein, this is a bad—"

The billionaire silenced him with a look. To Cooper, he said, "Would you give us a moment? I'd like to speak to Ms. Azzi and Mr. Kobb privately." He turned to face the girl. "Millie, would you bring Mr. Cooper to the executive lounge?"

Cooper shot a glance at Shannon, couldn't read her response. They'd formed something of a bond over the last days, but she didn't owe him anything. For a moment he considered refusing. But what would be the point? If he was caught, he was caught.

With exaggerated nonchalance, he stood. "Sure." Millie slid off the couch, her d-pad clutched tight to her chest. She walked to a blank wall. Part of it slid aside as she reached it, a hidden door he hadn't noticed. How much else had he missed?

At least the girl was going with him. Whatever she had figured out, she wouldn't be able to tell. He followed her in and found himself in another elevator. There were no buttons, no control panel. The muscles of his lower back tightened. He wondered if "executive lounge" was code for something.

Something like "interrogation cell."

You bought the ticket. Time to take the ride.

The last thing he saw as the door slid shut was Shannon looking over her shoulder at him, something inscrutable in her eyes.

Standing in the tiny box, he had a sudden vision of himself as though from a satellite. A close-up that quickly zoomed out: man in a box in a building in a complex in a city in a state in a nation—and an enemy of all of them. Panic slid slick fingers through his stomach. He took a breath, rolled his shoulders. Only way out was through.

Millie stared at the middle distance, her face hidden by bright green bangs. She looked so lost that for a moment he forgot his own situation. He wondered how many meetings she had sat through, how many billion-dollar deals. How many times her insight had led to someone's death. The weight of it would have been a lot for a soldier to bear. And she was just a child.

"It's okay," she said.

Cooper started. He wondered if she meant his situation or hers. "It is?"

"Yes."

He blew a breath. "All right. If you say so."

Again, he couldn't feel which direction the elevator was going, but it could only be down. And given the length of the ride, lower than the ground floor. Odd. And why a private elevator with a hidden door? What kind of executive lounge was accessed through the boss's office?

Ten more seconds, and the door slid open. Another hallway, but no sunlight or botanical garden here. They were in the basement, huddled beneath the humming power lines that drove the building.

"Go ahead," Millie said.

"You're not coming?"

She shook her head, still staring at the floor. "Go to the end. There's a door."

Cooper looked at her, then down the hallway. Shrugged. "Thanks." He stepped off the elevator.

"You should be careful," Millie said behind him.

"Why?"

For a moment, he thought she wouldn't answer. Then she raised her head, swatted a lock of green hair behind one ear. Took him in with those strange, sad eyes. "Everybody's lying," she said. "Everybody."

The elevator door slid closed.

Cooper stared at it. Slowly, he turned back and faced the dim hallway. He flexed his fingers. Wondered how deep he was right now. At least as far underground as he'd been above it a moment before. Something nagged at his subconscious, that hint of a puzzle piece that hadn't fallen into place yet, a pattern he could sense more than see. A hidden door. A private elevator. A child for an escort. A gifted, troubled child.

What was this place?

If this is the executive lounge, I'd sure hate to see the regular one.

He started down the hall. Thick carpet muted his footsteps. He could hear the rush and whoosh of air, ventilation systems of some sort. The walls were undecorated. He ran a hand down them: carbon fiber weave, very strong, very expensive.

At the end of the hall, a door swung open. There was no one standing there, and the room beyond it was dark.

With the feeling that he was entering some sort of a dream, he walked in.

CHAPTER 27

Data. Constellations of numbers glowing like stars, neon swipes of sine-curves, charts and graphs in three dimensions, hovering everywhere he looked. It was like walking into a planetarium, that darkened silence and sense of wonder, only instead of the heavens, it was the world hanging in every direction, the world broken down into digits and sweeps and waves. Cooper blinked, stared, turned slowly on his heel. The room was big, an underground cathedral, and in all directions, 360 degrees, luminous figures hung in the air. Things cycled and changed as he watched, the light seemingly alive, the correlations bizarre: population figures graphed against water consumption and the average length of women's skirts. Frequency of traffic accidents on nonrural roads between the hours of eight and eleven. Sunspot activity overlaid on homicide rates. A chronology of deaths in the 1941 German invasion of the Soviet Union mapped to the price of crude oil. Explosions in post offices from 1901 to 2012.

In the center of this circus of light stood the silhouetted ring-master. If he was aware of Cooper, he didn't show it. He raised a hand, pointed at a graph, swiped sideways, and zoomed to a micro level, red and green dots plotted like a map of the ocean floor.

The air was cold and smelled of…corn chips?

Cooper walked down the ramp in front of him. As he passed through a graph, the projections glowed in his peripheral vision, a neat line that swept across his body. "Ummm…hello?"

The figure turned. The ambient light was too dim to make out his features. He gestured to Cooper to come forward. When they were ten feet apart, the man said, "Lights to thirty percent," and soft, shadowless illumination sprang from nowhere and everywhere at once.

The man was thick around the waist, the beginnings of a second chin sprouting off the bulwark of the first. His skin was pallid and vaguely shiny, hair a rat's nest. He ran a hand through it with the jerky speed of a regular twitch. Cooper stared at him, the pattern beginning to come together, the truth of it huge and shattering and suddenly obvious.

"Hi," the man said. "I'm Erik Epstein."

Cooper opened his mouth, closed it. The truth slamming home, obvious. The structure of the face, the shape of the eyes, the breadth of the shoulders. It was like looking at the pudgy, nervous double of the handsome, assured billionaire he'd just left.

"The hologram," Cooper said. "It's a fake. It's all you."

"What? No. Huh-uh. Reasonable intuitional leap based on limited data, but incorrect. The hologram is real. I mean, the man is real. But he's not me. He plays me. He's been me for a long time now."

"An…actor?"

"A doppelgänger. My face and voice."

"I—I don't—"

"I don't like people. I mean, I like people, people don't like me. I'm not good at people. In person. They're clearer as data."

"But. Your…doppelgänger, he's been on the news. He eats dinner at the White House."

Epstein stared at him as if waiting for him to say something else.

"Why?"

"For a while I could just be in the data, but we knew people would want to see me. People are funny that way, they want to see, even when seeing isn't the point. Astronomy. The important information scientists get from telescopes isn't visible. Radiation spectra, red-line shift, radio waves. Data. That's what matters. That's what tells us something. But people want to see pictures. Supernova in vivid color. Even though scientifically it's useless."

Cooper nodded, getting it. "He's your color photo. What was he, someone who looked a lot like your high school yearbook?"

"My brother. Older."

That couldn't be. Epstein had had an older brother, a normal, but he'd died a dozen years ago in a car crash. "Wait. You faked his death?"

"Yes."

"But that was before anyone knew about you. Before you made your fortune."

"Yes."

"Are you telling me you two planned this twelve years ago?"

"Together we are Erik Epstein. I live in the data. And he is what people want to see. Better at talking to them." Epstein twitched his hands through his hair again. "Here." He gestured, and a vivid image appeared. The office upstairs, but from a different angle. Shannon in the chair, saying something. The lawyer, Kobb, shaking his head. Millicent hunch-shouldered, lost in her game. A security camera?

No—the angle was wrong. It was the view from behind the desk. The room as viewed by the hologram. By the other Erik Epstein.

"Do you see? We share eyes."

The enormity of it. For more than a decade, the world had watched one Erik Epstein, heard him talk on CNN, followed his political maneuverings to establish New Canaan, tracked his corporate takeovers, seen him board private jets. All the while, the real Erik Epstein had been out of sight. Living in this basement, this dark cave of wonders.

He wondered if anyone in the DAR knew it. If the *president* knew it.

"But…why? Why not just stay out of sight?"

"Too hard. Too many questions. People want to *see*." He said it nervously. "I like people. I understand them. But it would have been too hard. I didn't want press conferences. I wanted to work in the data. Do you know what Michelangelo said?"

Cooper blinked, thrown by the change in topic. "Umm."

"'In every block of marble I see a statue as plain as though it stood before me, shaped and perfect in attitude and action. I have only to hew away the rough walls that imprison the lovely apparition to reveal it to the other eyes as mine see it.'" The words running together. When he finished, again Epstein fell silent, waiting.

Whatever this is, it's important. One of the most powerful men on the planet is showing you a secret that at best a handful of people know. There's a reason.

Cooper paused and then said, "The way Michelangelo saw marble, that's how you saw the stock market."

"Yes. No. Not just that. Everything. Data." He turned and waved his arms in an intricate series of gestures. The whole room reacted, shimmering and twisting, a psychedelic light show of charts and numbers and moving graphs. A new set of data appeared. "Here. You see?"

Cooper stared, tracked from chart to chart. Tried to make sense of what he was looking at. *Do what* you *do. Find the patterns the way you can assemble a picture of someone's life from their apartment.*

Population figures. Resource usage. A time-lapse of Wyoming from above, taken over years, the brown wasteland sprouting a neat geometric pattern of cities and roads. A three-dimensional chart of the incidents of violence in Northern Ireland mapped against the number of British pubs and the average attendance figures of churches. "New Canaan."

"Obvious." Impatient.

"Its growth. There," Cooper said, pointing, "that's about the external resources the Holdfast depends on. External resources are weak points, dependencies that could be used against you. And…" He stared, feeling that intuitional leap, almost tasting it, but not grasping it. He strained, knowing as he did that it didn't work that way, any more than an artist could force a masterpiece.

New Canaan. This is about New Canaan. Only, most of it wasn't, at least not explicitly. The historical data. The Sicarii in Judea and the murder of priests in a crowd, the numbers rising, then the intersection of that line and the sudden plummet. Something called the Hashshashin plotted against Shia Muslims in the eleventh century. He didn't know what the words meant, or knew only fragments. *Hashshashin. Wasn't that the original term for "assassin"?* He thought so, but also thought he'd picked that up in a kung-fu movie. He simply didn't know enough history.

Forget what you don't know. Look at the patterns. What do they say?

"Violence. This is about violence." The words came out before the thought had finished forming.

"Yes! More."

"I don't…" He turned to Epstein. "I'm sorry, Erik, I can't see the way you see. What are you showing me? Why?"

"Because I want you to do something for me."

Favors for favors, sure. He'd watched the meeting upstairs. "You want me to do something in order to get your protection here, start a new life."

"No," the man said, his voice thick with scorn. "Not the lie. You don't want a new life here. That's not why you came."

Careful. This could all be a trap. What if he wants you to reveal your real purpose so that he can…

What? This man, this gifted and odd and immensely powerful man, would he really share his secret just to uncover you? Ridiculous. If he cared, he could have had you thrown out of the NCH. Or buried in the desert.

"No," Cooper said, "it's not."

"No. I know what you came for. It's in the data." Another whirl of his hands, and the room was suddenly filled with Cooper's life. A scrolling timeline of every recorded date of importance in his life, from his hospitalization as a teenager to his divorce from Natalie. A geographical chart of the people he had killed. A table marking the frequency with which his ID had been used to access the DAR bathroom, and at what hours.

A case-file note about Katherine Sandra Cooper, age four: "Subject related details of teacher's personal life suggesting strong abnorm tendencies. Recommend testing ahead of standard."

Cooper's stomach went cold. "You're looking at my child?"

"The data. I look at the data. It tells me the truth. Now you tell me the truth. Why are you here?"

He turned from the screens. Fixed the man with a hard stare. The feeling he had, it was like getting e-mailed a porn video that turned out to be his wedding night, as if some shadowy freak had been hiding in the closet with a camera. Epstein looked at him, looked away, shot a hand through his hair again.

"I'm here," Cooper said slowly, "to find and kill John Smith."

"Yes," Epstein said. "Yes."

"And you're not trying to stop me."

"No." The man tried a smile, his lips wriggling like worms. "I'm trying to help you."

■

Cooper walked down the hallway without seeing it. Trod the carpet without feeling it. Stepped into the elevator like a man asleep.

Tuned into Epstein's dream.

"It was never money. It was art. The stock market was marble and the billions my sculpture.

"And then the world took it away. My art scared them. Upset the way things worked.

"But it was never the money. The data, you see? It's the data. And so I needed a new project."

"New Canaan."

"Yes. A place for people like me. A place where artists could work together. Make new patterns and new data unlike anything ever. A place for freaks," he'd said, trying that smile again. "But then that upset things, too. Real art does. So I brought that into the pattern. In this new project, integrating with the rest of the world is part of the design. I realized people thought I was taking from them. I never wanted to take. It's not about the having, or the giving, it's about the *making*."

"What does this have to do with John Smith?"

"Look at the data. It's all there. Look at the Sicarii."

"I don't know what that means."

The man had snorted, a clever teacher with a dull student. "It means 'dagger-men.' In the first century, Judea was occupied by Romans. The Sicarii attacked people in public. Killed Romans, and also Herodians, those Jews who collaborated."

"They were terrorists," Cooper said, understanding beginning to dawn. "Early terrorists."

"Yes. Here." Erik had flicked his wrist, and one graph had expanded to fill the room in front of them. It was one Cooper had noticed before, a rising line marking murders. The line grew steadily...then intersected another line and plummeted. "You see?"

"They killed more and more people," Cooper said, "and then something happened." On intuition, he said, "The Romans decided they'd had enough."

Epstein nodded. "The Sicarii were hunted, pursued to the fortress of Masada, where they either were slaughtered or committed mass suicide. But look deeper."

"The rest of the Jews." It was coming clear to Cooper. "The Romans punished not just the killers, but the rest of the Jews." He turned to the man. "You want me to kill John Smith because if he keeps doing what he's doing, the government may turn against New Canaan."

"Will turn against. It's in the data. Extrapolating current terrorist activity and charting it against public countermeasures, mapped against similar historical datasets, there's a 53.2 percent chance that the US military will attack New Canaan within the next two years. A 73.6 percent within three."

Cooper had a flash of the briefings he'd seen, the preemptive plans, the missile strikes. *One thing the DAR has,* he'd thought on the way in, *is plans.* "So why not kill Smith yourself? You're the big man here. The King of New Canaan."

The abnorm winced. "No. It's not. It doesn't work like that. Besides. I like people. But people love him."

"You want him dead, but you're afraid that if you kill him, your...artwork...will tear itself apart." Cooper laughed grimly. "Because no matter how smart or rich you are, he's a leader, and you're not."

"I know what I am." There was the faintest hint of sadness in his voice. "I'm not even me."

The whole thing felt vaguely dirty, had the stench of palace politics about it. An odd reaction, Cooper knew, but he couldn't shake it. Still, the arguments made sense. And Epstein was right—if things kept going the way they were, New Canaan would be destroyed. And it might not stop there. Congress had already approved a bill to implant microchips against the carotid artery of every gifted in America. What was to keep those chips from becoming bombs?

He'd never thought of himself as an assassin. He'd killed when he had to, but always for the greater good. That was a certainty that fueled him. It was the only thing that kept him apart from John Smith. This, though, felt like crossing a line.

What line? You came here to do this.

Yes. But not for him.

So don't do it for him. Do it for Kate. And then go home.

"You understand?" Epstein seemed nervous on the point, afraid. After all, he had revealed not only his secret, but his agenda. The man might have an unparalleled head for data, but a chess player he was not, Cooper realized.

"Yes, I understand."

"And you'll do it? You'll kill John Smith?"

Cooper had started up the ramp. At the door, he'd turned, taken in the whirling chamber of data dreams and the man at the center of it. An architect trapped in a palace of his own design, watching a tsunami approach.

"Yeah," he'd said. "Yeah, I'll kill him."

The elevator doors slid open. Cooper shook his head to clear it, then stepped out into the office. The sudden sunlight was bright but not clean, the air beyond the windows thick with dust. Shannon had looked up at him, quirked that grin of hers. The lawyer had twisted his lips. From behind the desk, the handsome hologram of Erik Epstein gestured him in.

It was only Millie who understood, though.

CHAPTER 28

The lawyer ushered them back the way they'd come, down the sun-smeared hallway and the tiered stacks of plants. Cooper paused at the door of "Epstein's" office, glanced back at the hologram. The thin, handsome doppelgänger met his eyes, started a smile, and then canceled it. They stared at one another for a moment. Then, slowly, the faux Epstein nodded and disappeared.

In the elevator, Kobb said, "I hope you realize what an honor that was. Mr. Epstein is a very busy man."

"Yeah," Cooper said. "It was eye-opening to meet him."

Kobb cocked his head at that, didn't respond. Cooper had suspected the lawyer didn't know, felt it confirmed. He wondered how many people did.

The doors slid open on the lobby, the massive tri-d tuned now to a nature show, lush jungle green, monkeys perched in the crooks of tree limbs, gauzy light filtering from a faraway sun. Shannon tucked her hands in her pockets, craning her neck. "Funny. After the display upstairs, this isn't quite as impressive."

"That's for sure." He turned to Kobb. "Thanks for the time."

"Certainly, Mr….Cappello. A pleasure. You can see yourselves out from here?" The lawyer spun on his heel, already checking his watch as he strode to the elevator. Late for something. He seemed the kind of guy who ran through his whole life heading for something more important.

"You okay?"

"Sure," Cooper said. "What did you talk to, uh, Epstein, about?"

"You. He asked if I thought you were telling the truth."

"What did you say?"

"That I'd seen you attacked by DAR agents. That you'd had plenty of opportunities to make sure I got arrested, and that you hadn't." She grinned. "Kobb stopped just short of advising Epstein to have us both arrested. I don't think he enjoyed that meeting."

"I don't get the feeling Kobb enjoys very much." They strolled through the lobby, heels clicking on the polished floor. "He must be a kick in bed, huh?"

She laughed. "Three to five minutes of church-approved foreplay, followed by restrained intercourse during which both partners think about baseball."

"Mr. Cappello?"

He and Shannon spun, easy enough but both shifting weight, softening the knees, positioning themselves back-to-back. They'd grown used to each other already, knew which side to cover if something went wrong. Funny.

The woman who had called his pseudonym wore too much lipstick and her hair in a tight bun. "Tom Cappello?"

"Yes?"

"Mr. Epstein asked me to give you this." She held up a tan calfskin briefcase, smooth and expensive looking. Cooper took it from her. "Thanks."

"Yes, sir." She smiled vacantly and turned away.

"What's that?" Shannon asked.

He weighed the case and his words. "Epstein is going to help me. But you know. Nothing for nothing."

"What are you doing for him?"

"Just an odd job." He gave her a bland smile and saw her read it, understand. She was in the biz, after all. Before she could ask a follow-up question, he said, "Listen, I know we're all done, but..."

She tilted her head, the idea of a smile crossing her lips. "But?"

"You feel like grabbing a bite?"

■

After all the whirling forward-thinking of New Canaan, the café seemed downright nostalgic. It wasn't, of course—he hadn't yet seen one art deco sign here, one ironic T-shirt—but the place was simple and straightforward, with curved plastic booths and mediocre coffee in stained cups. The change was welcome.

"Are you serious?" He took a swig of the coffee. "Your boyfriend really said that?"

"Cross my heart," Shannon said. "He said my gift was clearly a sign of insecurity."

"You may be many things, but insecure ain't one of them."

"Yeah, well, thank you, but I spent the next three weeks in my bathrobe, crying and watching soap operas. And then I heard he was dating this stripper chick with huge..." She held her hands out in front of her chest. "I mean, like, watermelons. And it occurred to me, maybe the problem was that he didn't want to be with a woman who could manage to not be noticed. If his new girlfriend rubbed two brain cells together, she didn't have a third to catch fire, but she sure got noticed." She paused. "Of course, that was probably because she was always toppling over."

He'd been sipping the coffee, and the laughter made him choke and sputter. The waiter arrived and set their orders down, a hamburger for her, a BLT for him, the bacon brown and crisp. He snapped an end off, crunched it happily. In the background, some young pop group sang young pop songs, all heartbreak and wonder you could dance to.

Cooper took a bite of his sandwich and wiped his mouth. Leaned back in the booth, feeling strangely good. His life had always had a surreal quality to it, but that had only grown stronger in the last months, and even more so in the last days. Not two hours ago he'd been in the glowing heart of a temple of sorts, watching the world's richest man swim currents of data.

The thought brought him back to the briefcase on the floor. He slipped his foot sideways, touched it again. Still there.

Shannon had cut her burger in half and then into quarters, but instead of eating one of them she was picking at her fries.

"What's on your mind?"

She smiled. "I know that bugged your wife, but I think she was looking at it the wrong way."

"Yeah?"

"Sure. Instead of having to sit here for five minutes trying to think of a way to broach the subject, I can just look distracted until you ask me about it."

He smiled. "So you gonna tell me what's on your mind?"

"You," she said. She leaned back, put one arm across the back of the booth, and hit him with a level gaze.

"Ah. My favorite subject."

"We're done, right? We're square?"

"Square? Are we in a gangster film?"

"You know what I mean."

"Yeah," he said. "We're square."

"So we don't owe each other anything anymore."

"What are you really asking, Shannon?"

She looked away, not so much to dodge his eyes, he could tell, as to stare into some middle distance. "It's weird, don't you think? Our lives. There aren't that many tier-one gifted, and of those, there are fewer who can do the kinds of things we can do."

He took a noncommittal bite, let her talk.

"And, I don't know, I guess I've just found it nice to be able to know someone like you. Someone who gets what I do, who can do things I get."

"Not just gifts," he said.

"Don't talk with your mouth full."

He smiled, chewed, swallowed. "It's not just the gifts. It's our lives, too. Not many people get the way we live."

"Exactly."

"Well, this is sudden, but I accept."

"What?"

"Oh," he said, faking dejection. "I thought you were asking to marry me."

She laughed. "What the hell. Why not. Vegas isn't far."

"No, but it's pretty dull these days." He set down his sandwich. "Jokes aside, I know what you mean. It's been good, Azzi."

"Yeah," she said.

Their eyes met. A moment before, her eyes had just been her eyes, but now there was more. A weird sort of recognition. A yielding in both of them, an acknowledgment, and, yeah, a hunger, too. They held the look for a long time, long enough that when she finally broke it with a throaty chuckle, it felt like something he'd been leaning against had vanished.

"So what does Epstein want you to do for him?"

He shrugged, the game back on, took a bite of the BLT.

"Right," she said. "Well, not for nothing, but I hope it's something you can live with, and if it is, I hope you do it. And then I hope you take advantage of the chance you've got here."

"Here being…"

"New Canaan. I know there's more on your mind, Nick. Things you're not telling me. But this place, it really can be a fresh start. You can be whatever you want to be here. And be welcome."

He smiled—

Does she know?

No. Suspects, maybe. Fear.

And she called you Nick.

—and said, "Well, that's the plan."

Shannon nodded. "Good." She pushed her plate forward. "You know what? I'm not hungry after all." She wiped her hands on her napkin, tossed it on the plate, and kept her eyes off his. "Tell you what. Once you've given Epstein his pound of flesh, if you do start up a new life, maybe you and I can continue this conversation."

He laughed.

"What?"

"It's just…" He shrugged. "I don't have your phone number."

She smiled. "Tell you what. Maybe I'll just appear. I know you get a kick out of me doing that."

"Yes," he said. "I really do."

She slid out of the booth, and he joined her. For a moment they faced each other, and then he put up his arms and she slid into them. A hug, nothing sexual, but there were hugs and *hugs*, and this was the latter, their bodies close, testing the fit, and the fit was good. When she let him go, he felt the absence like a presence.

"So long, Cooper. Be good."

"Yeah," he said. "You too."

She walked out with a sway he could tell was calculated, but no less powerful for that. Didn't look over her shoulder. He watched her go and felt a tug in his chest, a yearning. She really was something. It was like meeting someone exceptional while you were married: the yank of possibility, the realization that here was another path your life could have taken.

Only, you're not married. You could be with her. It's just that she'll hate you.

He sat back down, feeling heavy. Finished his BLT. When the waiter came round, he thanked him and asked for a refill of coffee. No, nothing wrong with the burger, turned out his friend hadn't been hungry after all. Just the check, when you get a second.

After the guy filled his coffee and set the bill on the table, Cooper reached for the briefcase. The calfskin was so soft it seemed to hum beneath his fingers. He set the case on the table and took a casual glance about. No one watching. Popped the latches, raised the lid a few inches.

Onionskin papers, an envelope, a set of car keys. He opened the envelope, discovered it was an itinerary. Someone was arriving at a particular address the day after tomorrow. He had a good guess who that someone was.

The car keys had a tag with an address on it.

The onionskin was schematics for a building.

And underneath them, nestled in foam eggshells, was a .45 Beretta. The same weapon he'd preferred.

Back when he'd been a DAR agent.

■

The address on the car keys turned out to be a parking lot on the outskirts of Tesla, a ten-dollar cab ride. When he arrived, he repeatedly thumbed the unlock button on the remote and followed the honk to a truck, not one of the electric cars but an honest-to-God gas-guzzler, a spotless four-by-four Bronco with heavy tires and power to spare. Cooper climbed in, adjusted the mirrors, opened the briefcase, and started reading.

Like everything Epstein did, the information was clear and well calculated. It had all Cooper needed but nothing that gave it away. If someone had looked in the briefcase, they might have guessed he was a secret agent, but they'd have had no idea that they were looking at plans for the assassination of the nation's most dangerous terrorist.

There was a map recommending a route from this parking lot to an address in Leibniz, a town on the west side of the Holdfast. A three-hour drive that seemed to take him out of the way; a closer look at the map showed that it skirted a research facility that no doubt raised the security standard.

The itinerary indicated someone arriving in Leibniz tonight and staying in a house nestled up against the Shoshone National Forest. Photos showed a pleasant cabin atop a mountain ridge. A second-story balcony and lots of glass would offer stunning views of pine forests sweeping to cottonwoods at the base. Four tall fingers of rock jutted improbably up a mile down the ridge. No nearby neighbors. Schematics showed that the cabin possessed a few security upgrades—cameras front and back, bulletproof glass, steel-frame doors on the ground level—but nothing startling.

It belonged to a woman named Helen Epeus. He didn't recognize the name, but there was something there, some connection he couldn't quite grab. *Let it marinate.*

The documents suggested Epeus was a lover. The unnamed target had visited before, often arriving at night and leaving in the morning. It stated that a small security team would be there as well, but dryly noted that "their motion within the house seems restricted."

Translation: Smith doesn't want his security team watching him get down.

He took out the sidearm. Thumbed the magazine release. A full load, hollow-points. Body armor would stop them, but if they hit flesh, they'd shred on impact, tiny razors spinning inside fragile tissue. Two spare magazines, though why he would need that many rounds he couldn't imagine.

Cooper had been army, never trusted a weapon he hadn't disassembled himself, so he took a few moments to break it down. Everything was clean and cared for. He put it back together with practiced ease, then locked the safety and put it back in the case.

When he was done, the sun had dropped and the clock read two. He started the truck, revved the engine a couple of times for fun, and rolled out.

■

It was doable.

The drive had taken a bit under the recommended three hours, Cooper not opening the truck up, but certainly making the most of the smooth, straight roads. The scenery changed as he moved west, growing greener—not lush, but the air was sweet. The sky seemed bigger than it had a right to, and bright, with dramatic clouds forming high above the mountains to the west. He raced from cloud shadow to cloud shadow, watching the world turn colors as he went and trying not to think too much. He had that mission energy, that sense he always used to get when weeks of patterning a target were starting to click together, as though destiny was a bright neon line he could follow down the pavement.

John Smith. The man who had watched as seventy-three people were executed in the Monocle. Who had orchestrated a wave of attacks across the country. Who had planted the bombs at the Exchange in New York that had killed 1,143 in a blast wave that had shaken Cooper free of his real life and cast him adrift on this strange new path.

Even after everything Cooper had read about him, after every speech he'd watched, every friend he'd met, after talking to the shithead administrator of that academy in West Virginia, the real John Smith was a mystery. There were the facts: his gift for strategy, his success as a political organizer, his ability to inspire people. There were the myths, which varied depending on which side you were on. There were the rumors and the whispers. There was Shannon, saying he was a nice guy and believing it.

But the man himself? He was a play of shadows, a dream of a monster or a hero.

And tonight, at long last, Cooper would get to meet him. A guy who apparently had friends and lovers, who visited a woman named Helen Epeus in a lovely house atop a mountain ridge.

He got his first glimpse at it from the highway, though he didn't stop, just slid to the right-hand lane and stole glances. The town of Leibniz was ten minutes away, and most of the places out here had the look of cabins, people who wanted more separation than even New Canaan offered. It made sense; not everyone had moved to Wyoming because they believed in the cause. Plenty of residents fell in that thin space between libertarians and anarchists, liked the idea of a place where they could be left alone. Where the world wouldn't meddle. He had a feeling that if he took the Bronco down any of the dusty two-tracks he'd find himself passing No Trespassing and Solicitors Warmly Greeted With Gunfire signs, eventually ending up at lonely compounds where anything from isolationism to anti-Semitism could be pursued in relative peace.

The cabins this close to town didn't radiate that vibe, though. They were more luxurious. Private homes for nature lovers.

An hour's recon told him that the information in Epstein's briefcase was good. He could see why the man had been nervous, eager to gain his complicity. This was as exposed as a reclusive terrorist was ever likely to be. The forest would provide plenty of cover for a cautious approach; the security detail, while no doubt consummate professionals, shouldn't have any reason to expect an attack and would be easy enough for Cooper to get past. And while Smith was a strategic genius, and probably a decent fighter, head-to-head he'd be no match.

It was doable. He could get in, and he could kill John Smith.

Getting out was trickier. If he could manage not to raise an alarm, he should be able to reach Smith easily enough. But the man would doubtless be wearing a biometric alarm. The moment his heart went crazier than sex could account for, and certainly the moment it stopped, the bodyguards would come in heavy. There would be no sneaking out. It would be run-and-gun.

Figure it out as it comes. That's when you're at your best anyway.

Besides, doable was more than he'd ever had before. He'd go in tonight, finish his mission, and after that, well, things would take care of themselves.

Yeah? And if you succeed, do you think his organization is just going to announce that John Smith has been murdered? If you don't make it out, no one at the DAR will know what you've accomplished.

That made the next move obvious.

■

He needed a landline. The DAR monitored all mobile calls within the NCH, the Echelon II software churning relentlessly through a billion bits of data. And he'd be willing to bet that Smith had some routine surveillance of his own; the only way he could have continued to avoid capture was to have a steady stream of good intel. Using a cell phone was too big a risk.

Anywhere else, that would have meant a payphone. They were still around, if you knew where to look: convenience stores, malls, gas stations. Anachronisms, holdovers that no one had bothered to rip out. But this was New Canaan. In this nostalgia-free new world, not only weren't there payphones outside the gas stations, there were hardly any gas stations.

Cooper ran through and dismissed half a dozen plans: booking a hotel room, offering a homeowner cash to use their phone, breaking into an apartment. All risked drawing attention.

He was cruising Leibniz, just driving for the sake of it, taking the place in. It followed what he was starting to see as a pattern in NCH towns. Wind turbines to the west, massive water condensers on the east. Streets smooth and laid out in a perfect grid. An airfield for gliders, pay lots to charge electric cars. Well-designed pedestrian areas and public squares filled with bright young people moving with purpose. Mixed zoning, commercial and residential side by side; it would be an easy place to live, all the advantages of a city without the congestion and pollution. Come to New Canaan and help build a better world. Lots of ambition and energy, sunshine and sex.

He stopped at a hamburger stand on the outskirts of town, got a burger and a Coke, the latter more expensive. Ate sitting at a picnic bench gilded by the lowering sun. Across the street was a car dealership, small by American standards, the lot packed mirror to mirror with the tiny electric cars he saw everywhere here. His Bronco was unusual, but it didn't draw stares; the countryside was still pretty rough, and there were limits to what a...

Got it.

Cooper finished his meal, wiped his hands, and drove the truck across the street. The car salesman was the same as car salesmen everywhere: easy smile, quick to get personal, just delighted he'd dropped in. "I'm thinking of making the switch," Cooper said, pointing a thumb at the Bronco. "Gas is killing me."

"You'll never look back," the guy said. "Let's take a walk, see what moves you."

Cooper followed the guy around the lot, letting the patter wash over him. Mileage between charges, top speed, amenities. He sat in a sedan, ran his hands over the hood of a sporty two-seater. Finally settled on a miniature pickup with horsepower that made him snicker.

"I know," the guy said, "she doesn't look like much compared to that beast of yours. But she'll go off-road, handle light hauling. A perfect work truck, and if you ever need something heavier, you can always hire it."

The negotiations took ten minutes, and Cooper let the guy take him. When they were done, he said, "Mind if I use your phone to call my financing guy? My cell's dead."

"Sure thing," his new best friend said, not quite hiding his delight. "Step into my office."

His office turned out to be one in a line of desks in the open showroom. Not as private as Cooper might have liked, but private enough; salesmen weren't supposed to sit down, and the other desks were abandoned. His guy gestured him to his own chair, then left him with assurances that he'd be nearby.

The number he'd memorized six months ago and never dialed. It rang twice, and then a voice answered, "Jimmy's Mattresses."

"This is account number three two zero nine one seven," Cooper said.

"Yes, sir."

"I need to talk to Alpha. Immediately."

"Alpha, roger. Hold please."

Cooper leaned back in the sales guy's chair, the springs creaking. Out the front glass, he watched traffic pass, watched the clouds shift and change, rays of sunlight stabbing down from between them.

There was a click, and then Equitable Services Director Drew Peters said, "Nick?" The voice was familiar even now, quiet with the assurance of command. Cooper could picture him in his office, slim headset over neatly trimmed hair, the framed photos of targets on the wall, John Smith among them. *Is my photograph on that wall as well?*

"Yes, it's me."

"Are you all right?"

"Fine. I'm on-mission."

"What was that scene last week?"

"What?"

"Don't toy with me, son. On the El platform in Chicago. Do you know that civilians were shot?"

"Not by me," Cooper said, surprised at the anger sloshing in his gut. "Maybe you better talk to your goddamn snipers." He bit down on the instinctual *sir*.

"Excuse me?"

"I didn't shoot anybody. And you're welcome, by the way. For, you know, giving up my entire life and becoming a fugitive. You want to talk scenes? Okay. How about Chinatown?"

"You're referring to the detention of Lee Chen and his family?"

"Shoplifters are detained. This was a tactical response team starting a riot and kidnapping a family. That little girl was eight."

Heard himself say *was* instead of *is*, hated himself for it. "What are you guys even fighting for?"

There was a pause. In a clipped, controlled voice, Peters said, "Are you finished?"

"For now." Cooper realized how hard he was squeezing the phone and forced his fingers to relax.

"Good. First of all, by 'you guys,' are you referring to agents of the Department of Analysis and Response? Because you might want to remember that you are one."

"I'm—"

"Second, that was your fault."

"What?"

"You were spotted. What were you thinking? To pull that stunt on the El and then, that very same night, just walk down the street?"

"What are you talking about?" Replaying the night back in his head, the cool air, the Chinatown neon. He'd been wired, alert to any hint of recognition, had caught none. "No one saw me."

"No. But Roger Dickinson ordered the entire Echelon II network tasked to randomly scanning the video feed from security feeds across the city. More than ten thousand of them. An ATM camera caught you and Ms. Azzi walking side by side through Chinatown. Once he had that, Dickinson pulled footage from every camera for half a mile. Putting it all together took a while, which is the only reason you weren't caught."

Cooper opened his mouth, closed it.

"Your rules, Nick. Your fault." Peters didn't raise his voice, and somehow that made the words hit all the harder. "You laid out the parameters in the first place, remember? *You* told *me* that the only way your plan would work was if we went all the way."

"I didn't mean—"

"It doesn't matter if you meant it. All the way is all the way."

Part of him wanted to scream, to bang the phone on the desk, to stand up and grip the chair and hurl it through the plate glass window into the Wyoming sun. But afterward nothing would have changed. Temper tantrums weren't going to make a difference.

"Roger Dickinson, huh?" Cooper switched the phone again, wiped sweat from one palm.

"He's certainly risen to the challenge." Peters gave a brief, clipped laugh. "You may have been right about him wanting your job."

"I should have anticipated the cameras," Cooper said. "Damn. Damn, damn, damn."

"You're playing against thousands of people. I'd say you're doing very well."

"What happened to Lee Chen and his family? Never mind. I know the answer. Can you help them?"

"Help them?"

"They don't know anything. Truly. He's just a school friend of Shannon's."

"They harbored two of the most wanted terrorists in America. They got caught. They'll face the penalty. They have to."

"Drew, listen to me. The girl, Alice. She's eight years old."

There was a long pause. Finally Peters sighed. "All right. I'll see what I can do."

"Thank you."

"Now. What's your status?"

"I'm…" He took a breath, straightened his back. The anger that had seized him, it was easy to understand. Over the last few days, he'd seen the lie in a lot of the truths he'd held self-evident. But none of that mattered, not right now. "I'm calling because I've got my opportunity. I'm going after the target." A minor risk; even if Smith had a world-class intelligence network, it couldn't extend to the desk phone of a car dealership. "He dies tonight."

"So you've really done it," Peters said.

"I'm about to."

"You have your exit strategy worked out?"

"I'll jump off that bridge when I come to it. That's why I'm calling. Just in case. I wanted you to know that I'm living up to our deal." Cooper paused. "And I wanted to hear that you are, too."

"Of *course*, son." Peters's voice rarely betrayed emotion, but Cooper could hear the hurt in it. "No matter what happens, I'll do that. You're a hero."

"Kate—"

"Your daughter will never be tested. I've already taken care of the existing record, and taken measures to make sure that there will never be another. She's safe. I gave you my word, Nick. Whatever happens, I'll take care of your family."

My family. He had a flash of that morning, months ago, whirling his children on the front lawn of their house. One of them clinging to each arm, the weight of trust and love tugging at him with a pull he never wanted to be free of. The green blur of the world beyond them.

What you've seen has changed you. Fine. But that doesn't matter. You're not doing this for the DAR.

You're doing it for them.

CHAPTER 29

Back in action.

In his life, Cooper had killed thirteen—no, counting Gary on the freeway, fourteen—people. That made him neither uncomfortable nor proud. It was just a fact. He wasn't a violent guy, didn't get off on hurting people. He was a soldier. When he acted, it was for a reason, and it was to save lives.

And yet he had to admit it felt good to be back in action.

The last six months had seen plenty of excitement. Some of it he'd enjoyed, testing himself, building a reputation that would allow him a chance to get closer to John Smith. But at the same time, it had felt like a holding pattern, something he was doing while his real life was waiting. His real life as a father, and his real life as a government agent, as a man fighting for a better future.

As of tonight, the holding pattern was over. He'd have this one chance at Smith. Succeed or fail, this phase would be behind him. No more pretending, no more running.

Well, that's not quite true. If you fail, there will likely be some running involved. He smiled and killed the engine.

The ridgeline the cabin sat on backed up to the Shoshone National Forest. After studying the maps and satellite imagery

Epstein had provided, Cooper had settled on a narrow fire lane two miles from the house as a place to leave the truck. Earlier he'd stopped at a hunting-goods store in Leibniz and bought supplies, and now he stripped down to his skivvies and put them on. A thermal base layer, camouflage pants and jacket, a pair of Vasque hiking boots, and light gloves. He'd splurged on good binoculars, Steiner Predators, which had set him back two grand. Worth every penny—not only would the newtech lenses let him see in the dark, the chipset analyzed the image and highlighted motion. The guy behind the counter had said, "You looking to do a little nighttime hunting?"

"Something like that." Cooper had smiled.

"These are the ticket, then. Need ammo?"

"I'm good."

He checked the Beretta now, then looked at the spare magazines, decided against them. If he needed to reload, he'd already lost. Besides, they could make noise if they knocked into something. Cooper locked the truck, tucked the keys under the bumper, and started walking.

The air was crisp and cool, sweet in the way that air was supposed to taste but rarely did. He savored it and the clean movement of his muscles, the warmth in his legs as he climbed. He moved steadily but without hurry, and by the time he'd hiked up the back of the ridgeline, the sky had faded from indigo to purple and finally a velvety black. The moon cast sleek, wet-looking shadows.

The ridgeline was rocky, the trees old and bent with wind. The towers of vertical stone looked even more like fingers, the hand of a giant pushing up from below. Cooper squatted and glassed the area. It took him a few minutes to pick the right tree: an enormous Ponderosa pine about two hundred yards from the cabin.

Ten minutes later, he was perched on a broad limb twenty feet above the ground. His gloves were sticky with sap, and the rich, sharp smell of pine rang in his nostrils. Through the bunched needles, he had a perfect view of Helen Epeus's home. It was an attractive place with a boxy Pacific Northwest flavor to the architecture. Lots of glass and stylish cedar siding gapped in clean rows. The windows glowed a homey yellow. A cozy, serene spot… except for the man walking the perimeter with a submachine gun.

The gun was cross-slung, the grip in easy reach of the man's right hand, and judging by the way he moved, he'd reached for that grip before. The guard had a quiet ease and a ready alertness that Cooper recognized. A man who knew how to handle himself.

No surprise. But is he expecting anything?

A split-rail fence about fifty yards from the cabin marked the boundaries of the property. The guard followed the fence, moving slowly, checking shadows and keeping an eye on the road below. Cooper lay still on the branch, glad of the base layer—the night was getting chilly—and watched. The Predators traced a thin red outline around the man, reacting to his steady motion. It took the guard about eight minutes to walk a circuit, and while he varied his route, he rarely strayed far from the fence. A professional, but not showing any sign of anxiousness.

Good enough. Cooper turned his attention to the house itself.

The Predators went white as they adjusted to the change from darkness to light, and then he could see right in: Shaker furniture, shelves lined with books and pictures, a cottage kitchen with a half-full coffeepot. The second guard reminded Cooper of a drill sergeant: silver crew cut, lean muscles, ramrod posture. Sarge poured himself a cup of coffee, then turned to talk to someone Cooper couldn't see. That would be guard number three; while John Smith might be chummy with his security detail, tonight was about romance. Smith would be upstairs.

Okay. Three guards. A fourth was technically possible, but it would have been sloppy to have three inside and only one out, and Smith would never tolerate sloppy tactics.

The rest of the house looked as expected. The ground-level doors and frames were steel, and the locks heavy. A camera gazed down on the back entrance. In all, it was solid security, the kind of setup that would make a civilian feel safe. But a long way from unbeatable.

So the question is, how are you going to beat it?

A broad balcony hung off the second floor. A sliding glass door led to a bedroom, probably the master. The lights were off, the queen bed smooth. Unoccupied. He didn't doubt he could get up to the balcony. Only, what then? The door was likely locked, and the glass bulletproof.

It was too bad Shannon wasn't with him; he had no doubt she could stroll right past. He, on the other hand, might have to go in heavy. Sneak up on the exterior guard. With a little luck, he could take him down silently. With a lot of luck, the guard would have a key.

What if he doesn't? Or the doors run off a keypad? Or the security team all wear biometric sensors, so they know if a man goes down?

Risky. He was confident he could do the security team, especially if he took them by surprise. But while that was happening, what was to say Smith wasn't sprinting out the opposite door?

Still, what choice was there—

The light in the master bedroom snapped on, framing a silhouette. The sound of the glass door sliding on the track seemed loud in the Wyoming night. The figure was backlit. Another guard? Cooper refocused the binoculars.

And nearly dropped them. The figure wasn't security. It wasn't a stranger.

It had been seven years since the photograph that decorated Drew Peters's wall had been taken, a young activist addressing a crowd.

Five years since the massacre at the Monocle, that horrifying video he'd watched countless times, the calm butchery of seventy-three civilians.

Two years since the last confirmed photo, a blurry image taken at a distance as he climbed into the backseat of a Land Rover.

Now, through the wavering lenses of his new binoculars, Cooper watched John Smith step onto the balcony.

He wore jeans and a black sweater. His feet were bare. As Smith reached into a pocket and pulled out a pack of cigarettes, it struck Cooper how much older he looked. Like the pictures of presidents before and after their first term, Smith seemed to have aged two decades in a handful of years. His dark hair had salted, and his shoulders had a heaviness to them. But his eyes were sharp as broken glass when he snapped a silver lighter and lit his cigarette. The night vision optics amplified the flame to a halo of fire that seemed to engulf him.

Cooper stared.

The most dangerous man in America seemed at peace. He smoked meditatively, the cigarette pinned between his first two fingers. The night was too cool for bare feet, but Smith didn't seem bothered. He just stood there, staring out at the darkness.

It was unbelievable. A clean shot, no wind, adequate visibility, the target unaware. If he'd had a rifle, he could have ended a war with one squeeze of his finger.

But you don't have a rifle, you have a sidearm, and at this distance you may as well try to take him down with harsh language.

Half afraid that if he turned away Smith would vanish like some sort of demon, Cooper panned the binoculars. It took him just seconds to spot the exterior guard. The man was in the worst possible position, almost directly between the pine tree and the cabin. Cooper could go through him, but not without alerting Smith.

You get one chance. There's too much at stake to rush it.

He took a deep breath, calmed his nerves. Turned back to watch the man smoke. Despite the fact that he had been waiting for this moment, had been planning for it, he was staggered by the emotional punch of it.

Here was the reason, Cooper realized, that he existed himself. That he had done the things he had done and slept soundly despite them.

Smith was everything he had fought all his life. Not just a murderer, not even a terrorist—a hurricane in human form. A tsunami, an earthquake, a sniper at a school, or a dirty bomb in the water supply. A man who didn't believe in anything beyond his essential rightness, who killed not because it would make the world better but because he strove to make the world more like him. Standing barefoot under a stunning Wyoming sky, smoking a cigarette.

When he finished, he flicked the butt into the night, the ember wild and loose and momentarily bright. Then he turned and walked back inside. A moment later the light in the bedroom went out. John Smith—

It's only nine o'clock. Hours before he'll go to bed.

Smokers never stop at just one.

Who locks the door of a second-story balcony behind him? Especially when he knows he'll be back soon?

—was done.

Cooper hung his binoculars over a branch. He wouldn't need them again. Moving carefully, he began to climb. When his boots crunched dry soil, he dropped to a heel squat, his back against the tree, and waited for the guard to come around again.

When he did, Cooper started counting Mississippis.

At 100, he rose and started walking. He wanted to run, but couldn't risk either the noise or a turned ankle. It took the guard about eight minutes to walk a complete circuit of the fence. 480 Mississippi.

He kept his eyes down so that the light from the cabin wouldn't wreck his night vision, and checked his footing with each step. The moon was bright, which was good and bad. Good because he could keep a decent pace, bad because it meant he'd be easier to spot. A flush of energy ran through him, the world dropping away. It was just him and the silvered ground and the breath in his lungs and the pressure of the Beretta in his waistband. At 147 Mississippi, he reached the split-rail fence. The guard was out of sight on the other side of the property. Holding on to a post, Cooper slung first one leg and then the other, and stepped into Helen Epeus's yard.

That name, it meant something, but damned if he could remember what. No time. He took a moment to assess the situation—

The guard is a professional. A soldier of sorts.

Soldiers learn to work as a team. A team that divides responsibilities and then trusts each man to fulfill his part is far more effective than one where every man is trying to cover every angle.

He'll leave the security of the cabin to the security in the cabin.

—then dropped to his elbows and knees and started a fast army crawl toward the cabin.

At 200 Mississippi, the guard rounded the far side of the building. Moonlight danced down the barrel of his submachine gun. Cooper kept crawling. Rocks jammed into his knees, and something thorny tore at his gloves.

He could go faster, but didn't dare. It felt to him as if he was making a lot of noise as it was, scraping the ground with each move. He locked his core and checked his breath and pushed.

240 Mississippi. The guard was half a football field away. Cooper had made it about fifty feet, not quite halfway between the fence and the cabin. He lowered himself prone. The hard ground was cold through his camouflage. With an effort of will, Cooper closed his eyes. Even in the dark, few things were more recognizable to one human than another human's face, especially the eyes, which could catch any spare glint of light.

If he was right about the guard, if the man trusted his team, then his attention would be focused outward. He'd be looking for motion in the woods, not for suspicious shapes lying between him and the cabin.

250 Mississippi. A shuffling of footsteps. Rocks and dirt beneath combat boots. The man couldn't be more than twenty feet away.

A pause. A scrape. Cooper's nerves screamed to move, to roll on his back and pull the pistol and fire. Lying prone, unable to see, he was completely helpless; he was rendering his own abilities moot.

There's more to you than just your gift, soldier.

He lay still.

265 Mississippi.

270 Mississippi.

The footsteps resumed. Cooper began to breathe again.

At 340, he opened his eyes and rolled to a crouch. The guard was out of sight. After the total darkness, the cabin seemed ablaze with light, light streaming out the windows, light leaking under the doors. Light framing the balcony. He rose and walked toward the house, no longer worried about being seen. Even if the interior guards happened to glance at a window, night would turn the glass into a mirror.

He rolled his shoulders, shucked his gloves, and dropped them. Then he pushed into a hard run, straight at the wall of the cabin. At the last second he leaped, planting one boot against the cedar siding and pushing upward as he strained and turned.

His hands caught the lip of the balcony. He hung for a moment to combat the lateral inertia, and then he pulled himself up, first to the spindles, then the handrail, and finally over, crouching in the same spot John Smith had smoked his cigarette.

His breath came easy. His senses were sharp. He felt powerful and free and alive.

Cooper drew the Beretta and moved to the glass door. The bedroom beyond still swam in darkness. So far, so good. He'd made a little noise against the wooden siding, but not much. If you lived in a cabin in the woods, you got used to unexpected noises: animals on the hunt, windblown branches scraping the eaves, long-dead trees finally giving way.

Of course, everything depended on the glass door being unlocked. He was confident in the logic of his patterning, but, as always with his gift, it came down to intuition, not certainty.

So stop stalling and find out if you win a gold star.

He put his free hand on the handle and tugged.

The door slid easily.

Pistol in hand, Cooper slipped inside.

CHAPTER 30

The bedroom was dark, but his eyes were ready. A queen bed with plush linens and too many pillows. Unruffled; if Smith and his lady friend had been at it, they'd done it somewhere else. Nightstand by the bed, rocking chair in the far corner, hardwood dresser. Master bath off the west side. A painting, big, something abstract in dark colors.

He held the gun low and in two hands, his finger resting gently on the trigger. It felt good, molded for his hands.

Sounds: his own breathing, a little faster than normal, but steady. A television from below, laugh track to a joke he couldn't hear. The ticking of the clock on the bedside table. He hated clocks that ticked; every click a moment gone. Couldn't imagine sleeping in a room with one, drifting into unconsciousness to the sound of life slipping away.

No alarm, no sounds of panic.

He moved to the bedroom door, which was closed but not all the way. Slid along the near wall and glanced through the crack. A hallway. Keeping his right hand on the gun, he used his left to inch the door open. It swung in silence. The hallway was hardwood, newish. Good. Old hardwood creaked.

Light on his feet, joints supple. The hall ran a handful of feet and then one wall fell away, a railing with cables instead of wooden spindles. Light from below, and the television louder. A great room, connected by a spiral staircase. Three doors, one open; he could see tile on the floor, a guest bathroom. Cooper eased down the hall, setting each step with care. The next door, also open. He squatted low, glanced around the edge. Guest bedroom, dark. The last door was closed, a trickle of light glowing at the bottom. He moved to it, stood outside. No noise he could hear. He gave it a twenty count with breath held, then another thirty breathing. Nothing.

He put his left hand on the knob. Moved to the side of the door. Gently spun the handle, weapon up and sweeping the room as it was revealed inch by inch.

Bookcases, a leather couch, soft and expensive looking. Two chairs facing it. A lamp and an ashtray on a table beside the couch. A door in the far wall, closed, no light from below. A gas fireplace halfway up the wall, the flames dancing; twin flatscreens mounted above it.

Both monitors showing the same video.

Cooper slid into the room, weapon up, eyes forward as he closed the door behind him, and then moved to look at the flatscreens.

The video was taken from a high angle, and showed men walking through a restaurant. Something squeezed inside him as he recognized it. The footage from the massacre at the Monocle on Capitol Hill. He'd seen it a thousand times, knew every frame. What was—

Wait. The flatscreens weren't showing the exact same video.

At a glance, yes. The motion was the same, the angle, the footage of the bar and the patrons, the judge with his young mistress, the family from Indiana. But in the leftmost monitor, there were four men walking through the crowd. One in the lead, and three behind.

In the right monitor, it was only the three behind, all wearing trench coats.

In the left, John Smith wound his way through the crowd, his soldiers following behind.

In the right, the soldiers walked alone.

In the left, John Smith walked to the back booth where Senator Max "Hammer" Hemner sat.

In the right, the three men approached his booth, but at an odd, indeterminate distance. As though there was a ghost in front of them.

In the left, Hammer Hemner smiled at John Smith.

In the right, Hammer Hemner smiled at three men who had approached his table.

In the left, John Smith raised a pistol and shot the senator in the head.

In the right, a hole just appeared in the man's head, as if fired from elsewhere in the restaurant.

In both monitors, the three bodyguards shrugged out of their coats, revealing cross-slung Heckler & Koch tactical submachine guns. Each took the time to extend the retractable metal stock and brace the weapon against his shoulder. The red light of an exit sign fell like blood against their backs.

In both monitors, they began to fire. Their shots were precise and clustered. There was no spraying, no wide sweeps.

A vein thumped in Cooper's neck, and his hands were slick with sweat.

In both monitors, the video froze. Then it scrubbed back ten seconds.

In the left, John Smith raised a pistol and shot the senator in the head.

In the right, a hole just appeared in the man's head, as if fired from elsewhere in the restaurant.

In both monitors, the three bodyguards shrugged out of their coats, revealing cross-slung Heckler & Koch tactical submachine guns. Each took the time to extend the retractable metal stock and brace the weapon against his shoulder. The red light of an exit sign fell like blood against their backs.

The video froze, and scrubbed backward.

Cooper had the sudden sense he was being watched, whirled, gun up. Nothing. Turned back to the monitor in time to see the action again.

To watch the three shrug out of their coats, the red light of an exit sign falling like blood across their backs. Their weapons rising.

Pause. Scrub back.

The three shrug out of their coats, the red light of an exit sign falling like blood—

There's something wrong.

Not just that John Smith isn't in one of these.

Something else.

You were meant to see this. He knows you're here. This is for you.

But there's something else *wrong.*

—across their backs.

Pause. Scrub back.

The three shrug out of their coats, the red light of an exit sign falling like blood across their backs.

Pause. Scrub back.

The three shrug out of their coats, the red light of an exit sign falling like blood across their backs.

It was the same. The red light was the same in both videos.

But in the one on the left, the one he knew, John Smith was between them and the exit sign. His body should have blocked some of the light. Not enough to throw an obvious shadow, but still, the red shouldn't have reached them. Certainly not the one nearest him.

But if that was true…

Cooper stared, feeling as if the ground had slipped away beneath him, as if he had turned to fog and could slip insubstantial through all that he thought solid.

Then he heard the door open behind him.

He spun, reflexes taking over, the gun coming up, right arm straight, left cradling the butt of the gun, both eyes open and staring down the barrel at the man who stood in the doorway. His features were balanced and even, strong jaw, good eyelashes. The kind of face a woman might find handsome rather than hot, the kind that belonged to a golf pro or a trial lawyer.

"Hello, Cooper," John Smith said. "I'm not John Smith."

CHAPTER 31

Cooper stared down the barrel. Instinct had framed the sights square on the man's chest. John Smith stared back at him, one hand on the doorknob, the knuckles white. His pupils were wide and his pulse throbbed in his throat.

Pull the trigger.

From behind and to one side, Cooper heard an unmistakable sound. What his old partner Quinn had once described as the best sound in the world, provided you were the one who made it.

The racking of a shotgun.

Smith made the tiniest head nod. Without lowering the pistol, Cooper risked a fast glance.

Somehow, Shannon stood in the corner of the room. She looked small behind the pump-action, but had it braced perfectly, the butt against one delicate shoulder. The barrel had been cut down to almost nothing; it was more scattergun than shotgun. Even at this distance, with the right load—and it would be, he had no doubt—there was nothing he could do to avoid it. Shannon's gaze was steady and her finger had pressure on the trigger.

How did she *do* that?

"I don't have your gift," Smith said. "But I'm pretty sure what you're thinking. You're figuring that there is no way she can fire before you do. And you're right. You can probably get at least one. Odds are decent you kill me. Of course, if you do, it's certain that she'll kill you."

The world had gone wobbly and fast, everything blurring and blending. He felt like his life had become the video loop, pause, scrub back, pause, scrub back, nothing certain, everything changeable. The man was locked in his sights. Smith was nervous, that was clear. He might hope that Cooper wouldn't do it, but he wasn't certain.

Everything in Cooper screamed to pull the trigger, to take the shot and drop John Smith and be done with it. To end this before…what?

Smith spoke as if finishing Cooper's thought. "The thing is, if you do, you won't find out what happens next. You won't learn the truth. Though you've already figured out the first bit. Haven't you?"

One gentle squeeze of the trigger, then another as swiftly as possible. Hollow-point ammunition tearing through soft flesh, lead splintering to shivering razor blades, wide gaping wounds. John Smith dead. Mission accomplished.

That was all he had to do.

Pull the trigger!

He tried to speak, but only raw sound came out.

"Haven't you?"

Cooper said, "The video is fake."

"Yes."

"You were never at the Monocle."

"I was, actually. Half an hour earlier. I met Senator Hemner. I had a gin and tonic, he had four scotches. He agreed to support some changes to a piece of legislation, an early bill limiting testing of gifted. I thanked him, and I left."

Take the shot take the shot take the shot take the…

"Look at me," Smith said. "I know you can tell when someone is blatantly lying to you. Am I lying?"

A thousand times he'd watched that massacre. Looked for every clue, for any hint that could lead him to the man who had perpetrated it. He'd noticed the red light, but not that it should have been blocked. And how would he? It was only when compared with another version that it even seemed odd.

His version could be a fake. He's had time to do that, nothing but time—

But the official version is the one with the problem.

"There's more," Smith said. "A lot more. But you're going to have to put that down to hear it."

"Nick," Shannon said, her voice low but firm, tinged with a note of hope, maybe, or regret for something that hadn't happened yet but might. "Please."

He glanced at her. Saw that she would shoot him. Saw that she didn't want to.

A sudden wave of exhaustion swept him. A sense that the props that held him up had been kicked out.

But if this is true, it...

He stopped the thought. But lowered the gun.

"Thank you," Smith said.

"Fuck you," Cooper said.

"Fair enough. I'd feel the same, in your position."

Shannon said, "Cooper, how about you set the gun on the table? I'll set mine down, too."

He looked at her. She was back to calling him Cooper, he noticed, though it had been Nick a moment before. Funny, only Natalie and Drew Peters called him Nick. And now Shannon, exactly twice.

"How about," he said, "you go first?"

He waited for her to look at Smith. Told himself that if she did, he would snap the gun up and fire, execute his target.

Shannon bit her lip. Her eyes never left his.

She dropped the barrel of the gun, let it dangle from one hand. *Huh.*

Like a man in a dream, Cooper figured what the hell, set the safety, then tossed the gun on the table. What was the worst that would happen? They'd kill him?

They already have.

The thought came unbidden, a voice in a dark room. And just what the hell did it mean? He didn't know.

"Okay," he said. Trying for something like casual, but not sure he'd hit it. "Fine. Let's talk."

Smith seemed almost to sag, the tension streaming out of him. "Thank you."

"You weren't sure I wouldn't kill you, were you?"

"No. It was a risk. Calculated, but a risk."

"Why take it?"

"I wanted to meet you. No reward without risk."

"What did you mean when you said you weren't John Smith?"

"My dad's last name wasn't Smith. My mother never named me John."

"I know, you got it in the academy, boo-hoo. But you—"

"Kept the name they gave me. Yeah. Remember how in the civil-rights days, Malcolm X used to talk about giving up his slave name? Claiming his own? Well, I'll do the same, as soon as people like me aren't slaves. Right now, I want to remind everyone that I am what they made me."

"You're a terrorist."

"I'm a soldier on the losing side. But the John Smith you've chased, the monster who kills children, who murdered seventy-three people in the Monocle, he's not me. That John Smith wasn't born. He was created. Because he served someone's purpose."

Cooper could feel his gift surging, patterning, building from data. The same way it always did, the way he couldn't control any more than someone could choose not to be able to think. As always, the intuitive part of it was leaping ahead, building from the pattern, and he wanted it to stop, because if that was true, if this was true—

"*If* the video is fake," he said, knowing it was but not wanting to say it out loud, not sure of the reasons, "then who faked it?"

"Wrong question," Smith said. He slid a hand toward his pocket, froze, said, "I could use a smoke. You mind?" He didn't wait for a reply, but did move slowly, pulling out the pack and matches. Cooper catalogued the room, remembered the ashtray on the side table. *So why did he step out before—*

Because he wanted you to see.

He knew you were out there, and he gave you a way in.

Smith continued, lighting the cigarette around his words. "It's not who faked the video"—snap, puff, exhale—"it's who planned and executed the massacre. It's who recruited, organized, and armed a methodical, highly skilled hit team and sent them to murder seventy-two innocent civilians and a senator. Faking the footage was just the cover-up. And the payoff."

It was obvious and new at the same time, a paradigm shift that altered the whole world. Not just a faked video, but an orchestrated massacre. His gift filled in the pattern, dancing with new data—*stop*.

"Okay, so who…"

Smith walked around the end of the couch, flopped down on it. He ashed the cigarette and gestured to the opposite chair. Cooper ignored him. Smith said, "You play chess?"

"No." He did, but not the way Smith meant. No one played the way Smith meant.

"The secret to the game is that beginners—actually, intermediate players, too, and sometimes masters—they tend to look at just the one side. But the trick to chess is to be paying more attention to what the other side is doing."

"Okay."

"Right," Smith said. "Get to it. Fine. So, what did the Monocle accomplish?"

"It...a declaration of war. The murder of a senator who opposed you."

"There are plenty of people who hate abnorms a lot more than Hemner did. And why would I want to declare war? When I was fourteen, I played three simultaneous games of chess against three grand masters, and won them all. What are the odds that with no chance of victory, I declare war? No, you're still thinking with your side of the board. Who benefited from the massacre?"

You, Cooper wanted to say, but found that the word stuck. How exactly had Smith benefited? Before the Monocle, Smith had been an activist, a controversial figure but a respected one, and free. Afterward he had become the most hunted man in America. He'd had to abandon his whole life, to live for years as a fugitive with a target on his back.

"There you go. You're getting it."

"So what, you're not just a strategic genius, you're a reader, too?" The old smart-ass side coming out.

Smith shook his head. "I just know people. What happened after the Monocle?"

"You know what happened."

"Cooper," Shannon said. "Come on."

He glanced at her, couldn't untangle her expression. To her, he said, "Fine. I'll play. After the Monocle, John Smith became a national figure. A terrorist. He was hunted from one end of the country to the—"

"Yes." The look John Smith gave him was sad and warm at the same time, like a friend delivering bad news. "Yes. By whom?"

If this is true, it means that...

"No. I don't believe it."

Smith said, "Don't believe what, Cooper? I haven't told you anything."

—*Drew Peters, the day he recruited you. Saying that the program was extreme, but that it was necessary.*

The early days of Equitable Services, working out of the paper plant. The constant rumors of getting shut down. The limited funding. The investigation. The threat of a congressional subcommittee.

Then the Monocle.

Seventy-three people dead, including a senator, including children. At the hands of an abnorm.

A stunning validation of the vision of one man. One man who saw this coming. Who saw that the DAR needed the ability to go further than just monitoring.

That it needed to be able to kill.

Drew Peters, neat and trim, cool gray in his rimless glasses.

Drew Peters, saying that he needed believers.

Oh God—

"If this is true, it means that...that..." He couldn't say the words, couldn't let them float in the air. If this was true, it meant that everything else was a lie. That he hadn't been fighting to prevent a war. That he had been part of starting one. That the things he had done, the targets he had terminated...

The people he had killed...

The people he had murdered.

"No," Cooper said. "No." He looked at Shannon, saw nothing but sympathy on her face. Turned from it, recoiled, to Smith. And saw the same expression. "No."

"I'm sorry, Cooper, I really am..."

And then he was running.

PART THREE: ROGUE

CHAPTER 32

Out of the room, down the hall, through the bedroom, onto the balcony, over the railing, through the air, hitting hard. Behind him voices he was barely conscious of, a man, shouting something, something like *Stand down! Let him go!*, and the guard with his MP5 up but frozen, looking over his shoulder, Cooper thinking *slide-tackle to drop him, spin, elbow to the solar plexus, right-hand chop to the throat*, doing none of it, just sprinting past the stunned guard, the cold air slicing in and out of his lungs, his legs scissoring fast, feet slamming the ground, trying to outrun the things he'd heard, the pattern that formed in front of and behind and all through him, the gift that he couldn't turn off, the gift that had become a curse, the cold and relentless intuitive leap that put the pattern together, the pattern that had been right in front of him all this time but in the dark, brought into sharp relief by the illuminating influence of a handful of facts and a little nudging, all of which he could have done himself but never had, and the consequences of that, the unbelievable, horrifying, consequences—

"*I need true believers.*"

Drew Peters had said that to him the first time they met, and several times since, never so many that Cooper had thought it more than a call for a certain kind of loyalty, a loyalty Cooper possessed, a willingness to do hard things for a greater good. That was all it had ever been, never a delight, never. In the power, sure, and the freedom, the position, but never the act itself, not the killing but the cause. He had done what he'd done to stop a war, not to start one, to save the world, not to—

Flashes: the moon cutting silver swathes through swaying trees.

A branch he stumbled on cracking, the dry white interior like bone.

His hands, pale against pine bark.

Finally, a tiny stream glowing in the moonlight, the water burbling clean over rocks worn smooth. His knees in the water, the shocking cold of it.

If what they had shown him was true, then Equitable Services was a lie.

An extreme arm of a government agency asking for powers never granted another. The power to monitor, hunt, and execute American citizens.

An agency that was hobbling along. Barely surviving. About to be investigated. And then, suddenly, vindicated.

Granted enormous power. Unspecified funds. Direct access to the president.

Because of a lie.

John Smith didn't kill all those people in the Monocle.

Drew Peters did.

You have spent the last five years working for evil men. You have done what they asked you to do. You believed. Truly.

John Smith isn't the terrorist.

You are.

"Cooper?"

He heard her now. At a distance, looking for him. The sound of breaking twigs, the shuffle of dirt. She wasn't a ghost after all.

He knelt there, in the stream, the water soaking through his pants, the moon glowing above. Didn't want to be found. Didn't want to hear any more.

"Nick?"

"Yeah," he said. Coughed. "Here."

He scooped up double handfuls of water, splashed them on his face. The cold shocking, clarifying. Knee-walked out of the stream, dropped on the bank. Listened to her approach, and for once saw her coming, sliding lithely between the trees.

Shannon hesitated for a moment when she saw him there, then adjusted her course. She splashed through the stream, then dropped down beside him. He saw her think about putting a hand on his shoulder, and decide against it. He waited for her to speak, but she didn't. For a long moment they sat side by side, listening to the trickle of the water, burbling like an endless clock.

"I thought you were still in Newton," he said, finally.

"I know," she said. "Sorry."

"That thing you said. In the diner. About hoping I took the chance for a fresh start."

"Yeah."

"You knew I was coming here."

"He did. I was hoping…" She shrugged, didn't finish.

Somewhere nearby, a bird screeched as it dove, and something squealed as it died.

"A couple years ago," Cooper said, "I was tracking a guy named Rudy Turrentine. A brilliant, medical. A cardiac specialist at Johns Hopkins. He'd done some incredible stuff in his early career."

"The Turrentine valve. The procedure they do now instead of heart transplants."

"Yeah. But then he'd gone over to the other side. Joined John Smith. Rudy's latest design had this clever new gimmick. It could be remotely shut off. Send the right signal, and bam, the valve quit working. It was hidden deep in the coding, some sort of enzyme thing, I never really understood it. Point was, it gave Smith the power to stop the heart of anyone who'd had this procedure done. Potentially tens of thousands of people."

She knew enough not to say anything.

"Rudy ran, and I found him. Hiding in a shitty apartment in Fort Lauderdale. A multimillionaire, this guy, and a brilliant, and he was holed up above a payday-loan place in the part of town tourists don't go to." Cooper rubbed at his face, a trickle of water still left there. "My team surrounded the building, and I kicked in the door. He was watching TV, eating pork fried rice. It was greasy, I remember that. You could smell it. It struck me as funny, this heart specialist eating heart-attack fare. He jumped, and it went everywhere. A short guy, shy. He looked at me, and he…"

After a long pause, Shannon said, "He?"

"He said, 'Wait. I didn't do what they say.'" A sob came from somewhere. It took him by surprise, a sob like a hiccup, and he couldn't remember the last time he'd cried.

Shannon said, "Shh. It's okay."

"What did I do?" He turned to look at her, his gaze locked on her eyes glowing in the moonlight. "What have I done?"

She took a long moment before she spoke. "Did you believe it? That he could turn off people's hearts?"

"Yes."

"Then what you did, at least you thought you had a reason for it. You thought you were doing good. It's the people who lied to you that you should blame."

Cooper had a flash of Rudy Turrentine's arms, flailing in wild punches as he stepped closer, as he moved where the man wasn't swinging, as his own hands reached for the doctor's head, as they twisted, sharp and hard, fast, always fast, never making it take longer than it had to.

"I've done things, too, Nick." Her voice flat with effort. "We all have."

"What if he was telling the truth? What if he hadn't done it? What if, I don't know, some competitor had pledged millions in campaign contributions if Rudy Turrentine died?"

"What if you killed an innocent man."

"What if I killed an innocent *genius*. A doctor who could have saved thousands of lives."

It seemed there was nothing to say to that. He didn't blame her; he couldn't come up with a reply either. The water trickled, trickled, trickled away.

"I've been used. Haven't I?"

She nodded.

He made a sound that wasn't much like a laugh. "It's funny. All my life, the thing I've hated most was bullies. And it turns out, I am one."

"No," she said. "Misled, maybe. But you meant to do the right thing. I know that much about you. Believe me," she said, and did laugh, "I didn't want to think so. Remember on the El platform, I told you that you'd killed a friend of mine?"

"Brandon Vargas." The abnorm bank robber who'd killed a mother and her two-year-old. Reno, Vargas smoking a Dunhill behind a biker bar, his hands shaking.

"Once upon a time, Brandon and I were close. So I wanted revenge. John had told me that you were a good man, but I didn't believe it. I wanted you to be a monster, so I could get payback." She brushed hair behind one ear. "But then you turned out to be, well, you."

He weighed those words, the freight behind them. "Brandon. Was he really—"

"Yes. He really did rob those banks, and he did kill those people. The Brandon I knew was a sweetheart. He'd never have done that. But…he did." She turned to him. "Not every moment of your life has been a lie. Some of the things you did for good really were for good."

"But not all."

"No."

He rocked forward, hugging his knees. "I want it not to be true."

"I know."

"And if it is, then I want to die."

"*What?*" Her body tensed and her face changed. "You coward. You don't want to make it right. You don't want to fix it. You want to *die?*"

"How can I make it right? I can't take it back. I can't bring Rudy Turrentine—"

"No. But you can tell the truth."

It tripped alarms up and down him, a tingle and vibration up his spine. "What are you talking about?"

"Your boss, your agency—they're evil. They are everything you say you're against. You hate bullies? Well, guess what Equitable Services is?"

"And you have an idea how to fix that."

"Yeah. I do." She brushed the hair again. "There's evidence. Of what your boss, Peters, what he did. At the Monocle."

Now the laughter did come, though there was no humor in it. *Of course.*

"What?"

"That's why you really came out here, isn't it? You're step two. Step one, make me see the truth. Step two, set me on some mission for John Smith."

It was hard to gauge the full depth of her reaction in the darkness, but he could see her eyes change. Recognition, and maybe a sense of being caught. But something else, too. Like he'd wounded her.

"I'm right, aren't I? He wants me to do something."

"Of course," she said, and stared at him unblinking. "Why else would he take these chances? And I want you to do it, too. And if you're done with the woe-is-me bullshit, so do you. Because even if there is a step two, step one was *tell you the truth.*"

He'd been about to reply, to talk about how he didn't work for terrorists, but that hit like a kidney punch. The truth. Right. Cooper scooped up a handful of pebbles, shook them. Tossed them, one at a time, to plunk in the stream.

After a moment, Shannon said, "You remember what I said in that shithole hotel? We were watching the news. They were reporting on what we'd just done, and none of it was true."

Only a week or so ago, and yet it felt like a lifetime. The memory was clear, the two of them bickering like an old married couple. "You said maybe there wouldn't be a war if people didn't keep going on TV and saying there was."

"That's right. Maybe, just maybe, the problem isn't that there are normals and brilliants. It isn't that the world is changing fast. Maybe the problem is that no one is telling the truth about it. Maybe if there were more facts and fewer agendas, none of this would be happening."

There was something in the way she said it, clean and no bull, just fire and purity of purpose. That and the way the moonlight glowed on her skin, and the way his whole world had turned upside down, and the animal need for comfort, and the way she smelled, and the way she'd felt against him that night in the bar, and, tired of thinking, he just leaned over.

Her lips met his. There was no surprise and no hesitation, maybe just the hint of a smile, and that gone in the moment. Cooper put a hand on her side and she wrapped both of hers around his back and their tongues flickered and touched, the warmth against the chill of the night as sensual as it was sexy, and then she shoved him.

He fell, landed on his back on the hard ground, pebbles digging into him. Surprise took his breath, and for a moment he wondered what she intended, and then she climbed on top of him, her knees straddling his hips, her body writhing against his. Light and strong, delicate and fierce, her breasts raking his chest, those clavicles like the wing bones of birds, the taste of her.

She broke the kiss, pushing away a playful couple of inches. A knowing smile and a fall of bangs. "I just remembered something else you said."

"Yeah?" His hands slid down her back, cradled her midriff, slim enough his fingers almost touched.

"I said you must be a hell of a dancer. And you said, maybe if somebody else led."

He laughed at that. "Lead on."

She did.

CHAPTER 33

"Wake up."

Cold. It was cold. He heard the words through a haze, far away. Ignored them, grabbed at the covers and found—

"Wake up, Cooper."

—a clump of something like pine needles in his hands, and the bed hard. Cooper's eyes snapped open. He wasn't in a bed, and there weren't covers, just half-discarded clothing piled atop them. A pine grove, and the trickle of a stream, and Shannon making sleepy murmurs. A shape above him, a man.

John Smith said, "Come on. I want to show you something." He turned and started walking.

Cooper blinked. Rubbed at his eyes. His body had gone stiff and sore.

Beside him, Shannon stirred. "What is it?"

"We fell asleep."

She sat up suddenly, and the jacket they'd been using as a blanket slipped down, revealing her breasts, small and firm, the nipples dark. "What's going on?"

"He wants me to go with him." He gestured after the figure. The sky had lightened enough to bring faint color to the trees.

"Oh," she said. Still coming round. "Okay."

"I can stay."

"No." She rocked her neck to one side, the vertebrae cracking. Winced. "This is twice we've woken up badly. We're going to have to work on that."

"I'm willing to practice if you are."

She smiled. "You better go."

Smith had kept walking, wasn't looking back to see if he would follow. *Because he knows I will.* Cooper looked at her, saw that she knew it, too.

"It's okay," she said. "Really."

He stood creakily. Remembering the way they'd moved, like partners who had been dancing a long time. Her riding him under the moonlight, her head thrown back, hair flying free, Mediterranean skin gone pale against the spill of stars, the Milky Way. Both of them delaying, taking their time, slow fast slow, going until they were exhausted, and when they were spent, her collapsing against his chest. The feel of her sweet and warm, they wouldn't fall asleep, they'd just take a minute...

"Well, that was a first."

She quirked her sideways grin and said, "Imagine the second. Now, go."

He found his pants, pulled them on. She said, "Hold on." Reached a hand up and grabbed his shirt. The kiss was deep and sweet. His eyes were mostly closed, and when he opened them, briefly, he saw that hers were, too.

"Okay," she said. "I'm done with you."

He barked a laugh and stumbled after John Smith, buttoning his shirt as he went.

It was maybe four thirty, five in the morning. A thin mist hung low, and the sky had softened enough to hide the stars. His breath was fog. His head, too. He didn't push it, focused on motion, working out the cramps in his legs, getting some blood flowing. He knew the thoughts would come, and the memories, and they wouldn't all be of sexual abandon.

And by the time he'd caught up to Smith, he was…what? Not himself. He wasn't sure what that meant anymore. The self-assured agent? The idealist willing to kill for his country? The father who taught his children to hate bullies?

The most wanted man in America had his hands in his pockets and his eyes on the peaks Cooper had noticed the day before, the spires rising from the ridge like fingers. "How's your balance?"

Cooper looked at him, auditioned a dozen smart-ass remarks. Then he started moving, heading for the base of the tallest spire. Smith joined him. They didn't speak, just walked, the ground rapidly growing steep, tree cover falling away. At first Cooper's mind ran in a loop, replaying everything he'd learned the night before, looking for holes, desperate for them. Within half an hour, though, the incline had grown intense enough that thought was replaced with action, step step step breathe, step step step breathe. Soon he was using hands as often as feet, the rock rough against his fingers. The base of the towers was a scree field, loose flat stone that skittered and slipped beneath his feet. It was noisy and treacherous, every step holding the risk of picking the wrong rock and surfing it down, a sure ticket to a broken leg at the least. They were both panting now, Cooper's shirt soaked with sweat.

The fingers turned out to be towers of blocky boulders fifty yards high. Smith started on one side; Cooper pulled himself up the other. The grips were solid and broad, and he climbed with confidence as the ground fell away. There was a heart-stopping moment when a foothold crumbled, but his arms held, and he jammed his toes in a narrow crack and continued up. After a few minutes Cooper tilted his head back and saw that the top was only twenty feet above. Energy surged through him, and he pushed into motion. No way was Smith beating him there.

If it had been a race, they'd have needed a replay to confirm the winner. Cooper thought it had been him by a nose, pretty much literally, hauling himself face-first onto the rocky peak. And then they were sitting on top of the world and, for just an instant, grinning at each other, no thought behind it, no promises, just two men recognizing the essential stupidity and joy of what they had done together.

The summit was about eight feet wide. Cooper crawled to the other side and looked over, felt vertigo twitch in his belly for the first time. On this edge the ridge fell away dramatically, a sheer drop of four hundred feet. He pushed back and sat cross-legged. Dawn now, the sky bright, though the sun still played coy. "Nice view."

"Thought you'd like it," Smith said, looking at his hands. There was blood on them, a scrape, and he wiped them on his pants. "You okay?"

Cooper heard the multiple meanings in the question, had a flicker of insight into the man. There would never be just one thing happening here. Always levels. He couldn't turn off his gift for tactical thinking any more than Cooper could turn off his patterning.

Even now, patterning the man. "I just got it."

"Got what?"

"Helen Epeus. Epeus built the Trojan horse. And Helen, she was the reason for the war. There was no woman waiting for you. It was a joke."

Smith smiled. Layers of meaning. Who knew how deep they ran?

"So we're here," Cooper said, "for symbolic reasons, right? Two guys waiting for the sunrise. No baggage up here. Can't climb with it."

"Something like that, yeah."

"What you told me last night. It's true?"

"Yes."

"That's how we're going to do this. I want truth. No agendas, no goals, no manipulation. No underlying reasons, no rationalization. Just truth."

"Okay."

"Because, John, I'm in a ragged place, emotionally speaking. And it's entirely within the realm of possibility that I decide to throw your ass off this rock."

He saw the words hit, saw that Smith believed him. To his credit—whatever else he was, he wasn't a coward—Smith said, "Okay. But it goes both ways. You ask a question, I ask a question. Deal?"

"Fine. Did you blow up the Exchange?"

"No. But I was going to."

"You planted the bombs."

"Yes. I also had Alex Vasquez set to cripple military response at the same moment, and a few other strikes that I aborted."

"Why?"

"Because I got beaten." Smith scowled, and goddamn if there wasn't embarrassment behind it. "I hate to say it, but it's true. I underestimated the ruthlessness of my opponent. Fatal mistake."

"Explain."

"The Exchange had no tactical value, didn't hurt me per se. Destroying it was a symbolic stroke. But sometimes those are the most effective. I wanted to refocus the country on the idea that if there's going to be a future together, then we need to start thinking of it that way." Smith raised his arms up, stretching them out. "So I planned to blow it up. But when it was empty."

"That's easy to claim."

"It's not a claim, Cooper. It was the point. If we're going to coexist, the normal world has to stop trying to find ways to exclude us. Destroying the building was a way of saying that. But butchering a bunch of innocent people, what good would that do me? That would only hurt our cause. As, in fact, it did."

Shannon had said the same thing. Of course, she would have heard it from him. Cooper said, "You had to know that targeting it put innocent people at risk."

"A calculated risk. I wasn't *hoping* it would be empty. I *planned* for it to be."

"Nice work."

"As I said, I got beaten."

"What was the plan?"

"To release a video to every major media organization announcing that I planned to blow up the Exchange at two o'clock the following day. In it I'd say that any effort to disarm the bombs would result in me triggering them early. That they had until then to clear everyone out and evacuate the area."

"So why didn't you release it?"

"I did."

"You—what?" Cooper had been jumping ahead, old interrogation habits, and the answer threw him.

"I did release it. Sent it to seven media outlets. The networks, CNN, MSNBC, even Fox."

"But—"

"But you didn't see it." Smith nodded. "Yeah. That was where I got beat."

"You're saying that you sent the warning, and that none of the networks—"

"None of them aired it. Not one. Not before, and not after. Seven allegedly independent media organizations knew that I intended to blow up the building. They knew that it would happen around two o'clock. They knew that if they didn't broadcast it, people would die. Eleven hundred and forty-three people, as it turned out."

Vertigo strobed through Cooper again, though he sat nowhere near the edge. "You're saying someone *blocked* that story?"

"Yes. Spiked it seven times. My turn. Who has the power to do that?"

Cooper hesitated.

"Who can convince, or force, seven independent networks to bury a story? Could a rogue group do it? A terrorist?"

"No."

"No. Only someone in the system. Only the system itself."

"Drew Peters again."

"Maybe." Smith shrugged. "I don't know exactly. All I know is, when they didn't air that video, when I saw that the government wasn't evacuating, I realized what would happen if those bombs went off. And so I activated my contingency plan."

"Shannon."

"Shannon."

Cooper thought back to that moment six months ago, his running down the hall at her, Shannon looking up, telling him to wait, that he didn't understand. Jesus.

Would she have succeeded in stopping the bombs if he hadn't caught her? Was this one more load on his creaking conscience?

"So who benefits from something like this, Cooper? Who benefits from the Exchange blowing up?"

"You asked your question."

"Call this a follow-up."

He knew the answer, both the one Smith wanted to hear and the larger truth behind it. Yesterday, he couldn't have imagined admitting it. But this morning, as the first sharp rays of the sun split the horizon, he just said what his gift told him. "People who want a war."

"That's right. People who want a war. People who believe that it will make them richer, or more powerful. A few, even, who might truly believe that a war is necessary. But while there have been a handful of times in history when war truly was necessary, never, not once, has a war against our own children been justified. No, the people who want to start this war, they want to benefit from it."

"How did the bombs go off if you didn't trigger them?"

"Is that your question?"

"Call it a follow-up."

Smith laughed. "All five had a radio trigger with a specific code frequency. No one but me knew the code."

"So how—"

"Because I warned them."

He stopped talking, let Cooper work it out. "Your message gave someone enough time to find the bombs and break the code."

"Again, I didn't realize just how ruthless my enemy was. I knew they hated me, knew they wanted a war. But even I never believed they would blow up their own building, kill a thousand people, just to foster it."

"But…why?"

"Men will always find a reason."

Cooper thought about that. Thought that it was probably true. "Next question. What about the rest?"

"The rest?"

"The other things you've done. Assassinations. Explosions. Viral attacks. All of it."

A long silence. The sun broke the horizon, spilling bloody light across the east. As if on cue, Cooper heard birdsong, though he couldn't see any birds.

Finally Smith said, "Are you asking if my hands are clean? They're filthy. I'm sorry, but you wanted truth."

"You are a terrorist."

"I'm fighting a war. I'm fighting for my human rights, and the rights of people like me. I'm fighting for you, and Shannon, and the other million of us. Like your daughter."

Cooper found himself on his feet before he realized he'd moved. "Be careful, John. Be very careful."

"Oh, come off it." Smith looked up at him mildly. "You want to kill me? You can. I'm no match for you in a fight. I knew you could last night, and I knew you could when I brought you up here. You don't want me to talk about Kate? Fine. But I'm not the one who wants to put her in an academy."

"That's not going to happen."

"Why? Because you throw me off this rock?"

"Because…" Drew Peters's voice in his head. *Your daughter will never be tested. Whatever happens, I'll take care of your family.*

He sank to his knees. No more. Please. Enough. Not them, too.

I'll take care of your family.

"No one has clean hands," Smith said. "Not me, not Shannon, not you. But the system is the bloodiest. The new world is being forged one gear at a time, and those gears drip blood. My turn. What kind of world do you want for your abnorm daughter, Cooper? And while we're at it, what kind of world do you want for your normal son?"

He fought for breath. *I'll take care of your family.* In his effort to protect them, in his blindness, he'd left them under the protection of the most dangerous man imaginable. To protect his children, he'd let a lion into their bedroom.

No.

"This evidence," Cooper said. "Shannon said you had evidence. Of the things you're claiming."

"That's a longer story."

"I've got time."

"After I met Senator Hemner at the Monocle, I headed home. Never made it. I saw police all along my block, my apartment lit up with floodlights. I didn't know what was going on, but I knew enough to run. Which was what Peters wanted. What's the point of creating a myth like John Smith if you catch him right away? Better to let him run. To let him lurk out there in the darkness, a national boogeyman. More funding in it." He laughed without humor.

"So I ran, and I transformed myself from an activist into a soldier. I started building an army. And then I went digging. I wanted to know who my enemy was.

"It didn't take long to figure out that it was Equitable Services. Your agency benefited more than any other. But that wasn't proof. I had the why, and the who. So I went after the how."

"The how?"

"Someone had orchestrated the massacre. That same person had faked the footage of it. That was exceptional work. It had to be perfect, or as near as possible. That meant a gifted. A man who can do with image and media what I can do with a chessboard or what Shannon can do with a crowded room. That was all I needed to know to find him."

"What happened?"

"I asked him questions," Smith said dryly.

"You tortured him."

"No clean hands, remember? This man ruined my life and threatened the existence of my whole race. So yes, I asked firmly. He came clean about the forgery quickly enough."

The sun was moving fast now, the air warming every moment. Cooper stared into it, said, "If you had proof the Monocle was fake, why not release it?"

"What proof? The word of a twist to a terrorist, given under torture? Who would believe it? Would you? No one would have paid attention. I needed something more." Smith put his hands down and spun to face Cooper. "And I got it. This man, he also said that your director knew that if the truth about the Monocle ever came out, he'd hang. So Peters made sure he had protection."

"What kind of protection?"

Smith sighed. "That's the frustrating part. I don't really know. Video of some kind, that much is obvious. Something that he could use if the situation ever got dire enough. The forger claimed to have rigged the setup for Peters, but said that he never knew what the content was."

"And you believe him?"

"My questioning was…thorough."

I'll bet. Cooper put aside the thoughts of torture, focused on what Smith was telling him. Forced himself to be dispassionate, to work it like a problem. To let his gift run free. "So you know this proof is out there, but you don't know where, and even if you did, you don't think you can get to it. Not directly. You want me to do it for you."

"Yes."

"I don't have any idea where to start."

"You'll figure it out. That's what you do. The same way you could find Alex Vasquez. And think how much better you know Drew Peters."

He was right, Cooper knew. Already he could feel himself patterning. It wouldn't be at DAR headquarters, or at Peters's house. Both places could be locked down if things went wrong. Peters would have put it somewhere safe, somewhere he could get to it in the kind of dire times when he would need it. "Next question."

"I think it's my turn. But go ahead."

"What you're saying, it's compelling. Believable. But so was the story Peters told. So was Equitable Services. None of this is proof."

"That video is."

"But you haven't seen it. You don't know what's on it. For all *I* know, it proves you're the monster the DAR says you are."

"True." The man said it with the calm of a logician acknowledging the fallacy in an argument.

"All right." Cooper stood again, walked to the lip of the rock, stared down at the wide, bright world. "I'll find it. Not for you, and not for your cause." He turned and looked back at Smith. "But you better pray that video shows what you think it does. Because I know you now. I can find you again, and I can kill you."

"I believe you," Smith said. "I'm counting on you to take this all the way."

"Even if that means killing you."

"Sure. Because only someone that dedicated will have what it takes to face off against Drew Peters. Christ, Cooper. Why do you think I sent Shannon to bring you here in the first place?"

Cooper's hands clenched. A sick, floating feeling bloomed in his belly. "What?" His gift racing ahead again, providing yet another answer he didn't want. "What do you mean, 'sent Shannon'?"

"Ah." The other man looked disgruntled for a second. "Sorry. I thought you'd figured that part out already."

"What do you mean, 'sent Shannon'?"

Smith sighed. He rose, slipped his hands in his pockets. "Just that. I needed you, so I dispatched Shannon to get you. I sent her to that El platform, and I planned your route to me. I made sure you saw Samantha and the uses the world has for her. I had Shannon take you to Lee Chen's house so you could meet his daughter and her friends. I routed you through Epstein, because I knew he'd sell me out to protect his dream, and because I knew you'd never believe you could get to me without help. And I stood outside last night smoking a cigarette so you'd climb the balcony.

"I'm sorry, Cooper. I'm a chess player. I needed to turn a pawn into a queen." Smith shrugged. "So I did."

CHAPTER 34

Even now, three hours later, as he sat in a leather chair twenty thousand feet up, the comment still rankled. Which was pointless; Cooper had more important things to deal with than his injured pride.

It's not just pride. Being upset that John Smith out-planned you is like being upset that Barry Adams plays better football. It's just a fact.

No, it wasn't being beaten by Smith that stung. It was that for the first time since he and Natalie had split, Cooper had felt something for a woman. Yes, they were on opposite teams, and there were a thousand reasons a relationship wouldn't work, but still, those feelings had been real.

Unfortunately, everything they'd been based on was fake. Everything she'd told him was a lie. *Maybe even last night.*

He leaned back in his seat. Stared out the window. The jet was just cresting the clouds, baroque castles spilling below him. Usually it was his favorite moment in a flight, a view that managed to stir that childish sense of wonder that he was miles up in the air. But the intricate cloudscape did nothing for him now.

It's not just that you got used. It's that she used you.

This morning, on the rock spire, he'd told Smith what he needed, and had been unsurprised to find the guy had it standing by. "I'm sending Shannon with you."

"No," Cooper had said, "you're not."

"Listen, I'm sorry for your wounded feelings, but this is too important. You need her help. She goes."

"Sorry, I don't work for you. I'm doing this my way."

"Cooper—"

"Just arrange the plane." He scooted to the edge of the rock spire and hung his legs over. "I'll get to the runway myself."

"Talk to her, at least," Smith had said.

Cooper had ignored him, spun to grip the edge, and begun to climb down.

From above, Smith had said, "She deserves that much."

He'd paused, looking up. "Believe it or not, John, we're not all pieces on your chessboard. Just arrange the plane."

Just under three hours later he'd reached the airstrip Smith had told him about, a private field in the heart of the Holdfast, big enough to handle not only the gliders but an honest-to-God jet.

His was painted like a FedEx transport plane, flying commercial numbers. Clever—it was the aerial equivalent of a taxicab, a vehicle that could hide in plain sight. The pilot was waiting for him. "Hello, sir. I've got a change of clothes on board for you, and food if you're hungry."

"Thanks." He'd climbed the stairs. "Get airborne and get me to DC as fast as you can."

Fifteen minutes later he was back in civilian clothes—the sizes were perfect, of course—and the jet was racing down the runway. The pilot said it would take about four hours, longer if they had to circle when they arrived.

Which gave him four hours to figure out where Drew Peters would have hidden insurance against his sins.

Adding to the fun, DC was a risky place for Cooper. There were more cameras and more agents there than in any city in the country. If he were in Roger Dickinson's place, if he were hunting a rogue agent whose children lived in DC, he'd make sure the city was on constant alert.

Normally even if a camera picked him up, by the time that image was found and processed, he'd have moved on. But things had changed when he'd talked to Peters last night. If Cooper had actually killed John Smith, he would have called the department to arrange his safe return home. And he'd considered doing that, lying to Peters, saying that Smith was dead. But what if the DAR knew otherwise? What if they intercepted a call, or saw a photo? More important, lying to Peters was equivalent to throwing his hand in with John Smith, and Cooper wasn't ready to do that. Not until he saw the evidence. Better just to go quiet for now. The problem was that if Peters discovered him, he would assume that Cooper had been turned.

Have you? Been turned?

No. He didn't work for Smith, and while he understood the soldier-on-the-losing-side rationale, a terrorist was still a terrorist.

But you're definitely not a DAR agent anymore.

Which was all Peters would need to know. If the director suspected that Cooper was no longer his man, the gloves would come off. His picture would be flashed on every screen in America. John Smith had managed to hide from that, but Cooper didn't imagine that he could. No, his best chance lay in moving fast. Get to DC, get to the video, and make his moves from there.

Four hours to figure out where a digital file that could be stored on a drive about the size of a stamp was hidden in an area of roughly 7,850 square miles.

He'd come to that number by figuring that if Peters ever needed it, he'd need it fast. No more than an hour or two from his home or office. Figure a fifty-mile radius. Pi times radius squared equaled 7,850.

Calling it a needle in a haystack was an insult to haystacks.

So think. You've got...three and a half hours left. And if you're going to be playing against the entire DAR in their own backyard, it wouldn't hurt if you could grab an hour's sleep, too.

Obviously, the odds were better than the pure math suggested. He wasn't going to be randomly searching the terrain. He would be patterning Drew Peters, the same way he had once patterned targets for the man.

So. What did he know?

If Smith was right—if he was telling the truth—the video was some sort of insurance policy. Something that could protect Peters if the facts about the Monocle ever came out. That narrowed the search immensely.

It wouldn't be at DAR headquarters. Too exposed. Plus, if Peters were burned, the agency might be closed to him.

Which was a relief. If it had been at the office, there was no chance Cooper could reach it. Might as well have been on the moon. It was an odd synchronicity, but if Peters needed his insurance policy, he'd likely be in the same position Cooper was, a renegade hunted by all.

The same logic ruled out Peters's house. Or any property in his name: his lake house, his car, any athletic clubs.

Of course, this was the director of Equitable Services. He could easily have false documents. But owning property under a false identity was a big risk. Property meant a paper trail, and a paper trail could be followed. Especially one that smelled like corruption.

Okay, what about registering a safety-deposit box under a fake identity? Minimal chance of discovery. On the other hand, banks were closed at night and on the weekend. That delay could mean the end.

One of the safest ways to hide something was in a hotel. Check into a room, bring a few minimal tools. Remove a baseboard or the cover to a heating vent, and hide gear there. As long as Peters kept half an eye on the hotel, made sure that it wasn't about to undergo major renovations, it would be a perfectly anonymous hiding place.

Thing was, that presented the same difficulties in retrieval. Unless you rented the room in perpetuity, which negated the point, you couldn't count on being able to get back to it at a moment's notice. A hotel would happily book you in a specific room with a little notice, but if it was occupied, things got complicated. Yes, Peters could break in, but it would be clumsy, and Peters abhorred clumsy tactics.

A lawyer? Trusted family counsel, retained for years. That same person could be instructed to release it if Peters disappeared…

Only, this wasn't a private-eye movie. Peters didn't want the threat of vengeance after his death; he wanted to protect himself. And no employee could be trusted, not with something this important.

Out the window, the clouds had broken into clumps, the gold-green quilt of Nebraska or Iowa below him, that boxy and startlingly regular geometry visible only from above. He wished he had someone to bounce this off of, Bobby Quinn, or Shann—

Put her out of your head.

Which was like telling himself not to think about elephants. Immediately he was flashing back to the previous night, the way she had tasted, that mental Polaroid of her rocking back, sweat-slick skin outlined against the Milky Way. Had that been part of her mission, too? Smith had planned everything else, had plucked him up from an El station in Chicago and brought him to Wyoming. Was it possible that he'd sent Shannon to seduce him? To plant the seed of a mission, and then comfort him, tie Cooper to them?

It was possible. He didn't want to believe it, tended not to—he thought he knew Shannon, couldn't see her going with that—but it was possible. She could have been step two after all.

"Even if there is a step two, step one was tell you the truth." Her words in his head. And if she had lied to him, well, he'd lied to her,

too. The whole time they'd been together, it had been under false pretenses. But though he'd been lying to her about his mission, he hadn't been lying about who he was. Maybe she hadn't either. Maybe, like him, she was both a pro and a person, both a job and a life. Had it been a mistake not to include her? Until her, Cooper had never worked with anyone who could match him. And she would be a huge asset if he had to sneak into...

Enough. It was done.

So it wouldn't be at a hotel, wouldn't be with a lawyer. How about a friend, or a family member? Not his daughters, but a brother, say, or an old school friend. Someone who could be counted upon, who would never willingly betray him.

Problem was *willingly*. If Peters was in trouble, then his friends and family were, too. If someone suspected a friend had what they were after...well, normal people didn't resist torture.

Funny to be back on a private jet. It had started this way, the jet returning from San Antonio, where he'd followed Alex Vasquez. Alex Vasquez, who had told him a war was coming. He'd had no idea how right she'd been. He wondered, idly, if she had.

Cooper yawned. The seat was comfortable, and the last days had been long. The few hours of sleep he'd gotten had been on the cold ground, and not much good.

Okay, so figure it out. This is what you do.

Only, as always, his gift was something he couldn't control. Sometimes it made a wild intuitive leap that he knew was true before he had proof. Sometimes it just lay coiled and quiet, processing at its own speed.

Still, he had a sense that he was close, that he had the data he needed; he just needed to look at it from the right vantage point.

Tell you what, self. Figure this out, and you can go to sleep.

Peters's insurance would be geographically close. It would be somewhere he could get to night or day. Somewhere no one would stumble on it, ever; where the risk of that was essentially zero. It would not be in his name, or anywhere someone would think to look. Getting to it wouldn't require the help of another person.

What kind of place was essentially unchanging, always available, perfectly secure, and close at hand?

Cooper smiled.

Two minutes later, he was sound asleep.

CHAPTER 35

Full circle. Funny how life had a way of doing that.

He wasn't just back in DC; he was back in Georgetown, a couple of blocks from his old apartment, on his old jogging route. Cooper could picture that version of himself, a faded army tee clinging to his soaked chest as he rounded this stretch of R Street. This had been his favorite part of the run, a particularly scenic corner of intensely scenic Georgetown. The black wrought-iron fence on his right, the thick shade of old trees, the tidy, expensive row-house mansions on the south side of the street…and the elegant grace of Oak Hill Cemetery along the north.

He'd wandered through it a few times back then, read the pamphlet. It was old, dating to something like 1850. A gorgeously landscaped spread of gentle hills and quiet paths along the Potomac, dotted with old marble, monuments, and headstones for the gentry of two centuries past. Congressmen, Civil War generals, captains of industry…and bankers.

It was perfect. A brief walk from Drew Peters's house, completely unchanging, always accessible. The grounds might close, but Cooper doubted that meant more than an elderly watchman drawing a chain across the iron gate. Easiest thing in the world to find a patch of darkness and climb over. Kids probably did it all the time.

There was a map on a signpost near the entrance, with sections laid out in muted color: Joyce, Henry Crescent, Chapel Hill. The chapel was one of the cemetery's main destinations, and he remembered it being lovely, draped in ivy like a Romantic daydream. The map also marked some of the more famous dead.

Including Edward Eaton, "financier and attorney, undersecretary of the treasury to Abraham Lincoln."

Cooper started walking. The stonework and paths were marked by age, dignified like a worn patrician. He'd never really put much thought into where he'd be buried—had some loose notion of being cremated—but he could see the appeal in laying loved ones to rest here. It would be a pleasant place to imagine them.

Most of the grave sites were simple monuments, weathered stones with names and dates and often military rank. But here and there stone mausoleums nestled into the side of a hill or beneath a spread of branches. The one with EATON carved across the top had a stolid, bunkerish look. No elaborate statues or intricate carvings, just a pair of pillars flanking the door and a couple of small stained-glass windows. It spoke of stability and eternity, no doubt what Edward Eaton had in mind when he bought this house for the bodies of great-grandchildren whose parents hadn't even been conceived.

Cooper stood outside, his hands in his pockets. He wondered how often Drew Peters had come here, if he'd stood in the same place. Staring at the mausoleum where his wife lay.

Geographically proximate, unchanging, undisturbed, always accessible, and perfectly safe.

It fits. But would Peters really use it like that?

One way to find out.

The door was oak, dense and heavy, mounted on massive forged hinges that looked like they might date back to the founding of the cemetery. The lock was newer, a deadbolt that looked out of place. Cooper paused, glanced around. Some distance away, an elderly woman limped down the path, a bouquet of flowers dangling from one hand. There was the sound of a lawn mower and, more distant, a siren.

He knelt in front of the door and took a closer look at the lock. A year ago, when Cooper had needed to get through locked doors, he'd used a ram. Lock picking was for thieves, not DAR agents.

Then he became a thief. It hadn't taken long to learn; once you understood the fundamentals, the rest was just a matter of practice, and he'd had time. The lock was stiff, but he had it popped inside two minutes.

Cooper gripped the iron handle and pulled. With a rusty screech, the hinges gave. The door opened slowly. Sharp sunlight spilled into the crypt. The floor was stone, thick with dust, and the air smelled stale.

Here's another first.

He stepped inside the crypt and tugged the door closed behind him.

The bright sun vanished, but watery light filtered through the stained glass. If the light had been a sound it would have been a requiem, slow and quiet and full of loss. Cooper stood still and let his eyes adjust. The mausoleum was one room, thirty feet on a side, a bench in the center, ledges carved like bunk beds in the wall. Four high and three across, on all but the entrance wall, where the door took up one of the columns. Forty-four stone berths, all but two of them filled. Forty-two coffins, lying in orderly rest, names and dates carved beneath each one. A house for the dead. He felt a chill to think it, a primal shiver down the lizard part of his brain.

The light was too dim to make out the inscriptions, and he pulled out his datapad, uncrumpled it, and let the digital glow flood across the stone. The act felt strangely more offensive than breaking in had. Something wrong with introducing the modern world to this tomb, with using a device that couldn't have been conceived of when this place was built.

And then he saw that he wasn't the first to do it.

The box was about the size of a pack of matches, matte gray metal mounted just inside and above the door. No label, no LEDs glowing, nothing to reveal its purpose, but Cooper recognized it. It was government technology. Most of the box was a battery. The rest was a motion sensor and a transmitter. The thing was a long-term monitoring device, the kind you could put in a safe house for a decade and never think of again, just let it sit and watch, passive until it caught a hint of motion and broadcast its signal.

The monitor meant two things. First, that he was right in his hunch. The evidence was hidden here. The family might think to install a motion alarm in the crypt, but it wouldn't be DAR technology.

Which led to the second thing. The moment Cooper had opened the door, the monitor would have sent a blast to the director. His phone would be ringing, his d-pad pinging, sending one message:

Someone is where you don't want him to be.

Cooper's heart kicked up a notch. Peters was a man with astonishing power. The moment he got the alarm, he would dispatch a team, faceless, most likely, heavily armed men and women sent hurtling to this place. And because Peters couldn't risk a subject talking, that team would have shoot-to-kill orders.

On the upside, it does mean your brain is working. The evidence is here.

So get it and get the hell out. You've already lost about a minute. You've got…call it two more.

Shit.

He leaned in close, read the first inscription. TARA EATON, FAITHFUL WIFE, 1812–1859. The next for her husband, Edward Eaton, buried two years later.

Cooper spun, hustled to the other end of the crypt. Bodies would have been laid to rest in the order of their deaths, which meant that Director Peters's wife should be near the end.

The third to last, it turned out. ELIZABETH EATON, BELOVED DAUGHTER, 1962–2005. Above the inscription rested an elegant mahogany coffin, the wood still lustrous, though the top was covered with a thin layer of even dust. Cooper stared at it, struck by what he was looking at, a box with the remnants of a person in it, a woman he'd never met, mother to children who jokingly called him Uncle Nick, whom he'd tickled and wrestled and teased.

There was no time to wince over it. He started feeling his way around the coffin, fingers running over every inlaid detail, tracing the curves and edges. Tapping along the edges, feeling blindly on the sides. Nothing. He grimaced, then angled his head and leaned in over the box, feeling the cold stone above it, the dust in his eyes and nose as he ran his hands through darkness. He checked every edge, dragged his hands through the narrow space between the coffin and the berth wall.

Nothing.

Cooper stepped back. A spiderweb stuck to his hair, and he brushed it away.

There's one place you haven't checked…

He flashed to a fantasy of Natalie dead, hidden away in a room like this, and him sneaking in, breaking open the box, facing what lay inside…

The thought was repellent in every way. But it was possible.

Cooper had no tools, nothing to break the top open with. He'd have to throw it around, maybe slam it against the bench until the wood splintered, the remnants of Elizabeth Eaton jarring and tossing inside. An abomination, but the only way.

Except—

Would Peters have done the same?

No. He'd have brought tools. Cracked it open just enough, but still, cracked it open.

Has it been?

—that the seal on the coffin was perfect, the lid fitting the base so smoothly it was hard to see where one ended and the other began. Not only sealed; there were no signs of tool marks. Breaking the lid open would have left a mark.

His first thought was relief.

His second was frustration. Peters hadn't hidden what he was looking for in his dead wife's mausoleum. He'd been wrong.

Only, no. The monitor on the wall gave it away. The evidence was here. It just wasn't in her coffin.

Cooper stepped back, glanced at his watch. One minute left. He whirled, looked around the room. Forty-two coffins. A stone bench. He dashed to it, dropped down, checked the underside. Smooth. Same with the legs and the edges. Panic starting now. There was an iron crucifix above the door. He checked it hurriedly. Nothing.

Forty-five seconds.

It had to be here. Nothing else made sense. His gift had predicted it, the motion sensor had proved it, he just had to *find* it.

One of the other coffins? There were forty-one of them. No time to do even a cursory examination.

He stood in the center of the room, spinning slowly. Come on, come on. Willing his intuition to strike. Thirty seconds. He rubbed his hands together, dust flying.

Dust—

There's no way to hide anything here without disturbing the dust.

And no way to smooth dust out evenly.

So the best thing to do is clear it off entirely. Still a tell, but a less obvious one, especially as more dust settles.

—flying.

He sprinted back to the coffins. Elizabeth was third from last. The two after read Margaret Eaton, 1921–2006, and Theodore Eaton, 1918–2007.

There was dust atop both of them. Not a lot, but it hadn't been that long.

A half-forgotten conversation, one he'd probably never have remembered at all if it hadn't taken place the day his life exploded, the day he'd begged Drew Peters to protect his child. The director had told a story about his wife, the story that had triggered Cooper's being here in the first place. But he'd also talked about her father. What had he said?

"Her father, Teddy Eaton, he handled the private fortunes of half of Capitol Hill. God, he was a bastard. As his daughter was dying, the old man begged her to let him bury her with them. 'You're an Eaton, not a Peters. You should be with us.'"

Cooper smiled. It had nagged at him, the idea that Peters would abuse his wife's memory this way. It hadn't fit the pattern. But the old bastard who made sure Drew would never rest beside Elizabeth?

He dropped to a knee and felt around the back of the coffin. Spiderweb, brass hinge, old wood...and a strip of duct tape. He yanked it off, and a small object came with it. A memory stick about the size of a postage stamp.

A fine screw-you from the land of the living. Cooper would have admired Peters for it, but didn't have the time. He folded the tape over the drive, stuck it in his pocket, and ran for the door. Hit the heavy door at speed, his shoulder singing along with the hinges. Sunlight, sky, the wave of trees.

And a team of black-clad soldiers with automatic rifles, sprinting across the cemetery, moving between gravestones with no regard.

Cooper kept his momentum, spinning through the thin gap into the outside world. Made four steps before he heard the first shots. Something above him exploded, stone from the mausoleum raining down. He winced, pushed into a full-on run, everything he had. Reached the edge of the crypt, used a hand on the lip of it to spin himself around, trying to get the building between him and the commandos.

He wanted to get his bearings, move tactically, but couldn't risk it. The graveyard was hilly and filled with trees, and the crypts would provide occasional cover. At least it wasn't night;

the helmets the faceless wore included thermal optics, and against the cool of the evening his body heat would have shone like a laser.

A window shattered above him, the stained glass on the Eaton crypt. He hurled himself forward, stumbled for half a heartbeat on a root, felt more than heard a bullet pass above him. Darted left, then right, trying to present as tricky a target as possible. A sniper in a steady position wouldn't have trouble zeroing on him, but the agents had been running.

There was a gentle rise ahead of him, a nightmare, but the other side would provide a little cover. No choice. He slammed forward, boots rattling against the ground, the impact jarring up his legs. Breath coming hard, and panic sweat soaking his armpits. Sprinted diagonally across a row of headstones, leaped a short one, more gunfire behind, reached a tree, centripetally spun around the other side of it—*careful, do the same move too many times and they'll anticipate it*—but it worked this time, the thud of a round hitting the bark above him, and then he made the edge of the ridge and flung himself forward in a soccer slide tackle, low to the ground, stones and branches ripping at him.

Behind him, he heard the men yelling, knew they'd be spreading out in an arc, moving fast, trying to narrow his options. Cooper had his pistol, but the assault rifles they carried were capable of full auto and accurate to a mile.

Still.

He turned and fired twice directly at the roof of the crypt, then paused, fired again. Stone cracked and bullets ricocheted. The threat would slow them down, force them to move more carefully. It wouldn't buy much, though. He needed a plan.

The far side of the cemetery was bounded by the Potomac. If he could make it there, climb the fence, then…

Then what? A swimmer in open water was an easy target. Besides, it was the obvious move. Chase, and the target flees. Flee, and you can't think.

Cooper pictured the map he'd noticed at the entrance, the graceful regions nestled against one another, the famous dead, the chapel.

Worth a try.

He set off at a dash, keeping as low as he could without slowing down. Leaving the path behind and heading directly perpendicular to his previous course, not something fleeing people did. Adrenaline electrified his every nerve. The physical weight of the pistol in his hand and the emotional weight of the drive in his pocket. The smell of dirt. A gust of wind that lifted the tree limbs to dance.

A gunfight in a graveyard, Jesus Christ.

There was a row of tall tombstones with dates from the Civil War, and he angled behind them, moving fast. Through the trees ahead, a small hill, too perfectly proportioned to be natural, and the ivy of the chapel. He leaped a bench, landed moving, passing a tombstone with a slender angel beseeching the sky. Intuition made him glance over his shoulder.

The man was alone, probably the far edge of the arc. Fifteen yards away, atop the ridge. Black body armor and a good stance, weapon at the ready. The black helmet with its visor down, a blank-faced predator. His attention was focused on where Cooper was supposed to be, but intuition or his helmet optics must have screamed a warning, because he turned to look right at Cooper.

For an instant, they stood frozen. Then the faceless swung his rifle to bear, rocking his weight to his back leg, sighting down the barrel, zeroing in, gloved finger moving, and Cooper could see the path of the bullet, see it like it was drawn in the air, a line right to his chest, and without thinking he flung himself sideways.

Heard the crack of the bullet as he hung in the air, and heard its brothers, the man firing to follow him, the rush of air, the ground rising to meet Cooper, the angel staring at the sky, Cooper's hands coming up even as he fell, the pistol steady, the man in his sights. They both fired.

The angel wept stone tears.

The commando in black staggered as a hole spiderwebbed his visor.

Cooper hit the ground, the impact uncushioned by grace, knocking the wind from him. Kept the gun up as he watched the man fall.

He'd killed a DAR agent.

It was the first time. He had a sinking feeling it wouldn't be the last.

Then he was scrambling to his feet and running in a crouch, the chapel nearby now, the ivy waving in the breeze, the stained glass bloody in the evening light. He reached the edge of it, panting, ran around the far side, the bulk of it between him and the assault team, and only a fraction of a mile to the street.

To find Bobby Quinn leaning against the far side of a gravestone, most of his body out of sight behind the stone, a submachine gun braced on it. Leveled straight at Cooper's chest.

His former partner betrayed no surprise to see him. Had been expecting him. Of course. They'd worked together enough. He knew Cooper liked to double back, to misdirect. So he'd sent the team to cover the obvious routes, and then staked out his hunch.

"Drop the gun. Now."

Cooper considered making the same play he just had, a wild leap and a midair shot. But the situation was different. The faceless had been exposed and surprised. He'd telegraphed his intent with every muscle. Quinn, on the other hand, was ready and steady, with most of his body—and, more important, his body language— hidden. No way to read him if Cooper couldn't see him.

Besides. Are you going to shoot Bobby Quinn?

"I mean it. Drop the gun."

Cooper froze. Nervous energy crackling through him, his body rubbery. Had a weird desire to laugh. He dropped the gun. "Hi, Bobby."

"Lace your hands on your head, then get down on your knees with your ankles crossed."

Cooper stared at his colleague, his partner in a hundred missions, remembered the dark sense of humor of the man, the way he'd hold a cigarette for two minutes before he'd light it. How many times had they gone in a door together?

"Bobby." He struggled for words, wanted to explain the situation, the whole thing: going undercover, chasing John Smith, everything he'd learned since. Wanted half an hour in a pub, somewhere with oak and worn stools, coasters with the Guinness logo. Wanted to explain, to lay out everything that had happened, to make the man *understand*.

And then the laugh did hit him, nothing he could do about it. How many times had his targets wanted the same thing? How many times had he heard them say…

"Do it now!"

Cooper said, "I didn't do the things they say, Bobby." The colossal humor of it almost overwhelming him. What was the phrase the Irish used?

You want to make God laugh, you make a plan.

"Lace your hands behind—"

Cooper shook his head. "Can't do it."

"You think I won't shoot you?"

"I don't know." *But I do know that if I let you take me, I'm a dead man. And this evidence, whatever it is, it will vanish. Drew Peters will go on fostering a war. And I can't live with that.*

Even if it means I have to die with it.

"I guess we're going to find out." Slowly, hands at his sides, he started walking. Not toward Bobby, at a tangent. No time to talk, no time to explain. The rest of the tactical response team would have heard the gunfire, would be closing in on their dead comrade. They'd be here in seconds.

"Goddamn it, Cooper—"

"I'm sorry." He kept walking but met his partner's eyes as he did. "I promise you, I'm not who they say I am. But I can't stay to explain."

Quinn lowered the barrel of the gun a notch, pulled the trigger. A chunk of turf an inch in front of Cooper's foot detonated. "I know you can shoot out my legs, Bobby. But that's the same as killing me. You know those men won't hesitate. And if it's going to happen, I'd rather it was you."

"Cooper—"

"Make your choice, Bobby." He stopped then. Stared at the man. Trying to read his fate in the set of his partner's eyes, the twitch of the muscle in one cheek, the tension in his neck.

Finally, Bobby said, "Goddamn you." He turned, straightened. Put up his gun. "You've got three seconds."

A rush of emotion swept through Cooper. For a moment, he wondered if he would have made the same choice if their situations had been reversed. If he'd have had the courage to be a person instead of an agent.

A question for another time. He took the head start and set off at a sprint.

It was more like five seconds before Quinn started yelling that Cooper was over there, that he was by the chapel, and by that time the fence and the street and the wide world were in front of him.

CHAPTER 36

Cooper stalked the DC night with a bomb in his pocket and his head on fire.

Overhead, faint, he could hear the sound of an airship, flying low. Looking for him. There would be a sniper on board, and a high-res camera package, and if they spotted him, he'd never hear the shot.

Relax. You're just a man walking down the street. Just like all the others in this crowd. Don't run, don't call attention to yourself, and the odds of them spotting you are nil.

Well. Slim.

Any gunfight you walked away from was at least a partial success. But this one felt more partial than he'd like. Until he'd found the drive, he'd harbored hope that maybe Smith had lied, that the things Cooper had done were justified.

He couldn't shelter that hope any longer. Peters had sent a hit team. No hesitation, no orders to arrest. Just kill and clean it up later. Drew Peters was the bad guy. Which made John Smith… well, who knew what it made John Smith?

Worse, Cooper had hoped to get in and out unspotted. To have time to review the video before the DAR even knew he was back in town. But now not only would Peters know that his precious insurance had been taken—he would know who had taken it.

What would that mean? What would a man like Peters do next?

Cooper froze, every muscle locking like stone. Someone bumped into him from behind, and he spun, hands ready. A sad-looking man in a business suit jumped, his eyes wide. "Hey, man, watch where you're…"

But Cooper was already moving. Sprinting, despite the risk. A mini-mall was ahead on the right, one of those indoor places with a dozen fading businesses that never seemed to quite go under. He yanked open the door and stepped inside.

Muzak, and the multilayered reek of the candle shop by the entrance. A handful of shoppers wandering like zombies. His boot heels rang on the polished floor. A tanning place, a convenience store, a hair salon, a bright hallway leading to the bathrooms. Opposite them he found a payphone with a frayed cord, the phone book stolen long ago. He dug in his pockets. No change.

Back to the convenience store. He threw a ten at the vigilant-eyed Pakistani behind the register. "Quarters. I need quarters."

"No change—"

"Give me four goddamn quarters and keep the rest."

The man stared at him, shrugged, and opened the register in slow motion. Dipped in the drawer like he was pushing through water to do it. "Crazy, you are crazy."

Cooper snatched the coins and ran back to the payphone. Almost knocked over a suburban-looking chick with big hair, didn't slow.

He slotted two coins, then dialed Natalie's number. Held the phone to his ear, his heart going wilder than it ever had in the cemetery, his hands shaking, control slipping. Ring. Ring. Ring. *Come on, come on, come—*

"Hello, Cooper. Welcome home."

The world seemed to spin. He planted a hand against the wall. That voice. He knew that voice. "Dickinson."

"Got it in one."

"Where are my—"

"Children? They're safe. Safe as can be. Your ex-wife, too. All three are in the loving arms of Equitable Services."

Whatever happens, I'll take care of your family.

Cooper wanted to rage, to scream threats down the line. But it wouldn't do any good, he knew that.

Did it anyway. "Listen to me, you piece of shit, you let my children—"

"Shut up." Dickinson calm as the eye of the hurricane ravaging the countryside, calm as the iceberg ripping open the *Titanic*. "Just be quiet. Okay?"

He started to reply, managed to stop himself.

"Good. Now. This is simple. We're not gangsters, and this isn't a B movie. This is a situation you created. And it's a situation you can resolve."

Cooper bit his tongue, literally bit it, jamming his teeth down and relishing the pain and focus it brought.

"Here's how," Dickinson continued. "Just come in. Come in, and bring what you stole. Simple as that. I'm not going to bullshit you. You won't walk out again. But it will be quick, I'll promise that. And we'll let your family go."

"Listen to me, Roger, listen. Drew Peters is not what he says he is. He's a criminal. What I stole, it's a drive, and it's got evidence to back me up—"

"Listen to *me*, Cooper. Are you?"

"Yes."

"I. Don't. Care."

The second of silence that followed sounded like an earthquake.

"Get me? I don't care. It's not my job to care."

"Roger, I know you're dedicated, I know you're a believer, but what you believe in, it's all a lie."

Through the phone, a sound somewhere between a sigh and a laugh. "Don't you remember what I said that morning after Bryan Vasquez died?"

Cooper forced himself to think back. "You said you didn't hate me because I was an abnorm. You hate me because you think I'm weak."

"I don't hate you at all, Cooper. That's the point. But I believe. And you don't."

Cooper rubbed at his face with his hand. "Roger, please—"

The line was dead. He stood holding the phone to his ear, Muzak in the background, the scuff and squeal of dress shoes on the floor, the faint odor of disinfectant from the bathroom, his family held hostage by monsters.

You decided a long time ago that you'd lie down in traffic for your children. Every parent does. Time to pay that piper.

He dropped the phone and started for the exit. Felt relief, honestly. He was tired, so bloody, stoop-shouldered tired, and he'd been on his own too long. Die for his children? No problem. One dead twist, coming right up.

Do you really believe Peters will let them go?

Why not? It's me he wants. Me and his precious insurance, whatever it is. What harm can an environmental lawyer and two children do him?

He froze. What harm indeed?

Cooper turned and walked back to the men's room. Pushed open the door. A janitor was leaning against a mop.

"Get out."

"Say what?"

"Now."

The janitor took another look, then rolled his cart out, muttering something about crazy-ass people, he had a job same as anybody else. Cooper opened the middle stall and shut and locked it behind him. From one pocket he took his datapad, from the other the drive, still encased in duct tape. He peeled that off, dropped it on the floor. The chip he'd found on the back of Teddy Eaton's casket was a standard stamp drive, a terabyte storage, the kind you could buy in any drugstore. He slotted it, then sat down on the toilet.

The screen brightened, then started playing automatically.

The video showed two men talking in a bland room. One of the men was Drew Peters. The other he'd never met, but knew. Everybody did.

Cooper watched the video all the way through.

And when it was done, he hung his head, pressed his fingers into his eyes hard enough that black-and-white patterns danced. But not hard enough to erase what he had just seen.

He'd thought things were bad before. Bad last night, in Wyoming. Bad this afternoon, in the cemetery. Bad half an hour ago, on the phone with Roger Dickinson.

It turned out he'd had no idea what bad was.

There was no chance, none at all, that Peters would let his family live.

CHAPTER 37

He might have cried, sitting in that smelly toilet stall in the shitty mall in the heart of DC. He might have. He couldn't really say.

There seemed to be a few moments missing from his personal history. And he was having a hard time wanting them back.

What he did know was that at some point, he'd stood up, opened the stall door, and walked to the sink. Held his hands under the faucet until it finally came on, then splashed lukewarm water on his face. Again, and again. Paper-toweled dry.

Stared in the mirror. At a dead man, most likely, the father of murdered children.

But not a man who would go quietly.

Cooper tossed the towels in the trash, walked back to the pay-phone, inserted his last coins, and dialed another number.

■

Forty-five minutes later, he walked into a pub called McLaren's. Oak and worn stools, coasters with the Guinness logo. A smallish crowd of post-work drinkers, mostly men, mostly watching the game. He'd been there once before, years ago, some work party of Natalie's. Cooper walked to the bar, signaled the man behind it.

"What can I getcha?"

"You guys have a back room, right?"

"Yeah. Not open now, but if you want to rent it for an event, I can get you the manager's—"

"I'll give you…" He opened his wallet and took out a handful of bills. "Three hundred and forty bucks to let me use it for an hour."

The man looked left, then right. Shrugged, folded his hand around the bills. "Right this way."

He followed the guy around the end of the bar. The bartender jangled out a ring of keys, found one, and turned the lock. "You want anything?"

"Just privacy."

"Don't mess it up, okay? I'm the one who cleans."

Cooper nodded, said, "Privacy," then pushed into the back room.

It was a smaller twin of the main room. A bar along one side, the taps unscrewed, pitchers racked, washcloth dangling. Without anyone there, it had an air of sad expectation. Cooper flipped on the lights, then sat down at the abandoned bar. He laid his data-pad down, then spread his arms, put them palm first on the polished surface, and waited.

Ten minutes later, he heard the door open. Very slowly, moving only his head, he turned to look.

Bobby Quinn had on the same suit as earlier. His posture radiated fight-or-fight, and screw the other option. One hand rested on his weapon, the holster unsnapped.

"I'm not moving, Bobby. Legs crossed, hands on the bar."

Quinn glanced around the room. Didn't relax, but did step inside. He let the door click behind him, then drew the gun. Didn't point it, which was something.

"Half an hour," Cooper said. "Like I said on the phone. Then you'll understand."

His partner moved to the end of the bar. With his off hand, he reached around his back and came out with a pair of handcuffs. Slid them to Cooper. "Keep your right hand on the bar. Use your left to lock it to the rail."

"Come on, Bobby—"

The gun came up. "Do it."

Cooper sighed. He picked up the cuffs, careful to move slowly. Snapped them around his right wrist.

You do this, you're helpless. If you're wrong about Quinn, then it's all over.

He fastened the other end to the brass rail. Gave an experimental tug. A clang and a bite. "Better?"

Quinn holstered his weapon. Walked closer. His face was unreadable, too many things happening at once. "I'll give you your half hour, because I said I would. But when time is up, I'm going to call a team to bring you in."

"Like I said on the phone, if you do, I won't resist." He tried for a grin. "Much."

"You resist at all, and I'll kill you." It was a simple statement of fact, and all the more jarring coming from Bobby Quinn, to whom sarcasm and irony were akin to oxygen. "Start talking."

Cooper took a breath. "I've been in deep cover for six months. Since March 12th, when you and I almost stopped the bombing of the Exchange. I was inside. No idea how I survived, but I woke up in a triage tent. When I could walk again, I hitched a ride with a bunch of Marines and went to see Drew Peters. I pitched him a crazy plan: I'd go rogue. Everyone would blame me for the explosion. I'd become a bad guy. Be hunted."

He talked fast, didn't waste time on embellishments, just laid out the facts. His time on the run. Building a reputation as a thief. His coming-out party on the El platform. The trip to Wyoming. Meeting Epstein.

"Why? Why do all this?"

"I told you, so that I could get to John Smith and kill him."

Quinn shook his head. "That's the goal. I asked why."

"Oh. My daughter."

"Kate?"

"She was about to be tested. She would have been sent to an academy. Peters promised to keep her out." His stomach soured. *I'll take care of your family.* "Everything I've done, I did for her."

"Did you find Smith?"

"Yes."

"Did you kill him?"

"No."

"Ah-so."

Cooper started to lean back, stopped when the cuff bit his wrist. He said, "You don't believe me, do you?"

"No. And in twenty minutes, I'm going to bring you in."

"Jesus, Bobby. I've been a DAR agent for the last six months. I mean, teams came after me *four times.* Four. And in that time, I never killed one agent. Never even hurt one, more than his pride. Why do you think that is?"

"You just killed one." Quinn's eyes hard. "In the cemetery."

"Yeah," Cooper said. "Well, I'm not an agent anymore. And once you take a look at that"—he jerked his head toward the datapad—"I don't think you will be either."

"What is it?"

"Drew Peters's dirtiest secret. It's what I was picking up in the cemetery."

"I thought you were after Smith."

"So did I. Turns out, I was wrong."

Quinn wanted to pick up the datapad. Cooper could see it, could read it on him clear as morning sunlight. "Go ahead."

Bobby looked at him, and Cooper said, "Jesus, man, I'm hand-cuffed to the bar. What do you think I'm going to do, turn into a bat and fly away?"

A muscle twitched in Quinn's cheek, and Cooper realized his partner had been about to make a joke. He didn't, but Cooper knew the man, had sat alongside him for hours, days, years. *You're getting through to him.* "Okay, look, I'll do it. Okay?"

"Slowly."

Slowly, Cooper picked up his d-pad. Propped it on the rail so they both could see. Clumsy with his left hand, he activated it. Then started the video.

The same room he'd seen before, a hotel or a safe house. Matching furniture with no sense of style, walls painted putty. There was a window, and through it trees.

Director Drew Peters paced. He was younger here. The man's hair and style hadn't changed in the whole of the time Cooper had known him, but the lines on his forehead, the sagging beneath his eyes, those had deepened with time.

"When is this?" Quinn asked.

"Five years and between eight and nine months ago."

"How can you be so—"

"Watch."

On the screen, Peters walked to the table, picked up a glass of water, sipped at it. There was a knock on the door.

"Come in."

Two men in plain suits entered. The kind of men who looked like they were wearing sunglasses even when they weren't. They nodded at Peters, then checked the room. Finally, one spoke into a middle distance. "We're clear, Mr. Secretary."

A man walked into the room. Average height, good smile, conservative suit.

"Hey," Quinn said. "That's—"

"Yes."

That had been Cooper's first clue as to the age of the video. It had to be at least five years old, because the man who walked through the doors was, at the time, the secretary of defense. A connected man, a savvy politician, the kind people treated respectfully not only because he knew where the bodies were buried, but because he'd put his fair share in the ground himself. Secretary Henry Walker.

Only now, his title was different. It had been for five years. Since 2008…when he'd won his first presidential election. The first of two. Cooper had voted for him in both.

Even watching it again, knowing what was coming, how much worse things got, Cooper felt like he couldn't breathe. The president's famous March 12th speech echoed in his inner ear.

Let us face this adversity not as a divided nation, not as norm and abnorm, but as Americans. Let us work together to build a better future for our children.

A cry for tolerance, for humanity. A call to all people to work together.

A lie.

On the screen, the two men shook hands, exchanged pleasantries. Walker dismissed his security. Quinn said, "Okay, Cooper, other than the fact that I feel a little dirty watching this, what's the point?"

"I'll show you." With his left hand, he scrubbed forward to 10:36.

Walker:	It's the liberal hand-wringing that drives me batshit. Don't people understand that civil rights are a privilege? That when it comes to defending our way of life, sometimes they're a luxury we cannot afford?
Peters:	The public doesn't want to believe a war is coming.
Walker:	God willing, they're right. But I was always taught that God helps those who help themselves.
Peters:	My feelings exactly, sir.

To 12:09:

Walker: It's not that I hate the gifted. I don't. But only a fool doesn't fear them. It's a lovely sentiment to say that all men are brothers. But when your brother is better than you in every way, when he can out-plan, out-engineer, out-play you... well, it's hard to be the little brother.

Peters: Normal people need a wake-up call. They need to remember that our very way of life is at stake.

To 13:35:

Peters: Sir, I understand your desire to choose your words with care. So let me be the blunt one. If we don't do something, in thirty years, normal humans will have become irrelevant. At best.

Walker: And at worst?

Peters: Slaves.

To 17:56:

Walker: The thing is, there's two ways to go into a fight. You can do it wearing body armor and slinging a rifle, or you can show up in your skivvies. Not only that, but the guy who looks like he *can* fight rarely has to.

Peters: That's it exactly. I don't want genocide. But we need to prepare ourselves. We have the right to fight for our own survival. And this is not a war that can be fought with tanks and jets.

Walker: You've heard rumors about the congressional investigation into Equitable Services.

Peters:	Yes. But that's not why—
Walker:	Don't soil yourself. I'm not threatening you. But I do wonder whether this plan of yours is patriotism or self-preservation.
Peters:	Mr. Secretary—
Walker:	What's the target?
Peters:	Are you sure you want to know the operational details, sir?
Walker:	All right. You're right.

To 19:12:

Walker:	How many dead are you thinking?
Peters:	Somewhere between fifty and a hundred.
Walker:	That many?
Peters:	A small price to defend hundreds of millions.
Walker:	And these will be civilians.
Peters:	Yes.
Walker:	All?
Peters:	Yes, sir.
Walker:	No. No, that won't do.
Peters:	To ensure they're seen as terrorists, it has to be civilians. An attack against the military frames them as a military power. It defeats—
Walker:	I understand. But we need a symbol of the government there as well. Otherwise, it will seem random and unfocused.
Peters:	What about an attack on your office?
Walker:	Let's not get carried away. No, I was thinking a senator, or a Supreme Court judge. Someone respected, symbolic. And we'll need a patsy, too. A capable one who won't get caught right away. Someone to become the bogeyman.

Peters:	I have one in mind, sir. An activist named John Smith.
Walker:	I know of him.
Peters:	He's already made a pest of himself; it's only a matter of time before he would resort to violence anyway. And he's very capable. Once we tip him over, he'll play the part. Any, ah, symbolic target in particular?
Walker:	I can think of a few.

To 24:11:

Walker:	The key is to not let this get out of hand. We need an incident that unites the country, that justifies your work. Not something that kicks off a holy war.
Peters:	I understand, and I agree. Frankly, the gifted are too valuable to risk.
Walker:	Amen. But they need to be kept in their place.
Peters:	Sometimes war is the only route to peace.
Walker:	I think we understand one another.

To 28:04:

Peters:	I've already chosen a target. A restaurant. I've got teams ready.
Walker:	This is a hard assignment. Some of your shooters might flinch.
Peters:	Not these men.
Walker:	And afterward? Can you depend on their discretion?
Peters:	Depend on it? No. But I can assure it.
Walker:	Are you saying—

Peters: Operational details.

To 30:11:

Peters: Sir, I will handle everything. I will shield the administration in every way. But I need to hear directly from your lips, sir. I can't proceed on an assumption.

Walker: You're not recording this, are you?

Peters: Don't be ridiculous.

Walker: I'm kidding, Peters. Good lord, if you were recording this we'd both be up a creek.

Peters: True. So. Sir? I need explicit authorization.

Walker: Do it. Orchestrate the attack.

Peters: And you understand that we're talking about civilian casualties, maybe as many as a hundred of them.

Walker: I do. And I'm telling you to do it. As my daddy always said, freedom isn't free.

Cooper tapped the pause button. A freeze-frame of the two men shaking hands, the director leaning out of his chair to reach across the table.

Bobby Quinn looked like a man desperate to rewind his life. To go back and make a left turn instead of a right. "I don't believe it."

Cooper stared at him. At the topography of his facial musculature, the zygomatic major and minor, the buccinator driving the corners of his mouth. "Yes, you do."

"It's not possible," Quinn said heatedly. "You're saying that Director Peters planned the massacre at the Monocle?"

"The murder of seventy-three people, including children. Yes."

"But…why?"

Cooper sighed. "Because all the talk about preventing a war is bullshit. What they really want is to control it. They want to generate and maintain war at a low simmer. They want us all wound up and mistrusting each other. Norms and abnorms, left and right, rich and poor, all of it. The more we fear, the more we need them. And the more we need them, the more powerful they get."

"He's the president, Cooper. How much more—"

"That's right. He went from secretary of defense to president of the United States. What does that tell you? And remember Equitable Services before the Monocle? Limping along in an abandoned paper plant, no funding, no support, rumors of congressional investigations that could send us all to jail? Then an activist who had never been violent before all of a sudden walks into a restaurant and murders everyone. And, poof, the rest of the country starts seeing things Drew Peters's way."

"But what about the video from the restaurant?"

"The security footage is real. But Peters had an abnorm edit John Smith in later. The shooters work for Peters. Or did. I assume they're dead now."

"There you go," Quinn said. "If that video is fake, why is this one real?"

"Who could fake it?"

"John Smith—"

"No." Cooper shook his head. "The Monocle could be faked because Smith was relatively unknown, and the footage quality is poor, and especially because it was the DAR that did the investigation. But you can't fake footage of the president. There's too much of it available, too many ways to check it, too many people eager to. And why go to such lengths to hide a fake video?

"Besides. How many meetings have you sat in with Drew Peters? You really going to tell me that wasn't him?"

Quinn said, "So why isn't it encrypted?"

"I wondered that, too. But then I realized—it's an insurance policy. No doubt Peters has some sort of fail-safe that tells people where to find this if he dies mysteriously. If it were encrypted, it would defeat the point.

"This whole thing," Cooper said. "Everything we've done for the last years. All the actions, all the terminations. None of it was about truth, about protecting the public. They were just moves in a game we didn't know about, made by players who don't even want to win. No one wants to kill all the gifted. They just want to control them. And the rest of the country. And you know what? They do."

Quinn said, "The terminations?" Going through the same thing Cooper had the night before, the first nibbles of a horror that would soon sink its fangs deep. "You're saying that some of the people we killed, they—"

"Yeah," Cooper said. He pitied the guy, wanted to give him time to process it, to begin to deal with the enormity of everything. But that risked Quinn's freezing up, and there wasn't time for that. "And I'm sorry to say this, but it gets worse."

"How the hell can it get—"

"They have my children."

"They—who?"

"Peters."

"Come on, Cooper. That's paranoid."

"It's not. I called home. Roger Dickinson answered."

"Oh." Quinn stared. "Oh shit."

"What?"

His partner played with an imaginary cigarette and looked away. "I couldn't figure out why they'd put me in charge of the faceless at the cemetery. After all, Dickinson is the one with a hard-on for you. But just before Peters ordered me there, Dickinson left his office like his ass was on fire. Wouldn't talk to anyone, just bolted out. He must have been—"

"Going to my house. To kidnap my children."

"Yeah." Quinn turned to look at him. "I'm sorry, Coop. I didn't know. I would have stopped him."

"I know."

"So what, they want you to turn yourself in? Dickinson will kill you."

"If I thought it would save Natalie and the kids, I'd sacrifice myself. But they won't. By going undercover, I've given them too good a hand."

He watched Quinn work it out. "You're thinking that from the beginning, Peters let you do this because he'd win either way. Either you found Smith and killed him, or else…"

"Or else I volunteered to be the fall guy for real. Yeah. Everything I've done the last six months, it looks guilty. And now that I know about this?" Cooper gestured. "No, if I go in, they'll claim my cover story as true. Peters really will blame me for the March 12th explosion. He'll serve up my corpse to the media. A huge win for Equitable Services. Proof that the nation is in good hands. Billions of dollars in additional funding."

"And he can't have your ex going on CNN, saying that it's all a lie. Even if she's not believed, it spoils the PR value." Quinn nodded. "But how can he get rid of them? Kind of convenient if they just disappeared."

"Easy. I came back to kill them. Equitable Services tried to stop me, but they were too late. A tragedy, but at least they took down the bad guy. And perhaps if they had more resources…"

"But why would you kill your own—"

"Because I'm a crazy abnorm terrorist. Who knows how those people think? They're not even people."

Quinn said, "Jay-sus." He blew a long breath. "I don't want to believe this."

"But you do."

"I…" Quinn hesitated. "Yeah. I do."

"I need your help, Bobby. I need to get my children back. And then we have to make sure that this gets out. They can't get away with it. We can't let them."

"Do you know what you're saying? You're talking about taking on the *president*."

"I'm talking about two terrified children. And I'm talking about telling the truth."

"Coop, I want to help, but…"

"I know. But remember how I said I wasn't a DAR agent anymore? Well, are you? After seeing that? You've only got two choices, Bobby. You can pretend you don't know that everything you've served is a lie. Or you can help me."

It really was as simple as that, and Cooper made himself stop. All he'd wanted, back in the cemetery, was half an hour to make the man understand. Now he'd had it. There was no selling Quinn, no convincing him. No rhetorical flourish would make the difference, no appeal to emotion.

Either Bobby Quinn was a good man, or Cooper and his family were dead.

Quinn jammed the pads of his fingers into his eyes. "Shit." His hands muffled the words. "So what do we do?"

"Well, to start"—Cooper smiled and tugged at his wrist—"do you think you could unlock me?"

His partner laughed. "Sorry." He pulled the cuff key from his belt and tossed it over. "The truth shall set you free, right?"

"Something like that. That's our play, too. We use the video to set a trap for Peters."

"Sounds like you have a plan."

"The beginnings of one."

"Well, that's a relief. Sure, we're facing the most powerful covert organization on the planet, and in possession of stolen information that the president would nuke DC to keep private, but at least you have the beginnings of a plan. I was worried for a second."

"Hey," Cooper said, "the way I see it, the chance of success just doubled. Now it's the whole government against two of us."

"Three," said a voice behind them.

They both whirled. Quinn went for his weapon, but Cooper caught his partner's arm.

She stood with her hip popped, one hand leaning on the other side. A pose cocky and capable, her lips quirked in that sideways grin. "You left without saying good-bye, Nick. A girl might take that wrong."

Quinn said, "Who the hell are you, and how did you get here?"

Cooper said, "Hello, Shannon." She looked good. Damn good. He met her gaze, saw all the levels in it, strength, determination, and, beneath it, some hurt. He smiled in a way he hoped was apologetic, then said to Quinn, "She does that." To Shannon, he said, "When did you get here?"

"About an hour after you."

"Smith sent you?"

"No, asshole. I came because you need help. John just provided the plane."

"How did you find me?"

"I didn't. I found him." She jerked a thumb at Quinn.

"You're the girl from the Exchange," Quinn said. "And the thing with Bryan Vasquez."

"And you're Cooper's playmate." She pulled out a stool and took a seat. "So. What are we doing, boys?"

Cooper said, "Bringing down the head of Equitable Services and the president of the United States."

"Oh, good. I was afraid this was going to be dull."

"I try to keep life interesting."

"Any train rides planned?"

"If I tell you, it'll spoil the surprise."

"Don't do that. I love surprises."

"Time out." Quinn looked back and forth, forth and back. "Would you two quit flirting long enough to tell me what the *hell* is going on?"

"Bobby, meet Shannon Azzi. The Girl Who Walks Through Walls."

"Hiya," she said, and stuck out a hand.

Looking baffled, Quinn took it.

Cooper laughed. For the first time since he'd heard Dickinson's voice on the phone, he felt something like hope.

CHAPTER 38

"Jimmy's Mattresses. "

"This is account number three two zero nine one seven. I need to talk to Alpha."

"Hold, please."

The speaker of the disposable cell phone was tinny, but it would serve. They'd picked up a couple of them at a mini-mart en route to Quinn's apartment, a single in a Mount Vernon Square low-rise. Cooper had been there more times than he could remember, knew the furniture and the layout, had crashed on the couch. Quinn stared out the floor-to-ceiling windows at the night sky; Shannon splayed in a chair, one lithe leg up on the arm.

"Hello, Nick." Drew Peters sounded the same as ever. Calm, in control. The same as he'd sounded in the video, proposing the murder of innocent civilians. "Are you on your way in?"

"No."

"I see."

"I found the drive, Drew. Taped to the back of Teddy Eaton's coffin. And I've watched it. A nasty little snuff film."

"Omelets and eggs, Agent Cooper."

"Just Cooper. I don't work for you anymore."

"As you like. You understand the situation, though, yes? Roger was clear in his explanation?"

"Very clear. But we're not going to do it that way."

"What do you have in mind?"

"An exchange. The drive for my family."

"I don't think so. The drive is worthless. You'll have made copies by now."

"No. I haven't, and I won't."

A pause. "Why would I believe that?"

"Because you know that *I* know that even if this video got out, you could make sure that my family died. I mean even after you let them go. This would ruin you, but you'd still be able to act. Not all of your resources work for the DAR."

Another pause. "That's true."

"So here's the deal. We meet somewhere we both feel safe. You bring my family; I bring this. We all walk out. You get to go on running your evil empire. And my children get to grow up."

"I'm not sure you're in a position to negotiate. For now, your children are perfectly safe, as is your ex-wife. But Dickinson is a true believer. If I give the order, he won't hesitate to visit a host of violations on them."

Fire licked his belly and his knuckles went white, but Cooper kept his voice under control. "You'd suffer quite a few in prison, Drew, while your daughters grew up alone. And this posturing is pointless. We both know that you'll do anything to get the video back. And I'll do anything to know my family is safe. So let's cut the bullshit."

"All right. How about we meet at the Washington Monument? A public place."

Cooper laughed. "Yeah. And I'll never hear the shot from the airship. I don't think so. No, let's meet at the L'Enfant Plaza Metro station."

"Where you can have a news crew at the ready to film everything. I'm afraid not."

"Okay. We don't trust one another. So we set it up so that neither of us has time to prepare a surprise. You name a major street downtown. I'll pick an address. We'll meet in twenty minutes."

"Twenty minutes? No."

"I'm not going to give you time to get set up, Drew."

"I understand that. But I'm busy cleaning up your mess right now. There was a firefight in a cemetery in broad daylight. It will take time to make sure there's no connection to the agency."

"No connection to you, you mean."

"Those are the same thing. Let's meet in two hours."

"Fine. But we don't pick a location until the last minute. I'll call you. Have a street in mind, and don't mess with me. And if anyone in my family has so much as a bruise, deal's off and I burn you down."

"If you call this off, your family will suffer more than bruises."

"So we both better behave. I'll call in two hours. Agreed?"

"Agreed."

"One last thing."

"What's that?"

Cooper said, "How the fuck do you sleep at night, Drew?"

"With a prescription. Grow up. This is the way the world works." The director hung up the phone.

"Two hours." Quinn shook his head. "Just like you predicted."

"Peters is the head of Equitable Services and thinks like it. That makes him easy to anticipate. He wants enough time that he can use his resources, see if he can track me down without the hassle of meeting. There's always the chance that I screwed up, that someone caught my face on a camera, or that I was calling from a known phone number. A long shot, but worth checking, especially for a man with his own security force. But at the same time, he can't risk giving me enough time that I start to second-guess myself, decide to go to the media with the video. One hour isn't enough time, three is too long."

"What's to keep him from showing up at the meet with an army?"

"He knows I would spot them. He can't risk spooking me. And since he won't know the location in advance, he can't get snipers set up or teams in place."

"Still. He's got to know he's walking into a trap," Shannon said.

Cooper shook his head. "That's what we've got going for us. He thinks I'm working alone. He knows my capabilities, what advantages my gift offers. He can plan for that. Counter it."

"So because he thinks you're alone, he'll bring a small force, just enough not to scare you. And because you're *not* alone, you think we can take them."

"That's the idea."

"Gee," Quinn said. "It's a good thing you've got two other ass-holes wrapped up in this."

"Yeah," Cooper said. He locked eyes with his partner, his friend. He knew what it was Quinn was risking, the same as the rest of them. But while Cooper had no choice, and Shannon had her own reasons, Quinn was doing this because it was the right thing to do. *And because he's your friend.* Cooper fiddled with the edge of a cushion. Looked out the window. "Look, I want you to know—"

"Stow it," Quinn said. "Just make sure you pick up the check from now on."

"Beer's on me. Forever."

"You boys are adorable," Shannon said. "But this is stupid. If Peters picks a street and you pick an address, we won't be able to plan either. We'll be walking in blind."

"No, Ms. Mysterio," Quinn said. "That's where I come in." He glanced at his watch. "Speaking of. I better go to headquarters and gear up. Gimme that burner. I'll toss it in the river on the way."

"Be careful, Bobby. They don't know you're in this, but Peters will be on high alert. No wrong moves."

"I'll be in and out. Hell"—Quinn smiled—"I'll channel her."

■

Two hours.

A hundred and twenty endless minutes to pace.

He'd been moving ever since he left the mall bathroom, and that motion had given him something to think about. Now, though, there was nothing to do but wait. And in that stillness, his imagination kept painting pictures of his children. Of how scared they must be.

Dickinson won't have hurt them. He's dangerous, but he's not a psycho. He probably explained the situation to Natalie, let her manage the children. No point dealing with extra drama.

Even if that was true, it meant Natalie would be the one suffering all of it. No idea what was going on, what deals were being made, maybe even why they'd been taken.

Natalie was strong and smart. If things went the way he planned, she and the kids would be free in a couple of hours. She would be able to handle it.

But his daughter would know something was wrong. Kate was only four, but her gift was powerful. She would know that her mother was scared, would know that Dickinson was not a friend.

How will a four-year-old girl deal with that?

He couldn't think of an answer he liked.

"You should get some sleep," Shannon said from the kitchen, where she was rifling through Quinn's fridge. "Big night ahead."

"You too."

"I think your boyfriend is twelve. All he has in his fridge is chocolate milk, mustard, and beer."

"Yes, please."

She pulled out two bottles, twisted the caps off, and tossed them toward the trash. The kitchen had a pass-through to the living room, and she set his on the counter. They faced each other, the counter between them. Something always between them, it seemed like.

Shannon took a sip, tipping the bottle up and then wiping her lips with the back of her hand. She looked at him, and he could see her trying to decide what to say.

"I'm sorry," he said. "For leaving like that. It was stupid."

"Yeah. Why did you?"

"I don't know." He gestured with the beer. "I was confused."

"And now you're not?"

"No, I still am. I just don't care as much. I'm glad you're here."

"Because I can help you."

"Not only for that." Cooper paused. "While we're on the subject, though. Why are you doing this? Helping me?"

"Same reason I've given you every time you've asked. I'm more than willing to fight for my right to exist."

"Is that the only reason?"

She gave a noncommittal shrug.

"Let me try again. I'm sorry. I panicked. Everything happened fast, and Smith, the way he plays people. I couldn't be sure he wasn't using you to play me."

"You think I slept with you because he told me to?" Her voice was a knife wrapped in tissue paper.

"It occurred to me, all right? It seemed possible."

"Screw you, Cooper."

"But then, on the plane here, it hit me. The real reason I'd panicked. Yes, you'd been lying to me since we met. But I'd been lying to you, too. The difference was that you knew that, and I didn't. And I guess I just felt...stupid. Embarrassed."

"You're terrible at apologies, you know that?"

"Yeah. My ex said something about that." He tried for a smile, but it died on his lips. "Okay, truth?"

"Please."

"I really like you, Shannon. It's been a long time since I felt this way about someone. Years. Since Natalie and I split up. And this thing with you, whatever it is, it feels different. You understand parts of me that no one else does. And you're amazing at work. I'm not used to someone being able to match me."

"Arrogant much?"

"Come on. Tell me you don't know what I'm talking about."

"I don't have to. You're the one apologizing, not me."

Cooper took a pull on the beer, set it on the counter. "All right. Last try. You know last night when I asked you about the diner, about you saying you hoped I started fresh? I really, really wished I could do what you were suggesting. Walk away. Start a new life. And you were the reason."

Something in her softened.

Cooper said, "What we're about to try is insane. It's unlikely that we'll get out alive. But if we do, would you like to have dinner with me?"

Shannon quirked that smile. Took a sip of her beer. "Takes you a while to get there, but in the end you do okay."

"Is that a yes?"

"You think I'm amazing, huh?"

"Is *that* a yes?"

She shrugged. "If we're still alive later, ask me then."

CHAPTER 39

For all the frenetic activity of the day—the tourist-mobbed streets, the abrupt traffic jams, the motorcades that backed everything up, the eternal construction—at night, downtown Washington, DC, was calm. Restaurants did a steady business, cabs buzzed between hotels, men in suits and women in dresses strolled the sidewalks, but it felt like the pilot light of the city's furnace. Quinn returned with gear about nine; by nine thirty, the three of them were atop a parking deck in the heart of down-town. The skyline glowed 360, the most famous buildings in the world, bright white and spotlit. Bobby sat cross-legged on the hood of his car, laptop open. Shannon had climbed up on the concrete lip of the deck, was walking it back and forth like a tightrope, a five-story drop on one side and pure calm in her posture.

Cooper was reassembling his weapon. Quinn had brought it along with the rest of the gear. His trip to headquarters had gone without incident; he regularly requisitioned supplies like these, and the guards hadn't blinked. The gun was a Beretta, Cooper's preferred manufacturer. An agency weapon, and thus perfectly cleaned and maintained, but the army taught you not to fire a weapon you hadn't taken apart and put back together, and it was a habit he'd never tried to break. If nothing else, it passed the time.

Speaking of…

He glanced at Quinn, saw the man already looking at him. Nodding.

Cooper took out the second burner cell phone and dialed. Gave his code to the operative who answered, "Jimmy's Mattresses." Waited for Peters. When his former boss answered, Cooper said, "Couldn't find me, huh?"

"I told you, I was cleaning up your—"

"Yeah. What's the street?"

"7th Avenue, Northwest."

"Stand by." He muted the phone. "7th Avenue, Northwest."

Quinn began typing immediately, his fingers flying across the keys. "Let's see…"

Cooper stared out at the night, tapped his fingers. Five seconds. Ten. Fifteen. "Bobby…"

"Here we go. 900 7th Avenue. Hingepoint Productions, tenth floor. Give him…ten minutes exactly."

Cooper unmuted the phone. "900 7th Avenue, Northwest. Hingepoint Productions, on the tenth floor. 9:48. If you're not there by 9:49, deal's off."

"I need more time—"

"Negative."

Peters sighed. "900 7th Avenue, Northwest, confirmed."

Cooper hung up the phone. "Let's roll."

■

The parking deck had been at 10th and G, about a third of a mile away. Bobby had been right on the money. He'd been perusing buildings within a narrow radius for the last half an hour, preparing options on every street. The downtown was a snarl of one-ways and traffic lights, and since Peters would have to be driving—no other way to handle Cooper's family—Bobby had suggested turning that to their advantage, picking somewhere they could get to faster on foot. When it came to planning the logistics of an op, the man was unmatched.

The building was the tallest nearby. An office complex, and despite the hour, a number of the windows were lit up. Made sense. Official business hours might end at six, but in this town someone was always working late.

The lobby was at once attractive and bleak, a place meant to impress without creating the desire to linger. A janitor hunched over a floor buffer, polishing away the day's scuffs. Broad hallways branched off to elevators. Behind an information desk, a security guard in a navy suit straightened as they entered.

"Can I help you folks?"

"Department of Analysis and Response," Quinn said, and held up his badge. "Where's your security office?"

"Sir? I—"

"We don't have time to explain. Move."

"Yes, sir. Right this way." He slid off the chair, a little stiff but obviously fit. "What's this in regard to?"

"It's in regard to none of your business, son," Cooper said.

The man didn't like that, but didn't question it, either. Former military, Cooper could read in his posture, and used to following orders. Good. A building that hired soldiers and cops should have the security they needed.

The guard pulled a badge on a retracting clip, used it to open a low barrier, and held it in place while they all walked through. They strode past a bank of shining elevators, down a narrow hall that ended in a door that read AUTHORIZED PERSONNEL ONLY. A closed-circuit camera was mounted above it, pointed down. The guard knocked twice, then used his badge to open the door without waiting for a response. "This is our command center—"

Cooper chopped him at the base of the neck and stepped over his body as it fell. Took in the room without stopping, twenty feet square, two men in chairs in front of a glowing projection screen. He got to the first as he rose, punched him in the throat, then grabbed his lapels and hurled him into the other, the two colliding and tangling, an office chair rolling sideways at the impact, banging into a trash can, paper spilling. Cooper followed, dodged through the mess of arms and legs, and delivered a quick left jab and right cross to the other guard's chin. The man's head snapped back, cracked into the tile floor, and his eyes fluttered as his body went limp.

"Freeze!"

The third guard had been by a row of file cabinets at the back, out of his line of sight. Eating dinner, apparently, half a sandwich abandoned atop wax paper. The man had a Taser out and held in steady hands, aimed at Cooper, finger inside the trigger.

Quinn is standing behind me. I can dodge the electrodes, but he can't. A Taser is nonlethal and doesn't guarantee loss of consciousness, but it will scramble him, take him off his game.

And without him, this is over.

Cooper straightened slowly. Kept his hands up. "Listen—"

The guard twisted the Taser, pointed it at his own stomach, and pulled the trigger. Electrodes leaped from the barrel and jammed into his white dress shirt. There was a loud crackling and a flash of sparks. He went rigid, every muscle straining at once, and then toppled like a mannequin.

Suddenly revealed behind him, Shannon smiled. "Oops."

Amazing.

She winked at him, then dropped, took cuffs from the guard's belt, and locked him up. Cooper secured the others the same way. "Sedatives?"

"In the bag. Ten cc."

Cooper dug through and found a small black satchel with a hypodermic. He removed the cap, tapped out the bubble, then injected each of the guards in turn. By the time he'd straightened, Quinn was already in front of the projection screen, his fingers dancing through the air. "All right, all right."

"What have you got?"

"I got art, boss. I'm now the supreme commander of a nice suite of cameras and remote override on the door locks." The projection was four feet across, a glowing display hanging in midair. As Quinn moved and gestured, the screen responded, displaying video from various cameras: hallways, elevators, the lobby, all of it high definition and bright as a mirror. Satisfied, Quinn opened his laptop and propped it on the table. Dug in his gear bag and pulled out a small case. Inside, cradled in foam, was a row of tiny earpieces. He handed one to each of them. "Testing."

Cooper gave his partner the thumbs-up. Shannon said, "You boys do have good toys."

"Ladies and gentlemen, Elvis has entered the building," Quinn said. On the screen, two men Cooper didn't recognize stepped into the lobby. They wore jump boots instead of dress shoes, and they moved in graceful sync, checking the room, each knowing where the other would be looking. Each had a hand inside his suit jacket.

The next people through the door were his family.

Natalie was dressed in jeans and a sweatshirt, probably the same outfit she'd been wearing when Dickinson came for her. She looked lovelier than he remembered, but her face was pale and her shoulders tight.

Their children stood on either side of her, each holding one of her hands.

The world slipped and wobbled. Cooper felt a sick-sweet nausea, a blend of emotions competing at full force. It was the first time he'd seen them since the night everything changed, and he was shocked at how much they had grown. Todd was a full inch taller and ten pounds heavier, and Kate's face was losing the round softness of baby fat.

Six months, gone. The firsts that would have happened in that period, the laughter, the questions and fears and the ever-disappearing hours of them napping in his lap. The loss was palpable, tugged at him with physical weight.

Worse was the terror. To see them here, in the care of monsters, and to know that it was his fault. If anything happened to either of them, Jesus Christ, the world would crack, the sky would shatter, the sun would wink out, leaving nothing but a howl of wind across the emptiness.

As if to focus that fear, two more men stepped in behind them. Roger Dickinson, wary and alert, his quarterback good looks hiding a ruthless devotion that would make anything permissible. And Drew Peters, trim and neat as ever, cool gray as a winter morning. He carried a metal-backed briefcase that looked heavy.

I'll take care of your family.

"Okay," Quinn said, hands swirling in the air. The screen broke into quadrants showing external views. "No sign of other teams. And I'm monitoring DAR transmissions..." He looked at the laptop. "Got no notable action within half a mile. Looks like Peters didn't want to risk spooking you."

Cooper didn't respond, just stared. The two in front were good, he could tell. No surprise, but the fact that he didn't recognize them meant that Peters was using assets who weren't part of the conventional Equitable Services structure. *Probably part of his private team, the men he uses to clean up messes. They'll know what you can do and be ready for it.*

Two more men followed. One took up a position by the door; the other started toward the empty information desk. The advance guards headed for the elevator. Natalie stopped, turned over her shoulder to look at Peters. Said something.

"What's she saying?"

"Sorry, boss. No audio."

On the monitor, Peters shook his head. Dickinson stepped forward and put his hand on Natalie's arm. His fingers curled tight. Cooper fought an urge to punch the wall. The group began moving again, heading toward the elevator.

The janitor shut off the floor buffer and straightened. By his posture, it was clear he was asking them what they were doing. Without releasing Natalie, Roger Dickinson turned, pulled a gun from inside his suit, pointed it casually, and shot the janitor in the head.

At this distance, through the door, the bullet sounded like a firecracker.

On the screen, blood and gray matter spattered across the clean marble floors. The janitor crumpled.

Cooper was almost to the door before he realized he'd started moving. But Shannon was in front, wrapping her arms around him and planting a shoulder in his chest. "Nick, no!"

"Get out of my—"

"*No.* He's dead, and if you go out there, so are your children."

Cooper put a hand against her shoulder and—

Two men in front, ready. They'll be the first. Slide on the floor and fire, they won't be expecting it, you can take both.

Then stand up, run to the corner, take aim on...

Dickinson, a gun in his hand, standing beside your family?

Peters, behind them?

Two additional shooters in widely spaced positions?

—let it slip down her arm. He took a deep breath. Facing them now was suicide. Hell, that was probably even part of the point: Dickinson knew he was nearby, wanted to goad him into a stupid move.

"Cooper?" Quinn asked dryly. "We good?"

"Yeah." He shook himself free of Shannon, but gently, and she let him. "Yeah. What's happening?"

"Rear guard is moving on the body. Everyone else is heading for the elevator."

"All right." He took another breath, turned back to Quinn. His partner had cycled the images to follow the group's motion. The time code read 9:46. "You've got full control?"

"Just as God intended."

"Good. You can call the ball from here. Do you have a layout of the office?"

Quinn turned to the laptop, pulled open an architectural drawing, and made a few motions. "Hingepoint Productions. A graphic design firm. Their tagline is 'technology folds into art.' Cute, huh?"

Shannon said, "You can get a floor plan of any place? Just like that?"

"That's why we're Equitable Services, sweetheart."

Cooper leaned in. The diagram was simple enough, showed an open-plan office, rows of cubicles, the basic layout. "Can you pull it up on the cameras?"

"No. Building security covers common areas only. But I was able to remotely unlock the door."

"Okay. Shannon, you go up the stairs, I'll take the elevator. They're expecting me to be alone. They'll be keyed up and focused on me. Should make it easy for you to do your thing."

"They're heading up." Quinn typed in the air, and the whole screen filled with the inside of an elevator. The two shooters in front, then Natalie and his children, with Peters and Dickinson in back. One of the shooters pressed the button for the tenth floor.

There was no predicting the janitor. But everything else is going as you hoped. With Quinn watching from here and Shannon walking through walls, you can turn a losing situation into a winner. Let them get into the office and take position. You go in, draw their attention. Shannon gets behind, turns the tables. You finish it.

Drew Peters, you die tonight.

The elevator rose, the numbers changing. Second floor. Third. Fourth.

One of the shooters leaned forward and pressed a button.

The elevator stopped on the fifth floor.

"What are they—"

The two shooters stepped out. One turned and gestured to Natalie. She shook her head. The shooter drew a pistol. Pointed it.

At Todd.

There was probably only a hundred feet of distance between Cooper and his son, but it may as well have been a continent. Five floors of concrete and steel.

Natalie stepped between the man and their son. And then, as Cooper watched, she wound up and slapped him. Then she turned, took their children's hands, and led them off the elevator and into the hall.

Drew Peters pressed the button to close the elevator doors.

Cooper's brain was razor blades and electricity. Everything whirling and cutting, crackling and snapping. Distantly, he could hear Quinn saying what he already knew, that they were splitting up.

Peters has a plan of his own.

"Can you shut down the elevator?"

"I'll try, but I don't…" The floor numbers continued changing. Sixth floor, seventh floor, eighth floor…

Cooper wanted to scream, wanted to explode, wanted to flex his muscles and shatter the world. His family so close, and him helpless.

"I'm sorry, I can't do it, not before they…"

Ninth floor.

"Stop trying. Follow the others. Where are they going?"

Quinn gestured frantically, cycling through cameras so fast Cooper could barely process them, elevator, lobby, parking garage, rooftop, landing on an image of a hallway. The shooters moved away, one in front, one behind, his family in the middle. They walked to the end of the hall, turned the corner.

And were gone.

"Get them back!"

"That's the only camera we have on the fifth floor." Quinn's voice grim. "Cooper, I'm sorry. Looks like one camera in the elevator lobby of each floor, but that's all. Security for the common areas only. The offices would want privacy."

"How many offices on that floor?"

"Umm…ten suites."

Ten suites. Each with multiple places to hide.

"Let's go." Shannon's voice sounded pinched. "We can get to the fifth floor, work together. They won't be expecting both of us."

The elevator reached the tenth floor. Drew Peters and Roger Dickinson stepped off. They appeared in another monitor, the elevator lobby for that floor, and started walking. Peters transferred the briefcase to his other hand.

Cooper looked at the clock: 9:47. "No."

"What?" Quinn and Shannon together.

"I've got two minutes to get to that office. If I don't show up for the meeting, if I'm even a minute late, Peters will know something is happening. Best-case scenario, he'll call his team and they'll all abort. Worst case, he'll kill my family and take his chances calling down an army on this building."

"So…what do we do?"

"I need you to go after them." He turned to her. "You have to save my family."

Her eyes were wide. Scared, he realized, an expression he hadn't seen on her before. "Nick, I—"

He put a hand on her shoulder. "Please."

"What are you going to do?"

"Meet Peters. I'll buy you the time you need." Something dark and heavy slipped inside of him. "Get my family out of here."

He wanted to say more, to both of them, but there wasn't time. He just headed for the door. Shannon followed a moment later.

They moved swiftly down the hall to the elevator corridor and paused just before it.

In his ear, Quinn said, "One man by the elevator. The other is in the lobby behind the desk, pretending to be security."

Shannon said, "Is the elevator guard looking this way?"

"No."

She slid around the corner.

Cooper stood still, his body raging. The clock in his head counted down. His thoughts whirled, Natalie and Kate and Todd and men with guns and Drew Peters and President Walker.

This ends tonight. One way or the other.

"Shannon is in position. Go in two, one, now."

Cooper stepped around the edge of the corner. Shannon had shifted in where the guard wasn't looking, on the far side, and as Cooper started forward she coughed and pressed the call button. The guard whirled, one hand flying to his coat, and Cooper could read his thoughts, see him wondering how the hell this girl had gotten here without his noticing. Shannon smiled, just an office worker waiting for the elevator. The guard studied her, first relaxing and then stiffening when he heard Cooper's footsteps. He started to turn.

Too late.

Cooper grabbed his head in both hands and wrenched savagely, put all the anger into it, and the man's neck snapped and his body went limp and dead.

The elevator dinged. Cooper dragged the body on, pulling by the man's lolling head. Shannon pushed the buttons for five and ten.

"You two are scary together," Quinn said in both their ears. "Looks like the lobby guard didn't hear a thing. Good hunting."

The doors closed, and the elevator began to rise. Shannon said, "Nick, look—"

He cut her off. "You can do this."

"I just—"

"Listen," he said and then kissed her. She was briefly startled but returned the kiss, the elevator pinging off floors as their tongues danced. A kiss for luck and a cry for help and as clear a statement as he could think to make, and then the elevator stopped. He put one hand on her cheek. "I trust you."

She straightened her shoulders. "Buy me the time."

"Whatever it costs."

Shannon stepped off the elevator and turned right. Cooper pressed the door-close button, *come on, come on,* and then the elevator was in motion again.

Nothing to do now but wait for the future to arrive.

Six, seven, eight, nine, ten.

The doors slid open. Cooper took a deep breath and walked through them.

The hallway was corporate chic, gray carpet with a subtle pattern, beige walls, recessed lighting, a backlit glass display board listing the company names. Quinn said, "Turn right, third office on your left."

Cooper started down the hall. "Any sign of backup?"

"Negative. Local DAR frequencies are quiet, and the only phone I've monitored out of the building is on the third floor. A woman explaining to her husband that she'll be home late."

The office doors were heavy glass with bright metal handles, business names etched in the glass. He passed a lobbyist's office and a real estate firm, rounded the corner, saw the third. Hingepoint Productions, the first word spelled out lowercase and boxed in a design. A faint double chime pinged as he stepped through the door.

Quinn had said this was a graphic design firm, and the décor looked it. The near walls were painted a risky shade of orange that worked, and in place of paintings, skateboard decks were bolted to the wall, each a miniature work of art, robots and monsters, graffiti and skylines.

The floor plan had shown cubicles, but now he saw they were half-cubes, coming up maybe four feet. The ceiling was exposed, conduit and air-conditioning hanging from the girders. Quinn said, "I've unlocked all offices on the fifth floor. Shannon has checked the first—no luck. She's moving on."

Cooper moved down the aisle and stepped into the office proper. He could see clear across it in all directions. The studio took up a corner of the building, the exterior walls glass from floor to ceiling. With the overhead lights on, they were dark mirrors, bouncing the space back upon itself. In the precise center of the office was a long conference table surrounded by chairs.

Beside it stood Drew Peters and Roger Dickinson.

Cooper strolled forward. Calm and steady. Taking his time; the longer he could stall, the longer Shannon would have.

Dickinson looked the same as ever. Handsome, good posture, an alert readiness. His right hand was itching to jerk the pistol from his shoulder holster.

"Hello, Nick," Peters said. For the first time, Cooper noticed that Peters had a rodent-ish look. Something in his neat bearing and small mouth, his rimless glasses. The briefcase he'd been carrying sat on the table in front of him. "Nice to see you again."

The conference space was wide open. Cooper walked to the table. Stood opposite the two of them.

Remember, they don't know that you know, or that you have help. If they suspect either of those things for a second, this all comes crashing down. "Where's my family?"

"They're nearby."

"Not good enough." He took a step back, eyes forward.

"I'll prove it to you," Peters said, "but I'll need you to put down your gun."

"I don't have one."

"Of course you do. But it's okay. I'll go first." Peters reached for the briefcase, opening it slowly. The inside of the lid was a monitor, which glowed to life. The screen held white for a moment, then cut to a video feed.

Natalie sat in a leather chair at one end of a small room, Todd to her left, Kate to her right. The kids had pads of paper in front of them and appeared to be drawing. Kate, younger, was lost in it, but Natalie was leaning into Todd, trying to encourage him. Distracting them, Cooper realized, trying to keep them calm. The wall behind them was glass, the Capitol dome glowing in the distance. The two gunmen stood nearby, weapons out. One looked at the camera, the other at Natalie.

"That's quite a woman you divorced, Nick. A wonderful mother. And your children. Beautiful."

Cooper stared at the image, at his children, the reasons for every action he'd taken. Reason enough to set the world on fire. Natalie glanced up, directly into the monitor, as if she was staring at him.

How?

The camera, he realized. They would have set that up in front of them, and she was smart enough to know it would be for his benefit. It wasn't "as if" she was looking at him; she was staring at him. The look in her eyes a plea. Not for her, but for Kate and Todd.

A plea, and something else. What?

"Now. Your gun. Gently, please."

It wasn't that Natalie's eyes moved. They didn't. It was that she thought about moving them, thought about flickering them to the left. That thought translated into the tiniest subdermal motion, the kind of thing he could see.

The kind of thing she knows you can see.

She's giving you a hint.

Warmth bloomed in his chest. The women in his life were amazing.

"All I see is a conference room with the Capitol in the background," he said. "They could be anywhere."

"Let's not play games, Nick. You know how far I'm willing to go. Your gun."

In his ear, Quinn said, "Checking."

Cooper hesitated as if thinking about it. Then, slowly, he reached around his back and took out the pistol. Dickinson tensed, a coiled spring begging to explode. Using just his thumb and forefinger, Cooper set the weapon down and pushed it to slide across the table.

Quinn said, "Got it. Suite 508. The conference room is in the southeast corner."

Shannon said, "On my way."

Cooper said, "There. Now how about Roger does the same?"

Dickinson laughed. Peters gave his thin smile. "I don't think so. We're both aware of your abilities. Now, where's the drive?"

"It's safe."

"How nice to hear. Where?"

"If I tell you, how do I know you won't kill them anyway?"

"You have my word."

"That's not carrying as much weight with me as it used to, Drew."

"It's going to have to do. I told you, you're not in a position to negotiate. Give me what I want and I'll let you all go."

Dickinson said, "I bet it's in his pocket. Let me take him."

Shannon said, "Nick, I'm in the office, outside the conference room. Going now."

"No, Roger." Peters paused. Then he said, "Shoot Cooper's son on the count of three."

On the monitor, one of the guards raised his gun, pointed it at Todd—

The guards can hear him.

The speakerphone. The call light is on. They're listening in.

Shannon is stepping into that room now. She can take the guards...unless Peters or Dickinson yells a warning from up here.

Which they will if they're watching the monitor.

—as Peters said, "Three. Two."

"Okay!" Cooper took a quick step forward, and both Peters and Dickinson jumped, turned their full attention on him. "I've got it here." He reached in his pocket, felt the slim profile of the stamp drive. He didn't want to risk losing hold of it, even for a moment. It was the only proof he had of the monstrosity he had helped create. Once he let it go, everything could change. The only chance for some sort of justice could vanish.

It's justice or your children.

Cooper pulled the drive from his pocket. It took all his effort not to glance at the monitor. His children, helpless, and him up here, powerless, and Dickinson right there, hungry, his hand already flexing. Cooper kept his fingers curled around the drive, didn't let them see it. They wouldn't risk making a move until they were sure he wasn't bluffing. He held the moment as long as he dared, his heart pounding. Stepped forward, lowered his hand over the table. Opened his fingers.

The drive fell to the table.

Peters zeroed in on it, eyes hungry and triumphant.

A flash of movement on the monitor. Cooper told himself not to look, but it was too late, his gift beyond his control, needing data, reading situations.

Dickinson staring at him. Tracking his eyes. Following them.

They both watched as, on the monitor, Shannon threw an elbow into the throat of a gunman.

To the guards, Dickinson yelled, "Kill them!" as his hand flew inside his jacket.

Cooper spun and bolted for the nearest cubicle, leaving the drive on the table. A shot from behind, and drywall exploded. He kept moving, feeling Dickinson tracking him, firing again and again, not quite catching him, and then he was out of sight behind a low cube. He dropped to his knees and quickly crawled for the next one, bullets punching through the fabric walls.

Peters will go for the drive.

Nothing he could do about that. The conference room would be lethal. He wasn't a superhero who could dodge bullets. Being able to see where someone intended to shoot gave him a leg up, but against a professional like Dickinson, in an open space, it wouldn't be enough.

Had Shannon taken out both gunmen? No way to know, and no time to wonder. There was another shot, and another ragged hole blown in a fabric wall. A monitor exploded.

Cooper stayed low, hurried along the aisle between the cubicles. Pictured the floor plan, trying to place himself on it. The design studio was large, maybe fifty employees. The open plan meant that if he stood up, Dickinson would be able to see him. On the other hand, if he didn't stand up, his own gift was nullified. Without being able to see what was going on, he was just prey, scurrying from cover to cover.

He looked around. Two cubes near him, one stacked with papers and folders, the other neat and decorated, someone making an effort to turn a gray fabric cage into a cozy living room: a recliner, a lamp, framed photos on the desk. Nothing resembling a weapon in either, at least not a weapon he'd match against a handgun. Glanced upward: girders, pipes, hanging banks of fluorescent lights.

At some distance, a faint double ping. The door chime.

Quinn would have warned him if any more threats had come into the building. Which meant that sound was Peters leaving. With the drive.

Everything was falling apart.

Cooper crept into the well-decorated cube, took one of the photos off the desk. The glass was bright and reflected a ghostly image of him. He eased it up above the edge of the fabric wall. It was a long way from a mirror, but it gave a hint of what was going on, the overheads glowing in it, and motion, Dickinson somehow ten feet tall. The table. The agent had climbed on top of it for a better view. Cooper pulled the picture down before the man spotted it.

"Come on, Cooper," Dickinson said. "Come out and I'll make it quick. Just like your children."

Bile surged in his throat. He whispered, "Shannon? You okay?" No response.

Quinn said, "Coop, I don't know what's going on. I've got no feed, and she's not answering."

"I recognized your terrorist girlfriend," Dickinson said, "but I'm afraid she didn't make it."

It was a bluff. A way to taunt him into the open. It had to be.

"And that little stunt cost your family's lives. Sorry about that, but we did warn you."

He closed his eyes, leaned back against the cubicle wall.

"Ahh, don't sweat it, Cooper. Kids are replaceable. What's one or two gone?"

Nothing from Quinn. Nothing from Shannon. He'd caught only the tiniest flash of her on the monitor, a move to disable one of the guards, but there had been two in the room. Skilled killers on high alert.

His gift ran ahead of him again, collated the data, jumped to its conclusion.

Your family is dead.

Cooper had been at a scene once where a car had collided with an agent and pinned him against a metal barrier, shattering everything from the ribs down, severing both legs at midthigh. Massive physical damage, unsurvivable. What had haunted him most, though, was that the man was calm. He didn't scream, didn't seem to feel any pain.

Some wounds were too enormous to feel.

A strange dark purity flowed through him. It was almost sweet. If his family was gone, there wasn't much point in going on. Not many reasons to live. Just one.

You're going to die, Roger. And so is Peters.

He ducked low, left the cubicle, and scurried down the aisle. Kept his shoulder against the near wall, visualizing the angle Dickinson could see. Climbing on top of the conference table would give him the high ground, generally a tactical advantage. But it came with limitations, too.

A gunshot, and then another. Nothing exploded near him, though. Dickinson was blind-firing, trying to draw him out.

I'm coming out, Roger. Don't you worry.

He moved along the aisle back toward the entrance. On the wall between two mounted skateboards he saw what he'd been looking for. But it was a long, exposed sprint to reach it. No way to get there without being seen.

He dropped to a runner's crouch, ready to sprint. Then, with a looping toss, he threw the picture frame as far behind as he could.

Dickinson reacted immediately, twin gun blasts. Cooper didn't pause, just launched himself into a sprint for the far wall, covering a dozen yards in seconds. He heard glass shatter behind him, the picture frame hitting something. Dickinson would have processed it for the distraction it was. He'd have his gun up and be tracking, looking for motion.

It didn't matter. Nothing mattered now except killing. Killing, and the fact that Cooper had made it to the bank of light switches he'd spotted on the lobby wall. He smacked them all in one swiping blow. The fluorescents died.

Darkness fell, pure as fury.

Cooper turned and stood up. No need to hide now. When the lights had been on, Cooper had been prey, and Dickinson had been a predator.

With the lights out, Cooper was a shadow in the dark. And Dickinson was a silhouette standing on a conference table, bathed in the glow of the monitor Peters had brought. He may as well have been in a spotlight.

The agent had a gun in each hand, his own in the right, Cooper's in the left, and he raised them both and fired in the general direction of the light switches. But Cooper was no longer there.

And the twin muzzle flashes would only make things worse for him. Rob him of what limited night vision he'd have.

Cooper moved steadily, not running, not risking tripping or making a sound. Just watching Dickinson as he spun and flailed in the dark. By the time he reached the conference table, the other agent had realized his mistake. Dickinson jumped down, landing hard.

Cooper stepped forward and twisted the guns from the man's hands.

Then he put them both against Roger Dickinson's chest and pulled the triggers until the slides locked back.

What was left of the agent fell limp and wet. Cooper dropped the guns on top of him.

He walked to the table. To the monitor.

His family was dead.

Now he just had to face it. To look at the monitor and see the end of the world.

Cooper forced himself to face it.

The screen showed a conference room, the Capitol dome glowing in the distance.

It showed one of the shooters on the ground, splayed flat.

It showed the other pulling himself to his feet, woozy, his fingers scrabbling at the table for help.

What it did not show was the bodies of his family.

God bless you, Shannon. My girl who walks through walls.

"Coop?" Quinn's voice in his ear. "I just picked up Shannon in the number three elevator. She's got your family with her. She's bleeding pretty bad from the right side of her head—must have taken a hit that disabled the transmitter. But she's giving a thumbs-up to the camera, and everyone else looks fine."

For a moment he let himself feel it. A feeling as if he could flex and blow the roof open, a feeling like his heart might burst.

Quinn said, "Bad news is, I'm getting a lot of traffic on law enforcement frequencies. A small army is headed our way. Time to go."

"Where's Peters?"

"He's not with you?"

"No. And he's got the drive."

"*What?* How?"

"No time to explain. Has he shown up on your screens?"

"No. He didn't go through the elevator lobby."

The smart thing to do was get out, escape with Quinn and Shannon and his family. Hide somewhere and think of their next move. Let Peters walk away with the only evidence.

Cooper turned and ran for the exit. Through the lobby, out the door, the chime ringing behind him. "Quinn, are there cameras in the stairwells?"

"Negative."

Turned left on a hunch, kept going, found the stairwell at the end. He pushed open the door, stepped into a brightly lit concrete space. "Do they exit to the outside?"

"Yeah, of course, that's code in case of fire," Quinn said, and then, "Oh shit."

Cooper started down, jumping a flight at a time, his hand trailing down the metal railing. Peters would have made it to the street by now. Vanished into—

He couldn't be sure that Dickinson would take me. If he were, he'd have stayed to help.

Since he didn't, he suspected I might win.

And he knows that if I did, I'd come after him.

He won't do what you expect.

—the night. Cooper caught himself on a handrail, turned the other way, sprinted upward. His calves burning and lungs screaming. Past the tenth, the eleventh, the twelfth.

Quinn said, "Shit. Cooper, I've got a helicopter inbound, ETA forty-five seconds."

Sneaky, Drew. Very sneaky. Cooper said, "Good."

"Huh?"

"Get out of here. Get Shannon out, get my family out. I'll meet you at the rendezvous."

"Cooper—"

"Now. That's an order."

The flight above the twelfth ended in a door. Cooper hit it at a run, the thing flying open to expose the roof. Gravel and the bulk of industrial air conditioners, the sudden cool of the evening air and the buzz of the city all around, and, faint but growing louder, the whap of helicopter rotors.

The director was at the southeast edge of the building, in a clear space just barely broad enough for a helicopter to land on.

A flash of an image, San Antonio, the rooftop with Alex Vasquez. Chasing her to the edge of the building, her body a silhouette against the night sky.

Peters heard him when he was about ten feet away, whirled. He said, "No," and reached around his back. Cooper caught his arm, twisted it forward, then spun to bring the force of his other forearm down against the director's elbow, which snapped with a sick pop. Drew Peters screamed, and the gun dropped from his limp fingers.

Cooper held him up with one hand, then used the other to dig in the man's pockets. The stamp drive was in the front right. He took it, then gripped the man by his lapels and marched him backward. Three steps took them to the edge of the building. The skyline burned behind, a wash of lights on marble and monuments. The White House was lit from below, regal and imposing. He wondered if President Walker was there right now, if he was sitting in the Oval Office, or putting on a bathrobe and crawling into bed.

The chopper grew closer. A spotlight speared down from it, swinging back and forth, playing across the buildings. Hunting.

Peters's face was sheened with shock-sweat, his eyes wide. But his voice was strangely level as he said, "You want to kill me? Go ahead."

"Okay." He marched Peters a half step back.

"Wait!" The heel of the man's dress shoe slipped and scuffled at the edge. "This is bigger than you and me. If you do this, the world will burn."

"Still hoping I'm a true believer, huh?"

"I know you are."

"Maybe you're right. Maybe I still do believe. But not in you, and not in your dirty little game."

"It's not a game. It's the future. You're going to have to choose sides."

"Yeah," Cooper said. "I've heard that." He yanked his old mentor close, then shoved outward with all his strength.

As Drew Peters flew off the edge of the roof, he crossed the beam of the helicopter searchlight. A flailing rag doll a hundred feet above the concrete. And for a fraction of a second, the dazzling beam seemed to hold him up.

But only for a fraction of a second.

CHAPTER 40

It took him an hour and a half to get clean.

If done directly, the walk from the office building at 900 7th Street NW to the bench overlooking the Lincoln Memorial would take only about twenty minutes. Thirty if you strolled, enjoyed the route, which was one of the most famous in the world. Past the East Wing of the White House, the lights burning inside the windows at all hours. The Washington Monument, a spear in the heart of the night, the airplane warning light blinking slowly. The rippling reflections of the pond in Constitution Garden. The shiny black scar of the Vietnam Memorial bisecting the hillside. And finally the epic neoclassical bulk of the Lincoln Memorial itself. The broad marble steps leading up to the fluted columns, the colonnade glowing from spotlights within, somber old Honest Abe staring out in contemplation, as if weighing the country he had led.

But Cooper hadn't gone directly. His first priority had been getting out of the building. The stairwell had given him access to the street. From there, he'd headed north and then east, hearing the telltale sounds of converging force. Quinn hadn't been kidding about a small army; Peters must have summoned all nearby law enforcement. This being Washington, DC, the most heavily policed city in the nation, that meant not only DAR teams, but also metropolitan police, Capitol police, transit police, park police, the Secret Service uniformed division, and God knew how many others.

And as none of them seemed to know what was going on or for whom they were looking, the best description of it was "train wreck."

Cooper assumed that might have been part of the point, that Peters was focusing on getting maximum manpower in place and then quarterbacking from the air. The confusion would give him plenty of latitude to write the story however he liked—probably, that rogue agent–turned–abnorm terrorist Nick Cooper had kidnapped his family before being cornered in this building by Equitable Services. All the extra force would look good, a blow for interagency cooperation that still assured the real credit went to the DAR.

Sorry about that, Drew. I guess falling a dozen stories onto concrete is going to mess up your plan.

The good news was that without a quarterback, all those forces spent most of their time tripping over one another. Sirens and lights, SWAT teams and the faceless, barricades and badges. Cooper used the confusion to get a little distance, and after that, the rest was routine. He tracked in and out of buildings, rode the Metro one stop north and then two south, circled the same block twice in each direction, and then finally set off across the Mall.

An hour and a half later, he was sitting on the park bench, staring back at Abraham Lincoln. Still twenty minutes before he could rendezvous with Quinn and Shannon.

Twenty minutes before he could see his children.

Twenty minutes to decide the fate of the world.

Cooper had his datapad out, the stamp drive slotted. He'd logged on and prepped the video file for distribution. He'd learned from John Smith's mistake; instead of sending it to a handful of journalists who could be silenced, he'd prepped it for upload to a public video-sharing-system. All he had to do was press send and it would spread like wildfire. In an hour it would have propagated to thousands of people; by morning it would be everywhere, on every news channel, every website. The whole world would know the ugly truth.

All he had to do was press send.

What had Peters said? *"This is bigger than you and me. If you do this, the world will burn."*

It would certainly mean the end of this administration. A president caught on tape authorizing the murder of innocent citizens? He'd be crucified, face jail time, maybe worse.

All of which was fine with Cooper. But the problem with striking sparks was that fire wasn't easy to control. How far would this one go?

Faith in the government, already at an all-time low, would plummet. In their hearts, Americans already didn't believe that their leaders cared about them. People thought of politicians in the most jaded and cynical terms, and with some good reason. But it was a big step to discover the government was ordering their murder.

And Equitable Services. To have even a chance at survival, it would have to disavow Peters, claim he was a fanatic operating outside of bounds. But even then, the agency might be destroyed.

Which wasn't entirely a good thing. Yes, Peters had misused the agency. But the threat from violent abnorms was real. Maybe not every person Cooper had terminated was dirty. But plenty were. Without Equitable Services, there would be no one to contain them.

Not only that, but the video cleared John Smith of the Monocle. It turned him from a terrorist back into a freedom fighter, maybe even a hero. There were plenty of people who would look up to him. See him as a brave new voice. Maybe even a potential leader.

A scary thought. Smith had the intellect and acumen to lead. But Cooper didn't trust the man's heart. He'd admitted to planting bombs, to seeding viruses, to assassinating civilians. Smith was innocent of the Monocle, but he was plenty guilty.

Peters might well be right. Sharing this might well set the world on fire.

Of course, there's another option.

Cooper could put the video to work for him. By threatening to leak it, he could blackmail President Walker. Take over Equitable Services himself, run the agency the way it was supposed to be run. He could sit in Drew Peters's chair and make decisions the right way. Fight to prevent a war, instead of to prolong one.

It was a tempting thought. All his adult life, Cooper had fought to protect his country. First from external threats, in the army, and then from a much greater danger—its future. If straights and brilliants came to open conflict, it would be an unthinkably bloody affair, one that would turn fathers against sons and husbands against wives.

That would turn brothers against sisters. Would Kate and Todd someday have to take up arms against one another?

He couldn't let that happen. That was why he had done everything he had done. The good and the bad, the righteous and the misdirected. It had all been for that one belief—that somehow, some way, the children of this brave new world had to find a way to live together.

And if he used this instead of sharing it, he could help make that happen. Change the system from within.

Cooper looked up and out, at the velvety darkness of the Washington night. Low-bellied clouds shaded purple with light reflected off marble and monuments, off the machinery of government. Off a city that was supposed to stand for something.

From between massive columns, Abraham Lincoln stared out with a troubled expression. The bloodiest war in American history had happened on his watch, under his command. Could the country survive a second civil war?

He glanced at the clock on his d-pad. Time to go.

Truth or power?

Cooper thought of his children.

Then he pressed send, set the datapad on the bench, and left it there.

Maybe the world would burn. But if truth was all it took to start the fire, maybe it needed to.

Regardless, his part in this war was over.

■

Five minutes later, a cab dropped him in Shaw, on a quiet block of small row houses. Founded as freed-slave encampments, the neighborhood had once been the Harlem of DC—both the good Harlem and the bad Harlem—but in the last decades, gentrification had mixed things up, white professionals edging out blue-collar blacks. For good or bad, everything changed.

Cooper paid the driver and got out in front of a tidy Victorian. The ground-floor windows were bright, and he could see shapes moving inside. Quinn was leaning against his car, spinning an unlit cigarette. "You made it."

"Yeah. Took the scenic route."

"And Peters?"

"His route was scenic, too. But a whole lot faster."

"Been waiting to say that?"

"Little bit. My family?"

"Inside. I've been out here the last hour, haven't seen any signs of trouble."

"Shannon? You said she was hurt."

"Yeah, a nasty hit to the side of the head. Her ear's all bloody, but she's okay." Quinn smiled. "She's pretty pissed off about it, actually. I think the girl really believed she was invisible."

"She's damn close."

"That she is. Speaking of which." Quinn reached into his pocket, pulled out a stamp drive similar to the other one. "The security footage from 900. All cameras from half an hour before we arrived through departure. I wiped the local drives before I left. We're invisible, too."

"You're a goddamn wonder, Bobby."

"Don't you forget it." His partner put the cigarette between his lips, then took it out again. "So what do you think? Will the agency cop to what happened?"

"I doubt it. I'm sure some public-relations bright boy is working on the cover story now."

"'Director Drew Peters, infuriated by modern aesthetics, in protest shot up a graphic design company before hurling himself off the roof.'"

"Something like that." Motion caught his eye. The front door opening, and two figures stepping out. "We're safe here?"

"The house belongs to a friend of a friend, no connection." Quinn followed his gaze, saw Shannon and Natalie on the porch. The two women were talking, but even from here Cooper could read the stiffness in their postures, the awkwardness between them. *Ex-wife and new...whatever she is.*

Quinn seemed to see the same. "Yikes. That looks awkward. Better go before the knives come out."

"Yeah." He started up the walk, turned back. "Bobby? Thanks. I owe you one."

"Nah," Quinn said, and smiled. "You owe me a lot more than one."

Cooper laughed.

On the porch, Natalie tensed to see him. He could read her thoughts, same as ever. Could see the happiness in her, the relief that he was safe, and the anger over what she'd been put through in the last six months. Shannon had gauze on her ear and blood on her shirt. Her usually fluid posture was rigid.

"Hey," he said, looking from one of them to the other.

"Are we safe?" Natalie asked.

"Yes."

"It's over?"

"Yes."

"You're coming back to us?"

"Yes," he said, and saw Shannon stiffen further. "I guess I don't have to introduce you two?"

"No," Natalie said. "Shannon took care of that. She's amazing."

"I know." He let his eyes linger on the fine bones of her face. "You both are. I couldn't have done it without you."

He didn't really know what to say after that, and apparently neither of them did either. Natalie crossed her arms. Shannon shifted her weight from one foot to the other. After a moment, she said, "Well. I'll get out of here, let you be with your family." She held out a hand to Natalie. "It was nice to meet you."

Natalie looked at her, and at her outstretched hand. Then she stepped past it and wrapped her arms around the other woman. "Thank you," she whispered. "Thank you."

Shannon nodded, returned the embrace a little awkwardly. "Yeah. Your children are beautiful."

"And alive, thanks to you." Natalie held the hug a moment longer, then stepped back and said, "If you ever need anything, *anything*, don't hesitate. Okay?"

"Okay." She looked at Cooper. "See you around, I guess." Then she slid off the porch and started down the walk.

Cooper watched her and then turned back to his ex-wife. To most people, her pose wouldn't have given anything away, but he could read it all, a book he knew thoroughly. The honest gratitude coupled with the discomfort. It made sense; for the last six months, she had been living a nightmare, too, doing it for their children, the same as he had, and in some way, she must have been thinking of him as her partner in it. As a husband again, despite everything. It must have cut her to see the hints of his relationship with Shannon. And hurting her was the last thing he wanted to do. He'd explain, make it clear…

"The kids are all right?"

"They're…they will be. Want to see them?"

"Oh, God yes." He started for the door, then froze. "One second, okay?" Cooper didn't wait for an answer, just hurried down the steps, caught Shannon's arm. "Wait."

She turned to him. Her face unreadable. "What?"

He opened his mouth, closed it. Then said, "We survived."

"I noticed."

"And we saved the world."

"Hooray for us."

"So…"

She looked at him, quirked that half smile. "Yes?"

"Well, you said if we survived, you'd go out with me."

"No. I said if we survived, you could ask."

"Right. Well." He shrugged. "What do you say? Want to go on a date that doesn't involve gunfire?"

"I don't know." She struck a pose, paused. "What would we do without it?"

"We'll think of something." He smiled, and she smiled back.

"All right, Nick. But it better not be boring."

"Deal."

"Deal. Now go."

He nodded, started back for the house. Thought of something, turned. "Hey, wait, I still don't have your…"

Shannon was gone.

How does she do *that?*

He shook his head, grinned to himself, started for the house. The door was open, and he heard Natalie's voice, and then the three of them stepped out into the light.

Todd and Kate were both pale, and both had been crying. In that instant, he saw what had happened to them, all that had happened. The months he'd missed, and the pressure on them.

The horrors the world had wrought. And, worst of all, the things that had happened since yesterday, things they didn't understand, couldn't understand, but things that would mark them. They were wounded, he suddenly understood. Not physically, but not all wounds were visible.

The moment tore the heart out of him. A frozen instant that he would never shake.

Then they saw him. For a moment, they didn't know what they were looking at. It was dark, and it had been six months, an eternity at their ages, and for a second they didn't recognize him.

Kate was first, her eyes going wide. She looked up at Natalie, and then back at him, and then Todd said, "Dad?"

And then they were hurtling down the steps and across the walk and into his arms, and he was hoisting them up, all of them laughing and crying and saying each other's names and the warmth of them, the smell, the primal comfort, an emotional rush like he'd never known and always known, the thing that made everything worthwhile, and in that instant he realized he'd been wrong.

His part in this war wasn't over. Not even close.

His children needed a world to grow up in, a future worthy of them, and until that day his fight would never be over. As long as there was a war, he'd be in it.

But for a moment, as he hugged them so hard their bones pressed his, as Todd clutched his chest and Kate buried her face in his neck, as Natalie came down the steps and wrapped her arms around them all, as he smelled his son's hair and tasted his daughter's tears, the rest fell away.

The future could wait. For a little while, at least.

END OF BOOK ONE

EXCERPT: PROLOGUE FROM BOOK TWO

Enjoy an exclusive sneak peek at Book Two in the *Brilliance* Saga, coming 2014

On the monitor, Cleveland was burning.

Cooper watched the president watch it. Lionel Clay's face was drawn, his shoulders tight beneath his dress shirt. He stood like a man caught in a spotlight.

"The situation's getting worse." Owen Leahy pressed a button and the image shifted, an overhead view of a government building. Cold stone and columns, it was a gray island encircled by a sea of people, thousands of them, a mass of rough currents that formed no pattern. The secretary of defense continued, "City hall is surrounded. The National Guardsmen that were already on scene have secured the building, but they're having trouble getting reinforcements in. Cleveland PD has a riot team en route, but the mob is making it slow going."

"Where did the fire start?" The president spoke without looking from the screen.

"The east side, 55th and Scoville. A tenement building, but it's spreading fast. There are twelve square blocks burning, another twenty at risk in the next hour."

"Fire crews?"

"They're spread thin, sir, and they're tired. They've had multiple fires every day for the last two weeks. This is the first to get out of control. They're focusing on containment, with every station sending men, but the mob is—"

"Making it slow going."

"Yes, sir."

"Get the mayor on the phone."

"We've been trying." Leahy left the rest unsaid.

"The Children of Darwyn are behind this?"

"The COD are certainly involved. But there are too many people for it to be just them, and as you can see, the crowd is fighting itself." Leahy pressed another button, and the angle shifted, zooming in.

A camera drone, Cooper figured, unmanned and circling a mile above the scene. The video showed the front line of a pitched battle, men and women screaming at each other, whirling, spinning. A man in a leather jacket swung a baseball bat. A teenage girl, her face a bloody mess, leaned between two people pushing to get out of the fray. A white guy stood over a black man, kicking him savagely. A group rocked a car, bouncing and shoving and bouncing until it tilted up on one side, held for a moment, and toppled.

"The whole city is rioting?"

"A lot of people are out protecting their property, others are just watching. But everything within half a mile of Public Square is a mess. Intelligence estimates say as many as ten thousand rioters in the downtown area. And the power is still out. It will get worse when night falls."

"Why didn't the mayor call in more police right away?"

"We don't know, sir. But at this point, even if riot squads make it to city hall, they won't be able to do much more than secure the building. The mob is just too big."

"The democrats are going to have a field day with this," Marla Keevers said. The chief of staff had a way of turning the word 'democrats' into an obscenity. "You're going to take a huge—"

"I don't care about politics right now, Marla. One of my cities is on fire. Four hundred thousand people live in Cleveland. Is this part of a larger attack?"

"We don't know, sir."

"Why not?"

"It's chaos down there, Mr. President. I'm coordinating with the FBI and the DAR; we're hoping to have a better picture in an hour—"

"An *hour*?"

Keevers and Leahy exchanged a glance. The secretary of defense said, "Sir, it's time to take aggressive action. We should assume that this is the first step in an attack, maybe a national one."

The president said nothing.

"Sir, we need to act."

Clay stared at the screen.

"Mr. President?"

And as Nick Cooper stood beside a glowing Christmas tree in the Oval Office of the White House, watching the world begin to fall apart, he found himself thinking of something his mentor had said to him three months ago—just before Cooper threw him off a twelve-story building.

"Sir? What do you want us to do?"

His one time mentor had said, *If you do this, the world will burn.*

"Mr. President?"

The monitor had shifted back to a wide aerial view. The fire had spread, and thick smoke blotted out half the city.

"Sir?"

ACKNOWLEDGMENTS

There's an abiding myth that books are written solo, an ink-fingered dreamer stuck in a basement making it all up. The dreamer and the basement are both accurate, but I certainly didn't do it alone. My deepest thanks to:

Scott Miller, agent, buddy, and brother-in-arms, who not only didn't panic at my crazy left turn, but told me to write it, *stat.* Thanks also to the stellar team at Creative Artists, especially Jon Cassir, Matthew Snyder, and Rosi Bilow, who put the lie to all the jokes about Hollywood.

Reema Al-Zaben, Andy Bartlett, Jacque Ben-Zekry, Grace Doyle, Daphne Durham, Justin Golenbock, Danielle Marshall, and the rest of the Thomas & Mercer crew, who are passionate booklovers building a brave new world.

I'm fortunate to have two creative partners. The first is Sean Chercover, collaborator and heterosexual life mate, whose fingerprints are all over this book. Anything you didn't like was probably his fault. The second is Blake Crouch, who, at the summit of a fourteen-thousand-foot peak, helped me turn the slenderest fragment of a notion into a full-blown story...and then gave me the title. Drinks are on me, boys.

All the folks who read the book early and pointed out where it sucked, especially Michael Cook, Alison Dasho, and Darwyn Jones.

Jeroen ten Berge, the visionary behind the cover design.

Megan Beatie and Dana Kaye, gifted publicists and all-around get-er-done-rs.

Dale Rosenthal of the University of Illinois at Chicago, who, over Guinness, disassembled the global financial marketplace and then redesigned it abnorm-proof.

Kevin Anthony, who built the beautiful desk I'll be writing on for the rest of my life.

The crime-fiction community: booksellers and librarians, bloggers and reviewers, writers and publicists, but most especially the readers.

My brother, Matt, who devoured the book, carefully propped up my ego, then tore apart everything that didn't work. You're the man.

Sally and Anthony Sakey, better known as Mom and Dad, who gave me everything.

And finally, the two loves of my life: my wife, g.g., and our daughter, Jocelyn. Nothing would mean anything without you.

ABOUT THE AUTHOR

Marcus Sakey is the best-selling author of six novels, several of which are in development as films. His fiction has been nominated for or won an Anthony, Barry, Macavity, Strand Critic's Circle, Readers' Choice, Crimespree, Dilys, Crime Shot, Indie Lit, Romantic Times, and ITW Thriller Award. He lives in Chicago with his wife and daughter. Visit his website at MarcusSakey.com, or follow him on Facebook and Twitter, where he posts under the clever handle @MarcusSakey.